# Her

# Dark

# Inheritance

# Other Works by Meg Hafdahl

*Twisted Reveries*
*Twisted Reveries Volume II: Tales from Willoughby*
"The Pit" featured in
*Eclectically Criminal* compiled by Fern Brady

The Willoughby Chronicles
Book 1

# Her

# Dark

# Inheritance

## Meg Hafdahl

Inklings
Publishing

*Her Dark Inheritance*

Copyright © 2018 by Meg Hafdahl

Copyedited by Julian Kindred and D Tinker Editing
Formatted by D Tinker Editing
Cover Design by Verstandt

ISBN: 978-1-944428-25-9 by Inklings Publishing
http://inklingspublishing.com

First US Edition
Printed in the United States of America
22  21  20  19  18      1  2  3  4  5

*To Fox, my first*

# Contents

# Acknowledgments

Without others, I would have no reason to tell stories. I cannot do any of this on my own.

Thank you to Fern and Kelly C. for molding this novel into something better.

My RFW girls, I am humbled to be in a group of such supportive and lovely humans.

Luke, I want to be like you when I grow up.

My boys, thank you for the hugs.

Kelly F., I wouldn't want to spend long hours working with anyone else.

Thank you to Verstandt, everyone at Inklings, and my family, friends, and readers. I am grateful to receive all your support, kindness, and wisdom. It fuels me.

DAPHNE DIDN'T KNOW HER MOTHER.

It was a painful realization, the kind that created a sharp pang in the bottom of her belly. As a child, her mom had been the woman to caress her fevered forehead with damp washcloths when she was sick and cook homemade popcorn on Friday nights in a rusted pot. They had been close, friends even, but the truth was stripping away that certainty.

Daphne hovered now on her parents' front steps, remembering the recent emotional assaults inflicted on her by her mother. Secrets had begun to spill from her mother's affected brain like acid rain, burning through the reality Daphne had accepted as her life.

"I never really wanted kids." Jane Downs-Forrest had blinked at the blooming white serviceberry bushes outside her bedroom window. "Your dad persuaded me to keep you, though." She had tugged at the thin cap covering her bald head. "I wasn't fully convinced until you were at least five."

Her mom's wide smile had been so at odds with the words she'd spoken.

Daphne had frowned then. She had wanted to believe that her mother's constant stream of ugly thoughts were just random verbalizations created by the brain tumor. That her mother didn't really believe her own confessions.

But Daphne had been able to see the memories dancing across her mom's sallow eyes.

Jane had gripped Daphne's arm and whispered to her with sour breath. "I lost my virginity to my college professor!" A cough had racked her frail body. "I'm pretty sure it's the only reason I got an A in astronomy!" Jane had waggled her nonexistent eyebrows and snorted, as though life were a trivial joke. "So don't miss out; I'm sure you've got a cute one with glasses or something. Maybe in a tweed jacket with patches on the elbows."

Her mother was a stranger to her.

Jane had asked Daphne to visit after her eleven o'clock composition class. Daphne didn't want to. Her mother's bedroom, once a pleasant place with an oak four-poster bed and a collection of Yankee candles, was now a makeshift hospice that smelled of bleach and her mother's bedpan. And worse, the deep, cutting memories of her dying mother would surely keep Daphne up at night, chewing on Tums and wishing she had never known her mother's inner struggles. Watching her die of cancer was difficult enough.

But she couldn't ignore her mom's request.

When Daphne entered through the side door, her hands clenched around the straps of her backpack, she found her father hovering in the kitchen. It was the heart of the Forrest home, where they all had snacked and chatted and lived. Some of Daphne's childhood drawings were still taped to the wall amidst Jane's highly superior oil paintings. Adam Forrest spent most of his time standing at the kitchen's Formica counter, too anxious to sit or eat. Even his beloved herb garden out back had blackened and died.

"Hey, Dad." Daphne spoke in the hushed tone that had become the norm of their new life. "Mom told me to come home for lunch. She insists she has some really important thing to tell me."

Despite not being even the least bit hungry, she plucked a red apple from the ceramic bowl on the counter and bit into it. Her eyes flitted to her dad's face, watching for a clue. He stared past her though, his countenance the same tableau of agony and dread as his dying wife's.

"I'll drive you back when you're done."

"Thanks." She swallowed and began picking at the apple stem with nervous fingers. "I hope . . ." Daphne stopped herself. Her hopes didn't matter, not now. She had to listen to her mom's confessions, however hurtful or awkward it might be. Really, it was the least she could do.

Lost in his grief, her father didn't seem to hear her.

She walked down the hall, the apple stuck in her throat and the soggy core abandoned on a console table. Every day for the last few months, she had feared this walk down the darkened corridor. She wasn't certain, though, if she was frightened more by the prospect of her mother being dead in her bed or by her being alive.

Jane was propped up in her hospital bed. A blood pressure cuff was flipped over the edge of the railing, just visible in the darkness of the room. The collection of water glasses on the bedside table sparkled in the thin ray of sunlight that broke through the mostly closed curtains.

A yellow Post-It flitted down from the rail of her mom's bed on an imperceptible breeze. It landed, sticky side up, on the carpet a few inches from Daphne's feet.

She stooped and picked it up, turning it over to reveal a pencil sketch.

The drawn image was dark and ragged, wholly dissimilar from her mother's usual soft-edged depictions of rural life.

Daphne stared at the animal face within the deep circles—at the beady eyes and the thin black triangles that looked like infinite rows of teeth. A peculiar chill caused her fingers to become ice cold as she crushed the small piece of paper in her palm.

"Daughter." Jane no longer hid her bald head. The translucent flesh under her bulbous eyes showcased her blue veins. Her teeth stuck out from her emaciated lips, like a set of joke vampire fangs.

"Hey, Mom. You need anything?" Daphne slid her backpack off and set it on the carpet. She tossed the strange pencil drawing into the waste bin, hoping to forget how the deep grooves in the paper had given her a pervading sense of doom.

The discordant scents of impending death stung her nostrils. As she sat in the rolling office chair provided for visitors, a flash of a younger and healthier Jane Downs-Forrest raced across her mind. This was how Daphne would choose to remember her: the mother she knew with plump cheeks, lively blue eyes, and white wrists dotted with oil paint.

A pencil, ground down to a two-inch nub, poked out from under her mom's tower of pillows.

"No, no." The muscles in Jane's face twitched. "I just need to talk to you, to tell you everything."

Daphne held onto the arms of the chair, preparing herself for the assault of words.

"It's the true story of me."

Daphne thought she might miss her two o'clock American lit lecture. She rubbed her nervous belly.

"Daphne, I . . ." A line of drool ran down her mother's chin. Jane took a tissue and shakily patted it away. "Well, do you remember that I told you I was born in Iowa?"

"Yeah, you paint it all the time." Daphne pointed to a landscape above the dresser, framed in oak to match the furniture. It was of a field of wildflowers. A crumbling shed was in the foreground, encompassed by the brilliant pink light of the setting sun. It was one of Jane's personal favorites.

"Yes." Her mother gazed at her masterpiece. "That was a special place to me. I painted it from memory."

Daphne took in a sharp breath. She had assumed the painting was a beautiful fiction.

"Would you get it down for me? The painting?" Jane caught another errant dribble of spit with the tissue.

"Off the wall?"

Her mother gave a weak nod.

Daphne hesitated, feeling a touch naughty at the prospect of removing it from the wall. Carefully, she leaned over the dresser. On tiptoe, she lifted the heavy frame, which was about two feet wide, off the screws in the wall.

She had never been allowed to touch one of the paintings before, even in their frame. At art shows, her mother had always insisted she be the only one to set up her paintings. Even Daphne's dad was left to watch as her mom set them on easels and dusted the glass.

Jane's brittle mouth trembled. "Open it, from the back."

"Are you sure, Mom?" Daphne's hands hovered over one of the metal fasteners.

"Go on." She coughed.

Daphne carried the painting to the side of the bed. She knelt and removed the circular fasteners. With each one, she waited for her mom to bark from above that she was doing it wrong. Instead, the dying woman peered down over the rail, wearing a wan and unfamiliar smile.

"Take off the back and remove the protective matting," Jane instructed.

Daphne reluctantly obliged, worried her mother had finally lost her last shred of sanity. She lowered the heavy frame onto the carpet and pulled the painting out of its home. She flipped it over and looked at the haunting shed surrounded by the surreal pink light. For years, she had believed it was a setting sun that cast such deep shadows over the sea of flowers, but as it sat in her hand, she wasn't sure. From this close, she could see a swirl of black paint looming ominously over the landscape.

Her mom still smiled. "Turn it back over."

Daphne turned it over with cautious hands.

At the top, written in her mother's handwriting, was *4/15/01*. She scanned the thick ivory paper for more clues. At the bottom, written in translucent, ghostlike pencil:

Willoughby, MN

"Where's that? Willoughby?" Daphne's voice wavered as she pointed at the word.

Jane reached with her free hand, the other still clutching a tissue at her chin. Her sunken cheeks showed a hint of color. Daphne handed the painting to her mom and sat back down in the rolling chair. Her mind whirled with questions. She patted her empty pocket fruitlessly in search of a soothing stick of gum.

"That old shed was in Willoughby. I wonder if it's still there. I remember how hidden I felt inside. How safe and warm and concealed I was!" Jane took in a deep breath.

"Mom?"

"Hmm?"

"Willoughby? It's in Minnesota? MN?" Daphne used her feet to roll the chair closer to her mother. It snagged on the carpet as she forced it along.

"That's where I grew up: Willoughby, Minnesota." Jane sniffed. "I'm from Minnesota."

"You said you grew up in Iowa. You've always told me that."

To Daphne, a lifelong resident of Bellingham, Washington, there was no real difference between Iowa and Minnesota. It was all in the middle of the US, what her dad referred to as 'fly-over country.' What difference did it make? It seemed an odd thing to obscure.

"Well, why would you lie about that, Mom?" Inwardly, Daphne reminded herself to speak gently.

"Oh, my." Jane snatched at her blankets. "I'm cold."

Daphne stood and helped cover her mom's concave chest with a quilt. She then set the painting back on her mom's stomach so she could gaze at her work easily.

"Thank you, dear. My skin is just so very thin. I tell you, brain cancer is not for the weak." She returned the tissue to her wet chin.

"Why did you lie about where you grew up?" Daphne repeated. She sat back down on the edge of the rolling chair, attempting to keep it still.

"I suppose I didn't want there to be any way for you to connect me to it all. I was sure that eventually you would realize it. Or your friends or someone."

Daphne stiffened in the chair. She regretted the apple; it was barbed wire in her throat and her belly roiled. "I don't understand."

"Your dad told me not to tell you. He worries." Jane didn't look at her daughter. Her watery eyes, faded from their once-striking cerulean blue, regarded the oil painting on her lap. "But I know you can take it. You can handle it. You're stronger than I am. And I know you won't blame me or hate me." A droplet of saliva escaped Jane's tissue and soaked into the neckline of her nightgown.

"Willoughby is a tiny place on the western side of the state. I loved it. I thought I was going to live there my whole life, you know? Have kids there and maybe work as a veterinarian? I'd always wanted to do that. I don't think I've ever told you that. We'd swim in Cross Lake in the summer; the water was always really clear and the sand was good for making castles. Before I was born, there was a mill people worked at, but it burned down and the town stopped growing. I liked it that way: quaint and private."

Daphne leaned closer to her mom. Jane's voice was weakening with each sentence.

"There are farmers there, too, you know, growing barley and wheat and the like. My grandpa grew sugar beets. He taught me about hard work." A small smile pulled at Jane's crepey lips. It was hard to believe, Daphne thought, that her mother was only fifty-one years old. The cancer had pulled her through a sort of time warp, causing her to appear much older.

"My dad was a school teacher. I told you that and it's true. My mom stayed home. She was naturally domestic, unlike me, I suppose." Jane's eyes remained on the painting. "But I didn't tell you I had a brother, a twin. He was my best friend. We would play in the woods for hours. We had a fort we built up in a maple tree. We took good care of it, and I even swept out the leaves."

7

Daphne tried to imagine a small boy with chestnut curls and round cheeks like her mother, an uncle she had never known. "Did he die in the crash too?"

Jane emitted a rattling sigh. "No. There was no crash, Daphne."

Daphne's brain spun. She'd grown up believing her grandparents had died in a car crash when her mother was a teenager. A drunk driver had hit them head on, and they'd died instantly.

"They survived? They're alive?" Daphne stood up at the side of the bed. She didn't want to look at the painting on her mom's lap. It had gained a sort of eerie significance. A reflection of a place she should've known but didn't. Instead, she looked upon her emaciated mother. Jane raised her chin, and their eyes locked. Death swam in her corneas.

Jane motioned toward the buttons in the bed's plastic railing. "Daphne, dear, can you lower me? I'm getting tired."

Daphne ran her hand along the buttons and pressed the right one with her thumb until her mom lay flat. "Can you finish what you're telling me?"

"My family is dead." Jane clutched at her blanket. "They were murdered. Kyle too. His name was Kyle. They found his head apart from his body. It had been chopped off, you see—clean through." She tapped the painting with a yellow fingernail, indicating a spot of tangled flowers. "Right here is where they found him."

"Oh!" Daphne covered her mouth with a trembling hand.

"Daffy." Her mother hadn't called her that in many years. "Daffy, I must tell you." She grasped Daphne's hand in her dry claw. "I didn't do it. I didn't kill them."

Daphne swallowed down the sickly phlegm rising in her mouth. "Of course you didn't!"

"You must remember that I didn't do it, Daffy; I really didn't." Jane Downs-Forrest's gray eyelids drooped over her bulging eyeballs. "I'm only guilty of thinking and wanting."

Daphne sensed a presence behind her. Rhonda, Jane's hospice nurse, was in the doorway, dressed in her springtime floral scrubs and a bright-pink stethoscope hung around her fat neck. Her shift, Daphne realized, was just starting.

The nurse strode into the room on her soft shoes. "I need to take her vitals. Your dad says she's been having a bad day. And we better do a wipe down before she falls asleep."

"Wait, Rhonda," Daphne said over her shoulder. "She was telling me something."

"Daffy?" Jane whispered. "I know you won't blame me, because of that bad thing *you* did. You didn't mean to, honey, and I don't blame you, Daffy, just like you can't blame me."

Daphne panicked. Her mother's words, her bizarre story, were fracturing both her mind and her stomach. She ran, leaving Rhonda with her groggy mother, and rushed into the hall bathroom. She made it just in time, falling to her knees on the tile. Shreds of apple and the remnants of a blueberry muffin from the U coffee shop swirled within the ceramic bowl. Daphne hiccuped, praying for the panic to subside. Her doctor had called this uncontrollable purging a response to her untreated anxiety—an anxiety born from a traumatic event in high school. Whatever the cause, Daphne was never quite prepared for it.

A soft knock came from the bathroom door. "You all right?" her dad asked. Tears sprung from Daphne's eyes, falling onto the white toilet seat. "Daphne, you okay?"

"Gimme a minute." She spit the vile remnants into the bowl and flushed. Thankful to find a bottle of mouthwash under the sink, Daphne unscrewed the top and took a swig. Her body shook as she thought about the old shed at twilight, where her mother had felt protected and where a boy with her mother's face had been decapitated.

DAPHNE CLIMBED INTO HER DAD'S green Honda CRV on wobbly legs. She sucked on the peppermint he had given her, trying to concentrate on her upcoming American lit class. It was just a lecture day, thank goodness. She wouldn't have to participate in a small group or take a test.

"She told me." Daphne adjusted her backpack on the floor between her feet. She reached for her phone but then changed her mind, placing her quivering hands on her lap. Her emails and texts would only stress her out and give her overstuffed brain more unwanted thoughts.

Her dad tightened his grip on the steering wheel. "I guessed that."

"What is she talking about? Why would she say that? She said such awful things. Her parents—they died in an accident!" She felt hysterical, unhinged.

He scratched the graying hair by his ears. "Your mom is complicated. I'm sure you've figured that out by now."

Sometimes the slow, methodical way her father spoke was soothing, a powerful salve for her anxiety. At others it infuriated her. Currently, she just wanted to shake him until all her mother's strange secrets peppered out of him.

"She said she had a brother." Daphne peered out the passenger window at Marshall Street. Mrs. Andrews's tulips bloomed in her impossibly green front yard. The Pruitts' eldest boy pushed his scooter down the sidewalk with one hand while adjusting his headphones with the other. Oreo, a half-blind Boston terrier, barked lazily at the passing boy even as he lifted his leg on a porch post. "Is that true?"

Her dad drummed his fingers on the dashboard. "I told your mom not to tell you." He chewed on the inside of his cheek. "You deserve to know, that's true, but . . . ."

The rhythmic clacking of the turn signal filled the silence.

Daphne wiped a tear from her eyelashes. "Has everything she told me been a lie?"

"Don't be dramatic." He turned the car onto Sunnydale Avenue. "We all have pasts."

Daphne swallowed her mint, wondering if that was a pointed reference to hers. She stared straight ahead, terrified of catching even a hint of disappointment on her dad's face.

"There was some talk in the papers that she was to blame," he continued. "You know how they can be . . . nasty liars."

She nodded, knowing very well how desperate journalists could be to create a story out of nothing.

He merged onto I-5 in the direction of Western Washington University, cursing under his breath about the lurching traffic. "None of it matters, you know? It's ancient history. Your mom—she had this need to tell you. I guess I can understand it. Just don't let it get you all twisted up. You have finals to concern yourself with, and your future. Look ahead, Daphne. Don't let anything in the past weigh you down."

Daphne reached across the center console and squeezed her dad's right hand. How many times had he told her to let the past go? And how many times had she ignored him? "Thanks, Dad. You're right."

They shared a smile.

Yet the sharp, piercing pain in her belly only intensified.

WHEN THEY LOWERED her mother's body into the ground, Daphne could think only of Jane's claw-like hand grasping at her arm.

*You must remember that I didn't do it, Daffy.*

In the church, there was a blown-up picture resting on a wooden easel of Jane Downs-Forrest at a charity art event. Her chestnut curls skimmed her bare shoulders. She wore her beloved navy-blue strapless gown, which now dressed her dead body, and a string of pearls she'd received from Adam on their twentieth wedding anniversary. She smiled, obviously proud of the oil landscape behind her, which was marked with a *SOLD* slip.

Daphne couldn't look at her mother—neither the frail stranger in the coffin nor the picture of the woman who'd had a full, complicated life before Daphne even drew her first breath. Instead, as the pastor extolled Jane's virtues and joked about finding paintbrushes in heaven, Daphne stared at the landscape in the background of the photograph. A few brown curls obstructed the art, but she could make out another pastoral scene, this one of a picturesque river flowing beside the banks of a wooded area. An unexpected twist of charred wreckage could be seen through the weedy grass.

*That's where I grew up: Willoughby, Minnesota.*

FINALLY, THE SERVICE ENDED, and everyone poured out of the church. Many peered at Daphne sideways, uncertain how to speak to her. That, at least, hadn't changed.

She and her dad drove home in silence, followed by an endless parade of cars.

Painting buddies brought casseroles wrapped in tinfoil. They left them on the counter amid fruit platters and doughnut holes.

Her mom would have hated how they all dropped them there, with no order and at odd angles, hanging over the edge.

Daphne receded to the back porch, hoping to be forgotten.

She missed Bev. Her best friend hadn't been able to make it out, although she promised to come as soon as her finals were over. They were going to have a rom-com marathon, complete with Chinese takeout and sleeping bags.

Sometime later, her Aunt Lisa found her outside. "Cookie, dear? I made the toffee chip ones." She sidled up to Daphne on the wicker bench overlooking their fenced backyard. She held out a napkin stacked with four cookies.

"No, I've got a mint." Daphne stuck out her tongue.

"Ah, well." Lisa stuffed a toffee chip cookie in her mouth. "Everyone's eating 'em up in there. They were your mom's favorite, you know."

"Yeah, I know." Daphne tugged her black skirt down over her bent knees.

"She loved you very much." Lisa ate another cookie.

Daphne looked up at the looming Cascade Mountains. They were always with her, shielding her with their snowy peaks. "Mom never painted the mountains."

"What's that?"

"She never painted the Cascades. Or the ocean, either. Not once."

Lisa shrugged. "She preferred farmland."

The spring breeze lifted Daphne's blonde bangs. She could see the muddy grooves where her swing set had been. Years later, the grass still struggled to grow.

She remembered rocking slowly on the tire swing, listening to the cicadas in the heat of a summer day. She had been waiting for her mother to push her.

Jane Downs-Forrest had forgotten her promise to her seven-year-old daughter. That had been one of her bad days, when she had lain in bed with the covers pulled to her chin.

Daphne could still see her as she had been: young and healthy. Healthy on the outside, she realized now, but not within.

After an hour of waiting to be pushed—perhaps even longer—seven-year-old Daphne had crawled into her mother's bedroom, careful not to disturb her.

Her blonde braids had smacked her cheeks as she had risen onto her knees to see if her mom had fallen asleep.

Jane's eyes had been wide open. She had stared past her daughter as though there was something lurking in the corner of her room.

Daphne had shivered, looking over her shoulder at the empty wall. Saying nothing, she had crawled back out of the room and kept crawling until she had hit the living room couch with her forehead.

Then she had hoisted herself up onto the cushions and watched Nickelodeon until her dad came home.

Days like that—days when her mother fell into a sort of catatonia—came and went. No one ever mentioned them, though.

Daphne took another peppermint from her black clutch purse. She unwrapped it from the plastic and popped it into her mouth. The wrapper fell to the wood planks below them. Daphne reached to pick it up, but it scurried away in the wind.

"Do you know much about my mom? I mean, her life before she met Dad?" Daphne asked.

Her dad's little sister frowned. "I know her parents died when she was young, and she was from the Midwest." Lisa brushed cookie crumbs off her brown slacks. "Is there something specific you want to know?"

"She went to college here at WWU, right?"

"Yes, art history, I believe." Lisa wrapped the last two cookies in the greasy napkin and placed it in her cardigan pocket.

Daphne flipped the mint around her tongue. "Why?"

Lisa sighed. "I suppose artists like to know the background—"

"No." Daphne studied her aunt's face. "I mean, why would she come here?" She gestured toward the mountains. "She loved the plains and the woods. She painted them . . . God, every day."

Daphne's dad emerged from the house, his hands stuck in his pockets. She watched as his watery eyes searched for something to fix on.

"I hope everyone goes soon." He marched down the deck stairs and kicked softly at a tuft of grass growing through some cracked paver stones.

"Yeah," Daphne agreed as she crunched into her mint.

"Yeah, I can't sit around here anymore. Talking about her." His eyes continued to shift, from the bench, to ants marching on the cobblestones, to an invisible beacon far off on the horizon.

Lisa, small but stout, stood and followed him down the steps. She wrapped her short arms around her brother. "You'll be better tomorrow, Adam."

"Okay," he grumbled.

"Every day'll get better." She patted his elbow awkwardly. "Jane is here with us. She's watching over us and probably wishing you'd worn a better tie."

Adam pulled at his striped tie. He tried to smile, but pain flourished across his pale face.

Daphne tried to think of her mom, floating above her, hands on her hips. Pressure formed at the corners of her eyes. Daphne could cry if she let herself—a snotty, ugly sob. Not because her mother lay in a coffin, swimming in a formal gown that was much too big for her deflated breasts and inverted stomach. She could cry because her mother's story had finished before Daphne could even know the beginning. The end had come before Daphne was ready and, she suspected, before her mother was too.

WHEN EVERYONE HAD FINALLY LEFT, Jane's cat, a scraggy tom named Gopher, paced in front of his dish giving throaty mews. Daphne poured out the dry cat food, her sight clouded with tears and then disappeared into her basement lair—as her mom had often called it—and sobbed into her pillow. She cried until her stomach lurched. Her sorrow dissipated then as she distracted herself with keeping the nausea in check. Her chest ached as she struggled for fresh air. Her eyes felt raw, and her ruffled white blouse was soaked through.

She wondered, as curious Gopher jumped on her bed, how her father could sleep in the room her mother had died in, where her sick smell still lingered.

"Hey." She kissed Gopher's soft head. "It's all right, you know. It's gonna be okay."

The cat licked his paw.

Daphne noticed her laptop sitting on her cluttered desk. Its power light was flashing, and it looked rather forgotten under a pile of papers. For the last week, Daphne hadn't even thought about schoolwork. Even social media had been abandoned as she navigated the mire of her grief.

She grabbed the HP notebook and brought it back to her bed. After rubbing her tear-sodden palms against her comforter, she opened the laptop.

Google came up in a flash, waiting for her instruction. The cursor blinked in the search box. Daphne slowly typed *Willoughby, MN*. The first hit was the town's website. She clicked on willoughbymn.org.

WELCOME TO WILLOUGHBY!
A SMALL TOWN SURROUNDED BY BEAUTIFUL
LAKES AND DEEP WOODS AND FILLED WITH
FRIENDLY PEOPLE!

Daphne scanned over the list of government services and the tourist shots marked *CROSS LAKE AT SUMMERTIME*.

She stared at a picture of Willoughby School. It was an old boxy building reminiscent of a factory, flanked by two square chimneys. She tried to imagine her mom there, climbing the big steps with books in her arms. Maybe with pigtails swinging. She had never seen a photograph of her mom as a child—peculiar, she supposed, since her mother's past was now in question. As she attempted to picture Jane in her youth, skipping up the steps into the utilitarian school, Daphne could only discern her mother as a gray, skinny stranger.

With a sigh, Daphne left the town's official website and scanned the Google results page. There were a few headlines and obituaries:

*Year 2011 Marks 80th Anniversary of Culver Flour Mill Explosion*

*Seventeen-Year-Old Willoughby High Schooler Dies from Injuries Sustained in Snowmobile Crash*

*Willoughby Library Is the Place to Be!*

Daphne plugged in another search: *Jane Downs Willoughby*.
Nothing.
*Downs family Willoughby*.
Nothing.

A tingling, burgeoning panic made her limbs floppy. Her shoulders slumped as she blinked at the unhelpful computer screen. If her grandparents and uncle had died in an accident, surely there would be an article about it.

The search bar cursor winked at her, teasing.

*Murder Willoughby 1980s.*

A result showed at the top of the page from the Minneapolis Star Tribune:

*House of Horrors in Farm Town: The Search Continues.*

Shaking, Daphne clicked on the article.

*July 17, 1982*

*Willoughby, MN—The search continues for the culprit or culprits in the gruesome murder of the Bergman family. Gunnar, 43; Ida, 39; and Kyle, 16. The Bergmans' daughter, Caroline, 16, is the only survivor as she was out of the family home on the morning of July 13. The quaint community of Willoughby, off I-94 east of Fergus Falls, is reeling from the seemingly random attack on a school teacher and his family.*

*"This sort of violence doesn't visit us here in Willoughby," Otter Tail County Sheriff Robert Toft told reporters.*

*The police are still processing the scene, said to be a "tragedy beyond measure." The autopsies of all three Bergmans will be conducted by the end of this week, but there is no doubt as to the cause of death.*

*State police will join the county officers to assist in this most unusual and harrowing case.*

*The residents of Willoughby are shocked by this attack in such an innocent, family-focused community. Many have taken to locking their doors, an unusual practice in the heartland, until the murderer is apprehended. An impressive collection of flowers, handmade cards and stuffed animals have been placed on the sidewalk outside of the Bergmans' home. As Gunnar Bergman was an influential and well-loved teacher at Willoughby School, many of his students are in shock from such a horrifying turn of events.*

*Caroline Bergman, a minor, has been kept away from the media. Sheriff Toft told reporters that she is cooperating fully with the investigation and, although distraught, is doing whatever she can to help piece together what happened on that fateful day.*

There were more articles.

One headline flashed like a neon sign:

*Sixteen-Year-Old Deemed the "Minnesota Borden"*

Every shred of her consciousness begged Daphne not to read further.

Her finger clicked.

*July 26, 1982*

    *Willoughby, MN—In a dark and surprising twist, police and the farm community of Willoughby are focused on 16-year-old Caroline Bergman (pictured below), the only surviving family member of this summer's axe massacre. Some in town, and even around the US, have called Ms. Bergman the "Minnesota Borden," in reference to the notorious Lizzie Borden murders of 1892. Many have pointed out the similarities between this recent Minnesota horror and what happened in Fall River, MA, nearly one hundred years ago. The police say the investigation is still ongoing and there is no suspect yet in custody, but several residents of Willoughby have come forward, anonymously, to share the suspicion that has grown among the Bergmans' many friends, coworkers, and neighbors. Accusations have been made that Caroline was acting "out of character" before the murders occurred, and many believe that the police should abandon their working theory of a stranger passing through town and direct all the department's resources and focus on Caroline Bergman. One resident said, "We just want to find out who did this so we can all rest easy. That girl's alibi is thin, and she had the most reason."*

    *It is important to note: Caroline Bergman has not been charged with any crime as of yet.*

Daphne scrolled through the rest of the text until she found the grainy, black-and-white picture at the bottom.

*Caroline Bergman in happier times, ca. 1981*

It was her.

Daphne's mother.

Her hair was long and curled under her soft chin. She smiled with the ignorant joy of youth—unaware her family would be murdered with an axe and that she would die of brain cancer at fifty-one. Her dark one-piece swimsuit hugged her belly. A dripping ice cream cone drooped in her small hand.

Daphne's eyes stung. She opened them wider, taking in every detail of the photograph. Her mother squinted back at her in the long-ago sunlight.

On the right side of the webpage, there was a column entitled *Articles You Might Like.* The first one listed was *Unsolved Murders: Who Killed the Bergmans?*

There were many more articles, thousands, waiting to be clicked. Daphne snapped her laptop shut and kicked it to the foot of the bed. She covered her entire trembling body with the comforter. Gopher poked his pink nose inside and tickled her cheek with his whiskers.

She squirmed away from the tickle, closing her eyes.

*Caroline.*

The black type burned into her retinas.

*Caroline Bergman in happier times.*

Jane Downs-Forrest didn't exist. She never had.

Everything Daphne had believed to be true had shifted and fallen at her feet. She was alone, so completely alone that she was certain she had never been anything but an ignorant, blind child. Her mother was someone she didn't know. She had lived an entire other life before Daphne had come to be, and it wasn't boring or usual or even common.

Daphne searched her brain for what she knew about the Lizzie Borden case. She had watched a bit about it, years ago, on some cable channel. Her mother had come into the living room, she remembered, and had clicked the TV off. Jane—*Caroline?*—had said that was dark stuff, inappropriate for a little girl on a Sunday afternoon. She had told Daphne to go out to play, to get some sun on her face. Daphne had obeyed, though she had thought about Lizzie Borden, nearly in a trance, as she picked raspberries in their lush backyard. She had wondered why someone would take something sharp and use it on their parents. She recalled the black-and-white picture they had shown on the TV program, of Lizzie's dead dad lying back on an antique chaise, his face looking like a mound of raw ground beef. She remembered how they had said Lizzie could have done the murders naked because they never found any bloody clothes. That had stuck in Daphne's child brain, and it had turned over inside her for many nights thereafter, until she had finally asked her mom about it. She recalled going to sleep on a summer night, when it was still light out and the smell of distant barbeques trickled in through her open window.

"Mom, is that Lizzie Borden thing true? Did she kill her own parents?"

Her mother's blue eyes had grown stormy, and her apple cheeks had drained of color.

Daphne could remember that now. It hadn't seemed odd then.

"She was found innocent by a jury." Jane had smoothed the blankets over her only child. "So I think not. She was given a tough time by those around her. I think she was seen guilty in the eyes of those who didn't care to know the truth."

Daphne recalled how her mother had hesitated before kissing her. How she had appeared as though she wanted to say something else, like there were words on her lips, dangling there, wanting to be said, wanting to be heard by the little girl covered in a heap of stuffed animals.

Now Daphne prayed for the vomit to go away. Her mints, which helped soothe the torrent, were on the floor by the door, and there was no possible way she could crawl over there in her current state. She laid a hand on her agitated belly and breathed in and out.

Gopher purred beside her.

The floor creaked above her. Her father was moving with no purpose, circling her childhood home as though he might find his wife alive if he just kept opening cupboards and patrolling the hall.

She peeked her head out of the blanket and spied the laptop. All of this was the Wi-Fi's fault. Her whole life was crumbling beneath her because of a Google search.

Her dad would say she was being dramatic.

Daphne pulled the computer forward once more. It was hot and heavy in her hands. She opened a different browser to avoid looking at the string of articles. Instead she searched:

*Willoughby lodging.*

There was a single choice. According to Google Maps, it was a few miles from town on the far side of Cross Lake. It was only open in the spring and summer, and there was one picture of the motel and surrounding campsites. It looked like the sort of place her mom would avoid: a place that was probably cramped, old, and a bit dirty. Somehow, this attracted Daphne. She liked how the *MOTEL* sign was etched into a rough log and how the curtains in each room were a tacky powder blue.

Her mother was named Caroline Bergman. She recited this over and over, a mantra. Caroline's parents and brother were murdered. And for some odd reason, perhaps just because of the cancer eating her brain, her mother believed Daphne would think her guilty of such a horrible thing.

Daphne's mind clicked and turned. Her belly flipped.

Her father continued to pace upstairs, aimlessly, and she knew she was in danger of doing the same. After Daphne's bad time—not so long before her mother was diagnosed with cancer—she had thought she would walk forever, in the kind of catatonic state her mother would fall into, seeking nothing and achieving very little. Her fears had even come true. She had finished high school because she should and started college because she should, and she had sat and listened to her dying mother's confessions because she should. And they had all watched Daphne—the neighbors and friends and family—to see if she would implode, or worse explode and take them all with her down the darkened corridor of her life.

Daphne patted Gopher's patchy back. He raised his tail in delight.

"I'm crazy, I think," she whispered into his pointy ear. "But I have to . . . I have to know. I need to find out who Caroline Bergman was."

Daphne cracked her knuckles, readying them for another search. A new sensation surged through her sensitive stomach. It was excitement, she realized, a delicious hope that she had not sensed in a very long time.

# 6

DAPHNE FINISHED THE SHAKESPEARE FINAL with what she considered to be a rousing essay on Sonnet 18. Her only worry was that her penmanship had gotten sloppy at the end when her fingers cramped. But that hardly mattered as she walked across the quad in the morning sunshine.

Summer was imminent. Daphne could sense the heat through her skinny jeans. She stopped at the bus pavilion, mentally running through her wardrobe. She hadn't packed a suitcase in quite a long time.

Daphne's iPhone pinged in her back pocket.

*DAD'S CELL*

*How are you going to get around? Have you considered that?*

Annoyed, she unzipped the top pocket of her backpack and stuffed her phone inside. It lay in a crinkly wad of mints and empty wrappers. She grabbed a mint and slipped it into her mouth.

The phone pinged again before she could pull the zipper closed.

*DAD'S CELL*

*I love you and I just worry.*

A bus headed to the Bellis Fair Mall rolled up to the growing crowd. A few students climbed on, wearing the easy, relieved smiles of those done with the spring semester.

Daphne waited.

An anxious voice, deep within, urged her to alter her course. It asked her to stop the crazy plan she had set into motion. It would be so easy to give up. She could just stay home with her dad. He didn't need any more to worry about. So really it would be a favor to him. Wasn't that her responsibility? To take care of him? To distract him from reality?

She thought of the empty suitcase waiting on her bed. The same twin bed she had slept in since she had been freed from the confines of her crib. In the same spot, tucked against the basement's wood paneling. Her dresser, her vanity, all her things were just as they had been, unaffected by time. Yet so much had changed. Her backpack vibrated at her feet. Daphne fished out her phone and glanced at the caller. She was surprised that her best friend would call rather than text.

"Hey," she answered.

"Hi!" Beverly trilled. "Do you have a minute?"

Daphne watched the bus marked 11 ease up to the curb. "Yeah, just waiting to get home."

"Oh, well, um, how was your Shakespeare final?"

"Good." Daphne crunched her peppermint. "I'm just glad it's over."

"Great! I have something to tell you." Beverly's voice wavered, as it often did when she was nervous or uncertain.

"Okay . . ."

"Last night, Quentin and I went to that place Chester's—you know, where he took me on our first date. And like, I knew right when we got there something was up because he was just sweating. Like, his forehead was just wet, and I thought, oh my *God*, he's going to break up with me! Like, he's really going to do it this time! I know that's dumb, but that's what was going through my mind. So we sit at the same spot from our first date, and I'm like, holy shit here it comes, you know?"

Daphne sighed. "So did he?"

"No! Quentin proposed! He got down on one knee and the

whole bit; everyone watched. It was like out of a damn movie or something." Beverly squealed. It was a familiar, comforting sound that brought Daphne back to childhood.

"Oh. Oh, wow." Daphne paced the bus pavilion.

"Yeah!"

"That's just awesome, Bev. I mean, really, that's—"

"The ring is fucking huge! I'll text you a pic; oh my *God*, you'll die." Beverly laughed, the same high-pitched whoop she'd given when Daphne had tripped on her own high school graduation robe.

"You're getting married." The words didn't make any sense.

"Quentin is going to apply to the same medical residencies I am so we can be sure to get at least one together. Oh my crap, Daphne. You're the first person I called. I haven't even told my mom yet. She is going to flip!"

Daphne spied her bus as it made its turn onto campus. "Yeah. You should call her."

"Well, yeah, I am. But I just wanted to tell you first." Beverly's voice lowered. "I knew you'd be excited."

"Oh, I am." Daphne looked down at her brown ankle boots. "Really, Bev, that's so great. Send me the picture."

"You okay?" All the manic excitement had evaporated from Beverly's voice.

"Of course!"

"Really?" Daphne could visualize the arch of Beverly's eyebrow.

"I'm fine. You call your mom and we'll talk later." The doors of bus 23 sighed open. "I've got to get home to Dad, you know?"

"Daphne, I'm sorry." Beverly had switched to a somber lilt, her voice deep and cloying.

"Sorry? Why are you sorry for getting engaged?"

"No, I—" She cleared her throat. "I'm just talking about my mom and now I feel like shit, you know, like I don't know how to be sensitive. My mouth was just getting away from me."

Daphne stood back, letting others board the bus first. "You can talk about your mom, Bev. She's still alive."

A weighted silence ballooned between them. Daphne wanted to

say more, to assure Beverly that she was okay, that everything was okay. The reassuring words were swallowed by the rising sickness within her.

"All right, well, I'll send a picture."

"A picture?"

"Of the ring!" Beverly gave a casual giggle.

"Oh, yes. Yeah, please."

They said goodbye, and Daphne climbed up and scanned her student ID. She found her usual seat, close to the middle right door, and waited for the ding of her phone.

*BEV'S CELL*

A blurry photo of her best friend appeared. Beverly held her left hand in front of her cheek, showcasing a sparkling square-cut diamond ring.

Daphne held her finger over the text keyboard. The rumbling bus caused her hand to shake. The familiar sights of Bellingham, Washington, rushed by. Frowning, she typed a response that ended with five exclamation points and a smiley face.

7

DAPHNE'S SUITCASE WAITED ON HER BED like a gaping, ravenous mouth. She took a big silky wad of panties and tossed them in. She added a twist of tan B-cup bras. Then her black lacy one too—just in case.

Although her mom had been dead for two weeks, her presence remained in Daphne's basement bedroom like an unpleasant smell. She could hear Jane Downs-Forrest—not her weak, gasping deathbed voice but her strong living voice from before the cancer—telling Daphne to pack sensibly. To roll her socks and wrap each individual necklace in toilet paper.

It gave her a sick thrill to sprinkle her socks on top of the mountain of clothes.

Her dad knocked and simultaneously turned the knob. "Daphne?"

"Come in."

She barely recognized her father. He carried himself with an awkward hunch, as though he was too tall for every room. Even outdoors, he looked as though he were navigating under invisible hanging vines.

His eyes, normally brimming with good cheer, were veiny and shifty.

Daphne motioned toward her luggage. "I'm almost done."

"I'll drive you. You don't need to call a cab." He scratched his thin nose, his gaze falling on the messy suitcase.

"Thanks, Dad."

He nodded slowly.

Daphne could sense impending doom in the suffocating, pregnant silence. She stuffed a few paperbacks and empty notebooks in her suitcase and zipped it closed.

Her father hovered behind her like a hesitant ghost, unsure how to haunt her.

He coughed into the crook of his arm.

She stared at the silver *SAMSONITE* tag on her suitcase, wondering how she could convince him she wasn't making a life-altering mistake.

As though he had read her mind, he said, "Your mom wouldn't have wanted this—you going there."

A million responses trickled to the surface of her mind. She thought of telling him she didn't care what her dead mother wanted, but that, of course, wasn't true.

"I don't know. Maybe she'd like to know I'm there." She picked up the suitcase and set it on the floor. "I want to see it for myself."

"See what?" His troubled face was etched with newly formed wrinkles.

"I can read about what happened on Google, or I can go there." Daphne tried to pull the suitcase handle up so she could pull it on wheels. "You know I don't like reading articles on the internet; they're not always true."

Her dad leaned over and yanked up the suitcase handle for her. "How's this going to change anything? Going there?"

"Have you been there?" Daphne's hands fell to her hips, in a classic Jane Downs-Forrest pose.

He shuffled his feet. "No. Your mom never wanted to go back. She started a new life—her real life."

Daphne wondered how he could be so uninterested. He, she supposed, had had decades to get his questions answered. He had probably heard the story of the murders—and the accusations—a thousand times. Probably while his wife had lain next to him in the bedroom just upstairs, both of them gazing at the haunting painting of a creepy shed.

"Did you know they called her the Minnesota Borden?" She dared to look up at his strange, alien face. "Those hicks thought she killed her family."

His nostrils flared, and he scratched at his unshaven chin. "Yes. I know. That doesn't mean . . . she didn't kill anyone."

"I know, Dad." Daphne swung her purse over her shoulder. "Trust me, I don't believe any of that for a second. I'm going to Willoughby because I . . . I need to know about Caroline. It's where she's from, so in a way it's where I'm from."

His shoulders slumped even lower, causing his chin to skim his chest. "Daphne, your mom's name is Jane. Call her that. She had to change it, is all. It made her stronger to slough off that old name. You should be able to empathize with that instinct to hide, to start fresh."

Daphne bit her bottom lip, holding back the angry words that wanted to escape. There was part of her that believed he purposely brought up her past in order to wound her.

"And you must be able to empathize with my need to go. I need to see what she saw, and I want to learn about her past."

"I told you all there is to know. Mom hasn't been to Minnesota in decades." He gestured toward the paneled walls. "This was her home."

She glanced around her bedroom, only able to remember the bitter memories.

"I'm going," Daphne whispered.

Her dad nodded gravely.

She thought back to his words about her mom, about hiding and starting fresh. Perhaps Daphne was running away from the sour smell in their home and the soul-crushing image of her mom's empty dining chair. But at least she had a purpose. She couldn't reveal to her dad, though, that she wanted to search for clues in a thirty-year-old case in order to prove to everyone that her mom was not a murderer. Even saying it silently to herself was embarrassing. She was an English major, more comfortable in the U library than anywhere else. No matter how many episodes of *Law and Order* she'd watched, she was no expert on investigation.

Though she knew how inept she was, it didn't stop her. She had to go, if only to be somewhere new, near to her mom's heart, and far from where she had died.

# 8

"AH, GEEZ. I DON'T REMEMBER when the last time coulda been that I went there. No one hardly asks to go to Willoughby." The shuttle driver bit down on a frayed toothpick. "People like to go up there to the lake sometimes, but just locals, you know? People from that part of the state, you know?" Daphne was assaulted by the smell of an evergreen air freshener as the driver slid open the van door. She climbed up into the second row of seats and scooted far left, next to the window.

"Yup, Willoughby is small as can be. You're from Washington, right? Don't you want to go to the Mall of America instead?" He hoisted her suitcase into the trunk and slammed the door and then rounded the side of the van toward the open passenger side.

"No, thank you. Just Willoughby." Daphne buckled her seatbelt.

A slender, middle-aged woman stepped off the curb and squeaked, "This is the Minnesota Shuttle? Headed to Alexandria?"

"Sure are! You must be Nancy?"

The woman nodded, clutching her duffel bag to her chest as though it held precious jewels.

The driver slid the door closed and then crossed in front of the van toward his seat. He motioned for Nancy to join him up front as he yanked his own door open. "I'm headed west," he called over the hood. "I'll drop you in Alexandria first. Then that one back there is going to Willoughby, if you can believe it. First time in Minnesota, for crying out loud."

"Don'tcha want to go to the mall?" Nancy asked as she got inside. "It's the biggest in the US and even has rollercoasters." She glanced back at Daphne as she slipped in beside the driver.

"That sounds like fun." Daphne shrugged. "Maybe on my way back."

The woman looked back again at Daphne, a polite smile on her narrow face. "You've got family there?"

A moment of unadulterated panic shook Daphne's frame. The truth would not suffice. "Um, no." Daphne clutched her phone with a death grip. "I'm writing a book."

"Ah! A researcher, eh?" The driver shifted in his seat. His immense butt and meaty arms flowed over its edges. He pulled out into the congested line of taxis and shuttles leaving the airport. "What, about the mill or something?"

"The mill? No. I'm not really sure yet."

The driver huffed in response and then rolled down his window. "It's a beautiful spring day, ladies."

As they traveled away from the bustle of the Minneapolis-St. Paul International Airport, they were suddenly surrounded by the quiet consistency of American suburbs. Daphne thought it all looked like Washington at first: just the average urban expanse, filled with strip malls and townhouses.

Just as she had grown comfortable with the steady rush of Targets, McDonalds, and gated communities of identical houses, they left the metro area behind. She recognized what her mother had spent her entire life painting: the entrancing farmland of the Midwest. The farms gave way to crystal lakes surrounded by patches of enormous ancient pine trees. Daphne was reminded of her beloved Cascade Mountains looming over her existence, and she began to understand her mom's love for the farms and lakes and the timelessness of small town America.

They passed a crumbling, forgotten Dairy Queen. A limp vanilla-colored plastic cone on the roof had been sprayed with neon graffiti, reminding Daphne not to fully romanticize this bucolic piece of Minnesota. Although she could see the beauty her mother had fixated on for decades, she also had to remember the ugliness this part of the world had dumped so willingly onto Jane Downs-Forrest.

*Caroline Bergman.*

The name drifted to the surface of her thoughts like an untethered balloon.

Nancy and the driver spoke of sports, the weather, and his ailing sister in Duluth. After a while, they slowed and finally stopped in front of a casino with flashing lights and a packed parking lot. Daphne watched as Nancy slipped the driver a handful of ones and waved.

Daphne waved back, thinking how strange it was to wave to a stranger she would never see again.

They drove on.

The familiar symbols of civilization seemed to be fading. The towns were becoming smaller and farther apart.

Daphne noticed when they passed the first sign for Willoughby.

Willoughby/Cross Lake               30 miles

"About a half hour to go. Is there a motel?" The driver turned his head, his double chin grinding into his shoulder. He had found another toothpick and was inexplicably chewing on two.

"Oh, um, yes. Willoughby Motel—it's northeast, I think, on the lake."

"Ah, okay then, geez. Are you going to be all right up there?" He wiped his nose with his pale arm.

"Yes!" Daphne rifled through her purse but found only empty mint wrappers. Her stomach roiled. A dusty Tums finally rolled into her hand, sending a jolt of relief through her, and she popped it into her mouth.

"It's just—well, it's early season yet, so it's quiet up there, you know? Too cool for swimming yet, although the fishing's getting good." He took another swipe at his nose. "And you seem awfully young."

"I'll be fine," Daphne assured him.

This particular coddling had become an expected pitfall of being a young woman. She was small, five foot even, and had inherited her mother's round, youthful cheeks. People often mistook her for a teenager. Daphne resisted the urge to inform the fat man chewing on toothpicks that she was twenty-three years old, an age most people would agree made her an adult. Yet bringing that up seemed childish.

She looked down at herself, wondering if there was something she could do to seem older and more confident. She wore new black flats, a thin polka-dot ribbon tied into a bow on each shoe. Perhaps heels would help, she mused. They would give her an air of professionalism and make her taller. However, her mother had often paraded around on towering pumps, and as a child Daphne had quietly vowed not to torture her own feet.

For this momentous trip, she wore black skinny jeans, tailored nicely to her short legs, and her favorite blouse—silky white with black buttons and a matching collar. Gold key earrings dangled from her earlobes, and she had even taken the time to paint her nails a deep magenta.

She had done everything she could possibly imagine to appear as an adult, to look accomplished and mature. And to hide the truth. She was scared out of her mind to be flying alone, traveling by herself in a shuttle van across the state of Minnesota to a tiny town where she knew no one. Where bad things had happened, but where the truth of who her mother really was might be found.

They continued the trip in silence. When they turned onto the county road exit for Willoughby, Daphne slipped her phone into her purse and concentrated on the view.

The fact that her mother had witnessed the same trees and the same stretch of concrete created a hollow ache in Daphne's heart.

## WELCOME TO WILLOUGHBY!
### Population: 509

Her insides shriveled at the sight of the sign. The taste of the stale Tums lingered on her tongue. Any excitement she had held dissolved beneath the reality of what she had done so impetuously.

"Up by the lake you said?" The driver let out a deep, rumbling burp.

Daphne stared out her window. "Yeah."

Willoughby came into view. It was like a hidden secret, off the main highway, down a curving road, and tucked within the forest. A gas station was the first business: on the left, with Olson Auto Body connected onto the back. Daphne's eyes flitted from a rusted pickup with bald tires waiting in the gravel parking lot over to a farmer in dusty jeans and a baseball cap fiddling with the engine of a shiny tractor. They slowly crossed a road and went down the only business district in sight. Daphne made a mental note to eat dinner at The City Café, a small restaurant on the edge of Main Street. She'd had a hurried lunch at the airport and looked forward to sitting down and taking her time. There looked to be a closed sign on the café's glass door, along with a paper clock indicating they would reopen at four o'clock. Willoughby Grocery was next-door, an impossibly small place, but it would probably have a bag of chips and a loaf of bread for her to stock her motel room with. There was Knutson Drug with a colorful window display: *SUMMER IS ALMOST HERE!* A toddler, his diapers sticking out of the waist of his bright blue pants, flapped his chubby hands at the collection of balls and squirt guns behind the glass. As they drove past, the boy's mother looked up at the glinting windows of the shuttle van, her forehead crinkling.

The driver chuckled. "That's about it; blink and you miss it!"

They crossed Oak Street, and from the right side of the van, Daphne could see a beautiful gazebo, old-fashioned and surrounded by a spacious park. The sounds of children playing filled the air, and she could see the square brick building that, according to the website, housed every grade from prekindergarten through twelfth grade for the residents of not only Willoughby but also the rural community surrounding it. It seemed there was an afternoon recess and the young children were enjoying the bright sun and cool breeze of the late spring day.

"Oh!" Daphne had looked quickly to her left, up Ash Street, and was surprised to see an ornate Victorian mansion surrounded by a wrought-iron fence. It towered over its neighbors. Its old beauty was undeniable, yet incongruous in such a simple, quaint town.

*Quaint.* Her dying mother had used that word to describe this place. Reality smacked Daphne like a painful, unexpected wave. Her mom had walked that very sidewalk and had probably studied the swooping arches and gingerbread trim of that Victorian behemoth.

Daphne swallowed down a lump in her throat.

"All right, sign says to follow up this way." The driver pointed toward a rustic, weather-faded sign for the Willoughby Motel. Main Street curved, and Daphne could see sparkling light through the thick trees. It was Cross Lake, where her mom had stood in the sand dressed in a swimsuit and holding a dripping ice cream cone.

"This is Pelican River," the driver announced as they crossed a metal bridge with diagonal trusses. Daphne peered down at the narrow waterway, spying a young man with a cigarette hanging from the corner of his mouth standing on the clay banks. He held a fishing pole over the gently rushing water. His head moved along with the van, watching them with curious, beady eyes.

They turned onto a gravel road canopied by lush oak trees. For the first time since they had left Nancy at the casino in Alexandria, Daphne feared being alone with the strange man. If he desired, he could pull off the road now that they were deep in the rural woods and murder her. No one—probably not even the man fishing the Pelican River—would hear her screams.

Panic bubbled within her. She held her purse to her chest and ran her thumb over her cell. Finally, the old-fashioned L-shaped motel came into view through the trees. It was just like the picture:

small, clean, and rather charming. Blue curtains hung in each room, all closed.

"Here we are, last stop." The driver parked by the front office and trundled down from his seat. He stretched his arms toward the sky dramatically. After a few guttural groans, he opened the trunk and removed her rolling suitcase.

"Thank you." Daphne got out on shaky legs. She awkwardly removed a five-dollar bill from her wallet and handed it to the driver. "And I'm paid up on my credit card, right?"

"Yes." He scanned the length of the motel. "Here." He put a meaty hand into his pocket and fished out a card. "This is my number. I live in St. Paul, but I'm always driving back and forth past here a lot. Call me if you need something: a ride, or maybe help."

Help? She glanced at the card and slipped it into her purse, amid a mess of receipts and brochures. "Thanks again. I appreciate it." Daphne took her suitcase and rolled it across the gravel and up a single step to the motel office. The cynical side of her, powered by her mother's memory, wondered what sort of help a shuttle driver could give her. Yet another hearty part of herself was thankful to know someone, anyone, in this unfamiliar new land.

Daphne pushed through the screen door of the office. A woman dressed in a light cardigan and sporting a short, spiky hairdo stood at the front desk, a copy of Ann Rule's *The Stranger Beside Me* tented in front of her.

The shuttle rumbled out of the parking lot back toward Minneapolis, leaving an eerie silence behind.

Daphne stepped toward the desk and pointed at the book. "She's from Washington."

"What's that?"

"Ann Rule—she's from Washington state." Daphne smiled. "That's where I'm from."

"Yes, of course. You've come a long way, then." The middle-aged woman removed an enormous, leather-bound book from a drawer. She dropped it onto the counter. "You must be Daphne Forrest?"

Daphne gave a tentative nod, watching the clerk write in the ledger. She had never checked into a motel on her own before. A surge of pride that she was at least appearing to be an adult caused her to stand straighter.

As the woman scribbled notes, Daphne glanced around the cramped office. There was a dented coffee pot circled by a mismatched array of mugs in the corner.

"How long do you think you'll be staying with us?" The woman flipped quickly to another page of the ledger. "Looks like you're paid up through the thirty-first. That's, gosh, about two weeks."

"What do you mean?"

"Your dad called and paid for you through the end of the month." The woman looked up into Daphne's eyes and smiled warmly. "Adam, right?"

"Oh. Yes." Daphne sighed. "Okay, well, I'll let you know if it's going to be any longer."

Her moment of maturity fizzled. Of course her dad had had to meddle with her reservation.

The clerk took a key off the pegboard behind her. The display made Daphne think of a motel from a movie: how they all hung side by side with numbers on their attached plastic rectangles. "Your dad's just trying to take care of you."

Daphne nodded. She could sense the warm rush of embarrassment in her cheeks.

The woman handed the key to Daphne. "You're in twelve. That's at the very end, and it's the nicest, in my opinion."

"Thank you."

"Sign here."

Daphne scrawled her signature.

"I have to say . . ." The woman drummed her fingers on the desk. "We don't usually have young people like you staying here, alone."

"Oh?" Daphne patted her stomach; it was bubbling with anxiety underneath her blouse.

"It's just . . . I don't know what you're going to do here. Once it's warm enough you can swim, but that's probably a few more weeks yet." She frowned, causing the thin wrinkles around her mouth to deepen.

"I'm writing a book," Daphne explained. She had hoped to be anonymous here, a random face in the crowd. Immediately, it seemed her fears were materializing, that her presence was naturally conspicuous.

The woman nodded. "Ah." She squinted at Daphne. "About bad things?"

"Yeah, I guess." Daphne squirmed. She bent down and grasped her suitcase tightly. Under the woman's watchful scrutiny, she wondered if her round, childish cheeks would give her away? Would the first Willoughby resident she encountered realize she was related to *her*, to the town ghoul, Caroline Bergman?

"Bad things have happened here." The woman grinned. "But Willoughby is a wonderful place; you'll see."

"Yes," Daphne squeaked.

"Let me know what you need. I'm Maggie, and my husband, Jay, is lurking around here somewhere. Our sons come out and help from time to time. You can ask them for any assistance, as well." Maggie picked up her paperback. "It'll be pretty quiet here until school gets out, but then we get full of families."

A man appeared through the back door of the motel office, his salt-and-pepper hair stuck up in messy tufts. "Mags, I can't run to the Archer's 'til tomorrow. I don't want to be out at night. What if the truck stalls again?"

Maggie waved him away. "All right, then."

He produced a hankie from the back pocket of his jeans and wiped at his nose as he glanced over at Daphne. "The sun falls fast here."

"Jay, this is Daphne. She's staying with us."

"Welcome." He spoke through the red fabric. "We got coffee in the morning, if you drink the stuff."

"Thanks. I do. Nice to meet you both." Daphne navigated her luggage out into the sunshine.

As she walked to room twelve, she appreciated the weight of the key in her hand. The sensation of it, the rough line, oddly made her feel both free and grownup. It was strange, she knew, that this was her first venture away from home. Beverly was going to be an actual doctor and married. And here Daphne was: not in Cancun on spring break or visiting Beverly in California but officially in the middle of nowhere. Yet this hidden town had been the center of her mom's universe. A paranoid thought invaded Daphne's pleasant stroll to her room. She questioned if inside the office Maggie had returned to reading about the horrific reign of Ted Bundy or if she had leaned over the counter to gossip with her husband about their newest motel guest. Had they recognized that the daughter of Caroline Bergman, alleged axe murderer, had come home?

# July 4, 1982

CAROLINE USED TO LIKE the eerie atmosphere of the empty school, when everyone had left in a messy rush and the green linoleum was covered in rumpled notes and candy bar wrappers. It had been her kingdom. She had known every dull scuff of her shoe and even the stuttering whine of the janitor's polishing machine. She would circle the dark classrooms, forgotten for a while yet still somehow alive with energy.

When she was younger, she would play teacher in the kindergarten class, rubbing the chalkboards with her small hands and setting stuffed animals on the sharing rug. As she grew, she looked for interesting finds. She sometimes stole cigarettes from Mr. Sanderson's metal cupboard. She would smoke them in the gym—or once in the nurse's office as she lay on the sickbed, unraveling a long curl of scratchy gauze.

But ever since that horrible event two months ago, the overflowing trash cans and the sound of the dripping water fountains in the abandoned corridors carried a new, unwelcome feeling.

Caroline believed her dad hadn't known what she had seen that evening. This was only proof. He would never have voluntarily invited her to relive that moment.

"Carrie." Her father sat behind his enormous desk, his head barely visible between the neatly stacked piles of chemistry and physics textbooks. "Did you bring your friends? We can move faster—"

"No, it's just me," Caroline interrupted. She ran her hand over a sealed box of notebooks. "Kyle's coming, though. He was just helping out at Roger's."

Gunnar Bergman crossed his long arms and scowled.

Caroline took in a sharp breath. The sight of her dad's scrunched face brought an unexpected swell of anger to her heart. "He's coming," she repeated. "We can start anyways."

It was barely ten in the morning, yet the stale air of the school was muggy and clingy. A bead of sweat trickled theatrically down from the crux of her armpit and caught in the underarm of the new bathing suit she wore beneath her clothing. Caroline fanned herself, rustling her knee-length dress to get some cooling air. She wished she had waited to put her suit on until after she was at Cross Lake. But that morning she hadn't been able to resist modeling it in front of the mirror, making sure she looked desirable from every angle.

Caroline followed her father down the school's back steps to the gymnasium. Because it was summer most of the doors were locked. Gunnar handled a ball of keys in his palm, searching for the correct one.

Finally, as Caroline melted in the stifling heat, he located the gym key and pushed open the large door.

Caroline switched on the panel of lights.

Gunnar crossed the cavernous room, his loafers squeaking, and opened the two doors that led to the outside. Brilliant sunlight and fresh summer air flooded the gym.

"Grab what you can; we'll have to make a few trips." Her father used his authoritative teacher voice. It echoed off the painted brick walls.

Caroline found a wheeled cart bursting with colorful balls and hula hoops. She pushed it toward the open door, hoisting it up over the threshold. The wheels hit the grass with a dull thud. She tried to push it forward through the soft dirt, but it wouldn't budge.

"I've got it." Kyle appeared, panting. His bicycle lay on its side, the back tire still spinning. "Bess is back in her pen, but Roger said she'll probably get out again if we don't fix up that post. It needs some nails, is all; at least, that's what he said."

Gunnar hoisted badminton netting over his shoulder. "You're late."

Kyle rolled his eyes. "Let's get this moving." He grabbed the wheeled cart and pulled. It dislodged from the clump of dirt and grass.

Caroline smirked. She was happy he was there—happy she wasn't alone.

They left Gunnar behind in the gym as they maneuvered the cart, her pushing and him pulling.

As they passed the school's playground and rounded the trees, the smell of barbecued ribs tickled Caroline's nose. She had already planned out her paper plate: a healthy glob of Diana Maki's potato salad (it had the least amount of mustard), two of Doris Woodhouse's famous caramel rolls, and a nice heap of Dirk Ericcson's sweet honey ribs, with extra napkins on the side.

Caroline's stomach rumbled at the thought.

The Willoughby gazebo came into view. Red, white, and blue streamers wound artfully around each white pillar. Balloons stamped with patriotic stars swayed in the summer breeze, attached to each wooden stair with strings of ribbon. Small blond boys weaved in and out of the line of grills and picnic tables, their tiny fingers hovering over the triggers of their water guns.

Kyle walked backward, looking over his shoulder so he could dodge running dogs, old ladies in wide-brimmed hats, bags of fireworks, and coolers of beer.

Caroline's heart burst with excitement for the Willoughby Fourth of July Picnic, her town's finest hour. There were strangers sniffing the savory air and adjusting gingham table cloths. It made her proud that people came to *her* little town to celebrate.

"This'll work." Kyle parked the cart at the edge of the grass. A trail of children had followed them, eyeing the toys. A little girl who wasn't from Willoughby and who had red Popsicle juice lining her mouth reached out tentatively and touched a hula hoop.

Kyle smiled. "You can take it; just bring it back when you're finished." Caroline recognized their dad in him then, in the way his eyes narrowed into squinty lines.

The delighted children grabbed at the balls and paddles.

Unexpected sadness settled into Caroline's heart. Her smile faded as she watched them run off with their prizes, planning games of soccer or hopscotch or capture the flag.

"What's wrong?" Kyle asked, his eyes squeezed almost shut.

"I don't know." It was the truth.

Kyle was only four minutes older than her, but lately he'd acted like that difference was much greater. He nodded toward the children. "You wanna play something?"

"God, no!" A tell-tale pink crept across her full cheeks, though. They were her curse, those damn sensitive cheeks.

He leaned against the empty cart, a satisfied grin blooming. He surveyed the holiday festivities with the air of a timeworn grandfather bursting with sage advice.

Kyle looked even more like their father when he crossed his arms. He was six foot even, just like Gunnar. Instead of being awkwardly gangly like some of his taller classmates, Kyle carried the same quiet confidence of their father. They were both handsome, with matching masculine dimples in their strong chins. Caroline thought, as the sunshine sparkled through Kyle's honey-colored hair, that he and Gunnar were the true twins.

He kicked at something in the grass. "You think you'll stay here? After school?"

Caroline shrugged. Her mind had become suddenly occupied with whether she should tell him what she'd seen two months ago. The thought of saying it aloud, acknowledging it as reality, unnerved her.

Perhaps it had been a dream?

"I'm going to college. Maybe I'll learn about agriculture, and then I'll come back and help Roger or get my own farm." Kyle fished a lighter from the pocket of his jean shorts.

"Farmers don't go to college."

"Yeah." Kyle rolled his thumb over the trigger of the Bic, and fire blazed.

"If Mom sees—"

"I know." He stuffed the lighter back into his pocket. "You should go too."

"What? To college?" She shaded her eyes with her hand, watching Dr. Woodhouse and his wife, Doris, set up glistening caramel rolls in a line of crystal trays on a table beside the gazebo.

"To college, yeah. We can go together."

She thought about Greg for the first time since she had modeled her bathing suit in front of her full-length mirror. He could ask her to marry him after prom next year, and then if life was fair, Dr. and Doris Woodhouse would die or leave and Greg and Caroline could buy their mansion. She would keep all the furniture and art inside, and they would have kids—adorable, perfect children with Greg's innocent smile. And she would make Jell-O salad with grapes mixed in, and they would bring it to the Willoughby Fourth of July Picnic in Doris's sparkling crystal trays.

That would be ideal.

"I don't know. Seems like a waste of time."

"Just saying." Kyle rolled his squinty eyes again. "We should help Mom." He pointed toward the gazebo, where their mother wobbled on a stepstool, hanging a string of American flags above the entrance.

Her twin brother walked away. Caroline looked up at the cloudless sky and let the sun warm her face. Thoughts of Greg and living in Willoughby forever made her content. She removed the elastic tie that held her ponytail and let her brown curls fall down her back.

"Wait up!" Caroline chased Kyle, hopping over a mound of picnic blankets.

They helped their mother with the paper flags; Caroline held the tape. And then they returned to the school to lug sturdy chairs back for the old people. As soon as they placed them on the wooden floor of the gazebo, the elderly Willoughbians planted their butts.

The lunch line grew long with restless children and sunburned tourists. Caroline tiptoed into line, careful not to catch the attention of her parents, who would undoubtedly ask her to drag something else heavy across Willoughby Park.

"Hey, Carrie." Tiffany pinched Caroline's arm. "Coming swimming later?"

Caroline slipped the wide strap of her dress off her shoulder to reveal the pastel swimsuit underneath. "I got it at Penney's in St. Cloud."

"Nice." Tiffany sidled up to her.

"No cuts, Titty!" Will Dobson shouted from behind them. His younger brother, Dave, slapped his own knee, braying with laughter.

Tiffany swirled around and glared at the brothers. "Shut up, pizza face!"

Will's pimples burned bright red.

"Asses," Tiffany muttered under her breath as she turned back toward Caroline. "I'll be so happy when we can get out of here and find decent boys. No, not boys, real men." She looked down and adjusted her V-neck T-shirt.

"Speaking of . . ." Caroline bit her lip in expectation.

"Oh God."

"Is he coming?"

Tiffany frowned. "Sort of."

They moved a pace forward.

"Whadya mean?" Caroline pulled up the strap of her dress.

"Caroline . . ." Tiffany looked down at the sterling silver bangles on her wrist. She began to play with them, turning them around and around. "He's coming but he's, you know . . . I mean, you must know . . ."

A cold fist gripped Caroline's heart. "What?"

"Rosalee got her claws in him; everyone knows it. I'm pretty sure you'd have to be blind not to know." Tiffany tried to laugh, but it came out like a stifled sneeze.

A gap opened in the line before them, but Caroline couldn't move her unstable frame. Just Rosalee's name, spoken so casually, converted her into a limp dishrag.

"I'm sorry." Tiffany patted her awkwardly. "But you don't want Greg Brody."

"Shh!" Caroline recognized the heat rising to her face. Her cheeks were ready to betray her again, revealing her deepest emotions before she was ready to acknowledge them.

Tiffany hunched over to speak into Caroline's ear. "He's never going to leave Willoughby his whole life, and he'll probably be a farmer or just a drunk like ol' Dewitt. And you can tell he's going to be bald. I mean, someday he's going to lose that beautiful blond hair; you can just tell, Carrie!"

Caroline smiled. Tiffany always had a way of making her spirits brighten, even for a second.

Tiffany yanked her by the arm up to Dirk Ericcson's heaping pile of sweet ribs. They smelled like summer to her.

"Give Caroline an extra one, Dirk; she's blue." Tiffany handed him her Styrofoam plate. Dirk's eyes instantly flashed down to Tiffany's enormous breasts, squeezed into her too-small T-shirt. She had been having that effect on men since the sixth grade. Even Dirk, nearing sixty, was not immune to teenaged Tiffany's mature body.

"Ah, yeah, okay then." Using tongs, Dirk piled ribs onto the plate.

"Wow!" a familiar voice trilled from behind them.

Caroline turned to see Rosalee. She held a satchel full of beach towels. A cigarette was perched between her cupid-bow lips.

Caroline was sure her own cheeks were a vibrant shade of magenta.

"Wow!" Rosalee repeated.

"What?" Tiffany took the plate from Dirk. A drop of sauce dribbled down the side and onto the grass.

Rosalee blew smoke. "You girls need to slow down."

"What's that supposed to mean?" Tiffany set the plate down on Dirk's picnic table as though she were preparing herself for battle.

Rosalee smirked. The sight of her smug expression made Caroline furious.

"I'm just saying." She took the cigarette from her mouth and held it between her fingers. "You don't want to be fat for senior year."

Tiffany stepped forward, and Caroline thought she should hold her back. She would have been wholly useless though, as her body had become a wet noodle again, weak and tingling.

"Now that I think about it, I guess you're already halfway there," Rosalee spat.

"Rosalee Edwards!" a woman exclaimed from the crowd.

Everyone turned in a strange, nearly rehearsed unison to watch the unfolding drama.

Rosalee shrugged. "Just saying."

From the corner of her vision, Caroline could make out her father crossing the grass, his glasses glinting in the sunlight. She could see the strain in his jaw, and she knew that what was coming was inevitable. She couldn't find the strength to try to stop it.

"What's going on?" Gunnar approached Rosalee. "Is there a problem?"

Caroline could sense sweat, oddly cold, sliding down her back.

"Nothing, nothing." Rosalee looked up at Gunnar Bergman, her smirk still firmly on her tanned face. "No worries."

Tiffany pointed at her. "She's being a bitch!"

"Hey!" Gunnar boomed. "That's enough."

Something unhinged in Caroline's mind. She looked at Rosalee and fought the churn of physical sickness. Her father's words pounded in her ears.

"*Stop!*" Caroline screeched. She covered her mouth with a trembling hand.

Her father stared.

They all stared. She could sense them all: classmates, old people, all staring through her.

Dirk, frozen, held the dripping tongs.

Caroline's mother came stepping down the gazebo stairs, her head cocked toward the commotion.

A small child's laugh punctured the stillness.

"Go away, Dad." Caroline's voice was not her own. It vibrated in her chest, as though she was possessed by someone else, someone bolder, someone more like Tiffany. "I hate you." It came out as a husky whisper.

No one heard.

Her dad stood waiting with his fists clenched. If her tinny words had carried across to his ears, she knew he would have clutched her by the shoulder and screamed in her face.

"What?" Tiffany rested her hand on Caroline's shoulder. "What did you say?"

"Never mind." Caroline looked down at her cork sandals. The smell of the ribs had turned sour in her nose. It would have been nice, she mused, if the ground would have opened up and devoured her and everyone else in Willoughby. Then the rage would leave her body, as would the curiosity from their ugly, prying eyeballs. She had said *it*, however quietly, and she knew from the burst of fireworks in her ribcage that she had meant it.

A piece of her hungered to be heard. To speak louder and watch as her father realized how much she hated him. She forced that fantasy away.

"Get me out of here." The heat of rage and embarrassment was cooking her insides. Caroline leaned into her best friend, thankful for the comfort of Tiffany's familiar fruity scent.

Tiffany nodded obediently. "Let's go."

They intertwined their arms and marched away, together.

# 10

DAPHNE HAD BLOOD ON HER HANDS. It wasn't fresh. It was a viscous jelly, clumping between her fingers. She tried to wipe it off on her skirt, but the red clung to her skin.

Her mother appeared in the forest, peeking around the trunk of a peeling birch tree. She was young—younger than Daphne. Her face was porcelain and she wore a dark swimsuit. Dried ice cream was smudged at the corners of her lips.

"This way." Her mother's voice was scratchy, like it had been in the end. "Follow me, Daffy."

Daphne was weighed down by the blood. It wasn't just between her fingers; it was all over her, dripping down her dress like pancake syrup.

Her mother raced across the dirt. They were in soft soil, tilled it seemed for an incredibly large garden. It became mud, though, and Daphne was up to her knees in it. She trudged through it, wondering how her young mother could skip across it with such youthful grace.

Jane-Caroline laughed a child's laugh. "Come on!" Her voice rattled with death. "Come on and see her!"

At the end of the great pile of dirt was a house. It was slender, with a small porch and a puffing brick chimney. A short simple fence surrounded the lonely building. Her mother, barely a teenager, swung on the gate, kicking her legs and giggling.

"I'm waiting!" she croaked. "Daffy, hurry!"

The smell of rancid blood overwhelmed Daphne. It had soaked through to her underwear, and it squelched in her summer sandals. Her stomach churned as she fought through the last bit of dirt.

"Don't be slow. You're always very slow. I hate that." Her child mom frowned. The ice cream on her cheeks was no longer a faint hint of chocolate. It had turned into a deep red and was smeared from her forehead down to her chin.

Daphne reached out for the brick road, and she was suddenly standing on top of it. Her stomach roiled, and she wanted to leave. Yet the house with the dark windows beckoned to her.

Her mother had disappeared, and Daphne had never felt so alone. The forest was very far away and there was only the house, starkly white in the brilliant daylight. Daphne raised her hand to shield her eyes from the glare, relieved that the jelly blood was gone and her hands were perfectly clean.

She didn't remember going through the small yard and walking up the porch steps, but here she stood, in the front hall of the house. It smelled musty and of old, rotting meat. The heat was oppressive. Sweat trickled from her top lip, and she licked at the salt.

"Daffy?" Her mother sat across from her on the crooked stairs. An ice cream cone melted in her hand. "Why are you here still? You shouldn't be here."

Daphne wiped at her eyes. "I'm sorry, Mom."

Her mom pointed a sticky finger. "Look."

Daphne turned her head to see an old-fashioned parlor room. A vine-like pattern crawled up the wallpaper. An ornate couch with polished wooden feet was tucked in the corner.

She stepped toward the piece of antique furniture, curious about the man that lay outstretched upon it. He wore leather shoes, and he seemed to be asleep with his head propped up on a decorative pillow.

As Daphne inched closer, her stomach flipped and twisted,

indicating before she could really process it that she was seeing something wrong, something out of the ordinary. The man's hand was clenched in a fist. His face was a pulpy, indecipherable mess. Bits of teeth and bone stared back at her, broken pieces that made no sense in the soft tissue.

Her mother's dying voice shook the walls of the house. "Why did you kill Mr. Borden?"

"No, no, I didn't." Daphne tripped backward. She swiveled around, hoping to see her young mom on the stairs. She wanted a hug, a kiss, a reassurance.

Her mother was gone.

Instead, there was a woman in a white dress. It was buttoned up to her chin, and the lacy hem skimmed the floor where she stood. A pile of hair sat on her head, and she glared at Daphne with bulbous, veiny eyes. It was Lizzie Borden. Daphne recognized her from that documentary she'd watched so long ago. "Why did you kill him?"

"No . . . I . . ." Daphne looked down at the foreign weight in her hands. She dropped the axe handle, and the blade made an echoing metallic screech as it landed on the hardwood.

"Why did you kill him?" Lizzie Borden repeated. Her mouth was a dark hole with no teeth.

"No! I didn't mean to!" Daphne clutched at her belly. The nausea bubbled up into her throat. "I didn't mean to!"

Her body moved, falling toward the front door. She rushed down the steps. She tasted blood in her mouth. It singed her tongue, and she knew she was going to vomit.

"Why, Daphne? Why would you do that?" Her mother waited at the gate. She was her older self, fifty-one, with gray strands of hair twisting out of her bald head and black circles under her accusing eyes.

"I didn't mean to!" The blood had returned, old and gelatinous on her slick palms. "I didn't!"

And then a sound gripped her. It was as loud as a speeding train, shaking her body and ripping apart her brain. It was a sickening crunch. It pulled her away from the old house, up, up into the air and above the dirt and the strange, leafless trees.

Daphne woke with a gasp. She cried into the motel pillow, taking gulps of air into her aching lungs. Finally, she rubbed her eyes open and looked at her quaking hands.

There was no blood.

## 11

THE PANIC OF HER DREAM and the bald fear washed away. She was left with an overwhelming solitude that enveloped her in an unwelcome hug.

The evening light trickled into the motel room, illuminating the ratty pulled threads of the comforter over Daphne's legs. She had slept later than she had meant to, succumbing to the cool shadows and call of the empty bed.

Daphne stood. The thick-pile carpet tickled her bare feet. She unzipped her suitcase and dug until she found a plastic shopping bag. She unraveled it as she made her way to the closet-sized bathroom. The fluorescent light flickered overhead as she removed her deodorant from the bag. She rubbed it on her armpits, sniffing to make sure the salty tang of her nightmare had dissipated. She poured out the rest of the contents of the bag into the sink. Her bright pink tube of mascara looked lost in the chipped porcelain. Her eyeshadow had opened during the flight and had sprinkled light green powder on her toothbrush. Daphne frowned. She found her lipstick, a rosy shade called Eternal Flame, and dared to look in the mirror.

The quality of the light made her pale skin look a sickly green. Dark circles had sprouted beneath her eyes. She pressed her finger into the thin skin, thinking of her mother. Daphne did a full makeup overhaul, even stopping to tweeze a few errant eyebrow hairs. She brushed the kinks out of her blonde hair and smoothed down her bangs. The process of it calmed her. She took each tube, cream, and brush and placed them on a metal ledge next to a pair of plastic-wrapped cups. Later, she told herself, she would come back, fold her clothes, and place them with care into the provided chest of drawers.

It would make her mother happy. To organize. Daphne wasn't sure if that made her happy too or if it annoyed her that the ghost of her mother was always with her, whether in her nightmares or just to remind her to not be sloppy.

She needed fresh air and something decent to eat. Being away from the dim room would take her further away from the dream. The memory of it needled her, flooding her system with panic until she reminded herself that it wasn't real. It was all a terrible mishmash of Freudian imagery. Nothing more than a collection of random thoughts stored in a secret part of her brain, waiting to be unleashed on her when she was most vulnerable.

Daphne opened the door of her motel room a crack and looked out. The spring air had turned a bit cooler, which reminded her of the nippy ocean air she had grown up loving. The mature aspect of herself, the same piece of her that had lined up her makeup instead of leaving it in a clump in the sink, urged her to grab a sweater from her suitcase. She shrugged defiantly at the thought, confident that she could handle a waft of cool air on her own. She double-checked that her motel key was in the inner pocket of her purse and let the door slam shut behind her.

She stood awkwardly on the slatted deck that connected the rooms. The gravel lot was empty except for a few cars crowding the end where the main office stood. She watched as a chubby orange tabby sauntered down the rural road toward town. It swished its fluffy tail and stopped to sniff a fresh dandelion.

Daphne slipped her hand into her purse and felt for her phone. She slid it out carefully, not wanting to disturb the cat. She snapped a quick picture of it and sent it to Beverly. Her best friend would surely like it and know that Daphne was okay, that she was functioning with no mother. They could text about Gopher and Beverly's dead cat, Sweetie, and everything would go back to normal.

Daphne noticed the flash indicating low battery on the phone screen. She lowered her hands, knowing she had to save the phone's energy for the evening. "Crap." She should have plugged it in before she nodded off into her nightmare.

The orange cat abandoned its task and continued down the gravel path.

"He passes by every day."

"Oh!" Daphne instinctively clutched her phone to her chest as she turned toward the strange voice.

"Sorry, I just meant the cat." By the door marked with a 9, a young man stood holding a pile of folded towels. He was Asian, with dark cocoa eyes and a swish of black hair that was both messy and controlled. "He's friendly."

"Right." Daphne forced a smile. "I love cats. All animals, really."

"My mom told me to bring you more towels. She said you're going to be here awhile."

"Your mom?"

"Yeah, my mom and dad run this place. You know, from the front desk? Maggie? My mom's white, if that's what's confusing you." His eyes sparkled.

Daphne shook her head. "No! No, that's not confusing, of course! I'm just, yeah . . . I'm just new here and I'm out of my element."

He laughed. He was handsome and quite tall.

Daphne's cheeks flushed, as they always did in strained moments. A sneaky trickle of nervous sweat popped up behind her ears. "I'm sorry, thank you."

He stepped forward. "I'll just put these inside."

"Yeah." Daphne shuffled to the side, out of the way of the door. "Say, can you tell me how I can get to town? Is there a taxi service or something? Or Uber?"

"Uber in Willoughby?" He slipped a master key into the door. "Hell, no."

"Okay." Daphne tapped her fingers against her phone. "Is there someone I can call?"

"I told my parents we should have a rental car here. Maybe we could work something out." He pushed open the door and disappeared into the shadows. She felt embarrassed as she knew he was stepping over her disordered suitcase.

The man emerged from the room empty-handed. He closed the door and leaned his hand against it, looking down at her. "If I found a car for you, you'd bring it back, right?"

Daphne stiffened. "No. I mean, I can't take a car, thank you."

"It's really okay." He smiled down at her. "Otherwise, you'll have to walk, and it's muddy still. You'll get your shoes all, you know, messed up." He motioned toward her flats with the polka-dot bows.

"It's just that I don't drive." She felt incredibly young and stupid, like she was an infant. "I mean, I can but I don't. I don't have my license."

The young man opened his mouth and then closed it. He wanted to ask; Daphne could tell from the way he screwed his lips shut.

He let his hand fall from the door and stood up straight. "I'll run you in, then. Where're you going?"

"No, you don't have to—"

"It's fine. I'll drop you. That's part of my job. Probably?" He laughed. She liked the sound of it, happy and comfortable. "C'mon."

"I'm Daphne," she offered meekly, still mortified by her inability to drive.

"Edwin Monroe."

Daphne followed him across the gravel lot to a dirty Toyota Corolla. It was streaked with the mud he'd mentioned, making the car's actual color hard to pinpoint. As she grabbed at the door handle, an internal alarm pulsated inside her. This was what her mother had warned her against. Her mom's voice crackled in her head, telling her to stop all the madness, to not attempt to walk alone or, worse, be driven by a stranger around the backwoods.

She could call the helpful shuttle driver and ask him to take her back to the airport. She could do it now, before she had to explain to

Beverly where she was. Her father would be happy to see her. He wouldn't chide her for giving up. He would be relieved, though only half as much as she would be.

Daphne struggled to stamp down her mother's loud voice. It was difficult to discern the difference between her mom's paranoia and Daphne's own thoughts.

Edwin was young and nice, and his laugh made Daphne smile.

"Sorry, hold on." He squeezed in front of her and bent down to clean up the passenger side of his Toyota. Daphne took a step back and watched as he tossed a manila folder of paper, a handful of empty Target shopping bags, and a pair of sneakers into the backseat.

"Okay, that's as good as it gets." With a sheepish grin, he gestured for her to take a seat.

She smoothed her hand down her stomach to quiet it and sat, pulling the seatbelt across her. An intense craving for a mint gripped her.

He closed the door for her and rounded the car before getting into the driver's seat.

"Where to?"

"The restaurant I saw on Main Street. I mean, is there more than one?" She fiddled with the collar of her blouse.

"The City Café." He started the engine. "That's the only place to eat." His dark eyes gazed down the empty road. Daphne thought she could read a touch of shame in his expression. "Willoughby isn't exactly the capital of excitement."

She laughed, but it came out high pitched and sugary.

They rolled out of the parking lot.

She actually liked the smell of his cluttered car. It wasn't completely pleasant. There was a latent scent of gym socks, but she liked how it felt lived in, not perfect. A cinnamon-bun-shaped air freshener swung from the rearview mirror. Daphne glanced behind her and saw a pile of fast food wrappers in the back seat. She figured if he was a serial killer, he would have to be decidedly more organized.

Daphne tried to study him without staring. He wore well-fitting jeans that were frayed on one knee. The rips were not the fabricated kind. They came, she supposed, from real work around the motel. His T-shirt was plain white and a bit thin. She could see the tan skin of his chest through the fabric, especially when he inhaled before speaking.

"Can I ask?" His hand rested on the gearshift. "Why you're here? I mean, it's not my business. It's just, there's nothing to do. I mean, I'm back here to help my parents, but I wouldn't be otherwise."

"Did you grow up here?" Daphne asked. "Willoughby seems so nice for a child, sort of idyllic." She glanced at his profile.

He shrugged. "We moved here when I was eight. I thought we'd landed in the Twilight Zone. I was used to a big city: all the people and the places. Willoughby was just so small. I live in Minneapolis now, getting my master's in journalism at the Main U."

"Oh, me too. I mean, in Washington. I'm working on a literature degree. Not that I know what I'm going to do with it." Daphne kept a close eye on where they went. She wanted to keep track of each unique dip, curve, or fork in the road. Eventually, she would have to walk this route. There wouldn't always be a helpful stranger with a Toyota.

"I'm trying to be a journalist. I like writing about politics, crime, and all that stuff. Although my dad wants me to take over the motel eventually; he thinks I'm more responsible than my brother. Which is true." He glanced over at her, his chocolate eyes brimming with humor. "But I don't want to live here; just the summer is enough." They glided down the rural road and back over the bridge. The setting sun twinkled across what she remembered the shuttle driver calling the Pelican River.

"I like to write too." She pressed her hand against the inner pocket of her purse. She had run out of Tums and mints.

"No kidding. Fiction? Or are you a muckraker like me?"

Daphne hesitated. Headlines came to the forefront of her mind, written by overeager journalists who were more concerned with a salacious story than the truth about her mom. And Daphne remembered her own bad time, when reporters had said untrue things about her too. "Uh, both. I thought maybe I'd do some research here." The lie tasted like death in her mouth. "I'm writing a book."

"Willoughby is a fascinating place, even if it is small. I assume you're writing about something that happened here?" He took his eyes off the quiet road to observe her face. She turned away, fearful he would recognize her for what she was: a liar, and a bad one at that.

She organized her thoughts as the Main Street businesses came into view.

"Maybe. I'm not sure exactly yet. I guess I just needed some solitude." She chided herself for her sloppy story. Every day it would be easier, she assured herself. Through practice, she would learn to lie in a more authentic way. She would believe her own lies if she worked on them consistently enough.

If she really concentrated, she could even forget her mother had ever lived in this place. She could forget that she had been accused and shunned and had lost her family in such a savage way.

"Let me know if I can help out. I know quite a bit about the town history." He scratched at his clean-shaven jaw. "City Café, right?"

"Yes, please."

They slowed to allow a pair of teen girls to cross Main Street. He stared straight ahead. "So, you mentioned solitude. Like, do you mean away from your boyfriend?"

Daphne's stomach flipped and fizzled. Unlike her usual anxiety, it was a deliciously good ache, like a shot of adrenaline had swelled through her. "Ah, no, just my dad."

They both laughed nervously.

"Sorry, that was bad." He shrugged his muscular shoulders. "Anyways, the BLT is pretty good, or the grilled cheese."

They pulled up next to the curb, and he pulled the gearshift into park. Daphne glimpsed the door of the City Café, which was held open by a heavy potted plant.

He turned toward her, his eyes flitting all around the Toyota but never landing on her.

She unlatched the door of the car and swung it open. "Thank you, Edwin." She twisted around and held out her hand.

"You're welcome." He encapsulated her tiny hand with his own. "I'll pick you up here at eight thirty, okay?"

"Um." Daphne pulled her hand back. "You shouldn't feel like you have to. I mean, I can make my own way back."

Edwin's jaw tightened. "I don't think you should be walking around here at night. Not alone."

"Well . . ." She was certain everyone in the world must recognize how helpless she appeared. Was there a neon sign hovering above her, indicating how naïve she was? What was it about her that made everyone instinctually want to take care of her?

"Besides, you'll see everything by then." Edwin smiled. "Probably twice over. And this place shuts down quick. We're a farm town. No one walks alone around here at night."

She hesitated. Then she nodded. "Thank you. Yeah, eight thirty sounds great."

Daphne shut the car door and stood in front of the City Café. She waited, listening as Edwin made a U-turn behind her and headed back up toward the motel. She liked his smile and his easy laugh, though his warning against her being alone at night crept across her spine. It sounded like something her mom would have said. Jane Downs-Forrest had had an innate distrust of others.

*Caroline Bergman*, Daphne reminded herself.

Children screeched with happiness in the distance. A dog barked. The smell of greasy fries swirled from the doorway, causing her stomach to rumble greedily.

Every sound and smell of Willoughby reminded Daphne that her mother had spent her childhood on those very sidewalks. She knew her mom must have stood in that spot, perhaps happy or hungry. What frightened Daphne, down to the pit of her soul, was that she might remind the people of Willoughby of the woman who had raised her—the woman who had given her round apple cheeks prone to flushing. The woman they knew as an axe murderer.

# Edwin

HE MANEUVERED HIS COROLLA into a curved wayside about a half mile west of the motel. Rainbow splinters of twilight sparkled across the car's hood, blinding him as he shifted into park.

Edwin slumped down in the driver's seat and let out a wobbly breath. Both his hands came up to stroke his mop of hair. It calmed him to repeat the action several times, curling a few strands behind his ears.

He was acutely aware of how he would look to others: parked there beneath a drooping willow, blinking straight ahead at nothing.

As if in answer to his anxiety, a familiar rusted station wagon crested the hill behind Edwin. He watched through the rearview mirror as it slowed.

He didn't know the name of the farmer inside or of his moon-faced wife, whom he had often seen at the grocery store, carefully reading milk expiration dates while she held a sweaty clump of coupons.

Although he didn't know them, their faces and their Volvo wagon with the loose bumper that rattled in a rhythmic, musical beat, were a part of Willoughby.

More a part of it than he could ever be.

They both stared at Edwin as they drove by. The woman's sunburned elbow stuck out from her open window. She attempted a slight neighborly nod, but she thrust her chin out a bit too severely.

The movement appeared to be more of an accusation.

They were undoubtedly gossiping about him as they took a left onto the pitted dirt road toward their farm.

How he was unlike them. Asian, yes, but there was more than that.

A ping of hope brightened his mood. He let his hands fall into his lap as he thought of another *other*. Of the girl—a shiny bauble in a sea of bland. And it was not just because she was pretty—which she was, achingly so. But because she was unlike them too.

Daphne had this way about her, this unlikely flux of confidence and timidity, which was inherently intriguing.

The skin on his neck prickled at the memory of his fumbling, flirtatious words. And how he must have seemed to her, almost predatory in the way he had warned her.

He had sounded like one of them, a Willoughbian. And there was nothing more abhorrent to him than to be lumped in with their groupthink. With their matching suspicious head tilts, their glum, deeply sunk eyes, and their synthetic, insincere voices.

Seeing Daphne, how she had stared up at the City Café with a look of awkward apprehension, had created a fountain of emotions he hadn't been prepared for.

He had an instant tenderness for her and, too, a sort of necessity to take care of her. It wasn't that she seemed helpless; in fact, there was a blazing competency in her eyes that made him like her even more. His instinct for protection had been activated by the falling sun. It would be black soon. Not dark, not dimly lit. There would be an actual blackness that overwhelmed Willoughby in its entirety.

Edwin understood the black in Willoughby better than anyone. It was tethered to him, tugging at the corners of his mind, crashing through his body when he least expected, or wanted, it to.

Knowing that this blackness could take Daphne, that it could pierce through her as it did him, burrowed a hollow hole into his heart.

He clutched the steering wheel, cursing the shadows of night as they licked at the tires of his Corolla.

Edwin was determined to pull the beautiful stranger, Daphne, from the blackness. Before its teeth could sink in.

# July 5, 1982

IT WAS LATE, PROBABLY PAST NOON. Caroline could tell from the stale smell of pancakes, long ago eaten, and the tick of the clock echoing through the still home. Her mother sat in her lilac armchair, a needlepoint on her knee and a steaming cup of coffee beside her.

With cautious dread, Caroline slowly made her way down the groaning steps, unsure what to say or how to look at her mom.

"You're up." Her mom concentrated on the needle, pulling it up in a flourish. "Are you hungry?"

Caroline shook her head. A ball of lead had formed at the bottom of her belly. "Nope." Her tongue was a thick and scratchy lump.

Energy crackled in the air between them; unsaid words skipped off the wood-paneled walls.

Ida Bergman inhaled sharply and pursed her lips as she returned to her work. Caroline was used to this pressured silence. She had witnessed her mom use it against her dad, and Kyle too. There were times when her mother would yank at her needlepoint or beat the biscuits. Caroline wished her mother would accept her own rage and allow herself to yell and kick the cupboards. Ida, a first-generation American raised by stoic Finnish parents, was more measured than that, though. She seemed to have an infinite capacity for anger and

68

pain, trapping it inside her chest and letting it out in small puffs of steam that occasionally burned those around her.

In no mood to sense the steely resolve of her mother, Caroline turned from her place on the last stair and took the few steps to the kitchen door. She pushed her way in.

Water dripped from the faucet, reminding Caroline of her sandpaper tongue. She reached up and got a glass—the same bubbled cup she had used since she had first sat at the dinner table atop a pile of phone books. She filled it with water. It tasted of the well, tangy and metallic.

Kyle emerged through the screen door from the backyard, letting it slap back hard against the frame. "Hey!" he boomed. Her brother didn't fit in such a quiet and lifeless house. Caroline liked how he bustled through each room, too tall for the swinging lamps and too bright for the drab curtains.

"Hi," she croaked, taking another gulp of water.

"Drinky a little too much last night, eh?" His blue eyes squinted in their signature way. "Trying to forget?"

"Shh!" Caroline pushed at his strong shoulder. "Like I need to be in any more trouble."

"Kyle?" Ida's controlled voice trickled into the kitchen.

"Yeah, Mom. I got the post fixed up okay. Roger says you should let me go into town today. Since I'm so helpful, you know?" He poked his head out into the living room.

Caroline set the glass upside down on a towel.

"Oh, I bet he said that." Their mom had suddenly brightened. Kyle could elicit their mother's good humor quicker than anyone. "If you go to Fergus Falls, you have to pick up a few things for me."

"I can go?" He clutched the doorframe.

There was a pause.

"Please, Mom. We're going to see E.T. finally, before it goes!"

"Who?"

"Um, Carrie. Carrie, you're coming, right?" He turned and gave Caroline a conspiratorial wink.

"Yeah, Mom, please?" Caroline asked. She knew, of course, that her brother had another girl in mind. As awkward and unlucky as she was with boys, Kyle seemed to be supernaturally gifted with girls.

This made her think of Greg, trapped in Rosalee's vicious grip. Her heart ached.

"Watch your sister," Ida commanded. "Don't let her out of your sight."

Caroline wanted to swoop into the living room and stomp her feet as she reminded her mother that she and Kyle were the same age. That he was even sneakier and more troublesome than she was.

A red-hot anger prickled her skin.

Kyle beamed.

Caroline would have to find somewhere to spend the day, to help with her brother's ruse. It would've been nice, she thought, to really go to Fergus Falls and watch E.T. with a bucket of buttered popcorn and an enormous soda pop between her thighs. The Falls Five Theater even had air conditioning. This was only a fantasy, of course. She was destined to bum around the edges of Willoughby for the day, slightly hungover and very much embarrassed.

"Caroline, come here."

Steeling herself, she bit down hard on her bottom lip to keep all the words from spilling out. She walked slowly back into the living room, her hands balled into fists.

Ida sat stiffly in her chair, the needlepoint pushed to the side.

"You need to apologize to your father before you go." Her mother let out one of her roiling sighs of anger. "He's already at the school, so I will accept a written letter. A sincere letter."

Caroline knew her dad had not heard her most vicious words. But she also knew he had seen the anger radiating off her. And she had yelled at him to stop.

"Yes. I'm sorry." Caroline hoped to read forgiveness on her mother's face. But there was only controlled vitriol rippling beneath Ida's masculine features.

Her mother's nostrils flared. "You broke his heart. Speaking in that way, in front of everyone. And on the Fourth. You know the Fourth is a special day for him, for everyone."

Caroline swallowed. There were so many things to say. She imagined herself grabbing her mother's broad shoulders and shaking her.

*You're blind! YOU ARE BLIND!*

She would scream into Ida's face, spittle flying into her eyelashes. Or was it that she wasn't blind at all? Only willfully foolish and weak?

Instead, Caroline nodded in a gracious, sorry-looking way and slinked back into the kitchen.

Her brother hovered at the kitchen sink. Caroline surprised herself by walking straight into his chest and wrapping her arms around him. She forced the tears to stay away, just for a moment, and looked up at Kyle. He mouthed "Thank you" and kissed the top of her head.

She gave him a final squeeze and left the kitchen. There was a pull, inexplicable but very much alive, for her to go outside and breathe in the fresh air. She pushed through the screen door and instantly felt safer, herself. Her nightgown fluttered in the breeze, and for the first time in her young life, she did not care if the neighbors saw her in her nightclothes. She luxuriated in the feel of her toes in the grass as she took steady, calming breaths. The tears couldn't be staved off any longer, so she let them come. They were soothing and somehow grounding.

A small shed, where she had played house with Tiffany not too many summers ago, called to her from the end of their property. A ray of sunlight shone on its peeling paint. A squirrel, spooked by Caroline's footsteps, skittered up the side and watched her from the roof, panting.

The shed's door squealed on rusty hinges as Caroline pulled it open. A dirty window on the back wall, overlooking a field of wildflowers, was the only light. She scuffled in, crouching to avoid the spider webs. She closed the door and sat on the dirt floor. The air was moist, and she could taste mold on her lips. Her mind churned with a million thoughts. This place had been a safe spot for her. She had come here as a child when her mom's bottled anger and frustration seeped out onto them all. But she hadn't really needed it then. Life had been simple, and she had only had the cares of a child.

Now, she understood what a burden was, the burden of knowing. The bald and ugly truth had been thrust into her consciousness, and unlike her mother, she could not ignore it. This was a sobering realization that made the tears flow even more quickly. Did all of this make her a grownup? How nice it would be to be a child again. Even for just an afternoon, hidden in her shed. Tiffany had been a child along with her, before their boobs sprouted up and boys were at the forefront of their minds. A happy memory of sandcastles rolled across the surface of her brain, and Caroline was thankful for it.

She crawled to the back corner and scratched her nails across a piece of rotting wood. Her fingers seemed to remember what to do.

Kneeling, Caroline pulled back the panel and revealed her hiding spot. It smelled of soil. She pulled out a stuffed rabbit with torn ears and a loosely hanging eye. There was a soggy pack of playing cards and a frayed jumping rope. She searched for her journal and it was there. It had curled in the humidity, but the pencil markings of her childhood were still legible. She flipped through the drawings of wide-eyed puppies and crayon rubbings of leaves. There were empty pages in the back.

A violet-colored pencil rolled out of the hole and landed quietly on Caroline's leg.

She picked it up and blew the dust away.

The journal in her hands held endless possibility. If Ida had been in the shed with her, surely she would have encouraged her daughter to get started on the apology letter to her father. If Tiffany had been there, they would have ranked the boys in Willoughby School by hotness. Greg would have been number one to Caroline, of course.

She took the colored pencil and began a spiral on the center of a blank page. She created a sphere of loops.

Words threatened to come through. Descriptive words of what she had seen. Instead, she drew a dark hole, lined with uneven, dagger-like triangles.

This was her mother on the inside. The weak piece of her that refused to face the truth.

This odd drawing made her feel a bit better. It was like a catharsis. She had read that word somewhere.

Or even better, she thought as she ran a hand over a faded drawing of a rainbow-hued unicorn on the other page, she could draw what she had seen.

The idea both scared and thrilled her.

She could burn it after. She would. She would draw it just as she had seen it and then she would take Kyle's Bic and let the paper burn.

That would be the ultimate purge.

Caroline turned to another page and positioned the colored pencil in her hand. She let her mind slip back to that moment. She wanted to both picture and not picture the hazy memory. The violet pencil was wrong. Red. She needed red. So she reached up into the damp hole in hopes of finding a pack of more colors.

Her breath caught in her throat at the touch of something unexpected. She was sure there had been nothing so large in the hole just moments before. It was cold and smooth. She rose up on her knees and stuck her head inside.

As she squinted to see what was in there, the fear of a spider crawling up her nose flashed through her. She might have pulled her head back out, but the fear faded as she caught sight of what she had felt.

It glistened in a dim, eerie light. She wasn't certain where the light emanated from as the object revealed itself to her.

The pencil and journal fell from her hands onto the soft dirt floor. She needed both hands to yank out her new find. It was much too large to be in there. It was wedged tightly and didn't want to budge. She pulled, rocking it back and forth against the earth, until it popped out like a rotten tooth. The force nearly sent her onto her butt.

The axe was surprisingly heavy. She ran her finger over the grooves in the wood. It seemed familiar. The blade appeared dull and as rusty as the shed's door hinges. When she ran the pad of her thumb down the edge, it sliced into her skin, causing a teardrop of blood to drip from the swirls of her fingerprint.

It was sharp after all.

THERE WERE DEAD ANIMALS EVERYWHERE. Stuffed birds—grouses and ducks—forced into poses behind glass. There was an entire tableau, telling a story of survival in the Minnesota backwoods. The irony that they hadn't survived struck Daphne hard. They were stuck forever in a faux river, surrounded by old pinecones and synthetic grass.

"Find a spot!" called out a waitress, who immediately returned to sucking soda through a straw.

Daphne looked down from the taxidermy display that wrapped the ceiling of the City Café and surveyed the dinner crowd. A family with young children took up one of the few booths. A little boy messily nibbled applesauce from a spoon.

As she looked for a quiet place to sit, she sensed the stares from a group of farmers at the lunch counter. At least, she assumed they were farmers based on their sunburned arms and matching work boots. Each sat on a wooden stool, his head turned to look at her. The symmetry of their movements, as though they were mirrors of each other, creeped her out more than their lingering, curious eyes.

Daphne pulled at the collar of her blouse, suddenly feeling very naked. She swallowed down the sickness, telling herself she was silly for worrying. Silly to imagine that one of the men would stand up and point at her with a dirty finger. That she would read a frightening recognition in his eyes. That he would say, "You! You! It's her!" and they would all jump up and point together with their work-worn hands and chant in unison.

Then she would be shunned from Willoughby, just like her mother. She would be forced to run away, chased by angry citizens with sharp pitchforks and blazing lanterns.

One of them, wearing a faded Minnesota Twins baseball cap, swiveled back to his plate of greasy chicken-fried steak. The others followed suit, like paper cutouts of the same man, farmer archetypes with no seeming individuality.

Relieved, Daphne slipped into the back booth.

Her stomach demanded food, and her tongue demanded the calming taste of peppermint. After dinner, she would walk over to the drugstore she had spotted earlier and grab some mints and Tums—a whole stack of each. Her mouth puckered at the comforting thought.

The waitress slapped a paper menu onto the table. "Drink?"

"Iced tea, please." Daphne searched the table. "And do you have any sweeteners? Like Equal or Splenda?"

The waitress snorted. "Sugar?"

"Yeah, sure."

Her view consisted of the door to the unisex bathroom and the half wall that separated the diners from the kitchen. There was a single cook, flipping burgers with intensity. He didn't look much older than Daphne, perhaps in his early thirties. There was something, though, about the gray pallor of his skin and the dripping sweat on his chest that made her both sad and no longer very hungry.

He wore a crooked nametag on the strap of his apron, which had *JASPER* written on it in red Sharpie. She wondered why he bothered, being tucked away back there. And in such a small town, where surely everyone knew everyone else.

His eyes shot up and caught hers. She looked away instantly, pretending to find interest in the wallpaper.

The waitress returned with an iced tea and a bowl of sugar packets. "Have you decided?"

Daphne scanned the menu. "BLT. And fries with that, please."

"Okay. Anyone joining you?"

Daphne shook her head.

The waitress seemed to consider this. She picked up the menu and tucked it under her armpit. "Are you driving through?"

"No, I'm staying at the motel. I'll probably be in here a lot; there's no kitchen in my room and I can't cook anyways." Daphne offered a strained smile before taking the first sip of her tea.

The waitress, a curvaceous, middle-aged brunette, nodded thoughtfully. She crossed her arms over her plump breasts and tapped her sneakered foot against the floor. "Well, you're going to get bored fast." The menu dangled above her hip.

"That's what I hear." Daphne ripped open a sugar packet and poured the contents into her drink. The looming waitress made every movement awkward.

"I wouldn't go swimming. Cross Lake is still as cold as a witch's tit."

"Right, well, I'll manage." Daphne tried to sound casual. "I think I saw a library across the street; looks tiny, though. Do they have town information there? Like local interest books and articles, or that sort of thing?"

The waitress raised an eyebrow. "I haven't a clue."

The way the woman looked at her, confused and suspicious, made Daphne's sensitive belly fill with panic.

Daphne's inner mother nagged.

*You should have planned better, Daphne. You should have practiced your lies in front of a mirror. Written them down and learned them backward and forward. You are always so damn impulsive! It's narcissistic to think all will fall into place. These people—they'll figure you out.*

Yes, they would figure her out. They would know she was investigating what happened in 1982 and eventually they would see the resemblance. They would know. Daphne's back burned, as she thought of them all looking at her.

"Oh, well, I just like to read," she feebly offered to the perplexed waitress.

The buxom woman coughed. "Well, we open for breakfast at five, early for the farmers. And we do lunch from eleven to two, but then we close down 'til dinner time. Jasper needs a break every now and then."

The cook raised his head upon hearing his name.

"In a few weeks, we'll be open all day, once school gets out for the summer and we get the tourists, you know. And help from a few high schoolers. But of course, you won't be here."

The assumption made Daphne wonder.

"And we can deliver up to the motel if you need, for a fee."

"That's wonderful, thank you." Daphne stirred the sugar in with her straw.

The waitress walked away briskly, tossing the paper with Daphne's order toward the cook.

Daphne checked her phone, hopeful for a message from her dad or Beverly.

Nothing.

A wall of pictures in vintage frames, mostly in black and white, caught her attention. She scooted out of the booth and made her way across the restaurant, keenly aware of the turning heads and watchful eyes.

There were grainy photographs of men proudly posing with large dead fish. One gray photo in the center of the display showed the town's gazebo. It was draped with sheer fabric and surrounded with bouquets of cascading lilies. A long-ago bride stood on the steps, her face veiled.

Daphne ran her finger across the glass. She guessed the photograph was from the 1920s based on the way the bride's lacy dress skimmed her ankles. She wondered if her ancestors had been there—her great-grandparents, perhaps—drinking champagne from fluted glasses and breathing in the overwhelming scent such a pile of flowers would create.

She scanned the other photos in the haphazard display,

searching for something, or someone, familiar. They were all strangers. Strangers curled on picnic blankets, strangers kissing a baby's plump cheek, strangers gathered around a table in that very restaurant.

One photograph looked out of place, surrounded by a collection of hazy Polaroids from a 1970s era camping trip.

She nearly pressed her nose against the glass to get a good view of the sepia picture of a man posing with his foot upon a tufted stool. He was classically handsome, with an air of Clark Gable in his sly grin and sculpted chin. Daphne was no expert, but it appeared to have been taken around the turn of the twentieth century.

The photographed man's slight smile intrigued her, as she knew people of that time were known to have posed straight-faced.

Daphne stood back and looked up at the picture at the very top. She recognized the stately Victorian house she had seen from the shuttle's window. She stood on tiptoe, taking in the beauty of the garden and the ornate wrought-iron fence.

"Dat's Doris Woodhouse's place." The restroom door swung shut, and a large man shuffled up next to her. "It's a beaut. Damn shame she lives all alone in dat place." He hoisted his pants up over his drooping belly.

"It's gorgeous," Daphne agreed, looking sideways at the farmer.

"Oh yeah . . . . She owns dis whole town, really, Doris the old bat. Her mind's about gone out da winda, though!" The man chortled.

Daphne thought he sounded like a caricature, like one of those people with a supposed Minnesota accent she had seen on TV.

"Well, it looks like it should be a landmark, on a historical registry or something." Her eyes were drawn to a pulled curtain on the second floor. She was sure she could see the hint of someone peering out.

The man patted his belt buckle. "You got dat right, girl. And she's got another old one too that she charges to visit. What is it, ten a person? Dirk, is it ten to go in there? The one up Oak?"

"Huh?" An old man set down his hamburger.

"Ten bucks to go to Doris's house, the one she runs?" the man beside Daphne bellowed across the room.

"Oh, yeah, or maybe eight." The man named Dirk looked Daphne up and down. "You going over there?"

Every man at the counter had stopped eating, in their parallel way of identical action. They stared. The family in the first booth swiveled, curious.

Daphne shook her head. "I don't know. I don't know where you mean."

She turned toward the farmer at her side. He combed a hand through his scraggy beard. "Well." He nodded toward the picture of the Victorian. "Doris lives there, but she owns the murder house too. Where people go da . . . I dunno . . . da see where bad things happened." His face scrunched.

It was as though Daphne were moving, swaying from side to side in a dinghy on a rollicking sea. Her stomach slushed and foamed. "The murder house?"

"Yeah . . . . Awful things happened up dere, back before you were born, surely. A girl killed her whole family." He grunted. "Doris is a dark one. She snatched it up before anyone could buy it." He lowered his voice. "Not dat anyone wanted to. Oh, yeah, you can go dere and look at their furniture and where it all happened. And boy, the weirdos love it. Doris let's 'em sleep dere on Halloween! Dat's a lot more than ten bucks, though, yeah?"

Daphne hugged her body and made an effort not to look at the probing eyes she knew crawled all over her. She backed away from the pictures and the grinning farmer. Had he mentioned it because he knew? He was certainly old enough to have known her mother. Could he see the Caroline Bergman in her face? The fact that this was all a mistake, a misguided and naïve mistake, settled within her. She knew her father was right, that there was nothing that could come from the digging up of old memories. And she knew—*she knew*—her mother couldn't have possibly been the murderer, so what was even the point of such a strange trip?

"I don't think I want to go there." Her voice shook.

Jasper the cook dinged a bell. "Tiffany! Order up!"

The room fell silent, and Daphne slipped back into the booth. As the waitress trundled by, Daphne's mind begged her to get up and keep talking to the affable farmer, to act appropriately interested. She should pretend she had never heard of what happened. She should listen to his thoughts and do whatever sort of ill-conceived investigation she had come there to do.

But she pulsed with the realization that this was all real. That murder, bloody and ugly, had been there. That until that moment she hadn't really believed any of it. It had all been a story of something long ago, barely true.

The dusty stuffed ducks with glass eyes above her head reminded Daphne that in a small town, a place like Willoughby, murder remained. Time functioned differently off the main road. Her mom may have left them and the victims may have been buried, but the tragedy still rumbled beneath the surface.

As the BLT was placed in front of her, she could think only of the "murder house," a museum of the past, preserving the pain that had undoubtedly occurred within its walls. The pain that had followed Caroline Bergman all the way to Bellingham, Washington, that Daphne was sure had still remained even after her mother had become Jane Downs-Forrest. She could read the pain in the way her mother had treated her and how she would fall into an almost catatonic state, staring off into nothing.

Daphne recognized the pain because it was inside her own heart, a burden handed down to her.

An unwanted inheritance.

## 15

THE SUN DIPPED BEHIND KNUTSON DRUG, bleeding red light onto the cracked sidewalk. Her dinner was ensnared within her chest, a ball of bread and bacon unwilling to drop down into her inhospitable stomach. She tore open the cylinder of Tums she had purchased from inside and pressed two onto her tongue. The chalky taste reassured her that she was okay, that the world had not shifted once more to reveal another dark corridor of secrets.

Daphne loitered in the doorway, uncertain how to proceed.

*I'm in Willoughby and no one knows who I am. Why would they? And why would they even care?* She crunched down on the Tums, swallowing the shards and popping two more into her mouth.

*I'm in Willoughby, and everything is okay, and nothing bad is going to happen.*

A pharmacist in a white coat flipped the sign on the glass door from *OPEN* to *CLOSED*.

Displaced, Daphne wandered up Main Street. She liked sensing the weight of the mints and tubes of Tums in her purse as it brushed against her hip.

Across the street, a woman with vibrant, brassy-red hair was closing the library. She locked the door with a tangle of keys and stopped to smooth down a sign announcing *$2 USED BOOKS* taped to the front window.

"Excuse me?" Daphne called across the quiet street. "Hey, are you open tomorrow?"

The woman pivoted around on kitten heels, raising a hand to shield her eyes from the setting sun. "What's that?"

"Your hours tomorrow? Are you open?" Daphne balanced on the curb.

The red-haired woman, old but not quite elderly, stared. Daphne stared back.

"Ten to two," she said finally, her eyes still looking Daphne up and down.

"Thank you."

"Our hours change once summer comes. We don't usually get people here until it warms up. You're an anomaly."

This familiar sentiment, said by nearly everyone Daphne had met, made it seem like there was a script they were all reading from—a regulated series of remarks to make toward out-of-towners.

"Uh, well, you'll probably see me tomorrow." Daphne took a step back, aware of the familiar vulnerability that Willoughby had wrought. She wondered if all small-town people were so instantly questioning and suspicious.

She also wondered if her mom had treated strangers in the same way. If she had gaped at them as they dared to enter the invisible sphere that surrounded Willoughby.

"Wonderful." The librarian might have smiled, but Daphne had already looked away. She began walking up the street, east, toward the motel.

Daphne rubbed at her bare arms. A part of her, a large part, wanted to follow through with her plans and go to the library tomorrow and compile information about the Bergmans. But like the biting evening air, there was a part of her that niggled at her to retreat, to give up, to fall into her father's hug. She wished for nothing more than the familiarity of Bellingham, for even the strange smell of her mother's death that permeated her home. At least she would be safe, less exposed, less alone.

Daphne walked.

The imposing mansion loomed ahead, its impressive lawn and old-fashioned grandeur incongruous among the neighboring working-class bungalows.

Daphne stopped one block before the Victorian and looked up Oak Street at a row of such homes. Although the sun lingered, there were no children playing on porch steps or riding tricycles on the matching driveways.

The quiet ate at her. She slipped her hand into her purse and wiggled out a mint.

A hydrangea plant with newly budded flowers rattled. It was three houses up Oak, at the edge of the yard. The wide leaves scratched the sidewalk. Daphne dropped the mint as she watched the movement. That was not the spring breeze. Something was moving within the plant.

She moved toward it, unaware she was even walking. She kept her eyes on the bush. Its clatter was loud in the vacuum of the noiseless street.

It shook wildly.

She approached, fearful for some reason, though she couldn't guess why. A small voice within warned that it could be a dark and violent thing.

A random memory prodded Daphne. She hovered near the bush, remembering the Post-It note as she had crumpled and tossed in the trash bin. The drawing, her mom's last, had unsettled Daphne. Its scratchy, imprecise edges, and vague depiction of bulging monster eyes had haunted her.

And now, incomprehensibly, she worried that the vague outline of her mom's creation would propel itself from the foliage.

"Gah!" Daphne tripped backward as an orange flash jumped from the bush.

The short-legged tabby landed with a soft thump on the concrete.

Daphne's tense laugh echoed down the lonely street.

"Hi." She knelt and patted the cat's head. "Hi, kitty."

The cat sniffed Daphne's palm.

"You smell my BLT?"

*"Mew."*

"It's nice to see someone's around."

It was surprising, but it seemed to be the same cat that had been meandering outside the motel. It definitely had the same carrot stripes.

Daphne gave it a few more pats, letting the cat rub itself on her legs.

The whish and crack of a slammed door shocked her from the cat's calming company. She stood and saw a figure on the porch of the house with the hydrangea bush.

A shriveled old woman hobbled down the steps, a tissue pressed under her nose. She wore corduroy pants and an oversized knitted sweater with wooden buttons. "Oh, heavens! I'm afraid I'm going home for the night. It's going to be dark soon, and I'm very hungry for my supper. I'm having wild rice soup, I think, with cheese toast. Do you like cheese?" She gave a hearty blow into the tissue.

Daphne couldn't help but smile. "Yes, of course."

"Me too, on anything really. My husband said I ate too much of it, but he died first so I suppose he worried for nothing. His heart got him in the end, stress of life. He worked too hard. Typical doctor." She got to the final step and looked down at the brick path leading to the driveway. "This is a big step. It seems like it gets wider every day. I don't want to twist my ankle, or I'll be out here alone tonight, and they get so damn noisy at night."

Daphne glanced around at the empty neighborhood. "This isn't your house?"

"Nah." The old woman shook her head.

"Let me help you." Daphne rushed to her side, offering her hand.

"Thank you, dear, thank you."

She put her wrinkled hand, formed into a tight claw around the tissue, onto Daphne's. She wobbled as she stepped on the bricks.

"Okay?"

"Hm? Yes, I'm so sorry. I'm going home, and you're going to miss it." She released her grip from Daphne and stuffed the tissue in her cardigan pocket.

"Miss it?" As the words left her mouth, the realization shocked her. She knew who the old woman was, and more significantly, she suspected *where* she was. Daphne turned and took in the simple house. It looked like all the others on the short street, basic, with a detached garage and grass growing in tufts through the fissured driveway.

"Oh, it's Fox! Come here, Fox, and I'll give you a treat, little rascal." The woman, who must be Doris Woodhouse, as the farmer with the extreme accent had called her, fished out a cracker from the same pocket she had put her used tissue in. "I call him Fox because of his orange fur, and he's a sly one too!"

Fox sat on the sidewalk, his tail flitting, watching them both with the disinterested blink of all cats.

"Fox, I've got a cracker," Doris sang.

"You're Doris. And this is the . . ." Daphne swallowed down rising phlegm. "This is the murder house."

"I'd open it up for you to see, but I'm very hungry for my supper. I'm going to have wild rice soup." Doris crumbled the cracker and let the crumbs fall at Fox's feet.

"And cheese toast." Daphne had to get something in her mouth. Her breath smelled of vomit.

Doris's face brightened. "Cheese toast! Grand idea!"

Daphne tingled all over. "I'll walk you home. You live in that beautiful mansion, don't you?"

The old woman nodded slowly. The dying sun shone through the hairs of her chin.

"Yes, yes. It's not mine, really. Fred Willoughby built it before I was born and it's his, I should think. I'm just borrowing it."

"Well, it's very impressive." Daphne looked back again, at the less impressive house her mother had grown up in, at the yard she had surely played in. At the walls that had held her grandparents and her uncle before they died on a summer morning in 1982.

*Were they happy in there? Before the axe came down?*

Fox, the cat, nibbled on the cracker. Daphne's heart ached for Gopher and the musty silence of her basement bedroom.

"I'll let you in tomorrow; you can see it all." Doris led them back down to Main Street, walking surprisingly fast.

"Thank you." Daphne slipped a mint between her lips.

"I try to keep it clean, like your mother did. She liked it clean in there; she always kept a nice house."

Daphne froze. The pulsing beat of nausea swirled up through her body. "My mother?"

"Ida! She was a devoted housekeeper. Oh, she crocheted the most beautiful pillows and always had good Scandinavian meals— lutefisk done just right. We were friends; surely you remember?" Doris scratched her nose.

"Ida's not my mother." Daphne bit down with the hopes that the peppermint would soothe her tummy. It didn't.

Doris turned and looked into Daphne's eyes. She had been taller once; Daphne could see she had long, slender legs, but she was hunched over with the beginnings of a hump on her upper back. Her milky corneas searched Daphne's face, seeming to take in every line and swerve and pimple. The old woman took out the crinkled tissue and wiped at the corner of her mouth.

The action made Daphne think of her mother, dribbling saliva at the end.

The old woman's thin lips stretched into a shrewd smile, as though they were both in on some private joke. "Oh, Caroline, don't be cheeky! You were always mischief! A troublesome sort is what your mother always said."

Doris Woodhouse's snotty, cackling laugh startled a crow in a budding apple tree behind them. It thrashed its wings and flew above Daphne's head, abandoning them on Oak Street.

# 16

THE WORLD FLUXED IN AND OUT. She was on her knees in the grass, dry heaving. Every time the pressure rose up, she batted it back down. Tears pinched at her eyes and snot dripped from her nose. She had known all day that it was coming. She had known it was inevitable, yet she had hoped for it to be different.

For years, she had dealt with the tide of panic-induced vomit. It had been part of her since she was sixteen. From the moment her life unraveled, she had sensed the upset deep in her belly, a place where Tums and peppermint tea could not reach. How ironic, she thought feebly, that her mother had met with a similarly dark and unwelcome crossroads at the same age.

Daphne had walked Doris home, the last few steps agony as she held down the pounding ache of her terror. The old woman, oblivious, had patted her hand and repeated that she would show her the murder house in the morning. She hadn't called her Caroline again, but the name had been a foreboding storm cloud hovering over Daphne's head. She had known it was there, in her cheeks and perhaps in the manner of how both she and her mother cocked their heads to the side when thinking of an answer. But the storm had rained down upon her more quickly and more powerfully than she had ever imagined.

She had walked on rickety legs from Doris's luxe mansion and had finally stumbled into the grassy park, circling through the trees back toward town.

She let the gazebo hide her from the people. Not that there was anyone out in the waning twilight. Daphne had gone around to the back and rested her head against the cool wood. The vomit had come first, wet and sour, and now that her stomach was empty, she had fallen to her knees.

The muscles in her abdomen were finally unclenching, and she could appreciate the cool air on her cheeks. She spit and sat back on her heels, recognizing that her body was relaxing.

The tree-lined park began to look like a desolate forest as the moon commenced its alien glow. Tunnels of black twisted between the pines, and squat bushes hid the frenetic scurry of the nocturnal. A smell—not the bitter acid of her puke but something much worse—choked Daphne.

She scooted away from the mess in the grass, sniffing like a hound.

The revolting scent was enough to make her gag. With nothing left in her belly though, Daphne was immune to its putrid effects.

She wiped her nostrils with the back of her hand as her eyes stung from the mix of death and earth.

Her mind skipped, smoothly as a rock over the surface of Cross Lake. She thought first of her mom, swishing with formaldehyde as she was lowered into the dirt. Next, as the smell intensified, she lost herself in the memory of that drawing again. Yet this time, in Daphne's memory, the Post-It sketch was even more detailed. It had a snout, dripping with a glob of snot her mom had shaded expertly. And its black eyes were mesmeric.

Daphne trembled. She studied the darkness, the hazy peaks of the trees, and something else, something inside the blackness. It had a presence, and oddly, she knew it hated her. Its invisible disdain surged across the grass, rocketing up into her consciousness.

A single, needle-sharp tooth glistened in the murky infinity.

Fear for her life, never before so potent, caused Daphne to scuttle backward.

"Hey!" called a voice from behind her. "Daphne?"

She turned on her knees at the sound. Sudden relief wrapped itself around her terror, insulating her thoughts.

"Are you okay?" A figure in a white shirt and jeans walked down the slight decline from Main Street. She watched him through the intricately carved spindles.

"Edwin, hi." Daphne cleared her throat as she stood. The weight of her fear evaporated before she was on both feet.

As she steadied herself in the soft grass, she could not shake the notion that she had forgotten something.

A vital something.

"Is everything all right?" Edwin stopped about six feet from her, resting a hand on the gazebo's side.

"Yes," she squeaked, still tasting the acid in her teeth. "Why?"

He looked up at the last few streaks of magenta in the sky. "I was worried about you." He laughed. "I didn't see you, and it's past eight thirty."

"Oh." Daphne took three mints out of her purse. His concern annoyed her. No doubt it came from some misplaced belief that because she was a woman she needed saving. Beverly would have remarked that he needed to check his calendar: it was the twenty-first century and women did not need rescuing.

"You want one?" She showed him her handful of peppermints.

"Uh, yeah." He walked toward her and took one delicately from her hand.

She crunched the remaining two.

"Do you know Doris?" She surprised herself by bringing it up. Even the mention of the brittle old woman made her heart race.

Edwin popped the mint into his mouth. "It sounds like you're meeting the locals." He smiled.

"She's crazy."

He laughed so hard the mint nearly escaped his lips. "Yeah, yeah, she's a bit nutty, but she's really nice too. She takes care of everyone."

"Right, yes, she seemed really sweet." Daphne rubbed her palms together. Goosebumps were erupting all over, from both the cool night and her body's usual reaction to barfing. She was often chilled and dizzy for hours afterward.

"You're right though," he said. "Doris is crazy."

Daphne looked up at his face. The shadows of the night obscured him, but she could still see the expanse of his smile and his delightfully tousled hair.

Something clicked inside her. It was the same sort of disassociation she had experienced when she had decided to come to Willoughby in the first place. Like there were two of her, and one version of herself was dragging the rest of her along. She thought it must be adulthood, giving her a proverbial slap in the face.

"I threw up," she admitted.

It was the first time she had ever said those words since she'd gotten the flu in her childhood and crawled into her parents' bed with a shopping bag full of vomit. She supposed she had brought it for proof, but her mother had screeched when she realized what Daphne was carrying.

"Oh, no!"

"I threw up," Daphne repeated, making sure she had really said it.

"Damn! You didn't have the chili, did you?" He stepped forward, his face illuminated by a timed ground light that had clicked on beside the gazebo.

Daphne shook her head.

"Okay, well, I should have told you about the City Café chili. It gives everyone—literally everyone—the shits."

A smile, as unexpected as the words streaming out of her, popped onto her face. The apples of her full cheeks pressed into her eyes. "Yeah, you should have warned me."

He smiled back, and Daphne thought she might tell him everything. A portion of her, the logical, practical piece of her, had come unmoored at the sight of that smile.

The usual dizziness she expected after her panic-induced vomit

91

had burgeoned into something more. She was imbued with a jittery boldness that both terrified and exhilarated her. And there was something about Edwin's face, his crooked smile that began at one side of his lips before the other could catch up, and his thin white T-shirt that made everything worse. Or was it better?

He took one more step closer to her, and the concerned brow returned. "I knew you weren't okay. I knew it."

"I'm okay, I just . . . this happens sometimes, when I'm nervous or upset. Or confused, even." She had told herself this a million times, but she had never told another soul. Her dad knew. Beverly knew. Her mom had known. But they had never mentioned it. They had treated her like a closeted bulimic. And sometimes she wondered if they thought she did do it on purpose, that she actively chose to react to life in such an unhealthy way. Her mind screamed at the audacious way she spoke to Edwin, a stranger, about her reality. She chose to tell him because she was inexplicably comforted by him, drawn to him.

He looked into her eyes, and she thought the crushing sincerity in his face would surely kill her. "Can I help you? You must be nervous about something? Or upset?"

"No," she lied. It was worse than all the lies she had told that day. And somehow, she thought Edwin would be able to tell she was being dishonest. "I'm just . . . I think I'm just tired." That was true. Her limbs were floppy.

"Okay." He spoke softly. "I'll take you back to the motel." Edwin stretched his hand out for her.

That screeching mother inside told her to keep away, to not trust him. Strangers didn't hold hands.

Daphne dared to place her hand into his.

The dizziness was sharp, a real thumping pressure between her eyes.

They walked up the shallow hill toward his waiting Toyota. She looked up at the night sky and gasped.

"The stars."

"Yeah, small-town stars."

"Oh my God." Never in her life had she felt so small and insignificant. The vast spray of stars reminded her that she was both somewhere new and somewhere familiar. She had seen these stars—the way they coalesced in the black, creating swirling auras. She had seen them in some of her mom's paintings. "Have you ever believed that you didn't fit somewhere? Like you're, I don't know . . ."

"Out of your element?"

Daphne shrugged. "Yeah."

"Are you kidding?"

She looked away from the sky and turned toward Edwin, surprised by the cynicism in his voice. "What do you mean?"

Her hand quivered in his. She wasn't sure if she should take it back, away from his grip.

Edwin squeezed her fingers as though in answer. "I'm not just the only person in Willoughby who's Korean, I'm the only person in Willoughby who isn't white. And that includes my family."

A twinge of humiliation simmered in her belly. "I'm sorry. I'm stupid."

"No." He clutched her hand more tightly. "No, I just want you to know you're not alone. This place will make you think you are, sometimes." He motioned toward Main Street, where the shops were closed and the street lamps flickered dimly. "Willoughby—it's not good, Daphne. Do you believe that places can be bad? Like people?"

She shivered. "I don't . . . I've never thought about it."

"I can sense it sometimes, the ugliness. That's why I worried about you, I guess. Since you're new and . . ." Edwin trailed off.

"And?" She fortified herself, waiting for him to say what she knew he was thinking: that she was obviously naïve, foolish, a child.

"And maybe that's why you got sick. You can feel it too. Maybe that's what you're feeling."

GRAY-TINGED CLOUDS CREATED a canopy overhead as Daphne walked briskly toward the library. The morning air was moist with a hazy spittle of rain.

It had occurred to her to ask Edwin for a ride, but after he babied her last night, she hadn't wanted to seem helpless.

She regretted her outfit: a pair of light-wash skinny jeans, turquoise strappy sandals, and a pink tank top she had fished from the bottom of her suitcase. The warmth of the previous day had evaporated, leaving her chilled and soggy.

The sign reading OTTER TAIL COUNTY LIBRARY– WILLOUGHBY BRANCH came into view as she crossed Main. It was a slender brick building with a faded awning.

Yellow light spilled out onto the sidewalk through the front windows, making Daphne eager to get inside the comfort of the library's embrace.

A bell clanged overhead as she entered. It was a grating, shrill sound in such a tranquil place.

"Good morning." The librarian Daphne had seen the evening before stood alone behind a varnished maple counter.

"Hello." Daphne ran her hands through her dewy hair. She

glanced around at the many rows of books as she wiped her sandals on a straw mat.

"It's nice to see a new face." The librarian gave a warm smile as she rounded the tall counter and rested her elbow on the edge. She had a professional air about her, and she wore a well-tailored pair of slacks and polished black mules. In fact, she seemed to Daphne out of place in such a village, among farmers and vacationers. She was the human equivalent of Doris's Victorian mansion: a beautiful inconsistency.

"Really?" Daphne couldn't hide her surprise.

"It means summer is coming. My favorite time of year."

Daphne warmed, no longer etched with goosebumps from the icy morning. "Mine too." The library was homey. It was like she was in Bellingham and only a bus ride away from her dad.

"You must be on a mission." The librarian tilted her head, causing one of her owl earrings to clack against her shoulder.

"Sort of." Daphne stepped forward hesitantly, scanning the different sections.

"Mysteries are down that main aisle." The brassy-haired woman gestured toward a towering row of both hardcovers and paperbacks. "And we've got a halfway decent nonfiction section to the right there, near the children's corner."

Daphne nodded. "Local interest?"

"Yes, let me show you." The librarian led her through a row of books, her spicy, expensive-smelling perfume wafting up into Daphne's nostrils.

Against the back wall, beneath a corkboard covered in flyers advertising garage sales and babysitters, sat a table with books propped up on display stands. A few curled magazines were stacked neatly in between.

"If you give me a clue as to what you're researching, I could better help." The woman fidgeted with a thin book, shifting it back and forth on its stand.

Daphne stared at the black-and-white image on its front. It was of destruction: gnarled metal and burning wood. A man with soot on his face stood slumped in the background, staring past the camera.

"Well . . ."

The nattering, worrisome voice of Daphne's mom fought its way to the forefront of her consciousness.

*If you tell her the truth, she'll know. She'll know who you are and why you're here.*

This reminded her of Doris, of how she had recognized Daphne. Not in any sort of coherent way. Not in a way anyone would believe.

Daphne cleared her throat, which seemed to also clear the dark voice of her mother, like a vacuum sucking up cobwebs. "I'm writing a book on the Bergman case. The murders in 1982." Emboldened by the conviction of her lie, she straightened her shoulders and looked directly into the librarian's eyes.

"I see." The woman's irises sparked in what appeared to be a trembling excitement. "I'm afraid we don't have anything about that, specifically." She clapped her hands together. "We do have books about the county history, even one by a local author about the Native American massacre up at Cross Lake."

"Okay." Disappointed, Daphne picked up the book the librarian had been adjusting.

"That one is about the Culver Flour Mill explosion. It's a glorified pamphlet really, nothing very in depth." She tapped its edge.

"Seems interesting, though." Daphne flipped through the pages.

"Let me see." The librarian ran her finger over the spines of several books on the tabletop shelf. Daphne could tell this woman knew every single book and article in the building. There was nothing in the library unfamiliar to her. "Ah, yes. You can find some good city and county history here." She pulled out a heavy book with worn edges. "It has the general sort of stuff, nothing about the Bergman murders, but I believe there is a bit about the Bergman ancestors."

"What?" Daphne set the mill book back on the table, anxious to get her hands on this new find.

"The Bergmans were a prominent family here in Willoughby." The woman spoke with enthusiasm, her earrings jangling in rhythm with her words. "Caroline, the daughter—she was the last living one. I suppose you already know she ran off, not long after."

Daphne licked her lips, the sudden desire for a mint filling every thought. She mindlessly rooted around in her purse until she heard the comforting crinkle of plastic. "Yes, I did read that."

"And I assume you've already been to the house Doris runs?"

She slipped the mint onto her tongue, instantly grateful for its soothing effect on her gut. "Not yet."

"That will be the best place for you, really. Doris has collected a lot of information. The axe is even there."

Daphne's head snapped up. "The axe?"

"Of course. You do know what you're writing about, don't you?" The librarian tightly gripped the sides of the book in her hands, which was entitled *The Comprehensive History of Otter Tail County*.

"I guess I'm just surprised." Daphne didn't remember crunching into the mint and swallowing, but it was gone. "I assumed the killer left with it."

The woman closed her eyes and scrunched up her nose. She let out a dramatic sigh. "You have read about it all, haven't you? The Star Tribune in Minneapolis covered it for months, years even."

Daphne sensed a tell-tale flush creep across her cheeks. She felt foolish for her ill-conceived lie about writing a book. No one could believe she was researching a murder when she barely knew the specifics. "It's just . . . I don't trust reporters," she managed. "They don't always tell the truth, and I thought it best to come here, to the source."

A jittery excitement returned to the librarian's manner. "Are you really writing a book? About the murders? And it sounds as if you aren't necessarily sold on Caroline being the culprit."

Her worst fear was being realized. She had obviously not inherited her mom's ability to lie. It struck her in that moment that Caroline Bergman had become Jane Downs-Forrest seamlessly.

"Uh-huh," Daphne yelped.

"Oh!" The woman beamed. "Are you doing a sort of investigation, then? Like Miss Marple?"

Daphne didn't know who that was, but she nodded in agreement.

"Could I be of any help? I know quite a bit about it all. In fact, I knew the whole family!"

"Sure!" A smile erupted on Daphne's face. Maybe she wasn't such an awful liar, after all. And even better, the librarian had known her mother and showed no indication that Daphne's features were familiar.

The sloshing in her stomach calmed.

"I've always wanted to solve a mystery!" The librarian's chest swelled. Daphne caught a glimmer of her youth. "Wouldn't it be thrilling?"

The jarring trill of the bell sounded at the entrance.

"Moira?" a woman called from the front.

"Coming." The librarian's entire mien shifted. Her stoic professionalism returned as she handed Daphne the book. "Just a moment," she called in a sing-song voice, taking a second to smooth down the ripples of her fiery hair.

"I'll be back in a jiffy," she whispered, leaving Daphne alone in the back corner.

Daphne glanced down at the book in her hands, half listening to the conversation at the counter.

". . . he's getting lazy. Last week, he gave me Doug's mail and Doug got a package for Knutson." The other woman gave a husky humorless laugh.

Moira, the librarian, murmured something in response.

Daphne opened the front cover of the book. It smelled musty and the crepey, fragile pages made her think of her mother's gray deathbed skin.

An unexpected sadness deflated Daphne. She guessed it might be the library and the eager librarian. Moira was older than her mom, yet she was still alive. As was the book, in a way. It had probably been written decades before Caroline was born, yet here it was in her hands, still intact.

The two women continued to chat, mostly about the weather.

The stranger's voice weaved through the bookshelves, alighting on Daphne's ear. It sounded familiar, causing her to take a few steps forward and peer through an open slot between books. She spied the waitress from the City Café. She wore the same linen shirt and khaki pants. Her brown hair was brushed up into a utilitarian ponytail.

Daphne ignored their boring conversation and found more interest in the book. She slowly flipped through, stopping on captioned pictures of Willoughby, Fergus Falls, and a few other towns that made up Otter Tail County.

Turning to page 112, Daphne sucked in a sharp breath. It was the exact same sepia photograph she had seen in the café. The Clark Gable look-alike stared up at her, slightly faded by time.

Her eyes fell on the caption beneath: *Willoughby Councilman Calvin Bergman, ca. 1896.*

Blood rushed to her fingertips. She looked up from the page, glancing about the corner of the library as though a prank was being played on her.

It was so peculiar, to look upon a person from long ago and know they shared her heritage, her family.

On wobbly legs, Daphne carried *The Comprehensive History of Otter Tail County* to the front counter.

The waitress was still there, holding a pile of mail wrapped in a rubber band. "Ah, look who it is. Our first visitor of the season."

Daphne gave a slight smile in her direction. "Moira?" She turned toward the librarian.

"Yes?"

"This picture—it says this man's a Bergman." She slid the book across the counter to where Moira stood on the other end.

The librarian furrowed her brows as she studied the photograph. "Calvin." She looked up. "I believe he was the right-hand man, so to speak, of Fred Willoughby, our town's founder."

The waitress huffed. "Ancient history."

"Oh, come on." Moira frowned. "It's nice when young people show an interest in history. Don't you think so, Tiffany?"

Tiffany pressed her sizable chest against the counter and peered down at the book. "If you say so. He looks a bit light in the loafers if you ask me." She emitted another honking humorless laugh.

Daphne forced a giggle to be polite.

"Coming in today, girl?" Tiffany blinked rapidly.

"Yeah, soon. I'm starving." Daphne patted her stomach.

"All right, then. Moira, see you later?"

The librarian opened a pad of ink. "You know I never miss a fish fry."

Tiffany winked, swiveled on her heel, and pushed through the door.

Daphne watched as the statuesque waitress crossed Main Street in three, easy strides.

Moira pressed a stamper into the ink and rocked it back and forth. "I assume you want to take this one?"

"Please." Daphne drummed her fingers on the counter. She couldn't believe her luck, that there was a book about her ancestors and that Moira wanted to help her.

"Have you been to the police? For research?"

Daphne shook her head, instantly frightened by the prospect. "I don't even know what I'd do there."

A devious smile crept across Moira's lips. "Any good investigator starts there. Haven't you read any books?"

Daphne laughed, genuinely this time. "I'm new at this, if you can't tell."

The child-like exhilaration returned to the librarian's oval eyes. Her lips rose and fell as she seemed to speak to herself in a silent language.

"Here you are." Moira stamped the manila card on the inside cover. Daphne hadn't thought there was a library left in the country with such an archaic system. "If you want any others, you'll have to fill out a guest library form."

"Sure." Daphne slid the book to her chest. She knew researching her ancestors wouldn't solve the murders, yet she still sensed an undeniable pull to read about the man in the photograph.

She glanced out the glass front door at the brightening day. Sunlight wiggled through the separating clouds, shining threads of light on the hanging flowerpots.

A flood of luminous hope cascaded like frothy waves through Daphne's heart.

Perhaps she was right where she needed to be.

Moira leaned over the counter and placed her cold, manicured hand on Daphne's wrist. "Shall we go?"

"Go?" Daphne clutched the book to her breasts, staring at the librarian with both confusion and wonder.

The older woman let a toothy, obsequious smile burst forth. "I'll be your Watson."

"Um . . ."

"You lead, Holmes." Her hand vibrated on Daphne's skin. "Let's go to the police and see what we can dig up!" Moira whistled.

"Wait! I . . . what would I even say?"

"Let's develop a plan on the way. Oh! This is such a joy!" Moira clapped in a stilted rhythm as she made her way around the counter. Her purse was already hanging over her shoulder. She eagerly marched to the door in an excitable trance.

"Right now? We're just going to go now?" The waves of hope came crashing to a halt. The still waters of dread nearly drowned Daphne with paranoid thoughts.

Just the abstract image of the two of them walking through the doors of a police station and asking about a thirty-five-year-old murder made her tongue turn to sawdust. Words, wholly unhelpful, fizzled, and she was left with the realization that she had no control over the well-dressed librarian or what they were apparently about to do.

"Yes, no time like the present! It is all right, isn't it? That I help? I've been waiting for some excitement to come along, and here you are!"

Daphne shrugged. "I guess so. I mean . . . I could use some help." She had pictured a thousand different scenarios, all bad, yet nothing had prepared her for Moira's instant zeal. How had her innocent visit to a library suddenly devolved into an impromptu trip to the police?

They stepped out onto the wet sidewalk. The heady, pine-infused scent of a Minnesota spring clouded around them.

Moira locked the library's front door with an old-fashioned brass key. "The world is full of obvious things, which nobody by any chance ever observes."

Daphne stared, uncertain how to distract Moira from setting this bizarre plan into motion.

"That's from *The Hound of the Baskervilles*." Moira beamed. "We've got it in both hardcover and paperback. Tell me if you want a copy, my dear Holmes!"

"Maybe later." Daphne bit the inside of her cheek, fighting an urge to go running up Main Street, back toward the shadowy comfort of her motel room.

"Don't worry about a thing." Moira dropped her key into her clean leather purse. "I know people. In fact, Bob Toft is a friend."

Toft. The name blinked like a neon sign in Daphne's mind. It was familiar.

Daphne took in a deep, calming breath.

This was why she had come. This was why she was standing there, on the street of her mom's childhood. To learn, to investigate, to do something, anything, but rot away in her basement bedroom.

Daphne spoke in a measured, grownup tone. "So we're going all the way to Fergus Falls, then? To the county police? Or are we going to the Criminal Apprehension Bureau? That's hours away; I checked." She held the book as close to her body as she could manage, as though it would shield her from all the awkwardness that was to come.

"No need to drive all over the state! Bob Toft retired here, to Willoughby, of course." Moira smiled over her shoulder. It was a smile of giddy mania.

"I'm Daphne, by the way." She was a child, being led away from safety by the pied piper.

"Oh, yes, hello," Moira said absently as she hiked up Main Street, her heels clacking.

Daphne followed, straining to hear the librarian, who was murmuring something to herself.

It was a hissing whisper of incoherent words.

# 18

# July 8, 1982

IT WAS ANOTHER SCORCHER. Caroline had awoken with sweat pooled between her small breasts. She'd had a dream about her little hidey hole in the shed. In her dream, it was big enough to climb inside, so she had. Once tucked within the comforting, cool pocket of earth, she had realized she was stuck. Her mouth had been useless. She hadn't been able to scream, so she had clawed at the wood planks with her nails. Blood had poured from underneath her fingers, oily black blood.

The terror of her dream had lingered as she got ready for the day. She had washed her face with extra cold water before putting on her new swimsuit. It was pointless to wear it. She had bought it for Greg to see. But apparently, he only had eyes for Rosalee. If only he knew. If only she was bold enough to tell him what a foul bitch Rosalee was.

Caroline had been deep in thought when Tiffany met her at the corner of Oak and Main. They had cut through the shadowy trail to Cross Lake, sweating even in the shade.

"Would you tell him for me?" They were on the beach, listening to Tiffany's radio. They had set up in their usual dip of sand. Dolly Parton sang of the daily grind in *9 to 5*.

Tiffany was on her stomach, her feet in the air and crossed at the ankles. "Tell him what exactly?"

Caroline hesitated. She was on her back, enjoying the sensation of being blinded by the sun. She closed her eyes from the intense light and marveled at the speckles swimming beneath her eyelids.

"Carrie? What?"

"Just that Rosalee is horrible and she doesn't really like him, that she's just using him for the summer. And that she's slutty and bitchy and fake as hell."

"Carrie . . ."

"Well! It's all true!" Caroline flipped over onto her stomach.

"Of course it is, but Greg probably already knows all that. He doesn't care."

"What?"

"He just cares that she puts out, and she's the prettiest girl in Willoughby; don't forget that."

"Tiffany!" Rage curled up inside Caroline's chest. She punched at the sand with both hands.

"He's not going to marry her or anything. They're just screwing for the summer. You need to relax!" Tiffany knelt on her frayed towel. She searched through her oversized tote bag.

"Here." She plopped down a bottle of Miller Light in front of Caroline.

Caroline ran her bandaged thumb down the side. "Wha'? It's warm."

"Well, I couldn't bring the cooler; we're out of pop, so my mom woulda known." Tiffany produced a bottle opener from her massive bag and popped open her own bottle. White foam trickled down her hand as she settled back onto her towel.

"I'm still in trouble with my dad, so I don't think . . ."

"Trouble? Why? You didn't even do anything."

"You know my dad." Caroline picked at the tight strap of her suit. "I looked at him sideways, and in front of everyone. If Kyle'd done it, he wouldn't have cared."

Tiffany rolled her eyes. "Don't be so sure. And shit, Carrie, just drink the beer. It'll calm you down about Greg."

Caroline surveyed the beach. It was early yet, so there were only a few swimmers and a single distant boater. She'd at least be secretive about it. Tiffany popped off the cap, and Caroline hid the bottle between them, behind the bag. Once the foam settled, she took a long drink. It was warm, bordering on hot, and tasted like pee.

She wiped her mouth with the back of her hand. "Do you really want to leave?"

"What do you mean?"

"You wanna leave Willoughby?" Caroline slumped back down on her belly, so they were side by side.

Tiffany adjusted her sunglasses. "Yeah. I mean, there's nothing here for us, Carrie. There's just stupid, lazy men and mosquitos."

Caroline thought about her hometown. The sunlight twinkled on the lake. She shaded her eyes and looked at the towering pine trees, always there, surrounding Willoughby and protecting it, somehow, from the outside world. She thought about the field behind her house, how the land stretched out in brilliant eternity.

She loved Willoughby. She didn't love everyone in it. She loved Main Street and the Woodhouse's mansion and the gazebo, where Fred Willoughby's mangled body was found in 1900. She loved the Pelican River, how it curled and looped and led to the dense wilderness.

Sometimes, Caroline wished she could live there alone. That the population of planet Earth was eradicated by some disease for which she had a special immunity. She would live in her house and eat canned food at the City Café. She would skip across the grass in the park and twirl along Main, joyous from the freedom and the silence.

Maybe Greg could survive too. Maybe just the two of them. Then she would have the bravery to tell him about Rosalee.

As though her mind had created them into being, Greg and Rosalee appeared in the distance. They were holding hands as they came down the trail from town.

Inside Caroline, a mess of conflicting emotions formed into a sputtering volcano. The sight of Greg's sweet face sent goosebumps up her neck.

Yet Rosalee's long legs sashaying across the beach caused her jaw to tighten.

"Oh, no." Tiffany swigged her beer.

Caroline squeezed her fists.

"Don't look at them." Tiffany held her hand across Caroline's eyes. "Just ignore them."

Caroline swatted Tiffany's hand away. "God! I hate her so much!"

"Join the club." Her best friend sniffed. "Let's stare daggers at her until she feels all weird and leaves."

Caroline smirked. "Let's kill her."

Tiffany spit out a mouthful of beer. "*Ha!* Okay, once she goes swimming, you hold her feet and I'll sit on her ugly head." She wiped the drops from her cleavage.

"I thought you said she's the prettiest girl in Willoughby?" Caroline watched Greg kiss Rosalee's tan cheek.

Tiffany sighed. "Yeah, so she is. But why are pretty girls so horrible? It's like a rule that they have to be bitches."

"We really should kill her. We'd be helping humanity. And Greg. We'd be saving Greg from her."

Tiffany chuckled.

Caroline glanced at Tiffany. She envied her carefree nature. Tiffany was always the calm one, the friend to pull her back from the storm of her emotions. Caroline opened her mouth and then immediately cinched her lips. It frightened her to picture Tiffany's reaction to her thoughts. She yearned to speak of a plan, in a real sort of way, for getting rid of Rosalee. She thought about sharp things and, most of all, of Rosalee being trapped like Caroline had been in her dream. She wanted to imagine her swallowing dirt and struggling to escape a makeshift coffin. She pictured her long nails snagging on rotting wood and her tongue lolling out from between her dead lips.

Before Caroline could speak these dark thoughts, Tiffany changed the subject.

She wanted to talk about their senior year and Homecoming.

Caroline knew, too, that it was Tiffany's subtle way of guarding her from her own anger and jealousy.

So Caroline took a long drink of her warm beer and smiled. She played along, talking about formal dresses and corsages bursting with baby's breath.

Her eyes, however, were forced like magnets toward Greg.

He and Rosalee had found a spot of sand several yards away, their backs to Caroline and Tiffany. They laid out a towel to share and then snuggled up, their twist of bare toes grazing the water.

Caroline was sure she was going to explode into a thousand pieces.

". . . maybe we can go up to the cabin after, like have a party after Homecoming. If my mom thinks only girls are going—"

Caroline sat up. "I saw something."

"Ignore them, Carrie, please."

She shook her head vigorously. "No, I mean, I saw something bad before, a few months ago."

"Okay . . ." Tiffany pulled a bag of potato chips out of the tote bag.

"I haven't told anyone because, I don't know . . . I'm a scaredy-cat, I guess." Caroline thought maybe it would be easier to tell Tiffany than her brother. Tiffany would understand. She would tell her she wasn't crazy. She would believe her.

"Well, spill it!" Tiffany set down her snack and lifted her sunglasses to rest on her hairline.

"It's about my dad." Caroline luxuriated in the delicious sensation of immediate relief. Her muscles unclenched for the first time in months. This was the right thing to do. "He's having an affair."

# 19

DAPHNE COULDN'T SHAKE THE IDEA that she was losing control. That she had fallen into a slippery pit, which would churn her up and spit her out. It brought back the blood-tinged memories of her worst day. Seven years ago, when the true horror of the world had been revealed to her. Not in a subtle whiff of coming adulthood but rather in a violent, topsy-turvy wrenching that few had to endure.

For a moment, Daphne was sixteen again, curled up in the fetal position and wishing she could run away from it all.

Moira, seemingly ignorant or uninterested in Daphne's obvious distress, chattered on about detective novels as they drove down the pockmarked gravel road. "Poirot's sidekick is Hastings. I had a Pomeranian named Hastings for many years! Little lover, he was; he'd sleep right at my side. You know, Hastings—the character, I mean— is much like Watson, representing the reader. Miss Marple didn't have a particular helper; instead, she employed various ones."

"Ah." Daphne held her knees. The heels of her sandals threatened to slip from the edge of the passenger seat of Moira's pristine 1958 Plymouth Fury.

"I tell you, the sidekicks don't get their due. Dr. Watson is the most intriguing and complicated character Sir Conan Doyle ever wrote. In my opinion, that is."

"Moira?" Daphne dropped her legs and fished for the tube of Tums in her cross-body purse, thankful to wrap her hand around its cylindrical familiarity. "What are we going to do? When we get there? Will he even remember—"

"Oh! Oh, yes, he will!" Moira emitted a nasally laugh. "Murders like that don't happen every day. Not that Willoughby hasn't had its share of bad luck, but anyways, he'll remember. Toft will help us with your book; he's always had a thing for me, anyways."

"Okay. If you think so."

Moira took one hand off the enormous, retro steering wheel and pointed to a rusted mailbox. It was bent forward on its wooden post, reminding Daphne of an arthritic old woman favoring her cane. "Almost there."

Anxiety plucked at Daphne. It spoke to her in her mom's signature mistrustful whine.

*Where are you going? What are you doing? Who do you think you are? Sherlock Holmes? Really?*

"Say, would you maybe mention me? In the book, I mean?"

A lead ball of guilt dropped into Daphne's belly. "Oh, yeah, totally."

Moira gave a high-pitched squeal.

They turned onto a winding driveway canopied by elms and lined with worn birch logs. Moira caressed the Fury's gearshift as they chugged up a rutted hill.

Dew speckled moss crept up the chocolate wooden siding, making it seem like the cabin had just emerged from Cross Lake. Two folding chairs waited on the front lawn, their legs pinned to the ground by tangled grass. A glittering can of Miller Lite sat on one chair's arm, directing a ray of sunlight directly into Daphne's eyes.

"He retired here in '09." Moira pulled up to the attached garage and killed the engine. It hummed for a moment before dying out, not unlike a cat's warning growl. "He used to live in Fergus Falls, a few blocks from the station, but his wife died of ovarian cancer . . . God, around '02? I think it made him better, you know, to get out of that house and come back here to the lake."

"We should have warned him. That we were coming." Daphne flicked a Tums onto her tongue, pushing the chalky nub against the roof of her mouth.

Moira waved her hand dismissively. "He'll love it. The chance to talk about it. Bob loves a good mystery almost as much as me!"

The front screen door of the small cabin creaked open.

Daphne stiffened in the passenger seat. Thudding disapproval filled her entire being.

A bald, egg-shaped head stuck out from the opening.

Moira swung open her car door and leaped up, calling to the curious man on the covered porch. "*Bob?*"

"I thought that was your Plymouth." Grinning, Bob Toft stepped out into the burgeoning sunlight. The speckle of age spots on the top of his skull made a blotchy Rorschach test. "She looks damn fine. Heard her purring all the way down the drive." He was small and stout, with surprisingly muscular arms for a man in his seventies.

"Olson's keeping her running." Moira leaned against the car door's frame. "Though I take her to St. Paul every summer, for an annual."

Daphne pushed open the passenger door and practically slithered out of her seat, wishing she was anywhere but in retired Sheriff Bob Toft's driveway. She waited awkwardly by the Plymouth's apple-red hood, pretending to find interest in a set of wind chimes hanging from the eaves. It was made from antique spoons and pewter bells.

"Who's this? One of Glenda's?"

Moira giggled. "Nah, hers won't get this close to Willoughby. They're allergic to fresh air."

Bob gave a deep belly laugh.

"I'm Daphne Forrest." She raised her hand in a rigid wave.

"Hi." Bob regarded her with an intense, questioning gaze. Daphne hoped this was an inherent scrutiny, merely a reflex for a retired county sheriff. "Daphne, huh? You're not local. What are you doing riding around with this crazy woman?"

"Oh, heavens!" Moira feigned offense.

Daphne was infused with an intoxicating relief. His slyly searching eyes had not, it seemed, pinpointed her mom's cheeks or her own nervous energy.

"Honestly, I'm not quite sure." Her iPhone buzzed against her thigh. She ignored the sensation, though she was surprised it was even functioning in this portion of the damp forest.

"Daphne's being modest." Moira rounded the hood of her Plymouth and joined Bob and Daphne near the deck stairs. "She's in Willoughby to write a book. And I leaped upon her, begging to be involved!"

"Ah." Bob Toft's crescent eyes twinkled. He crossed his muscular arms, dotted with coarse white hair, over his camo-print T-shirt. "Who's minding the library?"

Moira ran a hand through her brassy curls. "No matter! That helper girl, what's her name? She'll be in soon enough."

Bob gave another hearty laugh, reminding Daphne of a convivial mall Santa. "I'm glad I'm retired, otherwise you'd run me ragged." He gestured toward a porch swing hanging from the ceiling by heavy chains. "Sit on down, ladies."

As she followed Moira onto the sloping deck, Daphne recognized the vibration of several text messages. She ran her hand against the soft side of her purse.

Bob leaned against the peeling porch railing. He slipped a pack of Camels from his T-shirt pocket, squeezing it to produce a cigarette. "You know, Moira used to bug me all the time." He fished a lighter from his jeans. "She should've been in law enforcement."

Moira sat primly on the edge of the metal porch swing. "Pooh." She snickered. "I prefer fictional cases. I mean, except in this instance."

"The mill?" He lit the end of his Camel, expertly sucking in the nicotine.

Daphne plopped down beside Moira, wondering what Willoughby's fascination was with the mill explosion.

"No." Moira poked her shoulder. "Tell Bob."

"I'm researching the Bergman murders."

His head snapped in Daphne's direction. The glow of his cigarette on the canopied porch created a surreal halo around his bald head.

Daphne forced down the slimy mucous that indicated her belly was going rogue. She clutched her purse tightly to her hip. "Moira said you could help me, maybe. She said you were the county sheriff in 1982."

His nostrils, stuffed with the same kind of white hair that covered his arms, flared. "I was."

"You must have a thousand questions!" Moira wiggled, causing the swing to stutter backward on the rusty chains.

"Yeah, um, yes." Daphne blinked at the retired sheriff, picturing what he may have looked like thirty-five years ago. It occurred to her that the small-town iciness she had been greeted with had melted away. Here she was, on Bob Toft's porch, in a position to find the truth.

Or at least some version of the truth.

A memory of her dark time, of when she was sixteen and scared to the core, drifted up, threatening to overtake her. She remembered the scent of old coffee and stale cigarettes. She remembered the police officers, their eyes shifting and their lips pursed.

Daphne concentrated on the tendril of smoke curling up into the jangling wind chimes.

Moira sighed. "Well, then."

"Oh, well, I guess . . . I guess my main question is, what do you think?"

"We should have paper or a recorder or something so you can quote him. She can quote you, right, Bob?" Moira steepled her hands as though forming a masterful plan.

Bob grumbled. "Call me anonymous."

"Ooh!" Moira steadied the swing beneath them by grinding her mules into the soggy planks. "Say an 'anonymous lawman.' That's intriguing, isn't it?" She turned toward Daphne, her eyes wide and her creased face flushed with what Daphne could only assume was excitement.

"Sure, yeah."

"What do I think?" Bob flicked ash into a Folger's coffee can by his elbow. "I think someone got away with murder."

Daphne nodded. "Who?"

"That's the million-dollar question, isn't it?" He sucked on his bottom lip, studying Daphne's face in his subtle, prodding way.

"Do you believe—"

"What?" Bob interrupted. "That Caroline did it? The daughter?"

Daphne shrugged one shoulder, uncertain, now that she had traveled over a thousand miles, if she wanted to know the answer.

"I don't know." He gave a rattling wet cough. "She looked like a deer in the fucking headlights. Excuse my French."

Moira screwed up her lips.

The retired sheriff dropped the nub of his cigarette into the coffee can and continued. "She cooperated with us. And the psychologist—some child specialist from St. Cloud—she said Caroline Bergman seemed genuinely upset by the whole mess. And Jesus, was it a mess."

Daphne trembled.

Bob blew air out of his hairy nose. "Can't say I blame her."

"Blame her?" Daphne could taste her discomfort, putrid on her tongue.

"Running like she did." Bob crossed one sneakered foot over his other ankle, in the effortless way of a confident cop. "We were doing everything we could, working nonstop. It was a month or so after, I think. Maybe just a few weeks. She just faded away."

Moira nodded. "Some people think she might have committed suicide. Either out of guilt or grief."

Desperate, Daphne plunged her hand into her purse and snatched out a mint. She smelled it for a second before tossing it into her mouth, letting the spicy scent ground her.

"I like to think she's happy somewhere," Bob added. "Living a life she couldn't have had here, with people whispering and shooting her dirty looks."

An image of her mom's gravestone wavered in Daphne's mind's eye. "Hmm, yeah."

"Frankly, the idea of her running away, starting some new life— it's laughable." Bob Toft fiddled with the Camel pack in his pocket, perhaps considering another smoke.

"Why do you say that?" Daphne tried to control the emotion in her voice.

"She was sixteen, a'course, a young sixteen. Caroline was one of those girls . . . oh, how would you describe her, Moira?"

The librarian tapped her chin, clearly enjoying the discussion. "I would say . . . well, Caroline was a quiet, weak sort."

"A limp noodle—that's what Smiley, the highway patrolman, called her."

Daphne's iPhone vibrated again, accompanied by the cascading tone of a phone call. "Sorry, I think I better take this." She leaped up from the swing, eager to get away from the curious-eyed sheriff and the overeager librarian, if just for a moment. The two of them talking about her mom that way—it made her feel like she was spying, doing something morally wrong.

BEV'S CELL lit up the rectangular screen.

"Hi, Bev." Daphne raced down the porch steps, finding refuge behind a pine tree adorned with several hanging birdhouses.

"Minnesota?" Beverly shrieked.

Daphne rested the back of her head against the scratchy bark. "Did my dad tell you?"

"He's shitting a brick, Daph. He thinks you're losing it."

Daphne laughed. "Maybe I am." Beverly's voice, however angry, instantly recharged her. Like maybe she hadn't tripped into another dimension.

"What the hell are you doing? I mean, you could have flown down here if you wanted a trip. I could have driven you around, at least."

There was an awkward beat of silence.

115

"Right."

"I just mean . . ." Beverly exhaled. "I just mean, why are you alone in the middle of nowhere?"

"Well." Daphne peered over her shoulder at Bob and Moira. They appeared to be deep in conversation. "There's a big mall here, like the biggest in the US."

"Uh-huh," Beverly said with her signature sass. "And is that where you are? Because your dad told me you're in some hick town where your mom grew up."

"So what?"

"Daphne, is that healthy? I mean, you should be with me or your dad. Not all alone, not now."

Daphne licked the minty flavor off her teeth, considering how to assuage Beverly's fears. She couldn't even calm herself.

But what she did know, as she stood under the dripping tree, was that she wasn't homesick or lonely or in need of her dad or Beverly or anyone.

That made her stand up straight. "I think this *is* what I need. I know it probably doesn't make sense."

"Fuck, no."

"I actually—like for the first time ever, I'm doing something, Bev."

Her best friend snorted.

"Call you later?"

"What're you busy doing? You can't talk now?"

"Not really."

"Call me soon."

"Yep." Daphne hung up and slid her cell back into her purse, taking a moment to suck in the fresh air.

She swiveled back around toward Bob Toft's cabin. Moira and Bob had descended the steps and were chatting by the Plymouth Fury's polished hood.

"Hey, sorry." Daphne couldn't help but notice she had been imbued with a sudden confidence. It was as though her brain had caught up to her body, like she could finally comprehend her surroundings. "You were saying, about Caroline, that you're shocked she ran?"

"Oh, right." Bob scratched at his loose jowls. "She struck me as too scared."

"She was like that even before the murders," Moira added. "Kind of moping around behind Tiffany, and Kyle too."

"Tiffany?" Daphne drummed her fingers on the passenger's window frame, hoping to appear casual.

Moira gripped her keys, looking like she was ready to leave. "Her best friend. You saw her just a bit ago, at the library. They ran around a lot. Caroline disappearing was hard on Tiffany. She searched for her for months afterward."

"She waits tables at the City Café." Bob patted his cigarette pack again.

"Right. Okay." Daphne's confidence faltered. Every time she assumed she was getting a handle on 1982, her foundation was shaken.

She allowed this knowledge to soak in.

Moira frowned. "Bob has to go."

"I know I look like a sluggish old man, but I have responsibilities. I don't want to be wandering around, alone, still working past nightfall." He winked at them both.

"Oh, okay, but just one more thing." Daphne thought she almost sounded like she knew what she was doing. "Is it worth it for me, do you think, to go up to Bemidji? To the Criminal Apprehension Bureau? Would they have files I could read?"

Bob chuckled, which turned into another wet, hacking cough. "You're serious about all this, huh, dear?"

Daphne simmered. "Yes."

"Listen, Daphne Forrest. They're not going to just hand over unsolved murder case files. It's still, technically, an active case."

His condescension provoked her. "There has to be some public record—"

"Hold on." Bob yanked up the sides of his belt. Daphne spied the butt of a revolver pressed against his hip. Once a cop, always a cop, she supposed.

"Gimme a minute to find it for you."

She and Moira waited by the car as Bob reentered the creaking screen door of his cabin.

"What do you suppose?" Moira buzzed.

Daphne was just as eager as Moira to see what Bob had for her. Despite her inner mom's criticisms, she might be making headway.

Three minutes later, Bob emerged holding a composition book with both hands. It was the old-fashioned kind Daphne's Shakespeare professor insisted on using for exams.

He stuck the notebook out toward Daphne, panting from his search. "Take it."

"Thank you." She flipped it open to the middle. Yellowing pages were covered in sharp, thin handwriting. "But . . . why're you giving it to me?"

"It's nothing official. Just my thoughts over the years." Bob raised his top lip in a sheepish smile. "Who knows, maybe you'll solve the whole damn thing."

"If only." Daphne squinted, trying to make sense of his notes.

"Well, it's Christmas in May!" Moira sidled up to Daphne to get a good look. "Don't you agree, Miss Marple?"

"Looks like it," Daphne managed.

Two words, underlined and circled in the margin of the page, caused her to sway, ever so slightly, into Moira:

## 20

DAPHNE'S CAVERNOUS BELLY ROARED. She hadn't eaten since before she'd retched behind the gazebo. Except for a steady diet of mints, of course.

Moira had gone back to the library, but not before yanking on Daphne's arm and reminding her she wanted to be involved every step of the way.

The City Café smelled like heaven. Daphne realized, as her eyes adjusted to the dimly lit restaurant, that the lunch special at nearly every spot was a bowl of beef chili sprinkled with cheese. Daphne grinned to herself. Apparently not everyone had gotten Edwin's memo about the City Café chili.

She hesitated by the register, wondering if she should slip into the back booth or plant herself at the counter. There she could better watch the waitress with stunned fascination.

Daphne flipped through her memories, backward and forward, trying to remember if her mom had ever mentioned a friend named Tiffany. It occurred to her, as she stood there sniffing in the onions and beans, that her mom had turned out to be an enigmatic figure. A shadow of a real person. Jane Downs-Forrest hadn't shared anything about her childhood. She had preferred to speak through her dreamlike landscapes.

"Hey, there!" The tall waitress slapped a menu on the end of the counter beside a display of plastic pastries. "Moira kept you a while."

Daphne nodded dumbly. She sat down on the circular padded stool. The library book and Bob's journal swung against her side. "Can you still do breakfast?"

"Uh-huh. What you want?"

"Eggs. Scrambled. And some toast and bacon?" Daphne tried to picture Tiffany as a teenager, as her mom's best friend.

"Sure thing." Tiffany winked. "Coffee?"

"Thank you."

Daphne watched as the waitress set to work. Tiffany bounced around the City Café with the confident ease of a woman who had waited tables her entire life.

She returned with a pitcher of coffee, pouring it precisely into a scratched mug without looking. "You're doing some local research, then, in the library?"

"Yeah, Moira was very helpful." Daphne fidgeted with the paper napkin rolled around a set of silverware. "I'm writing a book, so—"

"Is it about the mill explosion?"

Daphne forced down a laugh. Based on how many Willoughbians had asked her that, she was pretty sure she could make decent money selling them an account of the mill disaster.

"Um . . . no. Not exactly. Just about local . . . happenings." Daphne smiled.

Tiffany set the coffee pot on a cluttered shelf behind her. She grabbed a glass of soda hidden within a mess of rags and menus and took a long sip through the straw.

Daphne rolled the wrapped silverware up and down her place at the counter, chiding herself for not taking the opportunity to bring up the Bergmans. Tiffany would probably be the most integral person in Daphne's chaotic investigation. In fact, the waitress standing a few feet away probably knew more about her mom than she did. They had been teenaged friends, like the kind that probably shared secrets and talked about crushes and family strife. Daphne shuddered at the thought of how many secrets Beverly knew about her.

"You friends with Edwin?"

"Hmm?" Daphne glanced up at Tiffany.

"Edwin Monroe, the Asian kid?"

"We just met. At the motel." Daphne heard an echoing growl emanate from her stomach. She glanced over at Jasper the cook, licking her lips.

"Edwin's always creeping around here, writing up things for his blog. He has some unpopular ideas about Willoughby. Just ask his poor parents."

"Oh, yeah?" Daphne cocked her head, unable to hide her smile at the notion of Edwin bugging the locals.

"He just loves to drum up bad things, to make it seem like this town is the seventh circle of Hell." Tiffany slurped up the last few beads of soda from the glass. "He's just sore he got bullied when he was little. And over the whole Kasey thing, of course."

*Kasey thing?* Daphne filed that away for later.

"Say." Daphne's arms and legs tingled with fear. "Would you be okay if I interviewed you? For my book? You, well, you seem like you'd probably know a lot."

Tiffany drummed her sausage fingers on the counter. "Uh-huh. I don't know. Are you writing up bad things, like Edwin?"

Before Daphne could manufacture an answer, Jasper rang a bell in the kitchen.

"Order up!" he called over the sound of sizzling hamburgers.

"Lemme get your eggs, girl." Tiffany dropped her soda glass into a bin of soapy water.

"Did I hear my name?" Edwin appeared, dressed in the same jeans from the night before and a black short-sleeved polo. He plopped down on the stool beside Daphne.

Daphne fluffed up the hair on the sides of her face, hoping to hide her warm, rosy cheeks. "Yes, Tiffany was telling me about your blog."

The waitress returned with Daphne's meal. "You're not recruiting her, are you, Edwin? To write for you?"

Edwin leaned back, laughing heartily. "Maybe, Tiff. Maybe."

"Don't pump her full of strange ideas. She likes Willoughby, don't you?"

"Huh?" Daphne nearly drooled at the sight of her eggs. "Oh, yes! Everyone is so nice." She unraveled her silverware while nibbling on a piece of bacon. "And it's beautiful here. I hope to go to the lake today, to explore."

"See, I haven't been a negative influence." Edwin patted Daphne's bare shoulder, the tip of his finger momentarily slipping under the strap of her tank top.

Daphne grinned as she turned toward him, surprised by her own happiness. She liked the warmth of his hand on her skin.

She blinked, trying not to let her eyes linger on his handsome face. "Would you pass the ketchup?"

"The what?" His hand dropped from her shoulder as he twisted to look down the counter.

"The ketchup."

Edwin grabbed the bottle of Heinz and slid it toward her plate. He watched her, squinting, as she squeezed the ketchup onto her eggs.

"What! Why'd you do that?" he exclaimed.

Daphne flinched. "Do what?"

Edwin made a dramatic gagging noise. "Ketchup on your eggs? Are you high?"

"It's good! It's the only way to eat eggs, obviously."

"Obviously," Edwin repeated, running a hand through his lush black hair.

Daphne poked the eggs with her fork, scolding herself inwardly for allowing Edwin to distract her. He had a way of giving her sincere, deep looks with his cocoa eyes and making her forget why she was in Willoughby in the first place.

After she swallowed her first bite, Daphne glanced back up at

Tiffany. The waitress was watching her with a queer look. Her nostrils flared as she stirred a fresh glass of soda with a straw.

"You're not the first I've seen do that." Tiffany's bottom lip stretched into a sneering smile.

"Well, I've lost my appetite," Edwin teased.

Daphne took another bite, remembering her mom squirting ketchup on their eggs every Sunday.

Suddenly, another memory jolted her innards. She rested a hand on her belly, lost in the flashback.

They had been in the grocery store. It had been right after Daphne's own dark time, and she had been in her most depressed mood. She had had the hood of sweatshirt up over her head, and she had been praying no one would recognize her or her mom.

They had been in the aisle with the twelve packs of Pepsi and Coke.

"You know." Jane had stopped the shopping cart abruptly. "I had a friend who loved pop. We call it pop in the Midwest, not soda like out here. Anyways, she drank it nearly all the time. She could drink a gallon of it, I think." Something had flitted across her sky-blue eyes. "She was a good friend. I had a rough time and she was there. She was like Bev—how Beverly is good to you."

That friend now stood before Daphne, sucking down fresh soda and peering at Daphne as though she had said something peculiar. Daphne would have to figure out a way, somehow, to bleed the knowledge from her, to hear the stories of her mom's time in Willoughby. To find the clues that she knew would ultimately lead to the exoneration of her mother, if only in her own quiet knowledge. But that would be enough.

Edwin pointed to the pot of coffee. "Daphne's writing a book, you know."

Tiffany obeyed, pouring him a full mug. "So I've heard. She wants to interview me. But if she's hanging around you, then I'm not so sure. I've read that crap you write." Her hand landed on her plump hip, her nose and mouth twisting into an indignant knot.

"I only report facts. You know that." Edwin drank a gulp of black coffee.

Tiffany grumbled. "I'll think about it." She disappeared, leaving her soda glass behind.

Daphne stared at the fizzing 'pop' as she finished her breakfast, wishing, not for the first time, that her mom could guide her in the right direction.

## 21

ONCE DAPHNE FINISHED, she and Edwin walked out into the
sunshine. A woman with two small children waved from across the
street, right outside the library.

"Hey, Eddie. How's school?" She kept her palm flat on her son's
head, which magically seemed to keep him from wandering into the
street.

"Good!" he called across. "I'm home for the summer."

The woman observed Daphne like a bug in a jar, in the familiar
way she had grown accustomed to in Willoughby. "Say hi to your
mom for me; I haven't seen her in a while!"

Edwin agreed.

They walked along the sidewalk, in the direction of the motel
and Cross Lake.

"So, you want to interview Tiffany?" He looked down at the
loose shoelaces of his Vans sneakers.

Daphne deflected. "Eddie? Can I call you that?"

"Please don't." He smiled. "I'm really curious what you're up to.
I want to be in on the secret."

She watched as a Ford pickup zipped by, the bed full of
distressed antique furniture. "Moira does too. She brought me over
to Bob Toft's this morning."

"Whoa! Really?"

"Uh-huh." She stopped. "Did you know Tiffany was Caroline Bergman's best friend?"

Edwin took a few more steps and then swiveled toward her. "The Minnesota Borden?"

Daphne shivered at the moniker. "Yeah. They were best friends. At least, Moira says that, and . . . and I think that's true."

He tapped his chin. "You're writing a book about 1982—about what happened here?"

"Yes."

"But Tiffany will never talk to you."

"I don't know. I'm going to keep trying." She meant this passionately. So far, Tiffany was the closest person to her mother she'd found.

"It would be a good angle, the best friend. I know the police questioned her multiple times back then, especially after Caroline went missing. They thought maybe she knew where she'd gone. But it's not like she's going to give you anything too great. If she'd had information, she would've given it to the police back then and Caroline would be in prison."

Daphne tapped her sandal on the sidewalk, forcing herself to hold back. She wanted to convince him how wrong he was. How wrong they all were. There was no way Caroline Bergman could have killed anyone, much less her own parents and twin brother. And certainly not with an axe.

But Daphne was constantly questioning how she should act in this charade that she had fabricated. If she seemed overzealous, too fervent, it would be obvious why she was there. Well, she considered, perhaps not obvious, but she would surely slip up and refer to Caroline as her mother or say something equally incriminatory.

"So you knew that she was Caroline's friend?" she asked.

"I know a lot about Willoughby." He seemed very wise, standing there on the sidewalk with his arms crossed and a lock of his black hair fluttering in the wind.

"For your blog?"

"For the last few years, I've been compiling information about every tragedy that's happened in Willoughby."

Daphne looked over her shoulder at the tiny, quaint burg her mother had painted with so much care. Over the last day, she had grown comfortable with the idea that a murder—a brutal axe murder—had happened there.

Other tragedies, though—that was incomprehensible.

"You mean, like the mill explosion? Everyone brings that up."

Edwin, still the vision of wisdom, chuckled at her words, making her feel instantly ridiculous.

"The mill, yes, but . . . well, honestly, I thought you might know this, but there's a crap ton amount of tragedies here. I've been charting them back through our town history, and well, it's like I said before. Willoughby's a bad place."

He said it so seriously. It almost calmed her, to think that it was Willoughby that was innately wicked.

Despite Edwin's insistence that Willoughby was a bad place, she knew someone had held that axe. She knew that a person had driven the sharp edge into her grandmother, her grandfather, and her young uncle. And she knew it couldn't have been her mother—it just couldn't.

A realization hit her like a sledgehammer to the gut. If her mother hadn't done it—and she knew that was true—then someone else in Willoughby must have. And Willoughby was the type of place where people stayed for generations. Whoever had wielded that axe could still live on that very road. Daphne stared at the mesmeric spinning of plastic pinwheel flowers in someone's cluttered front yard. She wondered if the morning of July 13, 1982, had brought the same tickling breeze. She wondered if the same flowers had spun on Main Street, neon and everlasting.

# 22

# July 11, 1982

IT HAD BEEN ONE of those bizarre summer days when the oppressive humidity had given way to storms in the daytime. The radio had beeped and hollered to warn them all of the cyclones thrusting through the prairies of North Dakota, headed for the farmlands of western Minnesota. But as evening bled into night, the storms calmed, leaving only a rhythmic stippling of hot summer rain on the Bergman's roof.

Caroline stared at the yellowing popcorn ceiling above her. She laid atop the quilt on her bed. There was nothing else to do on a damp and lonely night. Her copy of *Northanger Abbey*, given to her with emphatic giddiness by Moira the librarian, rested on her lumpy pillow, open to the first page.

Ever since she shared her secret with Tiffany, Caroline had been infused with a marked levity. She was confident that by releasing the words into the ether, she had seized power back from the ugly thoughts that had monopolized her mind.

She had more time to think of Greg and the way his golden curls tufted out around his ears.

Most importantly, Tiffany had appeared to take on the burden well. She had listened to Caroline's entire story, nodding her head and sighing with displeasure in just the right spots. She never told

Caroline she was crazy. And she had been affected—truly hurt—that Caroline hadn't told her sooner.

"I just . . . it was so much to take in, I had to think it all through," Caroline had said.

Tiffany had frowned, her bottom lip jutting out in a pout. "Of course. It is a lot. I'm sorry you've been alone with this, but now I know."

So things were a bit better.

There was still a pain that surprised her in quiet moments, though. It struck a sharp stab in her stomach and then dissipated, leaving a hollow ache in her ribcage. She knew this would probably never go away. It was a growing pain, she supposed, her body's way of reminding her that she was no longer a child. That she was no longer free to believe in only the good.

Caroline searched her bedroom ceiling, looking for the shapes she had found as a little girl. She was sure a water stain had soaked through in the pattern of a toad on a lily pad. She had called him Sir Toad and had spoken to him in hushed whispers. As she strained to see it though, she found only vague brown blemishes.

She gave up and rolled onto her side. The spine of *Northanger Abbey* smacked into her cheek. She let it fall onto the wood slats of the floor—an inexcusable offense, to be sure, in Moira Kettlesburg's opinion.

Through her window, she could see the night was black, with a tinge of ochre blooming through the breaks of cloud. It was the strange twilight color that warned of storms. She knew this from her grandfather. He had told her to watch the hues of the sky, that the colors would tell her what she needed to know of what was to come, of what to expect.

Caroline pushed her bare feet into the folds of the quilt. A chill crawled up the milky white skin of her back. She thought perhaps she could fall asleep for a few moments, that she could exist in the peculiar, dreamlike bridge between life and sleep. But as her eyes grew heavy, she was stirred by an unexpected crash.

"Lightning?" Caroline asked the empty room as she sat up in a daze. But it had not been the cracked whip sound of thunder.

It had been a tinny crunch, and it had come from below her—downstairs.

Caroline heard the murmur of voices. Something was happening, something other than the quiet focus of her mother working on her cross-stich. Something other than her father's nightly ritual of reading books through the slim cut of his bifocals.

She hopped off her bed and crept across the moaning floor, twisting the doorknob and pulling open her door.

Directly across from her, Kyle's head stuck out of his room. He was leaning forward on tiptoe, peering down the stairs.

They shared a curious glance and then both snuck out. Caroline rested a hand on the spherical bannister, listening closely.

Their mother's voice trailed up the steps. ". . . pick it up, would you?"

Caroline squinted at shards of blue incandescent glass on the living room floor.

Kyle took in a sharp breath. "Dad's bluebird," he whispered.

It was their father's prized possession: glass blown by his own father and kept on a high shelf in the curio cabinet. How could it have possibly been broken?

They watched as their mother knelt on the floor, her housedress skimming the hardwood. Caroline could not see her face from this angle. She wondered what was etched across her mother's features.

Their father's voice, distressed and angry, filtered up toward them. Caroline wasn't able to discern what he was saying. A broom came into view, as well as her dad's legs. He was pacing with it under his arm.

He was angry. She could tell from the way he bore his foot into the floor. And from the growl in his voice as he mumbled.

Kyle wavered on the top step, no doubt thinking he should go down and help clean the mess. She was thankful he remained with her. They knew what was happening downstairs was not for them.

They would both be interlopers in something they couldn't understand.

Well, Caroline *could* understand.

She left her brother on the landing and slipped back into her room.

A smile bloomed across her face. She hoped her mother had taken a stool into the living room. She hoped she had stood on it as she reached for the bluebird and touched the cold glass. She hoped she had thrown it, full force, at the ground and reveled in the tinkling sound of it breaking into a thousand pieces.

The familiar stab sliced into Caroline's stomach, and she cradled her belly, waiting for it to lessen. Finally, her chest ached, and she knew she would soon forget the bad thing she had seen, at least for a few happy hours and she would be able to crawl under her quilt and dream of Greg.

She was compelled to distract herself. She crossed over to her window, wanting to suck in some fresh air. She wanted to smell the rich summer storm. She flipped the metal latch on the side and then cranked the handle below it. The air did not disappoint. It was earthy and surprisingly cool.

A yellow tint remained on the edges of sky, and Caroline had the urge to paint this moment. She wished she had a canvas and brushes so she could attempt to recreate such a beautiful and stirring sight.

Something moved down below in the Bergman's lawn. It was unmistakably alive. It was not a whippoorwill, although she could hear the bird's haunting chant in the distance. And it was not a lost cat, trailing through their yard toward the woods. It had the distinct secretive crawl of a human. A woman. She was obstructed by an overgrown bush, but the light of the downstairs illuminated a curl of her hair and a swish of her hip.

Another sharp wallop in the base of her belly took Caroline's breath away. Her mind whirled as the woman crawled away into the cover of the tall weeds. An alarm, rooted deep within, trilled a warning to Caroline.

The desire to forget overwhelmed her.

DAPHNE BROKE HER MESMERIZED GAZE from the spinning flowers. She studied Edwin's attractive face. "Do you have to work? Right now?"

He shrugged. "I mean, my boss is my mom, so not really."

Daphne motioned toward a city sign declaring *CROSS LAKE 1 MI.* "I think I'm going to go check out the lake."

He dropped his hands into the pockets of his jeans. "Are you inviting me?"

"Well, yeah. In a professional sort of way." Daphne's heart thumped against her ribcage from her sudden boldness. "I thought maybe we could look through this." She flashed Edwin the journal in her purse.

He scrunched his eyebrows together. "What's that?"

"Oh, no big deal. Just Bob Toft's personal journal on the Bergman case." Daphne giggled.

"Holy shit!" He beamed. "I've been trying to get that old fart to give me statements forever! How'd you finagle that out of him?"

"I don't know. Maybe because I was with Moira?"

Edwin peered down into her purse. "It's probably because you're cute." He sighed. "Figures."

At his compliment, a warm, delicious sensation flooded Daphne's body. "I think you're just jealous that I'm better at this than you."

"Okay, true. That was flagrant sexism." Edwin laughed. He fell in at her side as they headed out of town.

"Eddie?" Daphne teased.

"Ick! Don't call me that." He smiled. "How about Ed?"

"I like Edwin." Daphne shielded her eyes from the sun as they walked. "Edwin, who is Kasey?"

His sneaker skidded on the cement as he came to an abrupt halt. "What?"

They stood in front of a home with an abundance of dandelions edging the sidewalk.

Daphne regretted opening her mouth. She turned and looked up at Edwin's pained expression. "Tiffany, she mentioned Kasey. I'm sorry. She said the name and—"

"Right," Edwin interrupted. "I'm not surprised. Tiffany is like everyone else. She gossips."

"I'm sorry," Daphne repeated. "It's none of my business."

"No." Edwin chewed on the inside of his cheek as he seemed to consider what to share. "It's okay. Kasey was my best friend."

"Oh." Daphne took a tiny step toward Edwin. "Did something happen to him?"

"*Her.* She died when we were in high school. She . . . um . . . I'm not sure what happened." His lips pressed together tightly in a white line.

"God, I'm so sorry. I just lost my mom, so I know that must have been terrible." She braved another small step toward him, surprised she'd let such a private piece of herself slip out in front of him.

"Your mom? Shit! Are you okay?" His dark brown eyes swirled with empathy.

"Yes." Daphne lied. Changing the subject was vital; otherwise, she might be compelled by his kind face to say too much. "But tell

133

me about Kasey. What do you mean, you're not sure what happened?"

Edwin raked both hands through his hair. His eyes fell on an elderly man emerging from the garage door of the house they'd stopped in front of.

The man observed them with a curious glare as he unwound a tangled garden hose.

"Come on." Edwin grabbed Daphne's hand. Her skin tingled in his grip as he silently led her up two blocks and around the corner toward what was locally known as the murder house.

They stopped in front of an empty lot where a house had been torn down long ago. Scraggy grass nipped at Daphne's ankles. Edwin leaned in, close to her ear.

"Kasey died on a snowmobile," he whispered. "That's what I was told. But I don't . . . I just know it's not true." He straightened. "Does that make sense?"

"I guess." She swiveled around, looking at the weed-covered rectangle of land. "But why don't you want people to hear?"

Edwin's black eyebrows knit together in confusion. "Because I don't trust Willoughby. You shouldn't either."

An unpleasant chill skimmed across the back of her neck. Edwin spoke so earnestly that Daphne couldn't help but believe him. Before her mother's death and Daphne's own dark time, when the world was still a structured and predictable place, she probably would have thought Edwin paranoid.

"I'm sorry Kasey died. That's horrible." She reached out her hand and squeezed his elbow.

Edwin hung his head. A smile, tinged with sorrow, danced across his features. "She would have loved this, you know? Investigating the murders and reading Sheriff Toft's journal? We were going to be hard-hitting journalists together." He gave an embarrassed chuckle.

"I think I would have liked her," Daphne said.

"Edwin! Little Edwin Monroe!" a voice interrupted them.

They both turned to see tiny and feeble Doris Woodhouse

making her way slowly toward them. She shuffled up, extending her bare, wrinkled arms.

"Hey, Doris." Edwin embraced the old woman.

"You're coming to the house, aren't you? I'm opening it up for this one." She thrust a finger at Daphne.

Fear clutched at Daphne's abdomen. Doris had been the only one in Willoughby, so far, to recognize Daphne's lineage. And she was likely to mention it again.

Daphne could imagine the crushed expression on Edwin's face when he realized she was the daughter of a reviled villain from his hated hometown.

He broke away from Doris's aggressive hug. "Oh, sure. Maybe I can do a piece on my blog about the murders. I haven't done one in a while." He turned back to look at Daphne. "That is, if Daphne approves. She's writing a whole book."

Doris directed her beady gaze to Daphne. "Oh, is that so?"

"Yes," Daphne squeaked. "You can come, Edwin." What else could she say? *Go away because I don't want a confused old woman to reveal my lies?*

Doris clutched Edwin's hand and sidled up to his side. Daphne noted that he seemed to have a comforting effect on everyone.

"Oh, you'll love it, Daphne." Doris led them toward the Bergman's simple home. "Everything is just as it was."

Daphne let out a shaky breath. "Great."

"Oh, exactly how it was!" Doris peeked over her bony shoulder at Daphne and winked. "Just as you remember it, my dear. Just as you remember."

"You've seen it before?" Edwin asked.

"No. No, just the outside. I haven't had the chance."

Daphne was rattled by the old woman's haunting words. She clasped her hands together in a sort of prayer, attempting to keep herself calm as they drew closer to 415 Oak Street. She trailed behind Edwin and Doris up the cobblestone path to the front porch of the home her mother had grown up in. At first glance, it had the appearance of every working-class dwelling on the street. Yet as

Doris fiddled with the ball of keys in her aged hands, Daphne recognized the signs of a thriving business beside the front door. One sign read:

WELCOME TO THE SITE OF THE
BERGMAN AXE MURDERS!
SEP–MAY BY APPOINTMENT ONLY
JUN–AUG 9AM–5PM

On the other side of the door, above a plastic skeleton posed to give a creepy wave, there was another sign:

ADULTS: $8.50
CHILDREN UNDER 12 ARE FREE!
ABSOLUTELY NO PHOTOGRAPHY!
KEEP YOUR PHONE IN YOUR POCKET!

Daphne leaned forward and rubbed her thumb over a smudge of dust on the word *CHILDREN*. The thought of kids ogling her family's possessions sent a sickening pang through her tummy.

"Here we are!" Doris twisted the knob. Edwin pushed the door open and held it for Doris and Daphne to walk inside.

Daphne hesitantly crossed the threshold. She was instantly hit with the muggy scent of antiques. The stale smell brought her back to a consignment store in Bellingham, where her mother used to search through damp boxes for suitable frames for her paintings.

"Let me get settled a moment, and then I'll take you on a tour." Doris slipped off a pair of tan shoes designed for the aching feet of the elderly. "Don't touch a thing." She disappeared from the front entry, through the living room, past a staircase, and into the kitchen at the back of the home.

Daphne stood in awe, taking in each grain of wood on the paneled walls. The living room held a coffee-colored corduroy couch with orange throw pillows. A loosely knit blanket was thrown over the back as though it had just been wrapped around her mother's legs. An ancient television stood in the corner, its antenna pointed toward the ceiling.

"It's like a time capsule." Edwin kicked off his sneakers. "Doris is a fanatic about keeping it preserved. Apparently, a distant relative held an estate sale about a year after the murders and Doris freaked. She made them shut it down and bought it all herself. She donates the profits of the house to the town, though—to our library—and she bought the Willoughby Millers new baseball uniforms and equipment last spring."

"The Millers?" Daphne tilted her head. "Really?"

"I guess it's a little morbid. But they got their name before it exploded."

Doris returned to the small entrance after flipping on most of the downstairs lights. She silently pointed to a sign hung by a brass coat tree.

PLEASE REMOVE YOUR SHOES

There was a happy face with a wide black grin next to the words. Daphne nodded as she removed her black flats.

"Here." Edwin slipped a twenty-dollar bill out of his wallet and tried to hand it to Doris.

She refused to accept the payment. "Nonsense!"

He shrugged, returning the money to his back pocket.

"Now!" Doris clapped her hands together. "I want you to take a journey with me to 1982. Before both of you young things were even born."

"Doris has leftovers in her fridge older than both of us," Edwin whispered.

"It was hot that afternoon." Doris stood before them, clearly enjoying her role as Willoughby's murder historian. "Hotter than the Devil's armpit, as my darling husband, Franklin, used to say."

Edwin gave Daphne an amused glance. She tried to smile back.

"It had been a typical summer day. Visitors and locals alike were splashing around Cross Lake. There was no clue of the devastation to come." Doris looked down at the floor. Daphne could sense within her a genuine grief. "At approximately 1:12 that afternoon, sixteen-year-old Rosalee Edwards was heard screaming from the front lawn of this very home. A nearby neighbor, Donald Kettlesburg, came to her aid."

"A sixteen-year-old?" Daphne asked. "Not Caroline?"

Doris waved her arms. "Yes, yes. Listen.

"Rosalee was barely able to speak when Donald, the former principal of Willoughby School, came running toward her screams. Pale and frightened, she pointed toward the Bergman's open front door. Donald climbed the porch steps. He had an awful foreboding as he stood where you stand now."

Daphne glanced down at her feet as though answers were written on the hardwood beneath her toes.

"The tang of blood filled Donald's nose. He had fought in the Second World War and recognized the scent." The old woman paced before them. Daphne thought she looked like the evil witch in Snow White, grizzled, but with wide, curious eyes.

Doris urged them to move forward into the living room. They followed her as she stepped up beside the wooden staircase.

"This is where Gunnar Bergman lay." She ran a hand above the bottom step as though an invisible body still rested there. "Blood seeped down the steps and puddled on the floor."

Daphne squinted. She was certain she could make out the slightest hint of an outline on the oak. Vomit tickled her throat.

"Gunnar's face had taken the brunt of the attack. Donald wasn't even sure if the body belonged to Gunnar or his son, Kyle Bergman. They were both tall, and the body's face was no longer recognizable."

Daphne hiccuped. Her stomach roiled. She secreted a mint from the purse on her shoulder and slipped it onto her tongue.

"Next, he stepped into the kitchen, calling for Ida." Doris gestured toward the opening. Daphne and Edwin entered, with Doris right behind. It was a cramped kitchen, with a boxy toaster oven on the chipped counter and framed cross-stich patterns on nearly every inch of wall space. The table, tucked into a narrow nook, was set with melamine dishware in various colors. Daphne stared at a single plate. It was the color of lime Jell-O and had worn, scratchy edges. She wondered if her mother had eaten on that very plate. If she had scraped lasagna from that green plastic into her mouth.

"Ida lay on the kitchen floor. Donald slipped on the gore as he rushed to her aid. But she was clearly dead. The killer had sliced Ida's belly open with the axe, and once she was on the floor, the axe had been brought down onto her back as she most likely tried to escape." Doris stared at the kitchen floor as though she could see the murder playing out before her.

It occurred to Daphne that Doris appeared to be more lucid than she had the day before. It was hard to believe that the frail woman who had forgotten about cheese toast was the same woman before her now, recounting a decades-old murder.

"Was the blood coagulated when he arrived?" Edwin regarded the scene with a cool detachment.

Doris nodded. "It was beginning to, yes. It's believed they were killed in the late morning hours."

Edwin tapped his chin, thinking.

"And where was Kyle found?" Daphne steeled herself. It was the image of her young uncle losing his head that had haunted her since her mother had clawed at her arm with her dying hands.

Doris walked over to the back door of the kitchen. She pushed aside a ruffled curtain that covered a window in the door. Daphne leaned forward and looked out into the backyard.

"Beyond that shed, do you see the field of wildflowers?" Doris tapped the glass.

"Yes." Daphne peered out. She saw a peeling toolshed, and behind it was a sea of budding purple flowers. It was her mom's painting in vivid life.

"Kyle Bergman was decapitated out there. He was presumably running from the murderer. The axe, wiped clean of fingerprints, was found beside him."

Daphne stood back, quite finished with the macabre view. Her hand swayed toward Edwin. She wanted to grasp his fingers. She swallowed the instinct to grab for him and crossed her arms behind her back.

"And who do you believe did it, Mrs. Woodhouse?" Daphne looked into the old woman's wet, cloudy eyes.

Doris giggled as though Daphne had shared a joke. It was an odd warbled sound. "Many believe it was Caroline, the daughter who disappeared. Or a summer visitor, a stranger. I say it hardly matters! Time has forgotten, Daphne dear. We all forget!" Her wrinkled face curved into a toothy grin. "The dead forget too!"

Daphne glanced sideways at Edwin, hoping he wore the same confused expression she knew was painted on her own face. He gave an awkward smile, clearly used to Doris's ways.

"Let's go see the axe! If you look really, very close, you may see blood!" Doris, brittle and bent, pushed excitedly between Edwin and Daphne and back toward the staircase.

# 24

## May 4, 1982

IT WAS JUST LIKE KYLE to leave her alone. He knew she shouldn't be alone, not at night, but he left her on the corner of Main and Oak because Will Dobson had come by in his dad's Ford pickup and they wanted to drink a bottle of Jameson in the woods. Without her.

"You'll be fine!" Kyle said as he climbed up into the cab. The passenger window was covered in sheets of plastic wrap duct-taped to the window frame. Caroline had heard that Tammy Dobson broke the window with the heel of her sandal and their dad, Drew Dobson, beat the snot out of her. She was surprised Will had even been allowed to drive the thing. It was well known his dad was a drunken bully.

She crossed her arms and gave her best dejected frown, but they sped off anyway, leaving her in the dim light of the street, alone and chilled.

"Shit." Caroline hiked up the paper bag hanging at her elbow and let her cardigan sleeves fall down over her palms.

It was as though she were doing something naughty, stalking the streets of Willoughby all alone. Right at that moment, she was overwhelmed by the most peculiar sensation. It was the clashing notion that she was at once alone and being watched. Both unnerved her.

Caroline walked quickly toward the school, the paper bag of dinner leftovers swatting at her side.

She had been surprised when her mother had asked them to take a plate of food to their father. When he worked late, which was happening more often lately, he would just eat when he came home. But Ida Bergman had insisted.

Caroline smiled, happy to know that when she reached her father he would wonder where Kyle was. He would be upset that she was left in the dark, all by herself.

She shouldn't be alone.

Willoughby School came into view. Caroline crossed the street without looking. Any car on Main would be obvious, its headlights glowing and the purr of the engine filling the silence. She wished Greg Brody would drive up—although he didn't have a car, in her fantasy he did. He would be startled by her and hit his brakes. He would get out and check on her. Maybe his bumper would have swiped her knee and she would have the tiniest bloody scratch. He would say he'd have to carry her, although she wouldn't have been injured too badly. She would ride in his arms and smell his Irish Spring scent, and they would kiss in the moonlight.

Then she wouldn't be mad at Kyle for ditching her, or at her mom for forcing her to bring a cold plate of ham across town, or at her dad for working late all the damn time.

She jumped up the steps, two at a time, anxious to be inside, and pushed through the front door. The chain hung between the two doors, waiting for Gunnar Bergman to latch the padlock once he left. There was an eerie green light radiating from the back of the building. Caroline reminded herself it was just the nighttime lights. She had seen them before, but she still shivered as though someone had walked over her grave.

"Dad?" she called up the stairs to the second floor. Maybe he could come down and get his dinner; she was scared, for some reason, to go up there alone. The lockers lining the hall looked wrong in the pea-green light, and the school itself seemed like an alien place, a place she had never been. She wished Greg was there, or even her dead grandfather. Pop hadn't been afraid of anything. He'd lost most of his hearing and part of his right foot in the flour mill.

"Dad!" she yelled, louder this time. "I brought food!"

Silence.

"Shitty shit." Caroline sighed. She went up the stairs and reached the landing, turning to take the final steps. The light on the second floor was less green but dimmer, casting shadows on the linoleum. Her mind raced with all the terrifying possibilities. That she would find her dad in a pool of sticky blood, a knife in his back. That there would be a monster with wolfish eyes waiting for her at the end of the hall, hungry.

The second floor was empty. The door to her father's classroom, 212, was closed. She thought maybe he had left, maybe he had dropped by Willoughby Grocery before returning home.

A pang of terror rippled down from the base of her skull to the tips of her toes. She was alone. Alone. The chain was unlocked. Her father was an organized man, a man of precision. He would have locked it. He must be in his room. Even though it was darkened, he had to be in there.

Caroline let the paper bag slide down her arm, and she grasped the handle with her fingers. She thought it would be a handy weapon for when a monster sprang from a locker to eat her face. She could whack it with one of her mother's plates. Her mother would be upset about her family china; oh man, she would smolder.

That made Caroline smile.

Just like all the other classrooms, the door marked 212 had a window of obscured glass. It was the kind of glass that you could see hazy objects through, as though looking through the end of a beer bottle. Caroline had never bothered to try looking through them before; during the day all the doors were ajar. She realized, as she crept forward, that her father's was always open. Wide open.

Caroline touched the doorknob with her pointer finger as though she were worried it would be burning hot, as if from a fire within. She hesitated, not wanting to open it, not wanting to see.

There was a blurry light inside—the lamp on his desk. This only made the fear more palpable. The grownup side of her urged her to quiet the nonsense in her head; the monsters, shadows, and demons she was so afraid of finding were not real. The other side of her, the part of her that would develop into a brilliant landscape artist, blinked with urgency. Something was very wrong.

She realized there was a sound, and more than that, she knew what it was. It was the sound of her parents from the other side of her bedroom's thin wall, and it was the sound she'd heard at Cross Lake a few years ago, when night had fallen fast and she'd been alone—very alone—and she had stumbled across a writhing mess of beach blankets.

It was the sound of sighs and squeaks she knew she wanted to make with Greg, given the chance.

Caroline's skin crawled with disgust. She pressed her clammy hands against the door. The paper bag smacked into the wood, and she thought, for one agonizing second, that she was going to be found by the monster. Not the dark creature of her nightmares but the man she had thought for so long was God himself.

Although her sight was obscured and she had to stand on tiptoe, Caroline saw what she knew was happening. The twist of limbs, the rhythmic panting, and finally, to her surprise, the red high-top Converse sneakers. They were a blob of red, but she knew. They rested on the floor, waiting for the horror to end. Waiting to go back on the feet of the only girl in town who owned such shoes. Rosalee.

Rosalee. Rosalee. She hated her so much. She tripped back down the stairs and thought she could kill her. She could kill her with something sharp. Him too. It would be so good. To see the blade go into their skin, to shred them, to see red blood—as red as Rosalee's high-tops.

Caroline's brain pulsed with murder as she stumbled toward the front entrance. The bag of dinner slipped off her wrist and landed with a dull thud on the linoleum.

She stared at the school's door. She had just witnessed her father's affair, and inexplicably, she was frightened to go outside. To be alone in the murky night, or worse, to *not* be alone.

Galvanized by her spewing rage, Caroline ignored the warning in her heart and kicked through the door. She pounded down the steps and across Main, her mind hissing with fire as she thought of her father.

*Don't forget.*

*Don't forget what he is doing to us.*

*Don't forget how he chose Rosalee over you, over mom, over Kyle.*

*Just don't forget.*

# 25

AS THEY WALKED BACK to the Willoughby Motel, Daphne struggled to appear normal. She had seen her mother's bedroom, preserved by Doris Woodhouse for over thirty years. The image of the quilt her mother had slept under and her desk cluttered with ancient homework and dusty pencils had hollowed Daphne out. Then there had been the axe, tucked into the corner. It had been there, of course, because she had been the Minnesota Borden. Whether she was guilty or not, the strange people fascinated by true crime would come to Willoughby to see what they wanted to see: a murderous teenager.

"Why didn't the police keep it?" Daphne had asked as they had peered down at the murder weapon. "It's an unsolved case."

Doris had only chortled in response. In fact, she had laughed so hard that she had had to remove the crusty handkerchief from her pocket and blow her nose inside with a thundering honk.

Edwin and Daphne were both quiet, lost in their own solitary thoughts, as they made their way to the motel. Daphne wondered if he was beginning to suspect her motives. That perhaps he had seen a glimmer of recognition on her face at the sight of a painting in her mother's bedroom. The moment she had seen the brass frame hung above the squat dresser, she had known. There had been doubt that

Caroline Bergman was even her mother. She had seen her grainy photograph online, but Daphne had still held a small, pathetic hope that Jane Downs-Forrest had been another woman.

The painting, though, had proved it all. It wasn't as beautiful as her work at the end, before the cancer ravaged her nerves, but it was close. It was a landscape of swooping, artful strokes. It was the field of violet wildflowers that could be seen out her window, the exact perspective from up above. The place where her brother had taken his final breaths before someone plunged an axe through his young neck. The signature on the bottom right was a different name, Caroline B, but it was written in her mother's familiar curlicue letters.

Seeing it there, a few feet from where the axe was displayed for tourists' viewing pleasure, had been the final twist to Daphne's sensitive gut. She had wanted to vomit right there, on the scratched wooden floor of her mother's bedroom. Instead, she had excused herself and rushed downstairs to hug the toilet until it all came out. As she had clutched the porcelain, hearing Edwin and Doris pacing above, she had questioned her own motives. Why had she come on such a pointless errand? Beverly and her dad had been right.

More vomit had come until there was nothing left to gag on.

Weakened, Daphne spent the rest of the evening and night swaddled in the threadbare comforter of her motel room. She awoke many times, drowning in panic that she had forgotten something significant.

Half past eight the next day, she pattered across the narrow deck to the front office, groggy from her long night.

"Good morning!" Jay Monroe greeted her from beside a card table piled with muffins and a coffee pot, in the corner of the dim room. He poured steaming black coffee into his giant travel mug. "Sleep all right?"

"Yeah, comfy bed," Daphne answered politely, waiting awkwardly for him to finish.

"Splendid." Jay ripped open four Splenda packets at once and sprinkled them into his mug. "You're staying safe, aren't you? Not wandering around at night on your own?"

Daphne bit her lip, torn on how to proceed. She remembered Bob Toft mentioning the same thing—that he didn't want to be out at night, alone. "Are there wolves here? Or bears?"

Jay chuckled. "We're too far south for black bears." He blew at his coffee as he peered over the top of his mug with wrinkle-edged eyes. "What d'ya got there?" He pointed to the book tucked under Daphne's armpit.

"It's from the library. A local history book." She didn't like how he'd changed the subject. Edwin, his son, had done the same thing. He'd warned her about the nighttime like she was a little girl who might get lost in the dark.

She shivered at a foggy memory, of a threatening presence in a swirl of blackness.

"Edwin mentioned that you're doing some investigating." Jay left the breakfast table and began to pull out folders of paper from behind the front counter. "Moira, too. She was telling everyone at the fish fry last night, all excited; it's how she gets."

Daphne smiled as she placed the book down on a vinyl chair. "Moira's real nice. She wants to help." It unsettled her to think that she was a point of conversation at the City Café. She took a ceramic mug with the craggy outline of Minnesota on the front and poured herself a cup of coffee.

"Edwin wants to help you." Jay dropped into a swivel chair, drumming his fingers across a notebook.

Daphne looked over her shoulder at Jay. He was short, not much taller than her, with wild salt-and-pepper curls. "He knows a lot about this place."

The back door of the office swung open. Edwin and his mom, Maggie, entered together. Maggie nodded a hello to Daphne as she busied herself with some work beside her husband.

"Hey!" Edwin bounded toward Daphne. His happiness was infectious, causing Daphne's polite grin to stretch into a sincere smile.

"Hey." She dribbled the contents of a creamer cup into her coffee.

"What's your plan? Interviewing any suspects today?" He waggled his eyebrows.

She suppressed a giggle. "Moira, later, I think. I'm going to look over that book I got."

"Oh, okay." He tapped the toe of his Vans against the card table's leg rhythmically, watching as she helped herself to a lemon poppy seed muffin.

Daphne sensed his words unspoken. "Do you want to help?"

"It's obvious, huh?" He crackled with energy.

She motioned for him to follow her to an oval table pressed against the motel office's wall. She slid out the vinyl chair carefully, avoiding a spindle of brochures. Edwin sat opposite her, his knee pumping up and down.

Daphne opened to the precise page she was looking for. "This is Calvin Bergman. If I'm figuring the math right, he would have been Gunnar's grandfather, or great uncle."

Edwin studied the old photograph. "He looks like, what's his name? 'Frankly, my dear, I don't give a damn'?"

Daphne clapped. "Clark Gable! I thought so too!"

Jay and Maggie looked up from their tasks.

Daphne lowered her voice. "Moira said he was Fred Willoughby's right-hand man—I'm assuming Fred was a big deal around here?"

"Uh-huh." Edwin nodded. "He was a doctor who came here around the 1890s. This area was unincorporated—just a bunch of farms—and then they named the town after him. But he didn't last long. He died in 1900."

"Okay, I think I saw a picture of him." Daphne flipped through the pages, stopping to take a nibble of her muffin.

"Are you going to include the town's history too? In your book?"

"Maybe. Oh, here he is!"

She leaned over the table so they could both stare at the image of Fred Willoughby. He was a lanky man with a hooked nose, circular spectacles, and a pencil-thin moustache. His wife posed next to him in an austere gown of dark fabric. She was petite, pale, and rather mousey looking. They wore matching grimaces.

"Wow! Too bad they're dead, they look like a lot of fun," Edwin joked.

Daphne leaned in closer, reading the paragraph beneath the photograph:

*Revered physician and town founder, Dr. Fred Willoughby, became the first mayor of Willoughby, Minnesota. He is credited with both bringing modern medicine to Otter Tail County and commissioning the land along the Pelican River to be used for the commercial practice of flour milling. This would triple the town's population for a time in the early twentieth century, until the tragedy which occurred there in 1931 (see Chapter 12). Unfortunately, Fred Willoughby would not live to see Willoughby's economic growth. He died in 1900, shortly after the birth of his daughter, Francesca. In an ironic twist of fate, Francesca Willoughby—who went on to marry the Culver flour magnate, William Culver—died as a result of the mill disaster. She was Fred Willoughby's only child and last living blood relative.*

*Pictured (below) is Willoughby's first town council:*

*From left to right: Del Hart, Tony Shortall, Calvin Bergman, Foster Florence, Fred Willoughby.*

Edwin pointed to the group photo at the bottom of the page. "Here they are together, Calvin and Fred."

Daphne jumped up and stood beside Edwin to get a good look.

The five men were arm in arm, posed in front of a thicket of trees. Fred wore the same look of disinterest, while the others had varying degrees of smiles.

An odd compulsion prompted Daphne to ask Edwin a question. "Do you know any of these other last names? Descendants of these men?"

"Shortalls used to live here. Not anymore, though. Let's see . . . hey, Mom?"

"Hmm?" Maggie looked up from her work. She wore a pair of bifocals and a look of concentration.

"Ever heard of any Harts or Florences around here?"

Maggie twisted up her mouth, thinking. "Jay?" She tapped her husband's shoulder.

"Nah." Jay shrugged.

"Ask Doris." Maggie returned to her task, circling things on paper with a red Sharpie.

The mention of Doris made Daphne's mouth turn to dust. She didn't want to think about the murder house.

"Will you show me the mill? I'd like to see what all the fuss is about." Daphne shut the book and grabbed the remnants of her muffin. After the nausea-provoking murder house, she yearned to be outside.

"Sure! Bring that journal of Toft's too. We could look it over?" Edwin stood. "And let's sneak out of here before my mom puts me to work."

"I heard that," Maggie snapped.

## 26

"Here we go," Edwin said as they reached the wreckage.

The sun was unusually hot, and Daphne was already sweating.

"You can see here." He reached the end of the narrow path first. "There are still pieces of the waterwheel. Most of it fell into the river, but some of it blew back this way."

Daphne took in the twist of old metal and rotting wood. Several yards away, what appeared to have once been a grain elevator was now a dilapidated, roofless building crumbling in on itself.

*RILEY WUZ HERE* had been sprayed on the side in neon orange.

Daphne kicked a beer bottle with her sandal. She regretted coming down here. After her purge into the Bergman toilet the day before and her rotten night's sleep, she was still dehydrated and a bit wobbly.

Adding to her discomfort, there was a sinister atmosphere here that was thicker than the humidity.

"Caroline's grandfather. He lost part of his foot here." Daphne placed her hands on her hips, surveying the remnants of the wreckage hiding within the crawling weeds. The fact came to her mouth before her mind could even process it. It was something her mother had mentioned once, how Daphne's great-grandfather had lived through an explosion. It had to have been the one that occurred there, in Willoughby. "That must have been Calvin's son."

Edwin balanced on the edge of a steel beam resting in the soil. "That's funny."

"Hmm?" She could hear the river trickling beside them.

"You know about her grandfather, how he was injured here, but you didn't know where Kyle's body was found."

Daphne shrugged, uneasy.

"You know bits and pieces, but you don't know the whole story." Edwin jumped down from the beam. Sweat was visible under his floppy bangs. "You seemed upset in there, yesterday."

"It's disturbing, is all, being in a place like that."

His eyes searched her face. "You threw up."

Daphne bristled. The rhythmic cascade of the river pounded in her ears. "I just . . ."

The familiar tone of a ringing cell phone jangled in Edwin's pocket. He broke his intense gaze and slipped it out into his palm. "Oh, shit." He swiped to answer.

"Hey, Mom . . . yeah." Edwin turned his back to Daphne and looked out over the riverbank. "Yeah, yeah. I know. I'll pick it up on the way back. Yeah, promise."

Daphne stepped backward, wanting to give Edwin his privacy. She swiveled toward the decaying grain elevator, curious to search inside. She carefully stepped through the twisting, knee-length grass toward it. Crickets chirruped around her, and the air became dense against her bare skin.

A storm intensified within her. It was strange, unlike anything she had ever experienced. It was a heightening of her senses. She could smell the deep earthy scent of a smoldering fire.

Daphne closed her eyes and sucked in through her nostrils.

A far-off scream, barely audible, rattled her frame.

She opened her eyelids, jolted by an overwhelming heat, much stronger than the late spring sun.

Fire was all around her, lapping at her heels and trickling down like rain. She leaped back, tripping over a chunk of flaming wood, and landed on her butt. Terrified, she scrambled to her feet and searched behind her through the hazy smoke. Edwin had disappeared from the riverside. Her eyes were filling with water and her brain was coming unhinged. How had a fire started? And so suddenly?

"*Edwin!*" She choked.

Another anguished scream pierced through the cloudy smoke.

"*Edwin?*" It had to be him. He was on fire. He had come ablaze—spontaneous human combustion or something equally as horrifying must have been to blame. Daphne waved her hands in front of her face, pushing through the obscurity.

Her toes pressed into something soft. She bent over to see what was at her feet. It was a woman. A dead woman!

A break in the smoke revealed the singed ends of the woman's short, sandy-brown hair and her black lips. The rest of her face was a surreal lump, the consistency of candle wax. A spitting fire simmered along the fringe top of her sherbet-colored dress.

Daphne panicked at the sight of the woman's sloughed skin, dripping down into the grass.

The trimmed grass.

Daphne pinwheeled backward, trying to avoid getting the mess on her exposed toes. She became enveloped by black, gagging smoke.

She was lost.

"Edwin! Please!" She coughed into her elbow. The ground beneath her began to divot and slide. She fell to her knees, her mind swirling with questions.

"Please." Her lungs pounded with effort. She slid backward into a feeble crawl to get away from the fire.

As she clung to the ground, feeling her way through the muddled smoke, a foot stomped into a soft pile of cream-colored powder beside her.

*Flour,* she first thought.

Then a blaring alarm, not the kind she could hear but rather an internal jangling, tore open her mind.

The foot, attached to a leg she could not see through the strangling smoke, was wrong.

It wasn't human.

Daphne skittered backward at the sight of its putridity. Of its sickly pallor and spindly claws.

Suddenly, a tremendous force yanked on her body from below.

Daphne threw out her hands to find purchase. Pebbles and dirt rushed through her grasp as she slipped down an incredible void.

*I'm going to die.*

Her legs twisted in the wind and for one achingly long moment, Daphne believed she would fall for eternity. Her vision had been marred by the smoke, and she could only see the tears welling in her eyes.

Then she sensed the smack of ice-cold water against her side. She struggled to take in one last desperate breath before she was submerged. The freezing water squeezed around her entire body in a frigid embrace.

The water stung her nose. She opened her eyes wider, seeing the shadowy depths of Pelican River. A piece of white-washed wood sloshed beneath the surface alongside her. As she tumbled toward the river floor, she could make out the letters *IL* printed in black paint on the wood.

Realization whispered within her. She was drowning.

Daphne looked above her at the diminishing light. She was sinking into the abyss. Her arms began to thrash and her legs kicked. Bubbles emanated from her mouth.

She swam upward, frantic for air.

Finally, she sensed the euphoric release of pressure. Her head pushed through the surface of the river. She sucked in a painful gasp of air as she began a panicked doggy paddle.

The quality of the light surprised her. There was no obscuring smoke. Daphne swiped at her eyes with one hand and attempted to recognize her location. She was, indeed, in the Pelican River. She could see the far-off bridge beneath which the fisherman had sat as she had been trundled over it on her way to the motel.

*"Daphne? What the hell?"* Edwin's voice ripped through the water in her ears.

Daphne was too weak to call back to him, and the eroded banks of the river seemed too high for her to climb. She waved her hands up toward the blinding sun, unable to make out even Edwin's silhouette.

There was an echoing splash.

She searched around her, filled with dread that something *evil* had followed her. That an inexplicable fire would roar up from the lapping water and burn her flesh.

Edwin's head broke the surface about ten feet away.

"What are you doing?" Daphne paddled and kicked. She was certain if she stopped, she would sink like a stone.

"What are *you* doing?" Edwin swam toward her, his chin gliding above the water.

"I fell." The smell of smoke lingered in her nostrils.

"Jesus." Water dripped down his forehead, landing on his bow-shaped lips.

His strong arm curled around her middle. "Hey, hey." He held them both up by kicking his long, muscular legs. "Are you hurt?"

"I don't know!" She cried into the crook of his neck. "I couldn't see you! There's a dead lady up there; she was melting!" She jutted her chin up weakly toward the destroyed mill. There was more— another ugliness. It had left her, though.

"What? Oh my God." Edwin pulled her body into his. "Okay. Okay, come on." He turned her onto her back and hoisted her up under his arm. She squinted her eyes at the sun.

Edwin pulled her toward the riverbank.

"There was a fire. Did you see?" Daphne held tightly onto his shoulder.

"A fire?" Edwin paddled them up onto a narrow, sandy ridge. The steep grassy area where she had slipped was above them.

As soon as she was out of the river, Daphne's body erupted in goosebumps. She pulled her knees up under her chin and rocked back and forth to elicit the slightest sensation of warmth.

Edwin stood, wringing out the water from his T-shirt. "I'm really confused, Daphne."

"Me too." Her chin rattled. "Thank you, by the way."

He nodded absently. "There was a fire and a dead body?" He crouched down beside her. "I looked back and saw you. It looked like you . . . like you were fainting right over the edge."

She smoothed back her wet hair. "It doesn't make sense."

"And then I felt . . . I mean, never mind." He waved his hand.

"Felt what?" She licked at the water dribbling down her lips.

"Nothing." Edwin's warm eyes trailed down her face and landed on her legs. "Daphne, your knee."

"What?" Daphne lifted her head and saw a bloody gash just below her kneecap. "Oh, crap." She wiped at the wound with her soggy palm.

Edwin offered her his hand. "Show me what you saw." She grasped on and let him stand her up on frozen limbs. If Daphne hadn't just lived through such a terrifying moment, she would have found an excuse to press her head against his wet chest. Instead, she was determined to climb up the slope and find the dead woman in the fringe dress.

She started first, gripping tree roots to aid her ascent. Edwin followed behind, politely and awkwardly pushing up her thighs when she struggled to heave herself up.

As soon as she gripped the long grass and pulled herself up, she knew there had been no fire.

Daphne's mind whirled with confusion.

Edwin hoisted himself up after her.

She paced the field, trying to recreate her steps.

"You were on the phone." She pointed toward the rusted beam. "Over there. And I went this way, to check out the grain elevator."

Dripping, Edwin raced over and picked up his iPhone and shoes from where he'd left them on the precipice when he jumped in to grab her.

"I was going this way. And then . . ." Daphne stopped. She tried to remember. Her brain was in a vice. She just had to provoke it, make it happen again. Somehow, there had been fire and she had been there.

Edwin gently patted her back. "We should get you a change of clothes."

Daphne pulled at her sodden tank top, which clung to her bra. "Dammit."

He tugged at her shoulder. "You're upset, I think, and your mind . . . I think you got jumbled."

Daphne flared her nostrils, trying to catch the scent of a smoldering fire. There was only the moist earth.

She had seen the picture of the mill explosion on the front cover of the library book. It must've burrowed into her brain.

"My book!" Daphne clutched at her chest. Her cross-body purse had disappeared. "My phone! And, oh God! The sheriff's notes!" She whipped her head back and forth, searching for her possessions. The river gurgled beside them.

"Shit!" She desperately needed a mint. But they were all at the bottom of the Pelican River.

"I'M GLAD YOU'RE TALKING to me first. I worry about you bothering the others. Tiffany especially—she gets emotional, in her way."

Moira Kettlesburg twisted a silver band around her right middle finger as she spoke. She had arrived at Daphne's motel room at two thirty on the dot. They had agreed upon the time the day before. Daphne and Edwin had changed into dry clothes, and Daphne had taken a long nap. Her brain had needed rest. She had asked Edwin not to mention her strange daymare to Moira, or anyone. It was embarrassing enough that her vulnerability had been exposed to him.

"I've been thinking. I can understand why you want to know, Edwin, because you're from here." Moira glanced up from her sweating can of 7 Up and watched him. He paced the length of the motel room, phone in hand. "But, Daphne . . ." She turned her head and stared. "I don't see why you came all this way? Washington must have plenty of unsolved cases, fascinating ones just begging for a book, I'm sure."

Daphne sat on the edge of her bed, directly across from the librarian. A spiral notebook, opened to the first page, rested on her lap. Her pen was poised over the blank paper, waiting for something to induce her to write. But Moira's words wormed into her. The cracks in her story would appear before long in such a small place, where gossip must spread like a virus. People would talk, and Daphne knew that just because she was in a rural farm town, it didn't mean the residents were bumpkins. In fact, the well-tailored and eager woman before her emanated an adroit ability to deduce like her literary heroes.

"True," Daphne finally spoke. The pen trembled between her fingers. She quickly let it fall onto the notebook, "I guess I was searching for something far from home, a place I could investigate from the perspective of an outsider."

She was rather impressed with herself. She thought perhaps it sounded so good because it was partly true.

"I suppose the first part will be your impressions of Willoughby? What you think of our little burg?" Moira ran a fingernail across the top of the soda can, catching it in the tab.

*We call it pop in the Midwest, not soda like out here.*

Whenever her dead mom spoke in her mind, it was in her strange voice, the scratchy, frightening speech she used at the end. Daphne could hear it in her bones, an internal sound, like a gurgle of the stomach.

She pressed her lips together, purposefully trying not to look at the *pop* but rather to concentrate on the task at hand. "Oh yes, I'll talk about the dichotomy, of course: how beautiful it is here, how hard it is to believe anything like murder could happen here—"

Edwin snorted.

Both Daphne and Moira turned to look at him as he hovered by the motel room door.

"You don't think it's beautiful here, Ed?" Moira opened her *pop* with a punch and a hiss.

Edwin fiddled with the phone in his hand. "No. I mean, yes, I guess it can be, but I mean, can't you feel it? The bad—it's like a cloud or a fog, like a storm is always coming—or no, that it's always here."

Daphne swallowed down a sick rise of acid. She leaned over to the side of the bed and retrieved a stick of mint gum from her suitcase. She slipped it from the foil onto her tongue. Grief set in

160

over her lost phone. Immediately after falling into the river, all she had wanted was to call Bev or her dad. Not having it made her feel trapped, cut off from her life. Her stomach churned and cramped.

A smile spread slowly across the older woman's face, pushing the shallow wrinkles of her cheeks up into the corners of her eyes. "Tiffany told me, Ed—since I'm not one for computers—that you write about Willoughby like it's a person. An evil person." She seemed pleased by the idea, intrigued. She held up the can and took a long, thoughtful drink.

Daphne's eyes bounced from Moira to Edwin, certain there was a subtext she was missing. She wondered, as she got her pen and notebook back into place, if being an outsider in Willoughby was an insurmountable obstacle, as if she were studying an alien planet rather than the Minnesota town in which her mother had grown up.

"I don't—it's not like that exactly," Edwin sputtered. "I just— ever since I moved here as a little kid, I knew it wasn't a good place. And it turns out I was right. Do you have any idea how many bad things have happened here? For a place that, even in the summer, has less than a thousand residents?" Edwin walked toward the women. The passion in his voice and the determined jut of his jaw surprised Daphne. He had seemed to have a laid-back quality, a sort of slow, easy nature, but he had become jittery in the confines of the motel room. Now, speaking with Moira, he seemed agitated.

"I understand that too, Ed—why you would hate this place. The other children weren't kind to you." Moira's smile rapidly degraded into a frown. "If I were you, I wouldn't see the beauty, either."

Edwin stopped. The side of his leg brushed against Daphne's knees as he crossed by. He bent over the table, staring at Moira, who sat primly in the chair. "It's more than that."

Uncomfortable from the sudden tension, Daphne cut in. She had employed this same technique as an only child, thrusting herself between her parents when she could sense the mood change. "Let's talk about Caroline Bergman," she said with a forceful insistence. "You said you knew her? Did she come to the library back then?"

Moira brushed a red curl back from her forehead. "Yes."

Chandelier-style earrings jangled as she nodded. "She liked to read, just like her father, but as she got into her teen years, she began to come in less and less. The last book I lent out to her was *Northanger Abbey*. I remember because I thought she would really like it. It's a book with a touch of irony, and she had a keen sense of those things. She was clever."

Daphne was shocked by the pressure behind her eyes and the stinging inside her nose. She wanted to cry hot, fat tears at the sound of kind words about her mother. It was a pleasant notion, to know someone could see Jane Downs-Forrest—Caroline Bergman—for the complicated woman she was, not just a supposed murderer.

Edwin's shoulders relaxed, and he took a seat next to Daphne on the edge of the bed. He tapped the microphone function on his smartphone, recording Moira's words.

"I never did see that copy again. The following year, I went to the estate sale that Ida's distant relatives put on. I was hoping to get it back for the library. But it was gone."

Daphne tried to recall her mother's book collection. It was mostly a pile of dusty paperbacks wedged into her closet. Books had not held the same reverence in the Forrest household as art.

She wondered if Moira could tell she had lost her library book in the river. Like a special librarian sense.

"You said she came in less as she got older. Any thoughts to why?" Daphne let the notebook slide off her lap onto the bed. It seemed futile, to try to keep up with Moira's string of memories on paper. Besides, she knew she would remember it all; she would replay each word through her mind a thousand times that night. A million. Daphne sniffed back the threatening onslaught of tears.

"Well, I don't know. Typical teenager, I suppose. In the end, that summer right before it all . . . happened . . . I saw her—everyone in town did, at the Fourth of July picnic. There had been a ruckus and Gunnar had gotten involved. Caroline stared daggers at him."

"Was that unusual for her?" Edwin asked.

Moira took a sip of her drink. A bit of coral lipstick smeared on the can. "She looked up to him as a child, so yes, it was unusual. There had never been talk of discord in the Bergman family. Not until that day, and then they were all dead—except Carrie, of course—by the thirteenth. I think that's why people here, locals, were so suspicious of her right away, because that had been the first whiff of anything untoward. It was just a ripple, of course. A little blip."

Carrie. Daphne had never heard that nickname before. She kept trying to picture her mother's face, the soft cheeks framed by chestnut curls she'd had when Daphne was still small. Carrie. Before she had been ravaged by cancer. Before life had ripped her family from her.

Edwin leaned toward Moira, his elbows on his knees. "Did Caroline threaten her dad at the picnic?"

"No! It was just her look; it was all wrong. Like she was a stranger. Everyone nearby was taken aback."

There were so many things Daphne wanted to ask; she was giddy with the possibilities. Though she knew she had to proceed with caution. She could give herself away, and then, well, she wasn't sure what could happen but dark ideas floated up. She thought of being cast out. Sensing the warmth of Edwin's body beside her, she wasn't ready to be sent away from Willoughby. She couldn't stand the rejection the town would surely give if they all knew who she was. If they knew why she was truly there.

And that—the actual reason—floated up too, like a bubble on the surface of Cross Lake. She was there to find a murderer. Because Jane Downs-Forrest hadn't killed anyone. And to prove such a thing, Daphne had to find the person responsible. The Otter Tail County police hadn't managed that in over thirty years.

"Do you think"—Daphne bit down on her gum and tasted the minty flavor—"that Caroline really killed her family?"

Moira looked down at her hands folded into her lap. "They say that Ida was nearly split in two. And Kyle, his head was . . ." She cleared her throat. "Whoever killed them was angry. You don't hit someone with an axe that many times unless, well, unless you hate them."

Daphne rubbed absently at her belly. She tried to suck more flavor out of the gum to combat the nausea.

"But," Moira continued, "she wouldn't have—I mean, I really believe that she wouldn't have killed them like that. As I said before, and Bob was explaining, Carrie was weak. The thought of her acting in such a way—it doesn't fit. It's true the experts determined that it was a woman who had wielded the axe most likely, or a small man. Caroline . . . I think if she had really wanted to kill her family, she would have done it in a quieter manner."

Edwin scooted forward, his butt barely still on the bed. "So you think it's possible . . . ?"

"She was sixteen, a child. Is it possible? I suppose. A man driving a tractor claims to have seen her that morning walking toward her home."

Daphne and Edwin shared a glance.

"The police, ultimately, couldn't charge her, as you know. Until she disappeared, whenever Caroline was seen, cruel people would ask her where she put her clothes."

A tickle crept up Daphne's spine.

"If not Caroline, then you must have some guess as to who it could have been." Edwin reached over and set his phone on the table.

Moira glimpsed the phone, aware it was recording, and sighed deeply. "Everyone around here agrees it must have been her. That makes us more comfortable, I think. To believe it wasn't random. She disappeared soon after. Because they weren't able to charge her from lack of evidence, she was able to leave." The librarian blinked her thick lashes.

Daphne imagined her mother, young and scared, slipping away from Willoughby, the place she loved. If only things had been different.

Edwin stood. He picked up his phone and pressed the stop button. "Off the record, anyone you can think of? You're anonymous."

Moira rolled her neck. "There is someone."

The air in the motel room seemed to form a vacuum. Tiny motes danced in the jagged sunlight, and Daphne was sure the world had slowed, if only in that little piece of Minnesota.

"There was gossip, after the events of the Fourth. About Gunnar. That he was having an affair with one of his students."

"Jesus, a high schooler?" Edwin began to pace again.

Moira nodded. "I didn't think anything of it. Gunnar seemed like a good man, a family man, very intellectual too. He spearheaded the campaign for Willoughby to have its own library—a rare thing for such a tiny town. And after his death, the rumor quieted. There didn't seem to be any evidence, and as far as I know the police never pursued that route. It was probably just old hens, stirring things up."

"But you think it could be true?" Daphne searched Moira's pretty face. She wondered why such a poised and intelligent woman would stay in such a tiny town, without a husband or partner to share in her life.

"There was a girl. She had a reputation, and some believe it was her he was sleeping with. I think it's possible."

Edwin tapped his foot. "And you think she could be responsible for their deaths?"

"Well, you see, she was much bolder than Carrie, much more likely to let emotions get the best of her." Moira's smile returned, slow and sneaky, like there was a private joke for just her.

"Who? Who?" Daphne wanted to shake the librarian out of her proper posture. She wanted to slap her cheeks until she told her everything, every little detail of her mother, of that summer, of the grandparents she would never know. The ones whom she had, for so long, pictured as grim Iowa farmers, but who, as it seemed, had had rather more interesting lives than she could have known.

"You can't tell anyone I told you. The people here, they wouldn't like to think I'm one of those old hens, mucking things up from so long ago."

Edwin showed Moira the phone in his hand. "It's off."

The librarian leaned forward in her chair, the corner of her mouth twitching with what Daphne could only discern as excitement.

Moira was enjoying this, being part of a murder mystery, playing the witness. The woman's prim exterior sloughed away, and Daphne could see she was almost childlike in her buzzing exhilaration.

"Her name's Rosalee." Pink blossomed across Moira's brow and cheeks. "Rosalee Edwards."

Daphne scratched her chin. "Rosalee? I've heard that name before."

"Remember?" Edwin matched Moira's enthusiasm. "Doris said yesterday, during the tour, that Rosalee found the bodies!"

Moira grinned. "And Rosalee still lives here in Willoughby."

# 28

## July 12, 1982

THEY MET AT THE RUINS OF THE FLOUR MILL. It was an eerie place that most kids in Willoughby believed was haunted. Caroline's grandfather had been one of the lucky men to crawl out of the wreckage with his life. The grass had finally grown over the scorched earth, tangling around the forgotten beams and ancient machinery.

Tiffany waited with her hands in the pockets of her high-waisted nylon shorts. The stick of a lollipop protruded from between her lips as she watched Caroline climb over a twisted knot of metal.

Tiffany removed the red sucker and gave it a lick. "You're late."

"Yeah, yeah. My mom was being a bitch." Caroline pushed through the high grass. She stopped at the collection of tree stumps where Tiffany stood.

They each took a cautious seat on a stump, making sure not to be sliced by the ragged bark.

"I've been thinking about what you told me." Tiffany's knees pushed up into her soft middle. "About your dad."

Caroline picked at the moss on the side of her stump. She didn't want to revisit the pain of witnessing her dad having sex with Rosalee. Tiffany always seemed to have a way of whipping things up, of examining them until Caroline's head throbbed.

She attempted to change the subject. "Do you think there are ghosts here? Maybe, like the men who burned up? Or—my grandpa told me that some of them choked on the flour. There were mountains of it, he said."

"Carrie." Tiffany held the lollipop stick between her fingers and swirled it over her tongue. "We have to do something."

Caroline frowned as she glanced down at her white leather flats with eyelet cutouts. Her own shoes only forced her to remember the blur of Rosalee's vibrant Converse high-tops in her father's classroom. "Like what? Ask her politely to stop?"

Tiffany crunched down on her candy. She chewed slowly, watching Caroline's face. "We'll make her stop."

"Oh, really?"

"Well, you're not going to confront your dad, are you?"

Caroline shrugged. She had fantasized about revealing his indiscretion. It would be satisfying, she believed, to see the color drain from her mother's face. Maybe for once Ida Bergman would be infused with something more potent than apathy. More vitriolic than a broken bird. Maybe for once she would stand up from her chair, pink with rage, and scream.

*Scream.*

"I'm too chickenshit." Caroline sniffed the brackish moss underneath her fingernails.

Tiffany laughed. She tossed the lollipop stick at her feet, crunching on the candy. "So we'll make Rosalee pay for what she's done."

"Yeah." Caroline wasn't sure. She held rage toward Rosalee, certainly, but she thought her dad was the rotten one. He had allowed himself to be imperfect.

"I've got a plan. You're going to love it." Tiffany splayed out her legs. Somehow, she produced a can of Coke from behind a stump. It was her magical power, hiding pop all around her. "We're going to ambush her."

"What do you mean?"

Tiffany punched open the can of pop and took a sip. "She's gonna stop sleeping with your dad, and Greg too. We'll get you Greg, okay?"

Caroline wrinkled her nose. She wasn't sure she wanted Greg anymore. There was something upsetting about the notion that he was having sex with the same girl as her father.

"Okay," Tiffany continued. "First, we're going to get Pauline in on it. We have to get her to invite Rosalee to my house tonight."

"Pauline? We're going to tell her?" Caroline's stomach flipped. She stood up from the stump to stretch out her abdomen.

"She's Rosalee's friend. She'll get her over to my place. If we try—"

"We're not going to tell Pauline that Rosalee is . . . well, you know! We're not telling anyone!" Caroline fanned her hot cheeks.

Tiffany took another sip of Coke and set it down in the grass. "Okay, okay. We'll just tell her to invite Rosalee for a slumber party, and we won't involve her in the revenge piece of it."

Caroline took a shaky breath. She appreciated that Tiffany wanted to help her, but drudging it all up made her nervous. She wished she could forget it all.

"Tonight, after we've eaten pizza and played nice, we'll get her." Tiffany's eyes blazed.

"She's not even going to come, Tiffany! She hates us!"

Tiffany stood. She towered over Caroline. "I have pot. Pauline's going to tell her I have heroin too. You know she'll come then."

"Heroin?" Caroline screeched.

"Not really! It's a lie! But Rosalee is such a skanky bitch, she'll come. I promise, Carrie."

Caroline stared up at her best friend. Her breath smelled of Coca-Cola, per usual, but the rest of her face seemed foreign, like the husk of Tiffany had been filled with another. Her lush eyebrows jiggled, and her eyes—they pierced through Caroline like she wasn't even there.

"Okay." Caroline pumped her fists. "Then what?"

"First, we add my mom's eye drops to Rosalee's beer. It'll give her the worst diarrhea!" The edge of Tiffany's lip curled into a sneer.

Caroline smiled. That was a pretty good plan. How splendid it would be, to observe Rosalee squatting on the toilet in agony.

"When she's shitting her guts out, that's when we point it at her."

"Point what?"

Tiffany did a little spin on her heel. "My dad's shotgun!"

"Tiff—"

"Don't be a pussy! We're going to point it at her, right here." Tiffany pressed her pointer finger between Caroline's eyes.

Caroline instinctively pulled her head way. The pressure had hurt. "And?"

"And you're going to tell her exactly what you want. What you've been thinking since that day you saw her under your dad."

Caroline flinched. She saw the image of her father at the Fourth of July picnic, coming to his lover's aid. She hated him. She hated him more than Rosalee.

"You're going to tell her that if she doesn't stop fucking Gunnar, and Greg too, we're going to shoot her."

Something shifted within the dilapidated grain elevator ten yards behind them. It was the distinct sound of weight on broken twigs. Both girls froze.

"What the hell?" Caroline hissed.

"It was a bird probably." Tiffany waved her hands. "Or a coon. Never mind it."

Caroline stared over Tiffany's shoulder at the hollowed-out tower that had once housed mountains of flour alongside the banks of the Pelican River.

Maybe there were ghosts inside those walls. Watching them.

Or maybe it was something with teeth.

# Moira

MOIRA KNEW SHE SHOULDN'T go outside at night. Not alone. Yet she was still buzzing from the thrill of the afternoon. It had played out like a detective novel! And she had been the cool, mysterious witness! She wanted to write it all down or tell someone as she paced the length of her living room.

Her older sister—Glenda, that bitter old bat—was intent on souring her excitement. She drummed her yellow fingernails on the kitchen table, questioning Moira's sudden buoyancy. That was Glenda's way, Moira told herself as she slipped on her Minnetonka moccasins. Glenda was eternally suspicious and negative. She was unable to see the world as Moira saw it—like a beautifully paced book.

Moira left Glenda to watch *Dateline* and drink chamomile on her own. The house had become stuffy and rather confining.

She relished in the sensation of the night air tickling strands of her copper hair. As she walked, she replayed the scene in the girl's motel room from beginning to end. Moira was impressed with herself. She had parsed out the clues like a proper witness. This had been the most electrifying event in a very long time. Not that she had a good memory for things that came before. She was an expert on books, on the plots and the subtexts and which one a particular library-goer should read. But she had a tendency to forget the mundanity of the real world. That was for Glenda to recall.

Lost in her thoughts, Moira padded up the darkened Main Street. It was only a few minutes past nine, yet not a soul lingered around her. She finally glanced up at her library. It appeared altered in the moonlight. Somehow, her most beloved place in the world looked alien and sinister in the shadows, the front door a cavernous mouth. Perhaps she should go inside, turn the lights on, and read until she could calm herself from the day's excitement. Moira ran her hands over the pockets of her slacks.

She'd forgotten the keys.

"Maybe they'll come again? Yes! They'll have more questions." Moira spoke to the empty street. "They need me."

Edwin and Daphne would want her to help more, certainly! They would need her to recall the murders in great detail. She would sit with her legs crossed and slowly unravel her knowledge as they regarded her with wide eyes and nods of amazement. Although her memory was Swiss cheese, she still believed she could.

She could.

*I'm alone at night. I shouldn't be. That's wrong.*

The thought crawled up her spine like a fanged spider.

Moira halted. She peered down toward Olson Auto Body, suddenly afraid. The dim streetlamps illuminated a skittering paper cup on the other side of the street. The breeze pushed it far across the sidewalk until it rolled into the doorway of Knutson Drug.

*I shouldn't be.*

Moira swallowed down a lump rising in her throat. She felt foolish and, more than that, naughty. Glenda had told her to stay in.

She turned on her heel, suddenly craving the crushing imprisonment of her home. She wanted nothing more than to hear Lester Holt's booming voice on *Dateline* as she curled under her blanket and forgot the night.

"Forget. Just forget," Moira whispered.

She knew. As her feet settled on the pavement and she stared in the direction of her home, she knew she should never have been alone.

Not at night.

Not in Willoughby.

It was there. The vicious thing she knew would come.

But she had forgotten.

They all did.

Its yellow eyes bore into her soul. The stink of its skin, tangy and from the earth, filled her nose.

How naughty she had been!

Moira took a step backward. Her heart slammed against her ribcage as she watched it scratch toward her on wolf-like claws.

"I'll forget!" she screamed. She scrambled backward, tripping over a moccasin as it slipped from her foot. She landed on the sidewalk on her backside. She pivoted her head and looked up at her library with pleading eyes as though it could save her.

Now, she remembered. There were bad things that had happened in Willoughby, ugly things. Murder and hate were like warning wisps of smoke. This heaving beast before her was the fire. This monster that she had forgotten.

That they all forgot.

They knew, deep down in the basest hollows of their brains, that there was something lurking in the night. They knew, too, that this thing propelled them down a road of chaos and violence.

Though it was only when they saw it, as Moira did now, that the memory of its pervasiveness shocked them into a higher level of terrified consciousness.

"Please!" Moira covered her face with her hands. She was enveloped in the soothing blackness of her eyelids.

Then something viscous and pungent dripped down the side of her face, tinkling her earring.

*Drool.*

*It drooled on me.*

Moira clasped her hands over her eyes even more tightly.

It puffed its hot breath against her cheek.

She knew. She knew it was going to eat her with its razor teeth. She had seen them before, bloody needles that hungered for people like her. Naughty people.

*I shouldn't be alone.*

Sharp and ripping pain blossomed. It ravaged her left shoulder and shot up the muscles of her neck.

Moira screamed, but she knew no one would come.

Hot blood streamed down her arm and trickled down the ends of her well-manicured fingernails. Then it sprayed from her neck like a sprinkler on the fritz.

*It's a book. I'm only a character in a book.*

She slumped to her side, into its grasp. It gnawed on her head and she thought, as she died, that she could hear its thoughts pounding through its mouth and into her brain.

*Don't be alone, Moira. Not at night. Not in Willoughby.*

# 30

DAPHNE SQUEEZED HER EYES SHUT. She could still see the dead lady, her skin stripping from her body like a snake shedding. The hallucination haunted her, especially now that she was alone. Rolling over on the motel bed, she pulled her knees up to her chest. The injury on her left one wasn't too bad, more like a rug burn than a cut.

She would have to call her dad in the morning and beg him to send her cash until she could get Visa to send her a new credit card. Eventually, she would have to go to a bigger city and find a place to buy a new phone. Being an adult had its disadvantages. Her heart ached for her mother. She didn't yearn for her comforting embrace, because she had never really had that, but she did miss her mother's cool efficiency. She would have called Visa and produced a new phone for Daphne before the sun had dropped.

A soft rapping on the door stirred her from the frightening images. She jumped from the bed. "Yeah?"

"It's me," Edwin said through the door.

Daphne unlocked the deadbolt and let him in.

"Hey." He carried a paper plate covered in foil. "My mom wanted me to give you this. I told her you don't have any money for the City Café." Edwin handed her the still warm plate.

Daphne's eyes lit up at the sight of food. Her belly had been grumbling all evening.

"Thank you!" She tore off the foil to reveal a hearty slice of lasagna, garlic bread, and a serving of peas. "Oh my God, I'm starving."

"I figured."

She sat down on the end of the bed, taking in the scent of her dinner.

Edwin slipped a fork out of the pocket of his jeans.

"Oh, good. I thought I might have to eat with my hands. I wouldn't have hesitated, though." She took the fork and began to cut into the homemade lasagna.

Edwin sat down beside her. He watched as she took the first bite.

"Thank you, thank you," Daphne spoke with her mouth full.

"We'll tell Tiff tomorrow about your purse. She'll start a tab for you so you don't starve." He leaned back on his elbow.

Daphne nodded, scooping peas into her mouth.

"You're okay, right?"

She glanced over her shoulder at Edwin. He wore a maroon fitted T-shirt with *University of Minnesota* written in blocky gold letters. He watched her with his expressive chocolate eyes, concern creasing his forehead.

Suddenly, Daphne became self-conscious about the manner in which she was shoveling in Maggie's generous supper. She tapped the plate with her fork, forcing herself to eat slower.

"I'm okay." She wasn't sure. "Are you okay?"

He smiled. He had the sort of easy, cheerful smile that made his entire face light up with elation. "I'm definitely okay. I'm just worried, about what you said. About seeing a dead person and fire. It was right where . . ."

"Right where a mill exploded, killing dozens of people."

"Yeah." His eyes appeared to lose focus on her and slip away to deeper thoughts.

Daphne bit off a piece of garlic bread and swallowed. It seemed to stick in her throat. "What are you thinking?"

Edwin took in a sharp breath and sat up beside her. His knee grazed hers, and she wondered if the slight touch affected him the same way it did her.

"I'm thinking . . ." He stared at the blank screen of the tube television across from them. "I'm thinking it's a strange coincidence."

Daphne lowered the plate onto her lap. She stared at Edwin's serious expression.

"You think it means something?"

He shrugged. "I don't know. It's just . . . I think we should tell Doris."

Daphne turned toward him. "Doris?"

"We should tell Doris what you saw. She'll know what to do."

"Do? Edwin, I had a hallucination. I got strange ideas from all of this, well, murder talk. I was lightheaded."

"Yeah." His head dipped. He stared at his sneakers.

"Let's focus on our plan." Daphne stood and set the plate on top of the old television. She would finish it—probably lick the plate—once Edwin and his chiseled chin and muscular arms had left. "Tomorrow, we're going to find Rosalee. She found the bodies! And if the rumor is true, she was sleeping with Gunnar. She could be a suspect."

"A suspect." Edwin gave a breathy laugh. "Are we losing it?"

Daphne giggled. "Maybe. But I'm really glad you care about this stuff. And that, you know, you're helping me."

Edwin looked up through his lush black bangs.

Daphne bit down on the inside of her cheek, in abrupt and emergent need of a mint to soothe the fluttering within her. Though this sort of fluttering wasn't wholly bad.

Her eyes nervously darted from Edwin's face to the ratty drapes pulled across the window and then over to the digital clock on the nightstand. It read 9:06 p.m.

"I like helping you. This is a lot more fun than changing out toilet paper rolls all summer." He ran his shoe across the shag carpet.

Daphne laughed. She hoped it sounded casual and effortless.

Edwin stood. It was a tight room, so he had to stand awkwardly between the TV cabinet and the edge of the bed, inches from Daphne. She instinctively took a step back toward the bathroom, wondering what sorts of thoughts were swirling about in Edwin's mind.

His knees seemed to lock, and his hands were pulled into fists. His brow furrowed. "Shit."

"What is it?"

She could see the rapid rise and fall of his chest.

"Shit," he repeated. His eyes flitted all around the room, around her, through her. He swiftly dropped to his knees.

"Edwin? What the—"

"Shh!" He burrowed his hands into the carpet.

Daphne held her hand over her mouth, watching with wide eyes.

He put his ear to the floor and listened.

She strained her ears, but there was only the sound of the breeze, picking up outside and rustling through the towering trees that surrounded Willoughby Motel.

"Oh, fuck!" Edwin leaped up from his place on the floor and grabbed frantically at the doorknob.

The gentle flip in her stomach had transformed into a roiling torrent. Watching Edwin pull back the door with incredible force and run down the wooden deck steps made her tremble with fear. She stayed frozen in place before finally willing herself to move. To see what scared him so badly.

Daphne flew out of the motel room, her bare feet slapping against the steps. Edwin was crouched in the middle of the road, a dark figure in the shadows.

"*Edwin!*" She ran across the gravel parking lot, vaguely aware of the rocks cutting into the soles of her feet.

He seemed entranced, under some spell she could not hear or see herself. She ran up to him, looking both ways down the road to find the source of this madness.

"*Dammit!*" He pounded his fists on the pavement.

"A car's gonna come, Edwin! Get off the road!" Daphne wanted to pull his shoulder, but his face alarmed her.

"I can feel it, Daphne. Jesus, it's really loud this time." His voice cracked. Still kneeling, he covered his ears with both hands.

She hesitantly touched his back. "It's okay. It's okay, come on."

*"Go inside!"* He yelled as though he were in the eye of a deafening tornado.

Daphne shook her head. "You too! You come!" She wasn't sure he could hear her through his clasped palms. She tugged his arm and he followed.

She noticed as she led him back to her room that he walked as though he was off balance. Like the Earth was tilting under his feet and he couldn't find purchase. She held him up like she would a drunk.

When they got back inside, she latched the deadbolt and helped him onto the end of the bed.

He rubbed his face with his hands. "Fuck, I'm a coward."

She knelt before him. "What's wrong? What's going on?"

"I can still feel it." A single tear trailed down his cheek.

"Edwin, please tell me. I'm scared."

He clutched at his chest like he couldn't breathe. "Something bad is happening. Right now."

"Okay. Okay." Daphne scooted closer on her knees. She placed both hands on his thighs and looked up at his pale face. "How do you know?"

He flashed her a confused look, as if she had to be crazy not to understand his panic.

"Edwin, what did you hear? What did you feel?"

He took in a shaking, snotty breath. His eyes locked onto hers, and she could read the sincerity in their depths. "Willoughby," he said. "I felt Willoughby."

# 31

"HELLO? DAPH?" HER FATHER had answered after two rings. He sounded out of breath.

"Dad, are you okay?" The receiver of the motel room's phone smelled of stale cigarettes.

He chuckled. "Yeah, just puttering around in the garden, trying to get all these weeds torn out."

"That's wonderful!" Daphne grinned. "Will you plant gardenias this year?"

"Oh, we'll see. One step at a time."

It pleased her to hear his voice. It had lost some if its ghostly quality. He was coming back.

"Dad, I need your help."

"You coming home?" he asked eagerly.

She sniffed back tears. How nice it would have been, to go home and get under her quilt. To wrap the cloth around her head and forget all of this. "No. Not yet. But I lost my purse."

He choked. "What?"

"I know!" She shrugged. "Mom would kill me."

There was silence on the other end.

She gave an awkward laugh. "I mean she always said I was irresponsible about my stuff."

180

"Have you called Visa? And what about the police? Do you think it was stolen?" Her dad had slipped into his father mode, and she was happy for it. She had thought, after her mom's death, that he might have lost the ability to care for anyone.

"I'll call Visa. I'm sure I just lost it. Maybe it'll turn up." She pictured it bobbing down the river with a toad sitting atop the black leather, going for a ride. "In the meantime—"

"All right," he interrupted. "I'll wire you money. Where to?"

"I'll have to text you. I'm not sure."

"Text? So you still have your phone?"

"Oh, crap." She smacked her forehead. "I forgot. No, I'll just text you on Edwin's phone."

"Edwin?"

*Shit.*

She was like a teenager, caught in the act. "Uh . . . don't worry about it, Dad. He just works here at the motel."

"I'm glad you have someone to talk to," he said. "Is everything okay there?"

Daphne stared at the powder-blue curtains obstructing her view of the parking lot. She had been too nervous to pull them open and see what Willoughby had to offer this morning.

"Everything's okay."

"Okay, I love you. And miss you." Her dad sighed into the receiver. She could picture him leaning against the fridge door, twirling the old-fashioned phone cord around his palm.

"Love you too. Thanks for the help. Bye, Dad."

Next, she showered and got dressed in a pair of black leggings and a striped tee. Her eyes were hazy from lack of sleep, and her body ached from her adventurous dip in the river. Her mind, though, was focused on the task at hand. She was going to find Rosalee Edwards. And once she untangled the mess of the murders—by either finding the culprit or finding evidence to exonerate Caroline—she could leave this awful town and forget she had ever been here.

## 32

EDWIN SWEPT THE SLATTED PORCH. He turned when Daphne opened her door, blinking at her over his shoulder.

"Hey." She shook out her blonde hair. It was still damp from her shower.

"Hey." Edwin spun around and began to sweep his way toward her.

"Do you remember what happened last night?" She patted her side, searching for her lost purse. It was so peculiar not having her things. She didn't even have a pocket for gum.

Edwin glanced toward her motel room. A subtle smile danced on his lips.

A blush crept up her neck. Nothing like *that* had happened.

He dropped a dust pan onto the ground. "You mean the rumbling? What I felt?"

"Yes. Edwin, that was scary."

He was silent as he concentrated on the pile of dust bunnies.

Daphne set her hands on her hips. "You have to explain to me what that was. You can't just pretend like that was normal."

Edwin gripped the broom tightly. "I know. I know it's not normal." He frowned. "I'm not normal."

182

"I didn't say that." She couldn't stand to see the sorrowful wilt of his eyes.

"No, *I* did." He bent and picked up the full pan. "I hate this place. I've sensed that pressure since I was eight. It's like, I don't know, an earthquake. Sort of like soft tremors at first, and then it builds until I can't hear anything else and it's like—shit, like the world's going to open up into some big, fiery hole."

"Oh my God." Daphne's arms dropped to her sides.

Edwin set the broom against the wall and grabbed a limp trash bag from the porch floor. "I don't get it at school, in Minneapolis. I didn't get it before my parents bought this motel and we moved here, either." He emptied the dust into the bag.

"That's why you said it was Willoughby?"

He nodded.

"And you said it was like a warning?"

He took a seat on the top step of the stairs that led down to the gravel driveway. Daphne sat next to him, conscious of his proximity to her. He smelled of Dove soap and bitter motel coffee.

"One time, when I was about ten or eleven, I was playing in my backyard. We had a tire swing, and I liked to pretend I was an Ewok sometimes, living in my tree house. Or sometimes I played like I was Han Solo, and I'd use a stick shoved into my belt for my pistol."

"It's too bad we didn't know each other." Daphne tilted her head. "I used to play Ewoks too."

A wry smile pulled at his top lip. He looked down thoughtfully at his hands clasped together in his lap. "Well, I was going around in the swing—I really had it going—and then this vibration came. It didn't feel like it usually did, so I put my arm out to stop it. But when my hand touched the tree, it was like a shockwave. I had gotten little rumbles before and I had begun to figure out I was the only one feeling them, but this was stronger. Finally, the tire slowed, but by then my ears were ringing. It's kind of like being right next to a train or the engine of an airplane, I'd imagine. Anyways, I was a bit dizzy when I climbed down, but I saw someone standing there. It was Nicholas Shortall."

"Shortall? Where've I heard that?"

"In the book. It was the only name I knew, remember? Of that group of men, the ones with Calvin Bergman?"

Daphne nodded. "You said there aren't any Shortalls left?"

"Uh-huh. I'll explain. He was a grade higher than me, a chubby country kid. He got bused over to Willoughby from his family farm. Nick was the kind of kid with grease stains on his shirt because he could never seem to get all his lunch in his mouth. He got picked on for being fat, and I guess that's what made him treat me the way he did. Nick would trip me, and a couple of times he helped his buddies throw Chinese food on my head or down my shirt."

"God."

"So, he was standing in my yard, between me and my house, and as my eyes adjusted, I could see he had a knife in his hand. It was a bread knife—I remember it so clearly—with a serrated edge. He had it held up like he was Indiana Jones about to cut through a vine or something. Well, I was staggering around because it still sounded like I was next to a set of helicopter blades and the earth beneath me was shaking like crazy. Nick said something to me. His mouth was moving, and I could tell from his beady, little eyes that he had something bad on his mind. And it's strange, I know, but it was like the ground was speaking to me too. That's what I have so much trouble explaining to myself when it's over. Through all that rumbling and quaking, there are these vile words that come up and echo across my mind. *Chink. You don't belong here. Slit-eyes.*"

He paused.

Daphne opened her mouth to speak some reassuring axiom she hoped would come to her tongue, but Edwin continued.

"That's what kids said to me. Even grownups, like old man Dewitt. I heard all those things inside of me as I watched Nick Shortall. He started coming toward me, charging, and I just remember thinking, what is he playing? Why does he want to play with me? He hates me. Willoughby hates me. But then he got close and I could see deeper into his eyes, and I saw the sun glinting off the bread knife, and I realized. He was trying to kill me. He wanted to stick that knife into me. So I just took off running.

"I jumped over our short fence and just tore off through the woods. The throbbing had dwindled in my ears, and I could hear Nick close behind me. Honestly, I couldn't believe he had made it over the damn fence with that belly, but sure enough he was huffing as he ran. I knew where I was going, and I cut through Oak and zipped up to the murder house. It was summer, so I knew Doris would be there. And she was, waiting in the front yard for me like she knew I was coming. I just remember burying my face in her chest and crying. She gave me a handful of tissues and I told her Nick Shortall was trying to kill me, but that wasn't what I really thought. I thought Willoughby was trying to kill me.

"Nick never came out of the trees. I didn't see him until September, and then he just went back to tripping me and calling me names. He died our senior year. His dad ran him over with a tractor. Then his dad shot himself, or hung himself—I'm not sure. Their farm was sold off after a while. They were the last ones in the family."

Daphne exhaled, realizing she had been holding her breath for the last half of Edwin's story. She slipped her hand over his leg and grabbed onto his thumb. "Have you ever told anyone that before?"

He grabbed her hand and held it between both of his. "No."

"I'm so sorry that happened." Her heart ached for the little Korean boy who had been all alone. Although he had grown into an intelligent and capable man, she had witnessed the ghost of that boy as he spoke. She could see the fear and the hurt within him, as fresh as though it had happened a moment ago. "I can understand why you hate this town. I hate it too."

He smiled, showcasing his straight white teeth. "Already?"

"Yeah, already."

She scooted closer. If only she could tell him why. If only she could be as transparent with him as he had been with her. At the thrill of his hands encapsulating her own, she was induced to tell him about why she hated Willoughby, possibly even more than he did. It had sucked up her mom and spit her out. It had lulled Caroline Bergman into believing she could live and thrive there and then ruined her life and made her become the cold and detached Jane Downs-Forrest. It was Willoughby's fault.

Yet if she told Edwin that her mother was the Minnesota Borden, if only by reputation and not by any proof of evidence, he would reject her. Daphne was certain he would see her as a conspirator, as a part of Willoughby, the place he hated. And she had come to the conclusion soon after meeting him that being hated by him was not an option.

She ran his story through her mind, trying to make sense of it. "It's like a superpower."

"What?" He rubbed his palm over her knuckles.

"Think about it." Daphne watched as a van pulled into the parking lot. Gravel crunched under the tires as it parked by the office on the other end of the building. "It sounds like a special power, warning you of danger. You said last night that something bad was happening."

"Yeah."

"So you're like a superhero. Maybe you could use this for good."

"You believe me?" He turned, searching her face with warm eyes.

She thought for a moment. "Of course. Do you believe that I had that vision yesterday? That I saw a body? And a fire?"

"Yeah, I do. I think we should tell Doris."

"Okay."

They watched a couple with a collie on a leash get out of the van and enter the motel. An unexpected fear curled inside Daphne's belly. It scared her to think of all the people coming and going in Willoughby. It seemed too dangerous of a place for vacations and days on the lake.

"I'd prefer x-ray vision, though. Or being invisible. Oh! No! Flying! Flying would be awesome!" Edwin leaned back against the porch. He kept a strong hold on Daphne's hand.

Daphne laughed. "Will you help me talk to Rosalee? And then we can go see Doris. If you think she can help with whatever's going on."

"I know where Rosalee Edwards lives. We can go there. And yeah, Doris can help. I promise."

THEY DROVE TO THE OPPOSITE END of town and took a right up
Birch Street. Birch was lined with a tidy sidewalk and rambler-style
homes with well-trimmed lawns. As they slowed near the end of the
road, Daphne spied a gothic wrought-iron fence with
*WILLOUGHBY CEMETARY* written in swirly letters above the
gate.

"I'm pretty sure this is it." Edwin pulled his Toyota over to the
curb on the right, in front of a buttercream-yellow house with
distinctive curved shutters.

Daphne blinked at the open front curtains. "Now that we're
here, I'm not exactly sure how to—"

"Ask her if she was sleeping with Gunnar Bergman a million
years ago?" Edwin finished her thought.

"Right."

"Can we? I mean, it's not like she's going to tell us the truth."
He squinted at the house, his hand resting on the steering wheel.

"She was a child and he was an adult and her teacher. He was
the one doing wrong. She has nothing to be ashamed of."

Edwin shrugged. "Okay, but we still can't really bring it up."

"We'll see." Daphne cocked her head. "Do you know her very
well?"

"No. She teaches Sunday school at Willoughby Lutheran up the road, so I remember her from that." Edwin killed the engine and slipped the keys into his jeans pocket. Daphne opened her door and stepped out onto Rosalee's lawn.

A woman pushed open the screened door and poked her head out. "Hello?"

"Rosalee?" Edwin and Daphne approached the home.

"Yes? Is that you, Edwin Monroe?" She had a high, squeaky voice.

"Yes, Ma'am. This is my friend Daphne. Are you free for a few minutes?"

When she shaded her eyes from the sun, Daphne could see her natural beauty. She had porcelain skin and pouty lips that were the perfect shade of dusty pink. She wore a gold headband in her curled blonde hair, and her nails were manicured with French tips. Although she was the same age as Daphne's mother, she appeared to be in her forties. Daphne could not picture a starker contrast than that of Rosalee Edwards and her bald, dying mother.

"Is this for your blog?" Rosalee asked.

"Well, yeah." Edwin flashed his charming smile.

Rosalee watched Daphne with curiosity. "Uh-huh, I guess if it's only for a moment." She waved them inside.

The living room was narrow, with a big-screen TV mounted on the far wall above the mantle. Rosalee grabbed a mound of throw pillows from the corduroy couch and tossed them next to the brick fireplace to make room. "Take a seat, then."

They both sat on the couch, waiting as Rosalee settled in a glider chair across from them. Her back was to the bay window overlooking Birch Street. Daphne watched a little boy toddle along the sidewalk toward Main, dressed in a T-shirt and saggy diaper with his mom following close behind. He reminded her of someone named Oscar, a boy she had known, long ago.

She licked her lips, wishing for a mint or a spicy stick of gum.

"We're really sorry to bother you. To be honest, someone

pointed us in your direction." Edwin slipped out his iPhone and set it on his lap.

"Really?" Rosalee grinned. Her stained teeth were the first indication of her age. "I guess that's not surprising. Everyone around here is a gossip."

"Do you mind if we ask you a couple of questions?" Daphne asked. The words sounded abnormal coming from her mouth, like she was pretending to be on *Law and Order.*

Rosalee crossed her legs. The design on her bare toes matched the manicure on her hands. She wore a pair of khaki pants and a conservative blouse, with a tie at the neck. "I guess. Is this about the eighties?"

"Right. We're trying to gather information about the Bergman murders," Edwin said. "It's gone over thirty years without being solved."

Daphne glanced around the room, thinking about Edwin's choice of words. She realized maybe he did believe her mom could be innocent. Her eyes fell upon a collection of crosses in various sizes hung on the wall by the front door. A framed picture of Jesus sat on a small table underneath, next to a bowl of keys and change.

Rosalee fidgeted with her headband. "I'm not sure how much help I can be."

"You were friends with Caroline Bergman?" Edwin swiped the screen of his phone and jotted something down in a notepad app.

"Not exactly. We went to school together, and in a place this tiny you kind of have to be friends. You could have called us that in elementary, but by high school we'd drifted apart. She hated me."

Daphne sat up. "Why?"

"I was going with Greg Brody, and everyone knew she was in love with him. She thought it was a secret, but everyone knew. That's why they think she killed her family. At least, that's what I've heard. She did it for Greg, for some reason. Made sense to her, I guess. She was crazy."

Daphne ran a hand over her queasy stomach. As she continued

to look at Rosalee, she was disturbed by her yellow teeth and squeaky voice. Her beautiful features seemed to be waning in the sunlight. Wrinkles bunched around her eyes.

"How so?" Edwin typed into his phone.

"Listen. I was mean in high school, cruel to other girls. My grandma beat on me, and she was my only family." Rosalee studied her polished nails. "And so I guess I took it out on others."

The cycle of pain and hurt sounded familiar to Daphne. She thought back to the story Edwin had told. How that boy Nick had been teased and how that had compelled him to go after Edwin.

"So I'm not saying I was perfect. It took me a long time, and a lot of low points, before I embraced Jesus." Rosalee turned and gave the framed picture a loving glance. "The night of the twelfth, the night before the murders, I went over to Tiffany's house. She had told Pauline there would be . . . well, I'll be honest, at the time I was motivated by drugs. Shameful, I know." Her cheeks trembled.

"Pauline couldn't come and I knew Caroline would be there, but drugs would have been worth the awkwardness, as far as I was concerned. Anyways, the night was normal at first, just girls having fun. I even thought Caroline was getting over the whole Greg thing. But then I got sick. Really sick. Like the worst stomach cramps I've ever had, even to this day."

"What happened?" Edwin asked.

Daphne was having her own stomach cramps. She wondered how close Rosalee's bathroom was. If she was going to have to sit and listen to stories about her 'crazy' mother, she was going to need a toilet bowl.

"At first, I just thought it was food poisoning or too much beer. I went into the bathroom and tossed some water on my face, and that's when she kicked the door open."

"Who?" Edwin was typing furiously.

"Tiffany. She had a shotgun—her hick dad's, probably—pointed right at my head!" Rosalee's chest heaved up and down.

Daphne raised her eyebrow. "Tiffany?"

Rosalee nodded, her blonde curls bouncing. "Oh, yes. And Caroline was right beside her. They started screaming at me. I mean, just yelling bloody murder!"

*Interesting phrase.*

"Tiffany pulled back the hammer. I can still remember the sound. She said I better stop sleeping with him. She said she'd kill me if I didn't stop. She said Caroline had poisoned my drink to make me sick and the next step was a bullet in my brain. So I agreed. In my mind, I was thinking Greg was my boyfriend and they couldn't force me to do anything. But both of their eyes were crazy. And that barrel was staring right at me."

The room was silent for a moment as they all processed Rosalee's story.

"Wow. I've never heard this. Do you know if this is in the public record, Daphne?" Edwin kept his eyes on his phone as he took down his notes.

"No," Daphne replied weakly.

"So once you agreed to not be with Greg, did they let you go?"

Rosalee giggled. It was a creepy, juvenile sound. "That's the really, very strange thing." She reached down the tight neck of her blouse and pulled out a cross necklace. She rubbed the gold with her fingers. "They weren't talking about Greg."

Daphne sat forward. "They were talking about Gunnar, weren't they?"

Rosalee turned her gaze on Daphne. For a terrifying moment, Daphne believed she saw recognition in Rosalee's eyes. A realization that Daphne looked similar to one of the girls who had threatened her.

"Caroline got real close to me. Right up to my nose. She said, 'Stay away from my dad, you slut. Don't ever let me catch you again.'"

"Again?" Edwin, too, was on the edge of the couch.

"I have no clue what that meant, but I had a reputation." Rosalee tightened her grasp around the necklace. "I'm not proud of everything I've done. But I can promise you, my word to God, I never slept with Gunnar Bergman."

Daphne swallowed back the rising phlegm invading her throat. "Why do you think they thought you had?"

Rosalee shrugged. She kicked her foot as she spoke. "I've thought a lot about it. Especially after what happened that next morning: Caroline killing her whole family."

"Did you tell the police about their threat when Caroline's family was found?" Edwin asked. "I mean, you're saying that Caroline Bergman and her friend threatened you, say, twelve hours before the murders?" He seemed like an authentic journalist. Daphne thought he had a talent for knowing what questions to ask and when.

"Oh, of course. I told them the whole story, several times. I think it all just came down to the manner of the crime."

"How do you mean?"

Rosalee curled her lips back in a strained smile. "It was so gruesome. The police were struggling to pin it on her. But I think it was difficult to really wrap their minds around the idea that a petite teenager murdered her family with an axe. Even if she was a bit sullen. So they started looking for an outsider, and then, of course, Caroline vanished."

Daphne pictured her mother in their kitchen in Bellingham, scrubbing potatoes with a brush and listening to the King 5 local news. Jane had been boring. She had gone to bed promptly by ten every night. She had read *Reader's Digest* while she ate lunch, and she had worn the same Birkenstock sandals for six summers. Would Edwin and Rosalee be disappointed to know she had lived an average life?

Edwin cocked his head, causing his black bangs to flop to the side. "Do you believe Caroline killed them?"

"I was the same age she was. I was going through the same sort of things she was, growing up in this place, being both a child and a grownup." Her knuckles were strained around the gold cross. "And so I could imagine the rage she had toward her parents. I'd be lying if

I said I didn't want to hurt my grandma sometimes. I think she could have killed Ida and Gunnar. But what stops me from saying yes, fully, is Kyle. I heard his head was cut clean off, and I just can't . . . it's difficult to imagine her doing that piece of it. She was crazy, but not like that, not toward her brother."

Edwin typed something into his phone and then looked up at Rosalee. "Do you think it's possible that two people could have killed the Bergmans?"

This made the nascent nausea bubble up and threaten to spill out of Daphne. She hadn't considered two people. She hadn't considered anything, really, if she was being honest with herself. She had only considered that her mother could not be guilty.

Edwin had the ability to be professional, to view each witness with the lens of an outsider. The irony was that even though Daphne hadn't stepped into Willoughby until a few days ago, she was more a part of it than Edwin. She was part of Willoughby because her mother had been. She held less control over that fact than she held over her sensitive stomach.

"Excuse me. May I use your restroom?" Daphne stood, sensing a clammy sweat on her lower back.

Rosalee pointed behind Daphne. "Down the hall, second door on the right."

Daphne attempted to appear casual as she rushed down the narrow hall and pushed through the bathroom door.

*His head was cut clean off.*

The clam-shaped sink filled with water, and she splashed it on her cheeks and let it dribble down her chest. She stared at her reflection in the water-spotted mirror and could only see her mother. It was her mother in her round cheeks and the groove of her chin. It was her mother in her eyes, speaking to her.

*It wasn't me, Daffy.*

Her body ached to vomit. She thought of Rosalee, how she had claimed to have been poisoned by Caroline and Tiffany. Daphne had been poisoned. It was life that had pried her mouth open and forced her to drink its poison. Her body was constantly at war, trying to force out the bad, but the horror she had caused would never be purged. She really was her mother's daughter.

She glanced down at the toilet, which had a fuzzy pink cover on its lid. It was a small home, and they would probably hear her retching. And if they heard her, they would worry and fret and ask after her.

"Daphne?" Edwin softly rapped on the door. "We should probably get going."

"Coming." She swallowed down the salty taste and grabbed at the knob. Edwin stood in the darkened hall. The intensity he had directed toward their witness shifted toward Daphne. He watched her closely as they headed toward the front entrance.

"Thank you." Daphne opened the screen door and sucked in the fresh air.

"Yeah, thanks," Edwin added. "I know this stuff isn't fun to talk about."

Rosalee adjusted her headband. For the first time, Daphne noticed that her abundant blonde curls might be a wig. They had an unnatural wispy texture. "Are you putting all this on your blog, then? I read it sometimes. That one on the kidnappings in the seventies and eighties was fascinating. You have a way with words."

Edwin's face lit up. "Really? Yeah, well, I'm working on my blog, but Daphne here is writing a book."

"A book!" She wiggled her sharp nails in a sort of strange clap. "How exciting!"

"Do I have your permission to use your statements?" Daphne asked. She thought it sounded official.

"Yes! Yes!" Rosalee's yellow teeth appeared. "You, too, Ed. You should write the book together!"

"Wait." Edwin halted. "Doris told us that you found the bodies. Is that true?"

Rosalee's nostrils flared. A glassy sheen dropped over her eyeballs. "I didn't see much. I came over to . . . I don't know, tell them off or something. They'd humiliated me, and I thought if I went to Caroline's that morning, well . . . I saw blood through the door. And a bit of Gunnar. I think I stared at his dead arm for about thirty seconds, trying to make sense of it." She swallowed.

A memory threatened to pull Daphne down into a vile place. "I'm sorry."

Daphne and Edwin stepped down onto the cobblestone path that led to the sidewalk. Edwin slipped his phone into his back pocket. "Can we come back? If we have more questions?"

"Please do. And don't forget to talk to Tiffany and Greg. They can probably help you."

"Greg?" Daphne looked up at Edwin.

He scratched his chin thoughtfully. "Tiffany is married to Greg Brody."

"For thirty years." Rosalee held the screen door open with her bare foot.

Daphne's mind spun. "That's who Caroline had a crush on? Greg?"

Rosalee sighed. "Uh-huh. Everyone knew. Caroline was really obvious about it." She chuckled in her high, trilling voice. "Everyone was surprised when Tiffany and Greg got together."

"Yeah." Edwin still seemed lost in thought. "Thanks again."

"Sure, sure. Will I see you in church? It's been a while, Mr. Monroe," Rosalee chided.

"You sound like my mom," he joked.

Daphne waved goodbye as they walked to Edwin's car. Rosalee closed the screen and disappeared into her home.

Edwin set his hand on the passenger-side door handle. "Hey, can you drive? I was thinking I could read over these notes and—"

"I can't." Out of the corner of her eye, Daphne spied the small boy in the heavy diaper and his mother heading back up Birch.

"Right. I forgot." He pulled open the car door. "We need to talk to Tiff."

Daphne nodded, thankful he hadn't gotten stuck on her avoidance of driving. "Definitely. She was Caroline's best friend, *and* she's married to Greg."

"She's going to be a tough sell, though."

"We have to try."

Just as Daphne moved to sit down, the mother on the sidewalk called out to Edwin.

"Ed! Ed!" She waved her arms.

He turned. "Hey, what's up, Bella?"

The little boy stopped about three feet from them, one chubby finger planted up his nose.

"Ed, the library is closed!" Bella stepped up to her son on stick-thin legs. Her eyes were veiny and rimmed with red. "Oh!" She buried her face in her slender hands.

"What's wrong?" Edwin stepped forward. He patted Bella's shoulder. The little boy stood between them, peering between Edwin's legs at Daphne. He removed his finger from his nose and then stuck it between his lips and gave it a suck.

"Oh, Ed! It's awful!" Bella was the same height as Edwin, nearly six feet. She trembled like a child under his hand.

An ugly jealousy twisted through Daphne. It didn't bother her that he was touching the woman. It bothered her that he *knew* her. He knew her name. He knew her well enough to look concerned as she cried on him.

It was silly, she knew, to be seized by jealousy. It embarrassed her. But she had very little that she could consider her own, and Edwin was rapidly becoming an integral part of her troubled life. She had almost drowned in Willoughby—literally, even—but he had been there to lift her up, to buoy her. She needed him. As she watched Bella wipe tears from her cheekbones, she saw Edwin had that same effect on others. A green-eyed monster rose within her that she'd never expected was there.

"Can you tell me what's going on?" Edwin asked in a soothing tone.

The toddler wrapped his arms around his mother's leg.

Bella sniffled. "Moira."

Edwin and Daphne shared a glance.

"What? What about Moira? Is she sick?"

Bella shook her head. "I went and asked Glenda why the library was closed, and she was beside herself and said go ask Mr. Deacon!"

Edwin stiffened. His hand dropped from Bella's shoulder.

"I'm confused." Daphne knew she and the little boy were in the same boat. He pouted as he clutched at Bella and stared up at Edwin.

"Glenda is Moira's sister, and Mr. Deacon runs the funeral home." Edwin kept his eyes on Bella's tear-soaked face. "Are you saying—"

"She's dead!" Bella wiped her wet nose on her bare arm.

He took in a sharp breath. "Are you sure?"

"Glenda said it happened last night." Bella's lip quivered. "Oh my, I just saw her yesterday at the café! We have book club Thursday night!"

The boy began to sob between them.

"What happened?" Daphne closed her eyes. She could see Moira's swinging chandelier earrings and her vibrant auburn hair. She had been so alive. She had just been in Daphne's motel room, drinking 7 Up and discussing the case. "How could she die?"

Bella bent down and picked up her son. His diaper crunched under her arm. "I don't know. I just don't know. I have to go home and call Archie. I'm sorry." She rushed around them and headed toward a home at the end of Birch, where the cemetery gates cast an inky shadow across the lawn.

Edwin was frozen on the sidewalk, his back to Daphne. She hesitated, not sure how to rouse him from the shock.

"Last night," he muttered.

"Edwin?" She touched his arm.

He continued to stare at his feet.

"Do you feel something? Or hear something?"

"Nope." He rubbed his eyes with his fists. "No, but I bet Moira died just after nine o'clock."

"Oh my God." She stepped in front of him. "You mean, that's the bad thing? You said something bad was happening."

"I should have saved her." He ran his fingers into his hair and grasped tightly. "Shit. Shit!" He looked up. His stormy eyes stared through Daphne as though she were made of air.

"How could you know it was her? It could have been anyone!" As the words came spilling out of her, she knew she spoke the truth. It could have been anyone in Willoughby.

"I fucked up. I should have listened better. If I really concentrate, I can hear. I can get . . . I don't know, a glimmer of what's going on. I forget, though. I forget sometimes before I can get there, to help. Fuck." He crouched on the pavement.

She knelt down, the sidewalk scratching through her thin leggings. "We're going to figure out what happened, and we're going to make it better. We're going to help."

He bowed his head. "Moira's already dead!"

"Yeah, yeah, she is. But I think we can help everyone else. I know that doesn't make sense, but I believe it, deep down inside."

He extended his hand, and she grabbed onto it. "It makes sense," he whispered. His breath calmed, and he let his shoulders drop. "That makes a lot of sense."

Daphne bit her lip, oddly triumphant.

Maybe he needed her too.

# Doug Deacon

DOUG DEACON LIVED on the second floor of his funeral home on Main Street. He liked how easy it was to finish with his work and go up the stairs to heat a Hot Pocket in the microwave for lunch. When Doug flunked out of dental school, he had decided to give mortuary science a try. It had suited him. He preferred solitude. And it seemed his nostrils were not as sensitive to the pungent scent of death as others'.

His mother, a spindly, garrulous woman, had told him it was disturbing that he slept above the dead. She wouldn't step one craggy foot into his home. Until, of course, she died from complications of diabetes. Then he worked on her down in the cellar like he did everyone in Willoughby. He had laughed when he drained her organs, thinking about how she would have hated to know she was there inside his stone building. That she had become one of the dead people she had had such an aversion to in life.

On that late May morning, the bell attached to the front door chimed. Doug set down his electronic cigarette and cracked his neck. He stood from his computer desk, bleary-eyed. His day had started unusually early.

A voice floated into his back office. "Mr. Deacon?"

"Yup." Doug smoothed down his tie. He stepped out of his office and into the main showroom, to be flanked by sample-size caskets.

Edwin Monroe, the poor kid, hovered in the center of the room. Doug had pitied little Ed, although he was no longer so little. He had been like a beacon for the bullies, an *other* in a land of matching blonde children. The pretty stranger Doug had seen walking around Main was with him. At first, he'd thought she was a teenager. But under the flickering neon lights, he recognized an expression of harried worry, one reserved for adults.

"Edwin, I thought you were at the Main U." Doug clasped his fingers together into a steeple.

The tall Asian man forced a quick smile. "Summer break."

Doug's eyes fell upon the girl. "And who is this? Your girlfriend?"

She shook her head. "No, Mr. Deacon, we're here to ask about Moira Kettlesburg."

An unpleasant, tacky memory of torn flesh settled on the surface of his mind, like foam on a latte. Doug bowed his head. He studied his polished wingtip shoes. "News spreads fast."

"It's true? She's dead?" Edwin's voice cracked.

Doug looked up. This was the part of his job he disliked. Human emotion was sloppy.

"I'm afraid so. Glenda called me in the middle of the night. She was frantic."

"What happened?" Edwin and the woman asked in unison.

Doug rubbed his forehead. He could see, in his rather uncreative mind's eye, the remnants of Moira. She had been little more than a streak of nastiness, a mangled puddle. Though the vision didn't align with his logic. His thoughts were cloudy, and he wanted to lie down with a Hot Pocket and take a languid nap as he picked at the cheese. "Well, she *was* an advanced age, children."

"Moira?" The woman's eyes radiated suspicion. "We just saw her yesterday, and she was only in her sixties. What did she die of?"

Doug closed his eyes and tried to remember. He could see Moira, alive. He could see her glib smile and her pressed slacks. He could see her when they were in high school together, sitting on the gazebo steps with a giant, crusty book on her bare knees.

He was very tired.

"I, um . . . well, she had a bad heart, I believe. That's what Glenda told me." He thought about his feather pillow upstairs.

"So you verified that? You saw the signs of a heart attack?" Edwin placed his hand on the woman's lower back.

Doug yawned. "I cannot release that sort of information to you. I signed off on her death and brought her up to Fergus Falls to the coroner." He couldn't exactly remember seeing her dead body, but he could remember driving his hearse through the black night. He remembered the sunrise; tendrils of pink curling across the horizon.

"Fergus Falls? Why?" The small woman looked angry. He wondered why. She wasn't a Willoughbian. Maybe, Doug was tickled to imagine, she was in desperate need of a library book.

"Glenda requested her cremation." His eyelids were heavy. "I'm not equipped with a crematorium—"

"Already?" Edwin interrupted. "Is that normal? I mean, Jesus, she died probably, what? Twelve hours ago?"

"Or so." Doug flashed a toothy smile. "I'll be picking up her ashes later. Glenda will be coming in to arrange the memorial service this afternoon. I am bushed, and I need a nap before I deal with the bereaved. If you please." Doug stepped around the glowering woman and opened the front door of the funeral home.

"Mr. Deacon?" Edwin stepped out onto the sidewalk. The woman followed. "Can you assure me that Moira died naturally?"

Doug stared at the library directly across the street. A bouquet of daisies, wrapped in lacy ribbon, had already been placed on the steps.

A violent remembrance tugged at his innards. "If there had been any reason to suspect foul play, I would have contacted the county sheriff." The bell jangled above him as he closed the door. His mind swirled with exhaustion.

Doug climbed the stairs to his studio apartment. He shuffled past the kitchenette and crawled under the covers of his bed in his suit and shoes.

The mattress had never been so warm and welcoming.

He just needed rest.

And then, he was certain, the missing pieces would stitch themselves together.

Doug Deacon fell into a dreamless sleep.

# 35

DAPHNE COULDN'T BEAR to look at the library. She took a few steps to the left and went inside Willoughby Grocery. Edwin trailed behind, seemingly lost in thought. A Coca-Cola clock ticked above their heads as Daphne took in a quick appraisal of the gum selection.

"Good morning." A bland-looking man wearing a green apron stood behind the single checkout counter.

"Morning." Daphne grabbed two packs of spearmint Ice Breakers. She plopped them down and reached for her purse. "Oh, shit." It was still at the bottom of Pelican River.

Edwin stepped forward. "I've got it." He took a black wallet from his back jeans pocket. Daphne smiled at the *Star Wars* rebel alliance symbol on its side. He handed the grocer a wrinkled five-dollar bill.

"Thank you." She snatched up the gum and ripped the plastic off the top pack with her teeth.

"Did you hear?" The man punched buttons on the old-fashioned register. The drawer slid out, and he carefully counted the change.

"About Moira?" Edwin glanced out the window toward the library.

"A real shame. I don't know what's going to happen to the place." The man handed Edwin the money.

Daphne placed two rectangles of gum onto her tongue. She sucked the flavor until a welcome tang of relief flooded her body.

Edwin crunched his overstuffed wallet closed and slipped it back into his pocket. "She was a nice lady. I spent a lot of afternoons in that library, and Moira, she . . . she always welcomed me. Like I belonged there."

Daphne and Edwin walked back out into the sunshine.

"We need to talk to Tiff. And we should visit Glenda if she's not too upset to talk, and Doris too. We have a lot to do." He tapped his chin in a distracted manner as he spoke.

"Want a piece?" Daphne kept the gum packs close to her chest.

Edwin looked down at her curiously. "Uh . . . nope. Are you okay?"

"I don't know."

"Is the gum for your stomach?"

"It soothes it." She took in a fresh, minty breath.

"Were you going to puke at Rosalee's house?" he asked.

"No! No, I just had to . . . no."

"Daphne." He wiped at a bead of sweat that had pooled at the nape of his neck. "I think maybe there's stuff you're not telling me."

"It's hot," she blurted.

"I mean I told you about my thing. I told you about Nick Shortall and the knife." His eyes darted around her.

"I know." She bit down on the wad of gum. "I want to tell you everything." She believed that was probably the most honest thing she had said since she'd arrived in Willoughby.

"Why don't you drive?" His eyes finally landed on her.

Daphne tightened her grasp around the packs of gum. She was suddenly very hungry, as though she had been hollowed out and needed to be filled up to the brim.

An SUV drove by, toward Cross Lake. It hauled a pontoon boat behind it.

The heat was causing the summer season to start early.

She glanced across the street at a burgeoning crowd in front of Moira's library. A mix of farmers in frayed Lee jeans were speaking in somber voices.

An unexpected tear dripped down and dangled off her chin. "I'll tell you, but not here."

Edwin's face softened. "Let's go for a walk, then."

They left his car and trailed down Main.

Without looking, Daphne took a wide step over a dip in the sidewalk.

They made their way silently to the gazebo. Daphne didn't know she was leading him there until she saw its intricate rails and shingled roof.

They stepped up onto the stairs, and she read the plaque affixed to the side:

For My Darling Francesca,
May You Forever Be Shaded from the Rain.
Your Loving Father

"Who is the father?" She still held the package of gum in her fist.

"Fred Willoughby." Edwin sat down on a narrow cedar bench on the far edge of the gazebo. "Remember him from the book?"

"Of course. It said he died in 1900. Why do I feel like it was something mysterious?" Daphne sat down next to him. She let her package of gum, slick with sweat from her palm, fall onto the bench between them.

"Yep. Some strange thing, there's lots of theories. And remember Francesca? She died in the mill disaster."

"God!" She swiveled toward him. "What if that was her? Edwin! That *was* her! The dead woman I saw on fire!"

His eyes widened. "It'd make sense. Only a few women died there that day. It was mainly men."

Daphne picked nervously at a ball of lint on her leggings. A half-cloudy thought teased her. It was a sentence from the book that she had lost.

*She was Fred Willoughby's only child and last living blood relative.*

"Edwin?" She scrunched her eyebrows together, uncertain where her mind was headed. "Francesca, she was the last Willoughby?"

"Yeah."

"And Nick, the boy who bullied you, him and his dad were the last living Shortalls?"

"Uh-huh. I mean, I think."

"And the Bergmans, are there any more?" Daphne asked, knowing *she* was the last.

He shrugged. "If Caroline's still out there. What are ya thinking?"

Daphne shook her head. It was just a tickle of something, a fetus of an idea. "Don't know."

He turned his body toward her, his Vans grazing her ballet flats. "So, are you going to tell me the truth?"

"I was hoping you forgot."

He smiled in his handsome, tranquil way.

"You'll hate me." She used her tongue to press the gum against the roof of her mouth.

"I doubt it."

"Do you believe if you do something and you don't mean it, that it's like it never happened?"

His dark eyebrows knit together. "Well, whether you meant to do something or not, it still happened."

"Right." She blinked at the wetness pooling in her eyes. "My mom believed that. I mean, that if you didn't mean it, then it's like it wipes it clean from the universe or something."

"You didn't tell me how she died."

"Brain cancer." Daphne smooshed the ball of lint between her fingers.

Edwin scooted an inch closer. His leg touched the crumpled pack of gum. "Wow. That's fucking terrible, Daphne. I'm so sorry."

There was so much to say. And it was all terrible. In that moment, Daphne retraced her life. She saw her mother, wizened and dying. She pictured her grandmother, her grandfather, and her young uncle. They were chopped to death with a rusted axe. She thought of a little boy named Oscar. Death was her legacy. It was her past and her present. And as she looked out at Willoughby, she was sure it was her future.

"I was sixteen."

"When your mom died? I thought you said it was recently—"

"No. When . . . when something bad happened. Something else."

"Okay," he whispered.

"I shouldn't say that. Something bad didn't happen, just like that." She snapped her fingers. "I made it happen." Her jaw clamped down. If she told him about Oscar, would it all come out? Would she vomit out her words like she vomited out her anxieties? Would she tell him that her mother was Caroline Bergman?

She had a great distrust of herself. It was agony, not to know her own heart.

"Did you mean to, though? To make this bad thing happen?"

Edwin had this way of being both soft and hard, child-like and mature. Daphne thought of his charming *Star Wars* wallet and her heart burst and hissed like a firecracker. How could she tell him her entire mess? How could she drag him into her black hole?

She tried to concentrate on the gazebo's wooden planks, but her eyes were awash in tears.

When she opened her mouth, Daphne understood there was no turning back. She had chosen her course as soon as she had allowed herself to cry. Tears slicked down the back of her throat, battling with the rising vomit that always churned when Oscar came to mind. "No, I didn't mean to."

"Okay." He seemed unsure where to put his hands, finally clasping them awkwardly on his lap. "I think you should tell me, if you want."

Daphne didn't want to tell Edwin, or anyone. Yet she was imbued with a throbbing need to release it, as though it were figurative vomit of the mind. She leaned back, grinding her spine into the spindles of the gazebo. Every part of her was in pain.

"Beverly, my best friend, she got dropped off at my place so we could go to the mall." A tear caught in Daphne's eyelash. She swatted it away. "It ended up being the worst . . . not just day, but the worst time of my life. That morning, I was normal, you know? We were going to shop and eat froyo, just teenager stuff. The best part was that I finally had my driver's license."

Daphne could sense the brutality and the ugliness pooling at the bottom of her heart. Soon her soul would become withered and sooty as she remembered what she so ardently wished to forget.

Edwin placed his hands on hers. The contact of their skin caused her to suck in a hissing breath. She knew he would hate her or pity her, but she could not halt the barrage of words demanding to be liberated.

"We were joking around in my dad's van, just parked in the driveway." She threaded her fingers through Edwin's, knowing he would soon pull away from her. And she wouldn't blame him for it. "I was saying to Bev that we should run away, to Mexico or somewhere, just to escape from our parents and final exams. I really did take it seriously, though. I adjusted my mirrors and put my seatbelt on before I started the engine, just like in the driver's test." When Daphne closed her eyes, she could see the van's pseudo-wood dashboard and her dad's knot of keys in the ignition. The image was too visceral. She forced her eyelids apart, accepting the torrent of tears.

"I thought I did everything right." She didn't wipe at the snot bubbling in her nose because she didn't want to lose Edwin's hands. "I still hear it; it's a part of me, that sound." Daphne remembered her dream in the motel, how that wrenching, crackling sound had woken her. "I hadn't even reversed five feet and I heard it. Bev, too. She just started screaming like she knew what had happened immediately. I remember, for some reason, how her gum fell out of her mouth and got stuck in her hair. The glob of it was just swinging there."

She braved a glance up at Edwin. His eyes had darkened, and a frown pinched his normally sunny face. She had confused him.

Daphne tried to organize her thoughts, but they were emptying from her quicker than she could keep up.

"I kept thinking, as I put the van in park, that it was Marshall! It had to be him because he was this old, blind basset hound. And I thought, in that final moment before I really knew, that I had run over that poor dog. My legs were numb as I got out of the van, me believing I'd have to tell Mrs. Finn how I'd . . . I'd done that. But Beverly saw first. She was screaming so hard she was coughing too, and it was like the world had shifted. Like I'd unknowingly crossed this threshold into Hell. Because maybe, deep down, I knew it wasn't Marshall."

Edwin kept one hand wound around hers, while he used the other to collect the tears on Daphne's chin.

She glanced down at his glistening palm and believed herself to be the most undeserving human in Willoughby and, probably, the world.

"I saw the blood first, as I was rounding the back of the van. It was . . . there was a river of it. I'm sorry. Do you want me to stop?" She stared at a point on his chest, consciously not looking to see the disappointment in his eyes.

"No," he said firmly. "Go on."

"I'll never forget . . . it's like the gum, these images get burned inside. I'll never forget how I saw Thomas the Tank Engine. This toy was just sitting in this river of blood that was rushing down the driveway under my sandals. And it was like that toy train was looking at me. Just smiling. And that's when I got, for the first time, this hot, surging nausea. And it hasn't gone away. And I don't really want it to, because . . ."

*Because I deserve it.*

She couldn't speak the words around the gagging tears that filled her mouth and nose.

Daphne took a deep, aching breath. She tasted snot on her tongue as the final, piercing truth wriggled its way out. "It was Oscar.

I had pressed on the gas too hard. I hadn't looked in my mirrors well enough. I should have gotten out and checked before. It was so fast . . . his mom—they lived next door—she screeched. It was inhuman. She just kept calling me a murderer, over and over."

Daphne relived that moment, as she did so often during quiet times. She saw her own mother, emerging from their house. In the flurry of the waking nightmare, Jane Downs-Forrest had grabbed Daphne's shoulders and shaken her violently.

"It's all right! It's all right! You didn't mean it!" her mother had whispered, her breath hot on Daphne's pale face. "Don't listen." She'd covered her daughter's ears.

"Who's Oscar?" Edwin interrupted her violent reverie.

"A boy," Daphne answered. "A little boy who likes trains and sidewalk chalk. *Liked*. He . . . he was drawing on our driveway. At least I think he was." Her mind began to sketch a picture of Oscar, two years old with tight brown curls. A flash of Oscar's smile turned her insides raw. She had to fight to keep the contents of her stomach down.

Edwin gripped her elbows, pulling her to his chest. She soaked his T-shirt, sobbing into the crux of his armpit. He ran his fingers through Daphne's hair. "You were just a kid."

"I murdered a two-year-old." As soon as it dropped from her lips, Daphne knew she had never said those words aloud before. They tasted of salt.

"No," Edwin breathed. "You made a mistake."

Daphne raised her heavy, trembling head and dared to look at him. He was everything she wasn't. He was innocent, strong, and good. "I'm a murderer."

"No!" He shook his head emphatically. And she let herself believe him, for just a moment. "It was a freak thing. He shouldn't have been playing in your driveway, and you couldn't have known. It's happened to adults, Daphne. You have to forgive yourself."

She wiped at her soggy face with the back of her hand, shocked by a stirring niggle of hope. "I killed him. I didn't mean to, but I did. I can't ever drive again or trust myself."

He tilted his head, observing her with a look of concern she hoped would not slip into horror or pity. "It's awful that it happened. I mean that's tough stuff."

"You don't have to say anything—"

Their knees banged together as he drew her into a tight hug. "One horrible thing doesn't define you. You don't have to punish yourself."

She wanted to believe him so badly. Her heart sung at the pressure of his arms around her.

Edwin let go. "You went through all that? And your mom just died?"

"Uh-huh."

"And you're here in the middle of nowhere investigating an old murder?" The hint of a smile skipped across his lips.

Daphne sighed. "Yeah."

"You're stronger than you realize."

# 36

DAPHNE AND EDWIN SAT in silence for a beat, both listening to the nearby Willoughby School. Windows were open on the front of the brick building, allowing the din of the lunch hour to float across the park.

She could sense Edwin ruminating beside her, trying to find the perfect words. His eagerness brightened her spirit. "I'm actually glad I told you."

"Me too." He sniffed. Daphne realized he was suppressing his own tears.

He nudged her knee. "I think you deserve, like, a trip or something. Maybe to a tropical place where you can chill for a while?"

"Nah, I think I'm right where I need to be. Willoughby, Minnesota: the most fucked-up place on Earth."

Edwin laughed. "True. I'm glad you're here, though."

She felt worse, somehow, more than hollow. There was a deep hatred for herself, for every stitch of genetic makeup that formed her. She was everything a person would believe the daughter of a supposed axe murderer would be.

She was a murderer too.

Daphne grasped his arm and pulled him closer. His forehead

213

rested against her temple. She knew that, very soon, she would love him. It would be the sort of overwhelming love that transcended any emotion she held for her father or Beverly or even her mother on their best day.

"It was an accident," he breathed into her mussed hair.

The crunch of the van's wheel killing Oscar echoed in her soul. That sound would never leave her. She was sure, no matter how long her life lasted, it would always be just as vivid as it had been that day.

Daphne closed her eyes and saw the inside of her mother's childhood bedroom. Caroline had inhabited that room when she was sixteen, the age at which her life unraveled before her like a runaway ball of yarn.

It had to be a curse. Caroline had run away from Willoughby and changed her name to Jane, but the destruction had come with her. It was like a bad smell that lingered no matter how many windows you opened to freshen the air. Daphne was cursed from the moment she was conceived and carried by Caroline. An ugly thought bore through her, urging her to peek behind a dark curtain within her mind.

*What if she* had *killed them?*

It had always been there, this festering wound of an idea. Now, as she pressed herself deeper into Edwin's embrace, she accepted that it was possible. If she could run over a two-year-old drawing train tracks in chalk on her driveway, then her mother could decapitate her twin brother and bludgeon her parents.

Life was simply that precarious.

Edwin drew back. He gently turned her head so that she would look into his eyes. "It's okay. You're okay."

Daphne blinked away the tears.

He chewed on his bottom lip, observing her face. "Thank you for telling me."

"I'm sorry."

He patted her knee. "What for?"

"For being me, I guess." She was the most miserable creature in the world.

"Don't say that!"

Daphne sniffed up a drip of snot and looked over Edwin's shoulder, through the slats of the gazebo. A strange sensation overtook her. Willoughby School came into focus. The square building intrigued her.

"I need to go over there." She sensed a physical pull. Her body rose from the bench.

He glanced behind him. "The school?" He stood. "I don't think we should. Class is going for another week."

Daphne didn't hear him. Her eyes dried, and she could suddenly see every brick. The windows shone so brightly. And the rhythmic slap of the American flag sang to her in a wordless song.

The school wanted her.

She rushed down the steps and sprinted across the grass.

Edwin called after her, but his voice held no more importance than a flutter of wind.

Daphne was in a tunnel of senses. She could see only the front doors of Willoughby School, as though she were looking through the lens of a telescope.

The air stilled around her and then, somehow, it darkened.

Suddenly, the sun evaporated.

It was night.

It was just like at the river. She had entered a vision, somehow, and it was more real and vivid than her own life.

The cool breeze raised goosebumps on Daphne's arms. She reached the front stairs and ran up them, two at a time, until she felt the cool handle of the door.

Her tunnel vision broadened, and she could see all around her.

The full moon glimmered above, casting shadows across a painted sign on an easel propped beside the doors.

Willoughby Senior Prom
Class of '44
Give generously to our troops!
Donate for raffle tickets

A sickening alarm sounded in her chest. Daphne licked the gum in her mouth, trying to taste the last remnants of spearmint. It was a useless slug on her tongue.

She yanked the door open, still imperceptibly drawn to go within.

Red and silver garland was twisted around the stair railing that led upstairs. Bing Crosby's distinctive voice filled the empty corridor. She had watched his movies *Road to Rio* and *Holiday Inn* on Turner Classic Movies with her dad.

She held her breath, listening to the old-fashioned song for a beat.

Daphne took a step into the building. Bing's voice emanated from the end of the long hall.

Her stomach churned as she tiptoed toward the music. Her mind screamed. It could not begin to perceive what was happening. It was night when it had been day. It was 1944 when it had been 2017.

As she neared the end of the dark hall, the entrance to a gymnasium came into her view on the left. The music vibrated up her legs and filled her to the brim.

A barrel wrapped in butcher paper stood beside her. Daphne peeked inside. There was a heap of boxes, cans, and tubes.

She went to grab the box on top. It was Quaker Puffed Wheat with the familiar Quaker man in the black hat. Underneath was a grinning girl in pigtails tied with blue ribbons. The girl had a drawn speech bubble emanating from her smile.

*Be a proud American! Ration our supply!*

Daphne pulled her hand back as though the little girl would bite her fingertips.

She tiptoed forward and carefully stuck her head into the gymnasium.

Dim lights twinkled across the gym floor, revealing a crowd of couples swaying to the melody. One beautiful girl wore a slender dress with a cascading corsage dripping down her shoulder. Her date was in a suit that was a bit too large, his hair slicked back at his temples.

As the boy awkwardly twirled the girl under his arm, the girl's eyes fell upon the open doorway.

She squinted.

It was almost as if she *saw* Daphne.

Frightened, Daphne bolted to the right, down another corridor.

She rested the back of her head against a locker, trying to catch her breath.

The song ended and she heard polite applause. She screwed her eyes closed, trying to will herself, like Dorothy in the Land of Oz, back home. If only she had a pair of magical ruby slippers.

Something shifted at the opposite end of the hall. Daphne opened one eyelid, hoping to see the brilliant sun streaming through the window, to be back to reality.

The moonlight remained, creating an eerie glow.

An upbeat instrumental song began, something Daphne didn't recognize.

"Oh, yes! Yes!" A figure emerged from the darkness. It was an elderly woman with gray, ratty hair hanging in front of her eyes.

Desperate to hide, Daphne skidded up the hall and rattled the doorknob of the men's room. It mercifully opened.

She dove inside.

"Yes. Oh! I'm doing it! There's no stopping me!" the woman muttered as she made her way down the hall. She hadn't seemed to notice Daphne's scrambling. Daphne held the door open a sliver so she could hear.

A low, strict voice within her told her this was important, that she was seeing this for a reason. She wondered if this was what Edwin had meant when he said Willoughby talked to him.

The woman passed the restroom door. "Are you comin' along, then?" There was a thumping sound on the linoleum as she walked.

Daphne's body shook uncontrollably. She opened the door another inch.

The little woman, who was barely five feet and had what looked like a hump on her brittle back, dragged a shotgun behind her. Her twisted, arthritic hands held it by the stock, allowing the barrel to scratch against the floor.

Daphne drew in a frantic gasp of air, sucking her gum down her throat. She swallowed the lump, determined not to cough and catch the woman's attention.

"These troublesome youth! They have no respect!" The old woman stopped, about four feet past the door Daphne stood behind, and wiped her mouth with the sleeve of her sweater.

The music was loud, echoing through the bathroom walls, but the woman's voice pierced through the din.

The little old lady swiveled on her heel and stared down the corridor she had appeared from. Daphne thought she had heard her and was coming to shoot her or, worse, make her stay in that darkened school forever.

But the woman rocked back and forth, her hair smacking into her face. "I'm doing it. Right this minute."

That was the first moment Daphne believed the woman was talking to someone. She sensed a presence in the hall, someone other than just the old, unfamiliar woman.

It was the crushing sort of presence that filled her mind and body. Her thoughts were no longer her own. Someone had broken inside of her and was pulling wires.

Daphne was too afraid to close the door. She stood, motionless, waiting to see.

The smell invaded first, a powerful stinking scent that tickled her gag reflex.

A murky shadow shaded the old woman's frame. The gray strands of hair slipped to the sides of her face as she raised her head to regard the person—the *thing*—before her.

Daphne trembled at the reverence in the old woman's black eyes.

The thing stepped into her narrow view.

It was a monster. The kind she worried might lurk inside of her.

The very real kind that must have murdered a two-year-old boy with the tire of a minivan.

Daphne clasped her hand over her lips and dug her magenta-painted nails into the skin of her face.

The memory of a Post-It note scribbling—her mom's last—of a thing, a bad, ugly thing, clawed at her heart.

Slime dripped from the monster's needle teeth as it grew closer to the old woman. It walked on its hind legs like a man.

"Oh, yes, yes." The woman pursed her crepey lips. "I thought you'd come along! Old Hedda knew!" She tightened her grasp around the stock of the shotgun and turned back toward the open gymnasium.

The thing's wolfish snout sniffed the air.

Daphne was electrified with panic. It could smell her. It knew she was there.

The monster followed behind the shriveled lady, its serpentine tail coiling around its middle.

She sunk her nails deeper into the skin around her lips until warm blood speckled her face.

*You shouldn't be alone!*

*Not at night!*

*Not in Willoughby!*

It spoke to her without opening its circular, barbed mouth. It spoke with its mottled, greasy back to her.

Everything she knew, every experience she had lived, slipped from Daphne's mind. She knew only this monster and its dark, slimy thoughts. She could see only what the inside of its throat looked like in her mind's eye. It was what she would see when it ate her up.

*And then you'll be there with others, sloshing around in my stomach.*

Unrelenting fear tunneled up her esophagus. She bent forward and let the vomit pour onto the tiled floor.

As Daphne backed away from the mess, she glanced over to see the monster disappear. It crouched and then scuttled away on its leathery knees into the darkness.

She let the door close.

219

A sound ripped through the bathroom, and for the slightest second, Daphne thought it was the monster, clanging against the wall, pounding for her to let it in.

She was afraid she would.

Screams erupted, and she knew it must be in the gym with the kids. It might be eating the beautiful girl in the slim dress she'd seen dancing so happily.

After a few beats the thunderous *boom* came again, and she knew it was Hedda. Old Hedda was using her weapon.

Daphne was filled with helplessness. Her memories flooded back, and she thought of Thomas the Tank Engine grinning at her as the blood flowed underneath her shoes.

People were dying. Children. And she was hiding in the bathroom.

Perhaps she was here to save them. Was that her purpose?

No. No. Not someone like her. The universe surely could not be relying on someone like her to help.

Yet she couldn't stand there in the stink of her puke, waiting for Hedda to come blasting through the door.

She puffed out her chest and yanked open the door, jumping over her pile of vomit. Boys in suits or military uniforms and girls in colorful knee-length dresses poured out of the gymnasium doors. Shouts were heard and then another *boom* resonated.

A girl screamed.

A moment later there was one more *boom*.

Daphne ran to the opening, grabbing the doorframe as she peered inside. The crowd pushed through beside her, a clatter of yells and coughs and heavy breaths. A swath of crinoline scratched her leg.

She watched as a man jumped onto Hedda. They fell together onto the hard floor, like lovers embracing.

A rousing wartime song began to play on the colorful jukebox in the corner as they struggled.

The man—a teacher, Daphne presumed—straddled Hedda.

"No!" He grasped at the barrel as she swung it up toward him. "Hedda!"

Daphne could hear the desperation, and more, the disappointment, in his voice.

Hedda fiddled with the hammer.

The man slammed his fist into her left arm. Daphne could hear the crackle of the bone breaking over the haunting music.

The old woman didn't make a peep.

The gymnasium was empty except for the two struggling on the floor. Daphne watched, her mouth agape.

Hedda dug the muzzle of the gun into the floor and pushed her weight against it to slide out from under the man. He scrambled forward, grabbing at her wool skirt. She kicked him in the face so hard, her quilted slipper flew off.

"Stop! Stop this!" He grabbed at the surprisingly wily woman.

Hedda pushed her heels into the floor and crab-walked away on her remaining good elbow.

Daphne surveyed the gym floor, looking for some sort of weapon to give him. Forgetting that she was only an interloper, a viewer.

She saw the first body. A girl in a violet dress had a blackened hole in her middle. She lay flat on her back, her red curls splayed out around her pale face. Blood streamed toward a collection of tables.

There was a dead boy in a plaid tie splayed over a folding chair. The top of his head was ragged as a broken egg, his brains plopping out on a stark-white tablecloth.

Rage—a seething, fiery rage—pounded against Daphne's insides.

She rushed toward the man and Hedda, hoping to kick in the woman's teeth.

Time seemed to slow as she made her way across the floor and slipped in gore. She watched as the old woman yanked the shotgun up toward her own face.

"I forgot!" Hedda jammed the muzzle into her mouth.

The teacher was on his hands and knees, crawling toward her.

Hedda wiggled her big toe. She grazed it against the trigger.

"I mmomt," she said around the steel barrel.

The man reached forward.

Daphne tripped. She landed on the slick floor just as Hedda pushed the trigger with her toe.

Skull and brains splashed against the festive silver streamers on the wall.

The man let out an agonized scream.

Daphne raised herself up off her belly to see Hedda's body slump to the floor.

"Fuck!" the man roared.

Daphne's ears throbbed from the music and the shotgun blast. Daphne forced herself to stand. She turned to see the monster. It was watching them from the gymnasium doors, pleased with the death, sated. In fact, it seemed to suck in the bloody air through its barbed mouth as though tasting a fine wine.

She stared, certain it would come for her next. That death in the vicinity could not be as fortifying as a live, squirming body down its sharp gullet.

The doors closed on creaky hinges, by themselves. And the monster disappeared.

The music floated away and there was absolute silence. The smell of blood evaporated from her nose.

Daphne did a dizzying three-sixty. The teacher was gone. Hedda's headless body was gone. The streamers and bodies and jukebox were all gone.

She stood alone in the gym.

The air changed around her. It was a subtle shift in the pressure, tickling her eardrums and raising the hair on the back of her neck.

She thought she might scream. She thought she might drop to her knees and sob like she had when she was sixteen, when the shock had worn off and she had realized she was a murderer. When she had known that it really was little Oscar's blood on her sandals.

She knew she could fill the gymnasium with her tears and her snot.

Daphne's brain expanded. Her thoughts multiplied, stacking on each other in succession. Her arms hung slack at her sides as she made sense of herself and the new world she inhabited. All that she had known had been stripped away, like a lightning bolt tearing through the bark of a tree. Perception and reality folded in on each other, creating ripples of terror within her body and soul.

Time was not what she had believed. It had altered its linear course.

*Why me?*

It was one of a million questions.

Willoughby had chosen to show her something. The prom was important. The old woman and the presence . . .

Daphne tried to remember the other, the thing that had stalked behind the little old lady. It was amorphous in her mind, a darkness with no solid edge.

Whatever it was, it *made* her forget.

She knew this.

Finally, Daphne took one step, and another. Her ballet flats took her soundlessly to the gymnasium door that led back into the corridor of the school. She was sure the cool metal of the door handle would be refreshing against her palm, but her brain couldn't seem to process the tactile sense.

Instead, it was as though a ghost hand was opening the door and pushing her along the dark, lonely hall.

She passed a classroom with art pasted outside on a bulletin board. The sight of the pipe-cleaner grass and the cellophane sun tore into her mind and ravaged her thoughts.

*I'm not home yet.*

*We're not in Kansas anymore, Toto.*

A voice spoke from deep within her. It was not her own, yet somehow it was.

*Maybe I am home.*

Daphne made it to the front entrance of the school, although she couldn't remember instructing her legs to carry her there.

If she strained her ears, she was certain she could hear voices up the main stairs. It made her glad, to know she hadn't been sucked down into some sort of lonely parallel planet. Yet she knew someone like Hedda could be up there, with a shotgun, or something worse.

*Like an old, rusty van? With a big crunching tire?*

The words came up out of her mind unbidden. She wished she had never told Edwin. It made it all too fresh in her mind.

She really needed a peppermint.

Daphne turned, strangely compelled to go upstairs. As she placed her trembling foot on the first step, something caught her eye.

It glinted in the green light, waiting for her at the top.

She thought, at first, that it was extraneous information. Simply a bit of trash that invaded her already overfilled brain.

*Look.*

The voice inside urged her to pay attention.

*LOOK!*

Daphne climbed a few stairs, more aware than ever that she was alone. The people she had thought she'd heard must have been a pathetic invention of her fear.

Blue light flashed over the glass.

It was an empty bottle, precariously balanced on the top lip of the linoleum landing.

She hopped up the last stairs, bent down on her aching knees, and picked it up.

The Coke label was a bright red square on the neck, above a circular insignia. Daphne ran her thumb over the profile of a bird.

*IOWA HAWKEYES BIG 10 CO-CHAMPIONS 1981*

Her mind crumbled. She thought back to the cellophane sun. There had been something alarming about it, something dated and old.

Daphne raised the bottle up to her nose and sniffed the cola inside.

She was in 1982.

*1982. I'm in 1982. I know this.*

The Coke bottle slipped from her grasp.

Daphne flinched, expecting the glass to splinter. But the bottle toppled onto the hard floor, intact. She watched as it rolled away, pushed by the same invisible hand that had urged her up there.

It became a glimmering beacon as it spiraled down a darkened hall.

*I will follow it.*

In all her life, Daphne had not had such a powerful inner dialogue. And it was more than just herself. She knew that there was another—a separate but overwhelming connection that tethered her to Willoughby.

The image of an umbilical cord, veiny and taut, entered her mind.

She padded down the corridor marked *ARTS/LITERATURE*, squinting in order to see the bottle. It was a twinkle in the inky dark, leading her.

It somehow navigated around a trash bin, rolling efficiently.

*I am alone. I shouldn't be. I should never be alone.*

The tight hall was suddenly strangling. She was both exposed and smothered.

The bottle did one last whirling roll and stopped before a classroom door.

Daphne considered trying the handle, to see if the bottle was leading her to a clue.

But then an ugly, depressing thought came.

*I am alone.*

Her ears perked. She glanced down at the bottle. It remained at the bottom of the door, idle.

The air shifted, and she hoped it was a sign that she was returning home. She remained motionless, her head cocked and her tongue stale in her sour mouth.

*Hello?*

Daphne wasn't certain if she had spoken with her voice or inside her head. She knew it didn't really matter.

*I am alone, but I am always alone. That never changes.*

She smelled it first.

It was worse than the bitter puke she was often drowning in. And it was even worse than the metallic tang of Oscar's blood. It seemed to be both of those scents, mixed and magnified.

Daphne gagged. She bent over, holding her stomach, attempting to suck in fresh air.

A creature appeared at her right, slowly revealing itself from around the corner beneath a sign she could still read in the flickering, unreliable light: *SCIENCE*.

It crawled on four legs.

For one hopeful second, she thought it was the town orange tabby, Fox.

As it lumbered toward her, she could not ignore its stink, nor its wolfish eyes. It was much too large to be a cat, and its swinging, fleshy tail was not human.

It stood, six feet away, its hulking mass much too large for the school's hallway.

Daphne pressed the back of her hand into her nostrils. She couldn't take that smell.

*Fuck off.*

She said it without speaking.

Her boldness surprised her. She had said it because she couldn't really believe it was real. That it could hurt her.

It regarded her with its yellow eyeballs. It held a clawed, furless foot above the floor, contemplating.

The sight of its mouth—a deep, hollow tunnel of needled teeth—sent a shockwave through her.

She had seen those teeth before and forgotten.

She knew this.

Daphne knew, too, that it could fit her inside its maw. She would be eaten and digested in its blotchy abdomen, existing with the others in a stew of evil. A place she probably deserved to be.

*I said FUCK OFF.*

A single thread of pea-green saliva dribbled from its mouth onto the linoleum.

She had seen it with Hedda. It had been there, in 1944, reveling in the murder, tasting it, savoring it.

*You are alone at night. You should never be alone. Not here.*

It was inside her, crawling up through her brainstem and trickling down into her awareness.

Daphne stared into its milky eyes. She recognized a human reflection. It was frightened. Not fully, not even on the surface, but deep, deep down. It was a familiar expression. She had seen it on her mother's face when she had killed Oscar. Her mother had been frightened of her. She realized that for the very first time as she stood there now. Her mother had carried that deep fear with her always. Jane/Caroline had been a scared woman. She had lived as a runaway, as a coward. It hadn't been until the final days, when she was perhaps relieved to allow brain cancer to eat her memories, that the fear evaporated off her like water droplets.

*You were not expecting me. You didn't think I could be here, wherever this is.*

She took a step backward, if only to escape the putrid smell.

The monster understood Daphne. She could read that too. She wondered if Edwin had ever spoken to it, or Doris, or even Caroline.

No, she thought, her mother wouldn't speak to it. She was too wrapped up in her own weakness. She wore it like a shroud, ironically, until she died and then she left all her pain for Daphne to wear.

*I surprised you.*

She took great comfort in this.

The monster growled, raising its sinewy lips to reveal the complete and blinding darkness of its mouth.

She may have caught it off guard, but it was strengthening.

It set down its foot and began to lurch forward, bending at its waist.

Daphne knew it was preparing to run, to chase her, to devour her.

She squeezed her fists, glancing down at the Coke bottle in the pathetic hope it would lead her to a safe place.

It lay there dumbly, pretending to be inanimate.

Daphne turned on her heels. She leaped forward, drowning in the full force of her terror as her arms and legs pinwheeled.

Its hot, rancid breath curdled the air behind her.

She ran.

Willoughby School became a swirl of dark colors and glimmering lights.

There was a tug on her left ballet flat. It was sucked off her foot and into its slimy jaws.

She screamed inside her mind and pushed herself to run faster.

She flew forward, throwing herself at the staircase. The monster was right behind her.

*I'm sorry! I'm sorry I'm alone!*

She scrambled down the steps. Pain ripped through her chest; she had never run so swiftly.

Daphne's foot slipped on a stair, causing her right leg to bend awkwardly behind her in a painful display of the splits. She landed with a thud. Her tailbone throbbed as she bent forward, attempting to pull herself up with the banister. She immediately sensed a flourish of pain in her right ankle. Instinctively, she grabbed at the injury and was shocked by the cold weight of the monster's snout on her hand.

"Shit!"

She had twisted her body in order to grab her ankle and now had her back to the remaining stairs.

Before her brain could fire an appropriate action, it was on top of her, its mouth unhinging and preparing to swallow her.

The smell made her think of those final days, of her mother's bedpan.

She fell backward, the creature coming with her.

Daphne clenched her teeth, waiting for the agony of her head cracking against the floor. Instead, as she flew down the stairs backward, time slowed.

The edges of her vision narrowed.

Death, in the form of the stinking creature gnashing at her, was much too close.

Daphne turned her head, taking in the bizarre kaleidoscope of colors.

And then, there was someone else.

Standing by the main entrance, a bag in her hand.

She had round cheeks and brown hair.

Daphne knew.

She knew because this girl's eyes were swimming in fear and pulsing with anger.

*Mom.*

It was like the photograph had come to life—the one with the dripping ice cream cone.

The girl.

*Mom.*

DAPHNE SLOWLY CLIMBED out of the darkness. The light was foggy at first, and then it intensified, scorching her eyes. She screwed them shut and threw her arms over her face.

A constant, rhythmic clanging vibrated through her bones.

"Whoa! Daphne?" This voice was outside of herself, tinny and far away.

Daphne moaned and rolled over onto her side.

"Daphne!" He was closer.

"Edwin?" she asked in a whispering peep.

His presence enveloped her like a comforting cocoon. She blindly extended her hands, sunspots dancing in her vision.

"Hey." He gripped her elbows as he knelt beside her.

"It's so bright." The ground was hard beneath her.

"You passed out!" He pulled her body into a sitting position. "You ran this way, and then you just went down."

Her brain felt like a leaky faucet. She grasped for her memories, but they were dripping down into a black, bottomless drain.

Daphne rested her forehead against his collarbone, nuzzling her nose into his T-shirt. "I saw my mom."

"Your mom?" he repeated. "You saw your mom?" The words didn't make sense to her, repeated back like that.

"I . . . oh, Edwin." Her ankle throbbed.

"Your mom is dead." he reminded her. Like she could ever forget that shriveled woman and the tissue she pressed against her crepey lips to catch the dripping saliva.

She suddenly remembered a string of green sludge, plopping onto linoleum.

"Daphne, your ankle's bleeding. You were lying here, mumbling. I kept trying to wake you. It just started bleeding, like gushing out of nowhere. Do you remember anything?" His words came out in a manic stream.

She shook her head.

"We were on the gazebo, and you were getting upset. Do you remember that?"

She sniffled. "I think so."

"You ran away. You acted like you saw something, maybe? I followed you and then you fainted, just like at the river."

"How long?" She dared to open one eye. Edwin's head shaded her from the sun.

He ran his fingers down her spine. "I don't know, five minutes? No more than eight. I almost called 911, but you were breathing okay."

Daphne opened her other eye. She looked down at Edwin's knees. "Where are we?"

"The school. The playground. Daphne, what—"

"It was like the mill. It was just like it, except I'm having a harder time remembering." Her eyes flitted down to her ankle. It was smeared in red.

Edwin pulled back. He kept hold of her arms as he observed her face. "Tell me what you can remember. Did you go back? Like before, at the old mill?"

"Back?" She hiccuped.

He gave a somber nod.

"Yes. I think so. I saw two places, or times, I mean. Two different times." The gravity of her words seemed to weigh down her entire body. She wanted to fall back on the tarmac and take an extended nap.

"There was a prom. In the forties. I remember that." Her eyelids drooped.

"Prom?" His body stiffened. "When did you say?"

She was slipping into sleep. She had not been this lethargic after her vision at the river. This one had taken a steeper toll. "Nineteen forty . . . um . . ."

"Four?"

"Hmm, yeah. People died." She yearned for a pillow.

"Yeah, yeah, they did. Come on, you're falling asleep." Edwin slipped an arm around her waist and used the other to lift her legs as he stood.

She melted in his arms. It was nice to rely on someone else, to not be so alone.

"Edwin?"

"Hmm?" He held her as though she were a baby.

"Do you hate me? For what I told you?"

Edwin's eyes locked onto hers. "About Oscar? Never." His face didn't fall. He didn't look at her as though she were a bug, a monster, a thing with needle teeth.

"Are we going to a doctor?" Daphne lifted her head weakly and took another peek at her oozing ankle. There were several ragged puncture marks.

The shrill school bell sounded. Suddenly, a flood of children poured out a side door, excited for recess.

They stopped, staring at Edwin and the haggard, bleeding woman in his arms.

"Hey, kids." He adjusted Daphne's weight in his grip. "Beautiful day."

Daphne smiled. It was a strange sensation that stretched her cheeks.

How nice it would be, she thought, to be one of those children. To climb on the monkey bars in the warm sun and think only of hopscotch and cute boys.

"I'm not taking you to a doctor," Edwin answered in a hushed tone as he carried her around the outside of Willoughby School. "We're going to see Doris Woodhouse. We're not going to wait anymore." He held her more tightly. "She's gonna help us."

# July 12, 1982

TIFFANY SPUN THE DIAL on the TV until Tom Selleck appeared on the screen. "Yes! God, I love that fucking sexy moustache." She fell back onto the tan corduroy couch. "It's divine!"

Caroline nodded. She stared at the television, concentrating on a single blocky pixel of *Magnum, P.I.* "Yeah."

"I bet you Rosalee shit herself on the way home!" Tiffany opened a can of Diet Coke with a flip of her thumb. "She probably had to stop and poop in the Olson's garden!"

"Yeah."

Tiffany spun around, her pop sloshing out of the can. "What's wrong with you?"

Caroline shrugged. "I'm not sure."

"We *did it*!" Tiffany squeezed Caroline's knee. "We told that bitch off! I mean, did you see her face?"

"Yeah, I just . . ." Caroline couldn't express the icky apprehension crawling over her skin. Her mind kept bringing her back to that moment, to when she leaned in real close to Rosalee's face. She had threatened her, told her to stay away from her dad. There had been something wrong and unexpected in her expression.

Rosalee had been surprised.

"Carrie, you need to have another beer." Tiffany leaned back into the cushions of her parent's sofa. "Or two."

"Do you think I could be wrong? Like, what if my mind made me think I saw something I really didn't?"

Tiffany snorted. "Don't be a twit."

Caroline kicked her restless legs. She had had occasions throughout her life when there was someone else inside her mind, a separate voice. Could it make her see things that weren't there?

"I'm going to pee." She jumped off the couch, thankful for an excuse to stretch her muscles. Tiff had the ability to stay still for hours as long as she had a pile of pop within arm's reach. Caroline frowned at the thought of watching *Magnum, P.I.* for the rest of the night. She itched to do something, anything, else.

She trailed down the hall toward the bathroom, taking her time. The door sat crookedly at the end, across from Tiffany's parents' bedroom. Tiffany had busted the hinge when she kicked it in. It had been pretty cool, to barge inside as Rosalee was just pulling up her jean shorts. Her face had been funny; her bow lips stretched into an oval and her eyes like saucers.

It had smelled like shit in there, stinging Caroline's eyes. That had made it funnier, really.

She smiled at the memory. It had been nice to see Rosalee like that, cornered and scared. She had looked like she believed it, like she really thought they were going to shoot her.

Caroline wondered what would have happened if they had. If Tiffany had pulled the trigger and let the shot fly. It would have been satisfying to see Rosalee's brains on the mirror. Caroline would probably have been scrubbing the counter down with bleach right now if they had. And they could have thought up some clever way to hide the body. She had seen on some movie that you could bury it in a graveyard. Right on top of a body that was already there. No one thought to look there.

As she passed the open door to Tiffany's bedroom, something caught Caroline's eye. She stopped, transfixed.

The closet door was open. It was an accordion type door, pulled out on top of a mess of dropped clothes. The lightbulb inside was on, the string beside it twisting in an imperceptible breeze.

Caroline couldn't remember ever seeing that closet open before. She had spent countless hours in that rectangular room, playing Barbie dolls and gossiping about boys. She had fallen asleep on Tiffany's lumpy mattress as they listened to the *Grease* soundtrack and sneakily drank vodka mixed with orange juice.

But she had never seen inside that closet.

She stepped into the bedroom, navigating over the clutter. Her eyes stayed on the light bulb, even though it burned spots into her vision.

A car chase had begun on the television. She could hear the floor creak as Tiffany leaned forward and twisted the volume dial up. "You're missing it!" Tiffany called from the living room. "He's after the bad dude! Oh, shit!"

Caroline took in a shaky breath. She was doing something very wrong but very necessary.

She kicked at a bra on the floor that was curled up under the closet's door. Once it was dislodged, she was able to pull it open.

There was a typical collection of blouses and jeans hanging from wire hangers, and on the left, there was a box of old toys. Caroline smiled at the blue-framed Magna Doodle they hadn't played with in a long while. As little girls, they had used it to write secret messages to each other.

A red flash called to her from the right side of the closet. It was on the carpeted floor. She squinted, her eyes adjusting from the bright bulb.

There were two red things.

Red high-top sneakers with Velcro straps.

The ugliness burgeoned inside her, spilling and sloshing through every part of her.

Caroline's hands trembled as she bent over and picked the shoes up. They were in good condition, barely worn. They were size nine and a half.

She carried one in each hand back into the living room.

Tiffany was burrowed into the couch, an empty pop can against her meaty thigh. Her eyes were glued to the TV, with its enormous antenna pointed to the ceiling.

"Tiff-Tiffany?" Caroline stood at the arm of the couch.

"What?" She didn't look away from Tom Selleck's masculine face.

"Are these yours?"

Tiffany turned. "Yep. You like?"

Caroline forced herself to speak evenly. "I've never seen you wear them."

"I got them a few months ago. They're kinda tight, so I only wear them sometimes. My mom got them for my birthday, but I wanted different ones. She never listens to me. I told her—"

"Tiffany?" Rage heated Caroline's cheeks. She clutched the shoes in her fists, sinking her nails into the soft edges.

"What? Why do you look like that?" Tiffany searched around her seat for another can of pop.

*Rosalee's face. Her eyes. She was surprised.*

"I understand." She couldn't help the snarl in her voice. "I get it."

Tiffany sat up. "You are losing it. What the fuck is your problem?" She rolled her eyes.

Caroline's heartbeat thrummed in her ears. The pumping rhythm filled every part of her.

"You wanted to stop her from sleeping with my dad. You didn't want Rosalee to be with him."

Tiffany huffed. "Because you're my friend, and she's a bitch!"

"No." Caroline pulled her arm back and threw one high-top. It landed against Tiffany's stomach and rolled to the floor.

"Hey!" Tiffany stood up, shrieking. "What the—"

"You! You are the one! You had sex with him!" She wound up her left arm and threw the other shoe like she was the pitcher for the Willoughby Millers. It smacked into Tiffany's nose.

"Fuck!" Tiffany roared. She grabbed at her face. "Carrie!"

"Don't!" Caroline pointed her finger at her best friend. "I will *never* talk to you again." Her limbs were both tense and wobbly.

"Carrie, just wait." Tiffany's voice was an alien sound. It was quiet and shaky.

They stared at each other.

A commercial filled the silence. *"I'm cuckoo for Cocoa Puffs!"*

"You did, didn't you?" Caroline ran her hands through her hair. She had to keep herself occupied or she would leap across the room and pummel her fists into Tiffany's stupid face.

"It's . . . it's not like I planned on it happening."

Caroline hung her head. "I'm so stupid."

The strange, revolting sound of Tiffany's sobs mingled with the cereal jingle on the TV.

Caroline shuddered. "I'm going to kill you."

She rushed out of the house, forgetting her purse and her sandals. Tiffany's shouted "Come back!" trailed after her. Gravel cut into her bare toes as she crossed Ash and headed for the dark woods.

*I'm alone. I shouldn't be alone.*

Caroline breathed in the moist night air. The canopy of trees provided comfort, a sort of shield. Her thoughts flipped back and forth between her mother and father. She could not begin to guess which one she hated more. Her father had slept with her best friend, the girl she had grown up with from infanthood, and her mother . . . well. Her mother concentrated on her stitching and shoved it all down. She pushed it all deep down inside and sealed it shut, airtight.

She knelt down on a bed of pine needles and cried. Her chest hitched as she struggled for breath.

Hours passed.

*I am sorry. I'm sorry I'm alone.*

*No. No, it's okay.*

*Really?*

*Oh, yes. Yes.*

*Thank you.*

*But what are you going to do about it, Caroline? What are you going to do?*

Caroline sniffled. She looked up through the crooked limbs and clusters of leaves at a sliver of the sky. Glimmers of yellow moonlight were spreading above her.

It was at least midnight, surely.

Which meant a new day was dawning.

It was July 13, 1982.

# Doris

DORIS WOODHOUSE HAD FORGOTTEN HER TEA. She wrapped her age-speckled hand around the ceramic mug to feel the cool liquid inside.

She sighed. How forgetful she was becoming in her old age! If only Franklin had lived longer. He would have reminded her to drink her chamomile when it was still warm. He was a practical sort of a man, a doctor.

The old woman brought the mug to the sink and poured the muddy water down the drain. The tea bag plopped down into the plug. Doris figured she could fish it out later. There was no rush. Her life was a slow stroll. A lumbering march toward the inevitable last page of the book.

How she missed Franklin! He hadn't visited her in quite some time.

As she plodded out of the kitchen and down the oak-lined hallway to the parlor, she heard a jittery rapping on her front door.

"Oh, heavens." Doris buttoned up her loosely woven cardigan. She had known, when she had seen that girl poking about, that turmoil would soon follow.

Her muscles ached as she pulled open the heavy antique door.

240

Edwin Monroe rushed inside, the blonde girl hanging loosely in his arms.

"Doris!" His black bangs stuck up and his normally tender eyes were blazing wild. "She passed out!"

"Put her on the chaise." Doris waved a hand toward the ivory tufted sofa.

Edwin carefully set the girl down. He took a decorative pillow and wedged it under her head.

Doris stood over the girl, watching as her eyeballs revolved beneath her lids as though she were in the throes of an intense dream.

Edwin paced the parlor, running both hands through his hair. "She was mumbling, just random words, and then she just went limp," he whimpered.

"It's all right. She'll be fine." Doris pressed the back of her hand against the girl's forehead. She was slightly feverish.

"She ran toward the school and collapsed." Edwin stared into the hearth of the fireplace. "I was right over her, trying to wake her up, when all this blood just spurted out of her ankle."

"Goodness me."

"She said she went back, that she saw stuff."

"Back?" Doris watched the young man. He was agitated, pulling at his collar and biting into his lips.

"Doris, I think she went backward, like in time. I mean, not really, but like she saw it."

"Oh." She nodded.

Edwin crouched down beside the girl. "I told her you could help."

Doris was struck with the memory of Kasey, Edwin's best friend. He had lost her to Willoughby, and she could read on his face that he was terrified to lose this girl too.

"I hope that I can."

Sometimes, since she was nearing ninety, her mind was a maze. She struggled to access the proper channels in order to reach her thoughts. In this moment, it was a well-oiled machine. Both her vision and mind were clear.

"Will she wake up?" He held the girl's hand between his.

"Oh, yes. She has gone on a lengthy journey. One of the mind. I imagine she's experiencing something much like jet lag. She's exhausted, Edwin."

He exhaled. "Okay."

"She's an outsider, and like us, she has her sense." Doris herself was tired. She shuffled over to her favorite armchair and sat down. It pained her to see Edwin that way, frantic and worried. He was like a grandson to her.

"Daphne said she saw two places, or two times. She mentioned the prom. You know, in 1944?" He rolled up Daphne's black leggings to better show Doris the wound. "See, she got hurt."

"Ah." Doris frowned. She had seen these bites before, many times. "It will heal up."

"I think she needs stitches."

*If only Franklin were alive.*

"Maybe. I can do it, although my hands aren't as steady as they once were." She watched as a drop of blood fell on her Oriental rug. "You can assist me."

"I don't know; it could get infected. Maybe we should bring her to Fergus Falls—"

"It's a pity no one took over Franklin's practice." Her mind was slipping back into its intricate maze.

"Yeah." His eyes darted around the room.

"I have antibiotics. Don't fuss."

"You said she has a sense, like us? So you believe it? You think she really did see those things? That she saw the prom massacre?"

Doris drummed her knobby fingers on the chair's arm. "Of course. I believed *you*, didn't I?" How little and scared he had been! Little Edwin Monroe, running to her when he was bullied and when he realized the ugliness surging beneath him.

She hadn't told him how it pleased her, to know there was someone like her. She had been so alone, an unwanted anomaly in a bucolic place like Willoughby. And here had come this frightened Asian boy, more like her than her own husband and child.

"Yes. I'm glad you did." His face crumbled. He may have been a tall, strong man, Doris mused, but he was still just as frightened.

"Take a seat, Edwin. Buzzing around her isn't going to help anyone." Doris pointed to a hard-backed chair by the fireplace.

Edwin plopped down, his leg vibrating as he observed the unconscious girl.

"I knew when I saw her," Doris said.

"Really?"

"Quite. She's unlike her mother that way." Doris removed a tissue from her cardigan pocket and raised it up to her itching nose.

Edwin stiffened in his chair. "Her mother?" His foot was tapping violently against the rug. "She said . . . that's right, she said she saw her mom!"

"Hmm." Doris blew her nose. "Her mother had absolutely no sense. No intuition either, if you ask me."

He stilled his nervous movements. "She's from Willoughby?"

"Caroline? Yes. So in a small way, Daphne is too. Though she's really more of an outsider, don't you think?"

Doris watched as Edwin took a lingering look at Daphne. His cheeks paled.

"Her mom is Caroline Bergman."

Doris nodded. She was certain.

His shoulders fell. Doris recognized a flash of absolute anger as it crossed his features. She didn't like to see Edwin overtaken by such ugliness. He'd been a being of light for her within the murky confines of her home. Of *their* home—the dark and twisted landscape of Willoughby.

# July 13, 1982

CAROLINE CRAWLED OUT OF THE BRAMBLES, an infant slick with the remnants of a new and vast world. Her rebirthing had caused her thoughts to be swallowed, forgotten. The void of her mind held only the basest of desires. It was a glowing, burgeoning rage. It was a fire, kindled and stoked, licking the sides of her heart.

She knelt in the loose gravel of the road. The oversized KISS shirt she wore billowed in the dawn breeze. It was Kyle's shirt, though she could no longer smell the hint of his rank armpits. And her ears couldn't hear the steady thrum of the woodpecker, perched overhead on the dangling limb of an oak.

She perceived nothing but the developing patchwork of anger. It was being sewn together within her, a rigid and immovable force padding her brain like a quilted helmet.

Her body was pulled up, as though she were a puppet on a string. She stood, unseeing of the sun that crested the horizon. Her eyelids fluttered, and she walked in a halting, jumpy forward motion.

Her insides had been drained out, and she held only anger—an ocean of rage, rising and falling.

It waited for her on the road, standing impossibly upright, held by the same invisible puppet strings.

Caroline pushed her stringy, unwashed hair behind her ears and stared down at her axe. It wasn't in her secret place anymore. It was not stuffed down in the stinking, crumbling hole behind the rotten wood.

*That is mine*

It was her first real thought, tangible and fully formed.

*Yes. It is yours. I fetched it for you.*

Fetched! Like a dog! This made her laugh, yet no sound came out.

Caroline stopped. She circled her arms around the axe and brought it to her chest. She cradled it like a baby.

A flood of words and ideas filled the last few empty spaces inside her.

She thought it might all escape, plopping out of her nose and ears and pores. This was an unpleasant notion. Caroline wanted to keep all the anger.

It was both a comforting cloak and an impenetrable armor.

It made her stronger and happier.

She raised the axe up and rested the back end on her shoulder. It made her crack a smile, to imagine herself looking like a lumberjack in a KISS T-shirt.

The wood soothed her clammy palms. Caroline tightened her grasp around the handle and spaced her feet about a foot apart on the road.

Then she swung downward, bringing the blade clanging down on the pavement. Loose gravel sprayed up onto her legs.

Caroline frowned.

*I'm sorry. I don't want to hurt you.*

*No, it's perfectly fine!*

*I really don't want to hurt you.*

*Don't worry, I will heal in time. It barely left a scratch!*

"I don't want to hurt you," Caroline said aloud. She lifted the heavy axe back up onto her shoulder and lowered her head.

There was a scrape on Ash Street where she had let the blade fall.

Caroline rubbed her toe across the divot, blinking away a tear.

# 41

TIME WAS AN ELASTIC, UNDULATING LOOP. Her memories were shuffled, randomly, inside a bizarre photo album. Daphne was outside of herself, watching as she flipped through the plastic pages. There was the image of her mother in her swimsuit, wearing a youthful, naïve grin. There was an old, tattered picture of a bony woman with a shotgun in her mouth in 1944. And there was even a photograph of the dripping, liquid-like flames that had surrounded Daphne by Pelican Lake.

Although each memory and image was out of order, Daphne knew. She knew there was an association, an entrenched connection that could only be described as umbilical. It looped, like the softened construct of time, around her and the photos in her mind book.

Daphne floated up, away from herself holding the photo album, into a sea of billowy, darkened clouds.

Her eyes were open, yet she stretched them wider to see.

A dim light twinkled like a star.

"Ah, you are coming back."

Daphne breathed in an assault of perfume. She coughed.

"Do you need a tissue?"

It was an odd question. Daphne shook her head. Her tongue

tasted of pennies, and there was a ragged, sneaky pain crawling up her leg.

She rolled over, aware that her body was under a blanket and that her throbbing head was on a pillow. Her eyes focused on a brass bowl of potpourri on the bedside table. Sprigs of lavender and curls of bark overflowed, littering the doily beneath.

"This was my mother-in-law's room. Devorah. She had Alzheimer's, most likely. At that time, in the 1950s, she was just considered, oh . . . I don't know, old and forgetful." Doris Woodhouse's distinctive voice, a fusion of an elderly warble and the distinguished tone of an aristocrat, filled the small room.

Daphne stared at the potpourri, attempting to ground herself to reality. She spoke to herself, inside.

*I am safe.*

*I am in my time.*

*I am in Doris's Victorian. Upstairs, probably.*

She took in a gagging floral breath.

"Devorah died in this house. Franklin, my dear husband, too. But I can't let that bother me!" Doris emitted a wheezing laugh.

Daphne wiggled her fingers underneath the duvet. "Willoughby," she squeaked. "It's like that everywhere here, right?" Her throat was as dry as burned toast.

There was the sudden, jarring sound of Doris blowing her nose. "Yes. You cannot let it disturb your spirit."

Daphne turned over onto her other side in order to see Doris. Her muscles ached.

The elderly woman appeared small sitting in a plush armchair beside the bed.

As Daphne studied Doris's face, etched with deep wrinkles, her belly dropped. It was the jolt of realizing she had forgotten something essential.

"Doris, where is Edwin?"

The old woman wiped the end of her nose with the tissue and tucked it into the sleeve of her sweater. "He carried you here, but he left."

"Oh."

Doris screwed up her mouth. "I upset him."

Daphne frowned. She could remember her face pressed into his chest and the rhythmic sway of his walk as he carried her.

And then it had gone black.

Doris sighed, her shoulders slumping. "I told him who you were."

Daphne's head lifted off the pillow.

"What? Who am I?" The pain in her ankle intensified.

"You are Caroline."

Daphne sat up. "No! I am not, I am *not* Caroline."

Doris sniffed. "You are her daughter, which is the same thing."

Daphne's skin prickled with disgust and shame. "You know I'm her daughter?"

"Yes."

"How is that the same?"

Doris leaned back in the chair and giggled. "I used to pretend, too, that I wasn't my mother. She was a haughty woman, very concerned with appearances. I spent so much of my youth, and adulthood, rebelling against the notion that I could be anything like her. Yet there's no escaping such truths."

"Edwin hates me." Daphne wanted to die.

"Willoughby is much like a mother in that way," Doris finished.

Daphne slumped down into the musty sheets. She was alone.

"Oh!" Doris waved her arthritic hands in a flippant sort of motion. "Men are simple. Even Edwin. He will pace about and then he'll come back. I know these things. He had the face of a man who'll forgive."

Daphne's chin dropped to her chest. She should have told him!

"I stitched up your bite. It wasn't too bad. I've seen much worse, let me tell you."

"Bite?"

Doris pointed toward the end of the bed, where Daphne's feet curled underneath the duvet.

"If only Franklin had come by today, he could have helped! An unreliable doctor, if ever there was one! Although he would have probably just criticized my technique." She snorted.

Daphne was sure Franklin was dead.

"Tha-thank you." She lifted the blanket and peered down into the shadowy depths. Her ankle was wrapped in white gauze.

"Are you hungry?" Doris rose from the chair. It was a slow, arduous process that included a strong grip on the chair's arms.

Food, somehow, made Daphne think of Edwin. An arrow of pain and regret sliced through her abdomen. "No."

"I'll fix us some cornbread, I think. Yes, with creamed corn and sausages. Don't sausages sound tasty?"

Daphne shrugged. "Sure."

"Don't you get up. That ankle needs a respite, as does the rest of you! You were on a long journey."

"I was, wasn't I?" Daphne's mind slipped back. "Edwin said you could help me."

Doris slapped her knee. "I told you he's a typical man! I love Edwin, but he has such fantastical ideas." Her yellowed teeth appeared in a smile. "We women, of course, know the truth."

Daphne bit her lip. "Do we?"

The old woman straightened her aging back and looked down upon Daphne with sparkling judicious eyes. In that moment, Daphne believed she could see a glimmer of the woman Doris had been.

"The truth is that we can only help ourselves, dear." Doris gave a fluttering wink as she left the room.

Daphne held her eyes open, determined not to fall asleep. Or worse, to slip back onto the dizzying carousel of time.

She pushed herself up against the headboard of the antique bed. Her right ankle screamed and sizzled, as though it had been thrust into a campfire.

*Bite.*

There was no memory within her overflowing photo album of something biting her.

She wasn't brave enough to stretch down and unravel the gauze, either.

Doris's words reverberated through Daphne, filling every piece of her with an unlikely muddle of hopelessness and empowerment.

Edwin, like a hero, had rescued her from Pelican River. And he had carried her, bleeding, in his arms all the way to Doris's home.

It was sweet, noble even. Yet what Doris spoke was the truest sentence Daphne was certain she had ever heard.

She had come to Willoughby, alone. Her mind had been pulled backward in time, alone. She could only help herself.

And Edwin knew who she was. Doris was probably right about that too. Daphne could resist it, could turn her head away from the bitter medicine, but it would still be true.

She was, at least in part, her mother.

Daphne's eyes scanned the bedroom's wallpaper. It was a toile pattern, with identical farm boys tending to matching heaps of hay. They all held the same rake against their shoulders as they glanced to the side, beady eyes staring out from under their straw hats.

She was unnerved by the repetitiveness of the wallpaper clones. For the first time since she'd awakened, her stomach churned in its familiar anxious manner.

The window was covered in a thick brocade curtain that allowed for no guess at the time of day.

Daphne wiggled the toes of her right foot, checking to see if they were still there. She shuddered to think of Doris, shaky and a bit demented, sewing up her skin.

*Bite.*

She took in a hearty breath, suffocating on the potpourri and the stale sheets.

*If only I was home. If only I was in my cool, predictable basement. Dad and Mom would be overhead, their steps creaking the floorboards. I would see Oscar through the narrow casement, lugging a wagon of toy trains behind him with his pudgy baby hands.*

Tears came, fat, ugly drops cascading down her apple cheeks.

Doris stepped into the open doorway holding a tray of food. "Oh, goodness!"

Daphne wiped at her eyes. "I'm not hungry."

Doris continued toward the bed. "Nonsense. I made cornbread. It's only the Jiffy kind; I never learned how to do it from scratch. It's good Franklin isn't the picky type. He never seemed to mind that I was a godawful cook." She set the tray on the lumpy duvet, over Daphne's knees.

Daphne had the powerful urge to kick it off and watch the food splatter the disturbing wallpaper. Then she would overturn the bowl of potpourri for good measure.

Instead, she stared down at the plate Doris had prepared. The creamed corn was of a similar consistency to the vomit that had come up at Willoughby School in 1944. Although she hadn't really barfed then, had she? Because she was never there. She'd only watched it like a movie.

This made more tears puddle at the bridge of her nose.

"It's deer sausage, venison. I just heat it up, is all. Microwaves are handy things, don't you think?" Doris stood beside her, eagerly observing the meal.

"I'm not sure I can eat." Mucous ran down the back of Daphne's throat.

Doris settled back into the armchair. "Did you see bad things? Don't be scared. They happened long ago."

"They don't seem long ago to me."

Doris produced a shriveled tissue from her sleeve. She placed it under her nose, leaving a trail of white puffs across her upper lip. "Has this happened before? Before you came here?"

"No, never."

"I saw my grandmother after she died. She came to me and talked, as though nothing had even happened. It scared me so bad I piddled down my leg like a trembling Chihuahua." The old woman clutched the used tissue. "That happened to me even before I came to Willoughby. But once I arrived it grew worse. It's like a faucet:

251

some days it's turned on full power and I can see them all, somedays it's only a drip here and there."

"You see ghosts?" Daphne poked the square of cornbread.

"If that's what you want to call them. Edwin can feel things—"

"I've seen it."

Doris nodded.

"How is all this possible? How . . . how can we all do these things?" Daphne tore off a piece of the warm bread and rested it on her tongue.

"Good! It will make you stronger, to eat."

Daphne chewed. "Stronger for what? To get pulled back into some nightmare, again? No, thank you. I'm done."

Doris tapped her soft shoe on the hardwood. "Oh, don't give up. You've come for a battle, haven't you?"

Confused, Daphne tore off another piece and stuffed it in her mouth. It seemed she was hungry, after all. "I don't know what you mean."

"And you have your weapon." Doris's top lip curled into a devious smile.

Daphne swallowed the lump of bread. "Please, please, can you say what you mean?"

"Hey." Edwin stuck his head in the room.

Startled, Daphne clutched at the sides of the tray. "Edwin!"

Doris calmly observed him over her shoulder. "Did you get it all?"

"Yep." His eyes darted between Doris and the suitcase in his hands. He stepped into the room and set it on the floor and then swiftly retreated to the doorframe.

Daphne lifted herself up an inch to see. "My suitcase."

"That motel is much too far away. You may stay here, where I can tend to you." Doris scrunched the tissue between her hands.

"Thank you. That's very nice." Daphne settled back down and concentrated on the meal before her. It was beyond painful to consider looking into Edwin's eyes.

"I told you he'd come back," Doris announced rather smugly.

Mortified, Daphne picked up her fork and stabbed a deer sausage. She sliced into the meat, wondering if the action alone would make her puke.

Edwin stood in an awkward slump by the door. "I'm glad you're eating."

Everyone was obsessed with her eating. And they hovered around her, morose and speaking in cryptic clues.

How she would love to have a stable ankle on which to flee. She would run down Main until it became the county road. She would run, hot coals in her belly and a raging fire in her chest, until she was back in Bellingham. Until she was in her basement with her quilt over her head.

"Daphne?" Edwin's voice was raw and unmeasured.

She lifted her head and before she could fight it, her eyes were pulled to his cocoa ones like magnets. Everything she dreaded was swimming there: fear, confusion, anger, and hatred.

Her wet chin quivered.

Doris stood, in her slow and creaky way. "I'll get you some sausages. And a Coke, Edwin. That will taste good, hmm?"

"Yeah. Thank you, Doris." He squeezed his lanky body to the side to let her pass through the doorway.

As Doris padded down the hall on her squeaky house slippers, Edwin entered the bedroom. With a casual shrug, he leaned forward and dropped a pack of spearmint gum on the meal tray. He then sat on the arm of the chair lightly, as though he might need to jump up at any moment.

He cleared his throat. "How are you doing?"

Daphne crossed her arms over her chest. "You don't have to ask me that." She watched him from the corner of her eye.

"Well . . . I mean, I'm worried."

"Stop!" She balled her hands into tight fists.

"What?" He hovered above the chair's arm, barely touching its edge.

"I didn't tell you that I'm Caroline's daughter. I lied to you!" Her nails poked into the flesh of her palms.

Edwin sighed. "You don't owe me anything."

"Really?" The pain in her ankle had dulled, lingering in the background of her consciousness. "Really? You don't care?"

"I'm stupid. I probably should have figured it out. I mean, why else would someone from Washington care so much?" He gave a humorless laugh. "I know now, at least."

"God!" Daphne snapped. She clutched the tray of food and set it down on the bedside table. It collided into the bowl of potpourri with a clatter.

"Wh—" Edwin stood, watching her as she kicked the covers onto the floor.

"Quit being so fucking nice! Quit saving me and scooping me up and . . . and . . . thinking I'm helpless because I'm small or whatever." Daphne ignored her throbbing ankle and swung her legs off the mattress. She set her bare feet on the wood planks, just touching the twist of sheets she had flung aside. "Jesus, no matter what awful thing I say, you are just so *nice* about it!"

Edwin backed up, allowing her to stand.

There was an icy grip of agony as Daphne hobbled toward her suitcase.

"Where are you going?" A Tiffany-style lamp twinkled on the bureau behind Edwin, causing his face to fall into shadow.

She glanced down, realizing her black leggings had been removed. Her striped tunic barely covered her butt.

"Home." She knelt, favoring her gauze-wrapped ankle. "Once I have pants." Daphne unzipped her bag. She let her blonde hair hang down as she searched; it created a convenient curtain to obstruct her red-hot cheeks.

"Do you want me to be an asshole, then?"

The anger in his voice sent an unexpected yet pleasant quake through her body.

"Yes." She popped up, her ankle screaming. "Sure, yes." She held a pair of her jeans she had fished out of her suitcase.

"Okay." Edwin bit his lip. "I'm not rescuing you because you're small or because you look young. It's because you *are* helpless." He leaned back against the bureau. "You came here, lying to everyone, in order to find out what happened to your family, and you can. You have the key, somehow, to see what happened. But of course you're too scared to look. Not to mention, you made a mistake when you were a kid—something anyone could have done—and you've let that dictate your life. You don't even drive. So how are you going to go anywhere?"

Feeling like she'd been punched in the gut, Daphne goggled at him.

He took in a trembling breath. "You *need* someone to save you, Daphne."

He crossed the small room in three paces and left her alone, gaping and holding her pants.

A blind panic gripped her, churning her tummy and prickling her skin. Her open mouth tasted of death.

The pack of gum called to her from the tray, glinting in the lamplight like a tantalizing prism. She fantasized about the soothing mint on her tongue, but she couldn't take it.

Daphne clutched the metal sphere on the bedframe with one hand as she slipped a pair of skinny jeans onto her left leg. She then stuffed in her right leg, causing tears to well and catch in her eyelashes. She shimmied the pant leg up over the bulge of gauze, biting down on her cheek to stifle any yelps of pain.

She snapped the buttons of her fly and then grabbed her Samsonite, pulling it behind her on its wheels.

Edwin's words infected Daphne like venom.

She tested her right foot, walking to the open door. Pain zigzagged up her leg, a violent electricity.

She was resolved to not let this stop her.

The upstairs corridor of Doris's Victorian was awash in the distinctive salmon pink of an early summer evening. Daphne glanced around at the pristine angular ceiling and the plush Oriental rug running down the length of the hall.

An open staircase led to the main floor. Pushed against the stair rail was a small, child-sized bench holding a collection of antique porcelain dolls. Daphne blinked at a particular doll as it stared up at her with dead cornflower eyes. Two rectangular teeth were painted inside its open mouth. Its face, both human and not, unnerved her.

She screwed her eyes shut for a beat and then opened them again.

*. . . of course you're too scared to look.*

Daphne winced as she slowly made her way down the winding stairs. Reality was busting through her obstinacy.

*I have no money, no phone, no way out.*

She shuddered.

The stairs ended in a unique tiered landing in the front hall. It was a gorgeous room, with stained-glass windows and a portrait of a man in wire-framed spectacles. It was a man she recognized: Fred Willoughby. His grim and arrogant expression was identical to the one he had worn in her lost book.

Why did he seem important?

She shuffled to the front door, searching around the coat tree for her ballet flats.

Doris squeaked into the hall. "You're leaving."

"Yeah." Daphne kept her eyes on the floor.

"You didn't have shoes." The old woman spoke in almost a whisper.

Daphne unzipped her bag and removed a pair of silver flip-flops. She put them on, fumbling over the bandages, continuing to look away from Doris's probable frown.

"Thank you for the food and for letting me sleep, but I need to go home." Daphne gripped the door handle, praying Edwin wouldn't appear behind Doris.

"Oh, well, home it is, hmm? Shall I have Edwin accompany you? You don't want to be walking about. Your mother and father will certainly worry if you lose your way. Were the sausages too salty?"

"No. They were perfect." Daphne twisted the knob and walked out into the evening. She kept her chin plastered to her chest, allowing her blonde hair to hang down in obscuring strips. Edwin could be out there, hovering around the rose bushes in order to hit her with more of his painful truth bombs.

"Goodbye, dear!" Doris trilled from the front porch. "Come back tomorrow for sandwiches and chicken noodle soup. Campbell's, of course. I cannot cook a whit."

Daphne waved a limp hand in feigned agreement. It seemed Doris oscillated between enlightenment and dementia.

She unlatched the wrought-iron gate in the fence surrounding Doris's property and stumbled out onto the sidewalk. As she walked down the slight decline, the searing icy-hot pain of her ankle began to numb.

Fox, the orange tabby, sat flicking his tail at the intersection of Oak and Main. Daphne crossed the quiet road, her eyes focused on Fox's fuzzy ears.

"Hey." She had the urge to grasp his soft belly and cry into his fur.

*Cry later. Cry when you are far away.*

Fox regarded her with disinterest. He wiggled his nose, perhaps smelling a skittering rodent in the grass, and then padded away just as Daphne walked by.

She clamped down on a sob, trapping it in her chest.

Doris was nuts. Edwin too. Everyone.

Daphne walked down the north side of Main Street, her right flip-flop smacking into her sore heel.

If she had had that card from the shuttle driver, she could have called him and he would gladly have saved her. Or she could call her father to rescue her. A fantasy played in her mind, of her father in a rental car, pulling up to the curb. It would be worth his lectures to have a way out of Willoughby.

She couldn't let herself slip back into another hallucination. It was too unpredictable and much too frightening.

The tiny business district came into view. There was a crowd forming outside the City Café and a few stragglers across the street in front of the closed library.

Daphne steeled herself, knowing the only way out was through the group of Willoughbians.

Her rolling suitcase rattled behind her as she quickened her pace.

A farmer dressed in dusty Dickies with a fleshy, beet-red nose was the first to notice Daphne as she headed in their direction.

"Hey, girl, you're bleeding." He waggled a finger at her right leg.

Daphne glanced down at a bloom of red on the gauze. "Yep."

The others ceased their conversations and stared. There was a young man with acne scars twisting up his cheeks and a woman with a thick gray braid on her shoulder. There was a mom with an infant strapped to her chest and a little girl with puffy, tear-soaked eyes holding a stack of *Goosebumps* books that Moira would never stamp again.

Daphne sensed the pressure of all their eyes.

"You okay?" The mom stood on the steps of the café. Her baby fussed inside the BabyBjörn carrier.

Daphne realized she was talking to her.

"I'm fine." She continued on, aware that the citizens were silently stepping out of her way.

"Where the hell is she walking to?" someone murmured.

Daphne stopped. The sob lingering in her chest amplified the steady rock beat of her heart.

She swiveled, facing the sea of blank expressions.

"What? What are you looking at?" She trembled from her daring. "*What?*"

They seemed to blink in unison.

"Night's coming." It was the same farmer. "There's nothing that way, unless you gotta car to pick up at Olson's."

"I'm fine," Daphne lied. "*You* are the ones who need to worry." She gripped the handle of her suitcase protectively.

"What's that supposed to mean?" said the man with the acne scars.

"Moira *died*! And do any of you know why? Or do you even care?"

An angered voice erupted from the crowd. "Hey!"

Daphne had no control over her words. "There is something wrong here. Something really damn wrong." She waved an accusing finger. "All I know is that . . ." She pressed her eyes closed and was surprised by the image of needle teeth. "All I know is that if you choose to stay here, bad things will happen to you." Her eyes opened to the evening light swirling around them all.

"Are you threatening us?" someone bellowed.

Daphne shook her head weakly. Her eyes came to rest on the mom with the infant. A flash of acknowledgment passed across her pretty face.

Bad things, Daphne was certain, had already befallen her.

Yet she stayed. They all stayed, like scared children clutching at their mother's skirts. They knew nothing but Willoughby.

Daphne turned around. It was an awful, vulnerable intrusion to sense their eyes on her back.

A child's voice cut through the heavy silence. "You shouldn't be alone."

Daphne took in a breath and cinched her mouth shut, afraid to anger them any further. She walked ahead, toward the edge of town.

Relief would come when she crossed the threshold. As soon as she saw the back end of the *WELCOME TO WILLOUGHBY!* sign, she would let herself exhale.

# 42

## Edwin

WHEN FRED WILLOUGHBY DESIGNED his beloved Victorian manor, he had spent little time on the kitchen. The galley was known as the servant's sphere, a hidden sort of place where meals were magically conjured for the higher class. Later, when Doris Woodhouse became the mistress of Willoughby's most revered home, she held the same apathy for the culinary arts. Therefore, it was not as impressive as the grand front hall or even the study that had once been Dr. Woodhouse's exam room.

Edwin circled the length of Doris's cramped kitchen. It smelled of moldy tea bags and cornbread. He ran his hand across the butcher block island as he attempted to tamp down his frustration. When Daphne had popped out of the bed, tiny but furious, she had reminded him of Kasey. She had always been an unbending force of passion, whether it be ambition or rage. And this, he was certain in some indirect way, had been the cause of her death.

"She was mad at me for absolutely no reason!" He drummed his fingers on the wood.

Doris picked up a damp cloth from the sink and folded it in her wrinkled hands. "Oh, she had a reason. We always do. You should have walked her home, though, you stubborn thing. It's getting dark." She wiped at a spill of creamed corn.

Edwin didn't bother to remind her that Daphne was far from home. This happened often. Doris's mind would run like a well-oiled car and then abruptly sputter out and crash.

"I was mean to her." He spoke to himself. Doris was no longer driving on the proverbial road. "But it was justified. She asked for it, like literally asked for it. And to be honest, I think she needed it."

"Yes." Doris opened a drawer and poked around through a mess of serving spoons.

A dull ache pinched his temples. He knew Daphne had needed to hear the truth, yet he felt like such a prick for going through with it.

He thought back to the first time the ground had rumbled beneath his feet. Once he had been able to fully appreciate that he was alone in the sensation, he had been both terrified and confused.

Daphne had been thrown through time in vivid hallucinations— an unwilling passenger at the whim of Willoughby.

Perhaps, he considered, he had been a bit tough on her. Anyone with an instinct to live would run from that chaos. Edwin hung his head. He rubbed at the tension in his skull.

At first, when the sound winnowed into his ears, he thought it was only an audial memory.

"Doris?"

"Hmm?"

He stood up straight. "I think . . . I think I hear it."

Doris set down a ladle and cocked her head. "Naturally."

He didn't ask what that meant because he thought he already knew.

It was a deafening, invisible freight train. His head pounded with the assault of the sound. Doris's mouth moved, but he could only shrug in response.

An earthquake, the kind he figured could crumble buildings and create sinkholes, undulated beneath the linoleum.

Yet a tower of teacups remained still beside Doris.

The violent rattle vibrated up Edwin's body and caused him to bite down on the tip of his tongue. The metallic tang of blood trickled down his throat.

*Trouble, Eddie. Trouble is coming.*

The kitchen rocked. He lurched backward, nearly falling.

Once it was over, he would fix it; he would make everything okay.

Edwin bent over and grabbed his knees, allowing the tremors to wash over him.

# 43

HER DEAD MOTHER WOULDN'T SHUT UP. She appeared not as a ghost, like she would have for Doris, but instead as a stream of words in Daphne's mind. The loud and unavoidable memory of her mother's voice. It wasn't young Caroline, the teen Daphne was getting to know, and it wasn't her mother at the end, the one with the rancid breath and the bald head. It was her mother as she was while Daphne was a child. The practical, humorless woman who always had too much to do.

*You've gone and done it! Oh my, here you are on some dark road in the middle of nowhere, just asking to be raped and murdered. You might as well be holding a sign.*

Daphne tried to shut out the dialogue by thinking of anything else. She pictured a cheeseburger, but it melted away.

*Now what? You'll make it to the highway and find some pervert to drive you? Where? Do you even know which way to go? East or west? North or south?*

"Shut up, please," Daphne said to the dark. She was on the curving county road that led to I-90. It was a quiet thoroughfare, buffered by rows of mammoth pine trees. The sun had set, leaving several streaks of eerie light to filter through the pine needles. She thought her mother would have liked to paint such an intoxicating landscape, if cancer hadn't eaten her brain.

*Oh, Daffy, you can't handle all this. You need someone to guide you, to tell you what to do and how to do it.*

Edwin would probably agree.

Her father and Beverly too. Everyone in the entire world could probably come together and agree that Daphne was in way over her head.

At least she hadn't puked yet. Not even a dry heave.

A minivan's headlights momentarily blinded her. She reached up and shielded her eyes from the brightness.

It passed, on its way to Willoughby. Daphne wondered if the people inside the van had any clue that they were deliberately driving toward Hell. Or was Willoughby only Hell for some? Could a person grow up there, or even just stop and eat a tuna sandwich at the City Café, and be safe? Did any of those people in that crowd really believe there was nothing to run from?

As she distanced herself from the town, the events that had occurred seemed more and more implausible. Sliding through time on some crazy illusion couldn't really happen. She knew this intellectually, yet it had happened to her. She could still remember the crinoline of the girl's dress as she ran out of the prom, away from the madwoman with the gun.

Then Doris Woodhouse, the befuddled old woman, had treated it all like a normal sort of event. As though Daphne had told her she was dyslexic or nearsighted instead of a reluctant time traveler.

Daphne soldiered on, promising herself she would never go back to that awful place.

A foreign emotion saturated her thoughts. It was new and exhilarating. Her inner mother faded into white noise.

There was a glimmer of regret, as with every aspect of her life, but even more there was a swelling pride. It made her puff out her chest. She had done something. It was stupid, undoubtedly, yet necessary.

She was alone in the near-pitch darkness, on her way to nowhere.

The tunnel of trees buffered out any light or noise from I-90.

She wasn't certain how many miles it would be. Once there, she would have to stick out her thumb, she supposed, like people did to hitchhike in movies.

Tires crunched on loose gravel behind her. The vehicle was moving surprisingly slowly.

Daphne thought they may be decelerating at the sight of a woman hobbling along, so she moved farther off the road until her feet were tickled by clumps of ragweed.

Then the car pulled onto the curb behind her, and she could hear the idling engine and see the headlights streaming through her legs.

"Daphne?" Edwin called from behind her.

A puzzling concoction of rage and relief came at the sound of his voice. She kept walking.

"I'm good! You can go!" She prayed he wouldn't.

"Let me drive you. Please?" He was about twenty feet away. She hesitated.

"Please, it's for me, okay? I won't talk. Just tell me where you want to go, and I'll be like a mute Uber driver. You can sit in the back."

Daphne turned. She hated herself for doing it.

He stood behind the open door of his Toyota, his face obstructed by the glaring headlights.

Daphne wiggled her throbbing right foot. "What do you mean, it's for you?"

She could see his hand go up and swipe through his lush hair as he considered what to say.

"I might . . ." Edwin cleared his throat. "I might dive in to rescue people when they don't need it. I know that. But in my defense, you did say I'm like a superhero."

Although she couldn't see his smile through the light, she could hear it in his words.

"Yeah, okay." A piece of her cried at her giving up. "You have to admit, though, my powers are way cooler."

He laughed.

She wanted to run to him, wrap her arms around his waist, and bury her face in his chest. It was that same magnetic pull that had forced her to look into his chocolate eyes earlier, even when she had known it would cause her pain.

Her pride kept her from stumbling into him. She walked to the back passenger-side door of his Corolla and let herself in.

She pushed her bag down on the floor first and then moved a heap of food wrappers and notebooks out of her way.

As soon as her butt hit the seat, she was left exultant as the ripping pressure left her injured ankle. She bit her lip, careful not to show how grateful she was.

Edwin slipped into the driver seat and closed the door. They sat for a moment, both staring out the windshield at the empty road.

Without looking back, Edwin reached his long arm into the backseat and handed her his iPhone. "Type in where you want me to take you."

Daphne took the shining rectangle in her hand. It was a comforting object, a piece of reality that made Willoughby seem even farther away. She flipped it over and ran her thumb over the case. It was a cute cartoon of a wide-eyed Han Solo, blaster pistol in hand.

Edwin pulled out on the road and pressed on the gas, causing the trees to whip by Daphne's window.

She googled the address of the Western Union in Fergus Falls and plugged it into the map app.

"Here." She waved the iPhone between the headrests.

Edwin grabbed it and set it on his knee. "Okay."

She leaned back, hearing the crinkle of garbage around her. The pain in her ankle returned, somehow worse now that she was resting.

Her tummy rumbled, and she wished she had wrapped up the rest of the cornbread in a napkin and stuffed it into her bag.

Daphne studied the line of Edwin's neck. He sat stiff, nearly robotic, as he drove them in the direction of the highway. From her angle on the right side, she could see his profile too. A lock of black hair fell onto his brow.

Lights twinkled ahead. A blue shield-shaped sign marked 90 appeared as they slowed to a stop.

"You can talk." She slunk down into the seat, luxuriating in the soft fabric on her elbows.

Edwin flicked the signal lever and watched for an opening between cars. He then turned right, merging onto I-90 seamlessly.

Daphne thought about how nice and freeing it must be to drive. She could even remember the coolness of the steering wheel under her palms on her solo drive to the supermarket at sixteen. When she had arrived at Safeway, keys in hand like a grownup, she had been giddy with independence.

Edwin's words echoed inside her skull. He was right. She had given up driving because of a mistake, an accident. She had permanently grounded herself.

Daphne let her forehead rest against the glass. "I mean, if you want you can talk."

Edwin stirred in his seat. She liked how he had an undeniable energy. He had looked wrong before, sitting there like a statue. It was his nature to be moving, pacing. He was a thrumming livewire.

"I *am* sorry for what I said. I was being a dick." He glanced over his shoulder at her for the first time.

It relaxed her, to see his face emerge from the shadows. "No, I asked for it. And it was all true. You should go into psychology; you have an uncanny ability to understand people."

He laughed. "Thanks. Maybe it's just you I can understand." He returned his eyes to the road.

A wide smile surprised Daphne. It strained against her cheeks.

"Although what I said was maybe partly true, I also should have said it was brave what you did."

"Brave?"

"To come all the way out here to find out what happened for yourself. Willoughby, the people there, they don't like others. Also, if they knew you were Caroline's daughter, they could have gotten ugly. All these years later, it's still fresh for some. They think she got away with murder."

Daphne ground her left heel into a crumpled Big Gulp. "Maybe it was just stupid."

Edwin shook his head. "No. Definitely brave."

She sighed. "Except I'm running away."

"Anyone would."

They tunneled through the night.

They came upon a sign, lit by bulbs spiked into the grass below. Daphne stared at the image of two beer steins clinking together. A froth of bubbles cascaded down the side of one. The other had a drawing of a German girl in lederhosen. She had bouncy pigtails and a youthful grin. Her eyes reminded Daphne of the baby doll in Doris's upstairs hall. They were made to look human but held no life.

COME TO HISTORIC SONDERMAN'S TAVERNE!
OVER 30 GERMAN ALES ON TAP
BAVARIAN PRETZELS LIKE MOM USED TO MAKE
NEXT EXIT

"I've never been to a bar." She swiped absently at her aching ankle.

"What?" Edwin twisted his head to look at her. "Are you serious?"

"My mom's been dying for the last few years. Also, as you've pointed out, I don't drive."

He frowned. "Oh, right. Sorry."

"I've never been bowling, either. Or on a boat, even though I live near the ocean. I've never been on a rollercoaster or a motorcycle or even jumped on a bouncy castle . . . those look fun."

A pang of hunger knocked against her insides. It was a pleasant pain, much more welcome than her near-constant nausea.

"So, let's go." He clicked the turn signal.

"To the German place?"

"Yep. I'm going to buy you a dark beer, none of that Bud or Miller crap."

"Okay." The forceful smile returned, burning into her cheeks.

# 44

SONDERMAN'S TAVERNE WAS NESTLED into a bank of trees just off the highway. A gravel drive led down to its parking lot, where pickups and several semis were parked at odd angles on the unmarked dirt. It was a narrow trailer-shaped building draped with red and yellow lights. The colors of the German flag, Daphne noted as Edwin parked his Toyota.

He killed the engine. "Do you need help?"

"No." She swallowed. "I can walk. I just . . ." She didn't like the idea of going inside the roadside bar now that they were there. "I don't have my ID."

"I don't think this is the sort of place they care." Edwin opened his door and got out. He stretched his arms into the night air.

Daphne closed her eyes, attempting to will away the uncertainty beginning to bubble in her sensitive gut. It was time to do something different, to let life happen.

She stashed her suitcase under some of Edwin's trash to hide it from unsavory bar types and got out on wobbly legs. She was hungrier than she'd realized.

"Can you buy me a pretzel too?"

He nodded. His black hair was even darker than the sky around them. The red string lights shimmered across his face.

She followed him to the door. As Edwin reached for the handle, a man emerged. Loud modern country music spilled out. The man, barely of age, had a patchy orange beard and a *Game of Thrones* T-shirt with the wolfish symbol of House Stark covering his concave chest. He bobbed to the music, his bony shoulders going up and down like pistons.

"Excuse us." Edwin stepped out of the way.

The man, still bouncing, eyed Daphne. "Hey there." He spoke as though he knew her. "How are you?"

"I'm good." Daphne smoothed down her striped top, at once very conscious of how she must look after the longest day of her life. "How are you?"

"I was just leaving. Do you want to go to Amy's with me? It's girl's night; margaritas are half price. And the music is *so* much better."

Daphne opened her mouth to respond. Edwin looped his arm through hers. "She's good, dude."

The man shrugged. "Thought I'd ask." He held the door for them to enter and then danced away.

Daphne giggled. "You can't help yourself." They walked into the cramped bar, still arm in arm. Every stool around the L-shaped counter was occupied by various patrons, nearly all middle-aged men.

Edwin cocked his head. "I rescue. It's kind of my thing."

She liked the look of his arm in the crook of her elbow. "I guess that makes us a good team, then, since I need rescuing."

His head dropped lower. "Don't remember those things I said. Forget them."

At those words, Daphne was shot with a memory. Of the pain in her ankle, when something—

*Chomped!*

—caught on it. She had been on the stairs of the school, and it had been dark, and there had been a sudden bloom of agony.

She shuddered.

"You okay?" Edwin yelled over the clamor of the music and the conversations.

She nodded, tightening her grip around his bare arm.

"Here." He stopped and fished out a twenty from his *Star Wars* wallet with his left hand. "You order. Since it's your first time."

Daphne's heart raced. How silly she was! She was twenty-three years old. She should be able to walk into a bar with confidence. Yet she was an imposter. Everyone, she was certain, could tell she was a fumbling newbie.

"Um . . ."

"Push through here." Edwin pointed between two farmer-looking types planted on stools. "Say you want two beers, whatever's on tap that's an amber lager. And get a few pretzels with cheese." He let her go.

Daphne hesitated. Her mind outlined all the possible bad outcomes. What if the bartender asked for her ID? What if he blinked curiously at the notion of an "amber lager"?

Then Edwin set his hand on her shoulder and bent down until his lips skimmed her earlobe. "You have traveled through time," he whispered. "You got this."

Daphne was imbued with poise. She pushed herself between the stools and caught the bartender's attention with a casual wave. She ordered in an even voice, although her insides were vibrating with tension.

They carried their load back to a sticky table underneath a flashing *BIERGARTEN* sign.

She sat and devoured the first soft pretzel, not bothering to open the plastic cup of cheese dip.

"You can have mine too." Edwin pushed it toward her.

"No."

"Go on." He took the cap off the cheese and nudged it forward.

Daphne didn't argue further. Her stomach was begging for more doughy goodness.

He raised his glass mug to his lips and took a sip of beer. "Can I ask?"

"Hmm," she said between bites. "What?"

"What was she like? Your mom?"

She licked salt from her upper lip. "I don't know. When I was growing up, I thought she was so boring. She didn't spend time with me, really. After the accident, when I . . . you know, she kept trying to pretend it didn't happen. Even when she was diagnosed with cancer, she was always acting like it didn't matter. She wouldn't talk about anything. It's like she could willfully forget."

He scratched his chin. "When did you find out? Who she was?"

"A few weeks ago. Right before she died. It was our last talk. She said she didn't do it but . . ."

"But?"

"I don't know. I was here to prove her right. To make sure she hadn't really done such an awful thing, because I didn't think it was possible."

He leaned forward. "And now?"

Daphne stuck a finger into the liquid cheese and licked it off. "Even if she killed them, could I blame her? Or is it like what I did? Was it an accident, like lifting your foot off the brake?"

Edwin's mouth became a serious line. "Taking an axe to your family is not in the same category as what you did."

"Okay, but Willoughby. It has this power. It makes the ground beneath you shake, and it makes me—God, I saw things! Could it make people do things they don't mean?"

A whip-fast memory seized her like electricity, making her insides chatter. She saw that old woman, Hedda, shuffling beside something sinister. Whatever *it* was, her mind held a veil over it, like a pixelated bit of video.

As the memory evaporated, Daphne stared back at Edwin, whose eyebrows arched into a sharp V. She studied him as he considered her question. Everyone behind him—a large group chortling in the corner, an awkward pair on a date flipping through a karaoke song list, a silent man in a neon trucker hat—was different from him. Edwin seemed to have grown so accustomed to being the only person of color in a room that he didn't seem to notice it now. She thought of the bullies he had encountered in Willoughby and was filled with fury. Daphne suddenly wished she could go back in time to see him as a child, to comfort him, and to kick all the bad ones in their teeth.

"It could. It would go along with my research, that there are more tragedies in Willoughby than statistically expected. Way more. It's just hard to accept that a town—*a place*—could force someone's hand."

"Right. Yeah." Daphne looked down at the empty parchment paper, sad to see she had no more pretzel left. She drank a gulp of the beer. It tasted awful.

"No, huh?" He brushed his fingers through his thick hair, in his attractive way.

"It'll grow on me. I can tell." The first rush of alcohol traveled through her veins. "Edwin?"

"Uh-huh." He took another sip.

"The prom." Daphne's shoulders slumped at the memory "I saw an old woman. She shot teenagers. And herself."

He cleared his throat. "Hedda Steenson."

"Yes! Hedda! Why? I mean, why would I be shown that? Like the mill explosion. There must be a reason. Like your power, the shaking, it warns you."

An uneasy air flickered between them. She read a hesitance in his eyes, a desire to stay away from reality just a bit longer.

"I wrote a blog piece about it a few years ago. She was a retired teacher and, well, no one knows why, but she showed up and shot up the place."

"Do you know their names? The ones who died?" The compulsion to ask such a peculiar question surprised her.

"Uh . . . no." Edwin shrugged. He squinted at her, surely wondering the same thing she was.

*Why would their names matter?*

"I can pull up my article, though."

Daphne clapped her hands. "Oh, yes!"

He swiped across the screen, taking a few moments to find it.

"Okay." He read through it quickly. "Oh, here we go. It was five kids: Eugene Dewitt, Ruth Hart, Patricia Carlson, Irene Donahue, and Herbert Perry."

"Hart!" Daphne stomped her uninjured foot, causing a few patrons to glance in their direction.

"Hart?" Edwin looked up from his cell. "Who's that?"

"Remember?" She was giddy with the discovery. It meant something! It had to. "In that photograph, pretty much the only one we looked at before I lost that book. The men, it was Bergman, Shortall, Florence, Willoughby, and Hart!"

He sat back, his eyes darting from left to right as he processed what she was saying.

"You saw Francesca's body at the mill. And you saw the prom." He counted on his fingers.

"And *you* told me about Nick Shortall. How his dad killed him, and then shot himself."

Edwin pressed his thumbs into the corners of his eyes, clearly trying to find a connection, a reason.

"Did you write anything else about the victims? Ruth Hart, anything about her?"

Edwin scrolled through his article. "Ruth, seventeen, was said to be a songbird," he read. "She had designs on leaving Willoughby for Hollywood, to achieve her dreams of headlining studio musicals. Although she was orphaned by a tragic boating accident in which she lost both parents, Ruth was known to her friends as bubbly and optimistic."

"Oh my God." Daphne took another sip of the lager. She hoped it would calm the storm within.

"She was the last Hart, maybe?" Edwin chewed on his cheek.

"Just like Nick and his dad were the last Shortalls. Francesca the last Willoughby. And—"

"You." His breath hitched.

"Me. I'm the last Bergman."

*They all died in awful, untimely ways.*

They sat in silence for a beat. Daphne shook her head a few times, attempting to dissuade herself from making shaky connections. There was no reason the photo held any importance. And wasn't it to be expected that descendants of those men would both live in Willoughby, and die?

Yet there was a tinny, mouse-quiet voice inside her that assured her she was on the right path.

"I don't want to go to the Western Union," she blurted.

"Okay."

"And I don't want to go back to Willoughby."

He set the mug down. "Should we live here? In this biergarten?" He gestured to the flashing tube lights above.

She appreciated that he was making a joke. It buoyed her, held her up from the darkness threatening to pull her down.

Daphne smiled. "Maybe." She scooted her chair forward until their knees were touching.

It would be nice, she thought, to live there and eat pretzels for every meal. They could wash dishes and then lay beneath the counter, falling asleep to the steady, warring flash of blue inside and red and yellow outside.

It would be nice to live there and forget.

# July 13, 1982

SHE HAD CRAWLED INTO THE SHED. It was a comforting, shadowy tomb. The axe lay beside her, wrapped in a dusty woven blanket she had found in her hiding spot.

Caroline couldn't remember putting the blanket there. That musty hole provided, it seemed, whatever it was she would need.

She leaned her head back on the soft earth floor, sensing every bump of the ground on her skull. It was early yet, before her mother would patter down the stairs in her slippers and make a pot of bitter coffee. Then her father would rise. He would surely greet his wife with a scowl and a grumble. He was a fake man, a phony. Caroline wasn't even sure that if she split him down the middle, blood would spill out. She thought maybe he was stuffed with straw, like the Scarecrow in *The Wizard of Oz*. Although it was not a brain he was missing. It was, like that poor Tin Man, a heart.

The axe whispered to her.

"Yes." She stroked its sharp crescent blade. "I know."

Her mother knew too. Caroline could read it in her shifting eyes. Ida was a cornered animal, skittering away from the truth.

Caroline had been doing the same. She had made herself believe it was that slut Rosalee. That had made it better, for a while. To think her dad had been trapped in a tacky web of lust, unable to twist himself free.

But she knew the truth.

She fell asleep for a moment. She dreamed of paint—dripping, churning paint.

By the time she woke, the axe had escaped its blanket. It leaned against the whitewashed wall, as though it were spying through the loose slats.

". . . shh! Keep your voice down! Jesus!" A man's voice—her father's—filtered into the shed.

Caroline crawled toward the sound. She peeked through where the axe was looking. There were her father's hairy legs as he stood on the back steps. She could make out the bottom edge of his boxer shorts.

"You better get this under control!" a girl hissed.

*Tiffany,* the axe told her.

"I will! By ending this." Her father stepped down, and she could see the bottom of his belly in his white undershirt. It was heaving in and out.

"Ha!" Tiffany came into view. Caroline recognized her silver bangle and, of course, a glass bottle of Coke sloshing in her hand. "You keep saying that, over and over, after every time, and then you crawl back."

"No," her father's whisper sliced through the morning air. "No. Not again."

Tiffany laughed. It was a squeaky, humorless whistle. "Bullshit."

"Tell her you were kidding. Tell her anything, but not the fucking truth." His hand was a crimson fist.

"She's dumb enough." Tiffany swung the bottle. "But why lie? If we're gonna be together."

It was his turn to laugh. "That'll never happen. You must understand that much."

They stood silent. Caroline held her breath, listening.

*That bitch! Oh, that slutty, awful bitch!*

Caroline wrapped her hands around the axe to shut it up. To strangle out its words.

*You should do her first. Oh! Hack off those boobs, the ones your daddy likes to grab onto. Right, Caroline? RIGHT?*

*And don't forget Daddy, Mommy, and Kyle too! Everyone!*

She squeezed, grinding her nails into the wooden handle.

*No. I won't! I won't hurt anyone.* She spoke to the axe without opening her mouth. *I can't do that. I'll just forget, is all. Just make me forget. Please. Make me! Make me!*

DAPHNE WAS BUZZED on one mug of beer. She tingled with happiness.

"Well?" Edwin stood beside his Toyota, keys in hand. "Where to?"

They stood in the quiet parking lot of Sonderman's. Music and revelry thumped inside.

"Where do you live? I mean, when you're not helping at the motel?" She rested against the hood, giving her ankle a breather.

"Minneapolis, near the U. That's almost three hours away. Oh, and about that, I'm pretty sure my mom is going to fire me."

Daphne's brow furrowed. "Oh, no! Is it my fault?"

Edwin shrugged. "You brought me into all this, so technically . . ." His smile lit up his face.

She turned and looked up at the moon. Edwin had a way of making her feel at once very young and very mature. "I'm sorry. But you do love all this, don't you? Investigating and finding clues?"

He was beside her, drumming his fingers on the hood. "Is it obvious?"

"Yep." Daphne forced herself to continue staring at the moon. If she looked at his face, so very close, she would dive headfirst into his twinkling eyes like a drunken fool.

And she was just slightly buzzed.

"If only there were a rollercoaster nearby," he said, "so you could mark another first off your list."

She could sense the heat of his body and smell the musk of his skin. Her heart ballooned, pressing against her ribs. Her chest ached and quivered.

"I would probably be too afraid to get on." She lowered her gaze, pretending to find interest in picking at her thumbnail.

"No. I don't think so. Not anymore." He was right beside her, his knuckles grazing her thigh.

Daphne remembered the sensation of his breath on her ear when he had reminded her she was a time traveler of sorts. That she could do anything.

*You got this.*

She lowered her left hand until she touched his warm skin, threading her fingers through his. He let out a soft breath.

"Edwin?" She turned, despite herself. He looked upon her with shining affectionate eyes. It was difficult for her to speak with her heart bursting and rattling within her. "We can go back in the morning. I want to go back. I'm going to find out what happened, somehow, by figuring out how to see it. To see 1982 for myself."

"Good. That's good." He swallowed, and she knew his mind and body were abuzz. And she knew it wasn't the amber lager.

Daphne reached out with her right hand and clutched the side of his black T-shirt, pulling him closer. At that moment he seemed ten feet tall. There was no way she could close the gap between them on her own, even on tiptoe.

Edwin, flushed and breathing heavily, read her mind.

He pressed his forehead to hers.

Daphne reached up and curled her arms around Edwin's neck.

His hands ran up her sides, feather light, and landed on her cheeks. He stood back, regarding her with his firework eyes.

Edwin lifted her chin and kissed her. She recognized urgency from the pressure of his lips.

An incredible sense of belonging plucked at the chords of her soul.

She pushed her fingers into the hair at the nape of his neck. Since she had met him, she had craved the touch of those thick black strands.

Edwin pressed his body into her, causing her butt to grind into the front wheel well of the Corolla. She broke away from his lips to take a quick breath, and suddenly his hands were on her thighs as he lifted her up onto the hood.

They kissed deeply. Daphne held Edwin close, cinching her legs around him. She ignored the cry of her ankle and the faraway din of the German bar.

He pulled back, panting. "When you left . . ." He spoke huskily. "Everything shook, how it does, and I was so afraid. I thought something was going to happen to you."

She pawed at his chest. "I'm okay." She was petrified of everything, of even ordering beer on her own, yet she was not frightened by Edwin's touch and proximity.

The air was too cold between them.

Daphne hugged Edwin, pressing her ear against his heart. It thwacked unsteadily against his ribcage in the same jerky, nervous motion he used while pacing.

She was glad he shared in her jittery euphoria.

"If you go back tomorrow and try to see . . ."

"I will." She smelled peppermint and beer on his shirt.

"Then you have to promise," he whispered gruffly in her ear, "that you'll be safe, Daphne. Think about your ankle."

She closed her eyes, remembering the sharp pain in her vision that now throbbed here, in her real life and time.

An unnamed and invisible threat snaked across her memory.

# July 13, 1982

THE WALLS OF THE SLOPING SHED, the mocking axe, her trembling hands—everything was cloaked in a red, hot rage. It was as though she were looking through a shard of crimson glass.

Anger and pain squirmed inside her, threatening to push itself from her weak body.

"Tiffany?" she managed. "Tiffany? Psst!"

Her best friend, the girl she loved most in the world, halted in front of the door.

"Hey!" Caroline whispered.

"Carrie?"

"I'm in here."

She could see a swish of Tiffany's long brown hair as she looked over her shoulder toward the back steps.

Caroline's father had gone back inside the house.

The door creaked open. Tiffany stuck her face inside. "Carrie?"

"Yeah, c'mon."

Tiffany, dressed in jean shorts buttoned high on her waist and a lacy tank top, slipped into the darkened shed and closed the door carefully behind her.

Caroline glanced down and saw she was wearing the red high-top sneakers.

Vicious lightning flashed across her vision.

"What the fuck are you doing in here?" Tiffany still held a glass bottle of Coke.

Caroline ground her bare feet into the axe handle. "I'm standing on this, so it'll shut up already."

Tiffany blinked. "Is it talking?"

"Yes."

"You heard all that, didn't you? Your dad and me."

"Yes."

Tiffany let out a great big sigh.

"It's telling me to kill you." Caroline pushed down all her weight on the axe. It sunk deeper into the chalky dirt.

"Oh?" Tiffany gripped the neck of the Coke bottle so tightly, her knuckles faded to white.

Caroline nodded.

"Are you going to?"

"It's talking to me, right here." She tapped at the space between her eyebrows. "It's like my brain, but it's not me. It's the axe."

Tiffany gave a calm, measured nod. She set the Coke bottle down on a table littered with long-forgotten projects. "I hear talking, sometimes."

"Yeah?"

"Uh-huh. At night sometimes, when I go out to smoke on the curb or walk alone to . . . well, walk to see Gunnar."

*Gunnar! How easily she says his name.*

Caroline knelt. She ran her palm over the weapon.

Tiffany took a step back, the heels of her sneakers pushed into the rotting door.

"You know what, though?" Tiffany gulped in air. "It's not the axe, really. It's you."

"No."

"Yep." Her voice cracked. "Think about it, Carrie. The axe can't make you do something you don't already want to do. You hate me for what I did."

Caroline sunk down into the grime. She pulled the axe into her lap like a child.

"It can whisper to you. It can be like a friend, like . . . like a mom. It can help. But it can't make you be someone you're not."

Caroline concentrated on the dust motes between them, swimming in the shafts of light. "I don't hate you."

"Jesus! You must."

"I hate him."

Tiffany breathed in through her nostrils. "Well, yeah, you should. He's the monster you know. He's the real fucking monster."

"Her too." Caroline pinched her eyes closed, rocking with the axe.

"Her?"

"Ida." She had never referred to her mother that way. "She sits in her chair and punches a needle through cloth, and she just pretends. She knows. I know she knows. Ida just lets it all happen around her. She sits and forgets."

Tiffany's lip curled into a grimace. "Bitch."

They nodded in unison.

"I can't do it, though." A tear blazed down Caroline's cheek. "I want to. My heart wants to . . ." She didn't finish her thought aloud because, in that moment, it struck her how much like her mother she truly was.

*I can't do it because I'm frightened I won't forget. I'm terrified I'll remember it all.*

The anger clawed and thrashed. It could not be contained for long.

# 48

IT WAS THE SORT OF DREAM in which she knew she was dreaming. This, however, did not ease Daphne's mind.

She relived the prom of 1944 over and over. Every time she thrust herself at the old woman with the shotgun, she was spun back to the beginning. Then mercifully, she was let go. She stood, alone, on Main Street. Something was with her, trailing her, eating her thoughts and digesting them in its invisible stomach.

Then she was sixteen, and Beverly was beside her in the van. They were chattering about boys and nonsense. That same invisible force was pushing them backward. Until the sound, the one that haunted her with its squelching pop, thundered around them, as if amplified by a million speakers.

Daphne woke with a start, slamming her knees into the glove compartment.

"Shit!"

Edwin stirred beside her. "You okay?"

Early morning light filtered in through the windows.

Daphne rubbed her tired eyes, surprised by the wetness on her lashes. "What if I go back to the wrong place? What if I see what happened in Bellingham? Over and over? See Oscar. And I know I'd try to stop it every time. Even though I can't. I'd try even though it's just like pictures in a book. That's what that guy says to the boy in *The Shining*. Have you seen it? He says it's like looking at pictures in a book."

"No." Edwin sat up in the reclined driver's seat. "I don't know how this works, but I think it probably only functions in Willoughby. Seeing Willoughby."

She curled toward him. "I don't want to see the murders, either, but I have to."

"I understand. I do. If I could go back and see what happened to Kasey, I would. And I would try to save her too, even though I couldn't . . ." He drifted off in thought.

"But if you actually had the ability to intervene," he added, "like I said, you shouldn't." He wiped a tear from the side of her nose. "You must know about the butterfly effect."

"Of course. I know."

"And what if by saving that boy, you killed more people?"

Daphne looked down at her hands. She would sacrifice her life for that boy. She would trade places with him in a heartbeat. Yet Edwin was right. If she could affect the past, if she played with time and cause and effect, she would put more people, possibly more children, in harm's way.

So whether or not she could affect the past didn't matter. She couldn't be a time traveler, just a time observer.

"That ankle is proof, though, that you can get hurt in your visions. Somehow."

Daphne sniffed in some tears and pulled the lever on the side of the passenger seat up to get it into a sitting position.

"Listen, I've been doing some research while you were snoring." Edwin chuckled.

Daphne rolled her eyes. "Yeah?"

"I found the obituaries of the teens who died at the prom." He handed her his phone.

Daphne glanced down at a black-and-white article. It was from an Otter Tail County archive site.

A young boy posed for a formal photograph. His hair was combed neatly, and he had a distinctive gap between his two front teeth.

### HERBERT PERRY
#### *1928–1944*

*Herbert, beloved son, has been called to Heaven. Services to be held at Willoughby Lutheran on the 29th of May. Herbert is missed by his classmates and fellow team members of the Willoughby Millers and, most of all, by his devoted mother, Amelia (Florence) Perry.*

An image of a cracked-open skull with escaping brains caused Daphne to shiver. "He's a Florence."

Edwin took his phone and slipped it back into his jeans pocket. "It matters. I don't know why." He shrugged. "But I think it does."

"I think so too."

"I think it means you're in danger. That the descendants of those men . . . that Willoughby—or someone or some *thing* there—doesn't want you alive."

Daphne wondered if the cancer in her mom's brain wasn't so random after all.

Edwin placed his hand on her knee. "I wish I could go with you into your vision or hallucination." He bit his lip, staring out at the wall of trees.

She wished he could too. She had no control of when and where she was sent to, and certainly not who came with. It seemed Willoughby would decide whether to let her see that which she so desperately wanted to witness.

*Or did she have a way to force it along?*

That deep, intoxicating yearning to run returned.

A painful memory came too. It was of that foolish teenage discussion she and Beverly had been having moments before she became a murderer.

They had wanted to run to Mexico, away from research papers and parents. They had wanted to drive the open road, free and untethered.

"Eddie?" She grinned.

He chuckled. It was a sweet, innocent sound. "Ugh, yes, Daffy?"

That was her mother's pet name for her when she was little—and at the very, very end.

"I want to drive. Now, I mean, if you'll help me."

His relaxed smile tightened into a questioning purse of his lips. "Definitely. You don't need my help, though; you already know how."

Daphne got out of Edwin's car and stretched her sore muscles. They were parked about four miles down the winding gravel road from Sonderman's at a makeshift campsite. They had chosen it for its encapsulating shield of trees. It seemed to be preferred by locals, as it abutted a twinkling brook and was littered with several soggy firepits and loads of beer and soda cans.

Edwin joined her at the trunk.

"Can you make sure there's nothing here?" Daphne squatted and looked between the back tires. "Please?" The only conceivable way to exit was by reversing. If she went forward, they would crash into a pile of lumber.

He gave a somber nod.

Daphne stood and extended her hand.

He set the keys in her palm.

A hairy, monstrous dread scurried up her spine.

"I don't want you to stand there, though." She ran her thumb over the serrated edge of the Toyota key.

Edwin planted a kiss on top of her head. "Get in and start up the engine. I'll make sure no one . . . and nothing is behind you, okay?"

Daphne got into the driver's seat. It was still warm from Edwin's slumbering body. How strange, she thought as she tested the firmness of the brake pedal, to be sitting on this side of a car.

She adjusted the rearview mirror to her liking and strapped herself in.

"Step away, okay?" she called through the open door. "I'm going to turn it on." She couldn't have him standing at the bumper like that, not with the engine going. Just the thought made her shudder.

Edwin obeyed, giving the car a wide berth. "Go ahead." He was to her left, watching from the tangled grass.

"There's nothing back there?"

"Nope, I have a good view. There's nothing."

As Daphne slipped the key into the starter and twisted, a pleasant realization came to mind. Her stomach didn't ache. Aside from hunger the night before, it hadn't flopped or fizzled.

She had even gone without the soothing taste of mint on her tongue.

Daphne exhaled as the engine came to life.

"Okay, jump in." She beckoned to Edwin. "If there's nothing there."

He shook his head. "Nothing." He skipped over the pile of logs in front of the car and got into the passenger side.

Daphne closed her door.

"Let's go to Willoughby." Edwin's smile had a hint of sorrow as he clicked in his seatbelt.

"My foot is on the brake, right?" She knew it was, but she needed him to say it.

"Yep."

Her hand shook as she clutched the gearshift. She stared at the R with intensity.

"Here we go," she breathed.

Daphne pulled the gearshift into reverse and inched the car backward, keeping her eye behind her and her foot pulsing the brake.

"Once we hit the gravel, you're going to steer us to the left," Edwin instructed.

A bead of sweat popped from her brow. Her armpits, too, were clammy. Every few seconds, she wanted to thrust the car into park and give up.

She wished for her quilt from her basement bedroom, to throw over her head and hide.

The crunch of the gravel sent a shockwave through her cells. At first, when she heard the tire scraping, she was certain she had hurt someone. Then she let the delusion dissipate. It was an ugly thought that deserved to be shredded and thrown away.

Daphne steered them up onto the road and pushed the gearshift to the *D*.

It was time to drive.

# 49

## Doris

DORIS WOODHOUSE AWOKE, cheerful to be alive. At her age, every morning, every meal, and every cogent moment was a gift.

She peeked around her bedroom to make certain she was alone and then began the arduous process of her morning routine. Her joints cracked like bubble wrap as she shuffled down the corridor in her terrycloth robe to her bathroom.

Just as Doris placed her wizened hand on the brass knob, there was a terrible racket downstairs.

"All right!" She knew it was Edwin. He had a quick, anxious way of moving. His uneven knocks peppered her front door.

Doris circumvented the bathroom and made her way down the curving staircase to the main floor. She gripped the rail with each step.

Finally, she reached the door and unlocked the knob.

Edwin and his friend—Doris could not recall her name—burst into her front hall.

The girl was buzzing with a sort of prideful, draining energy, like she had just run a marathon or slain a dragon.

"Doris, sorry, did we wake you?" Edwin squeezed her shoulder a touch too roughly.

"Nah, but my bladder is as tight as a drum. May I?" Doris gestured to the powder room down the corridor by the kitchen.

"Yeah, yeah, go. Sorry."

Doris wiggled her nose, pretending to be inconvenienced. The truth was, she was overjoyed to have Edwin visit. He lived away, in the city, and she missed his warm soul in the winters. She tried to convince him every summer to stay for good, but he didn't see the beauty of Willoughby. Not like she could.

She padded off to the bathroom. Everything was a production at her ungodly age. Just sitting on the toilet required a Herculean effort.

As she sat on the cold porcelain, waiting for the last squirts, she held her breath. Her ears were pretty decent most of the time, so she could hear Edwin and the girl. Caroline's girl.

They were developing a whole plan. A lethal one.

Doris scrunched her gray eyebrows together in concern.

*Foolish children.*

She flushed, pulled up her cotton panties, and washed her hands with lavender soap, all while figuring out the best way to help them.

". . . then you hide. Wherever you go, you hide. Keep thinking about your ankle. That you can get hurt," Edwin finished as Doris stepped into the front parlor.

Doris twiddled her translucent fingers. "Hide. That's amusing."

The girl, a petite thing with her mother's round cheeks, cleared her throat. "Doris, can you help me? I want to go back and see who murdered my family."

"I believe I told you before." The old woman plopped down in her favored chair. She tucked the edges of her robe together for modesty. "You're alone in this. Just as I am alone in mine, and Edwin as well."

The girl and Edwin shared a suspicious glance. "There isn't anything you can tell me?"

Doris rubbed at her temples. There was much to tell. So much so that she often felt her brain was flooding with memories. She swam through them, over them, under them—navigating as best she could.

How could she make this girl understand? Even Edwin grappled to comprehend Willoughby, and he had been in its orbit since he was a child.

Her mind was relatively clear that morning, which made Doris grateful. "Does it matter who killed your grandparents and your young uncle?"

"Yes." The girl stood by the unlit hearth. The gauze on her ankle had unspooled, catching on the heel of her thong sandal. "It matters to me."

Doris attempted to outline her thoughts before they flitted away like dandelion puffs on a strong breeze.

"I cannot help you get where, or rather when, you are going. Just as you cannot help me speak to the dead." At the mention of this, there was a familiar icy intrusion in her beloved home. Someone was lurking about. "In order for you to fully conceive of what you are doing, I must tell you this: Willoughby does not impose its will. It has no will of its own. It is a place."

They both blinked at her, unbelieving. She empathized with their disbelief; it was easy, at first, to see Willoughby as inherently evil.

"What I'm saying is that Willoughby itself has no mean intention."

"Ha!" Edwin paced the room.

"My husband, Franklin, was born and died here. He was a lovely man, a doctor who treated those who couldn't pay. He complimented me every day and never once raised his voice in anger." Doris got lost, for a moment, in good memories. "Dear." She turned her creaky body toward the girl. "Don't you agree, there are decent people in Willoughby? Your mother, she loved you."

The girl—*woman*, Doris corrected herself—was straining to hold the tears in her wet eyes. "Yes."

"And this man here, Edwin Monroe, you love him?"

Both Edwin and the woman gave nervous, high-pitched laughs.

*Daphne. Her name is Daphne.*

"Um . . . uh-huh. Yes." Daphne glanced at Edwin from the corner of her eyes. Her cheeks burned rosy pink.

Doris chuckled inwardly at their coyness.

*Foolish, foolish children.*

"So you must admit, we are not all bad."

"True," Daphne agreed.

"But so many awful things have happened here. Murders, bizarre accidents, pain. We're a town of a few hundred." Edwin raked a hand through his hair. "Moira just died. She was one of the good ones."

Doris tapped her slipper on the floor. "Yes. Willoughby, in part, is to blame. It's just a bad piece, though, a rotten tooth."

"In part?" Daphne grasped the mantelpiece as though she were aboard a rollicking ship.

Doris cracked a thin smile. "It only means to help."

The young people shared another glance. They thought she was off, drowning deep down in her dementia. If only they could see into her clear and level head.

Then Daphne gasped. "You said last night that Willoughby is like a mother."

"Did I? That's rather clever of me, yes." Doris patted her belly. She wanted some peanut butter toast.

Edwin stopped and grasped the back of a Victorian, high-backed chair. "I'm confused, Doris."

The old woman was growing weary of their pointed stares. "The bad people and the weak people—their thoughts are the loudest, don't you see? The ones who wish chaos upon the Earth. And it is this combination of the bad and the weak that is the most potent and dangerous." She straightened her back against the chair. "All you can see, from your side of it, is the death. The others—they are assuaged, comforted. They appreciate the rules, enforced with cruelty, and the forgetting. The forgetting is for the good and the bad, because Willoughby is a rather coddling sort of mother."

At this, Doris could sense the fracturing of her thoughts. She slumped forward and took in a gulp of air. "Remember this, if you go seeing back in time. It is the bad and the weak who cry the loudest."

Edwin crossed the room and wound his arm around Daphne's.

Doris was cloudy inside, stormy. She needed tea and toast. It was all she could think of: the crunch of the bread and the steam of the drink. "I'm famished. You may clean yourselves upstairs, if you like. After toast, perhaps, I'll check your ankle, if you don't run off too quickly."

"Thank you," Daphne replied in a tinny yelp.

Doris left them in the parlor. On her lumbering way from the front of the manor to the back galley, she forgot they were even there.

# 50

AFTER THEY SHOWERED, Doris gave them the keys to the murder house. There were no scheduled tours, and she was rather zapped of energy.

"Dear?" She stopped them as they crossed her vast front lawn. Her age-flecked eyeballs concentrated on Daphne. "Do be careful."

Still brimming with the heady zeal of her drive, Daphne waved in agreement. Once she had parked at the curb in front of the mansion, she had been imbued with a jittery invincibility. It was still there, stroking the flames of her determination.

There was no way to know if being in proximity to the house would work. She had gone there before, and nothing had happened.

Yet she had to try.

As they stepped inside her mother's childhood home, Doris's cautionary words came back to her. She carefully rolled her injured ankle, questioning all that she knew about reality. If she could be injured in a vision, could she be killed?

And who would be doing the killing? Not whoever split her family open with an axe. That was impossible. But maybe an interloper, like her?

Edwin strolled into the living room—a shrine to the past. "I was thinking that when we were in here before, getting the tour from

296

Doris, that that must have been difficult. I mean, to stand here and listen to what happened to your family. And to keep it a secret, about Caroline being your mom."

It took Daphne a moment to ground herself. The walls, the shag rug, the tube TV, everything around her had been touched by her mother. "I shouldn't have lied." She rubbed her belly. The relentless threat of vomit was coming back, full force. "I just . . . I'm so fucking scared that if she *is* to blame, if she did do all this, then there is this unavoidable snag in my, um, DNA. Like, in a way, I *am* her."

He paced, poking his head into the kitchen and then returning to Daphne. "My birth parents rolled me up in a towel and left me in the back dumpster of a Bibimbap restaurant. I was two months old. They could have brought me to an orphanage, or even left me inside the place. But they threw me out." His nostrils flared with anger. "I'm not them. I'll never be them. We become who we are by the choices we make."

Daphne turned his words over. Was she just imagining, then, the tether between herself and the home she stood in?

They walked together, from room to room. Daphne was prepared at any moment to slip away into the tunnel. She stared at random objects, willing herself to go. She wanted to get it over with, to rip off the Band-Aid. That is, if Willoughby would allow her to see what she wanted. There was no guarantee.

Doris had helpfully wrapped up her ankle and given her a dose of antibiotics from an old-looking prescription bottle. And Edwin had slipped a pearl-handled folding knife into the back pocket of her jeans, mumbling about how it probably didn't make sense to bring a weapon into a vision but that it couldn't hurt to try.

Edwin patted the arm of the sofa. "You should lie down, in case it comes on quickly. You could bang your head or something."

Lying down in the hot room and listening to the tick of the clock sounded like torture.

She suddenly needed fresh air and space.

They walked into the kitchen.

"I'm going to go outside. Alone." They gazed out the back

kitchen window at the overgrown field of wildflowers. It was where Doris had told them young Kyle had been found.

Edwin twitched, visibly resisting the urge to argue. He hopped from foot to foot as though standing on hot coals and not pea-green linoleum.

"Do you feel anything?" she asked.

His face softened. He glanced down at his feet and then up again, right into her eyes. "I—"

"I mean, shaking? Like your warning thing?"

His shoulders dropped. "No."

"Maybe it won't happen at all, then. It seems random." But she'd already begun to recognize the hypnotic pull of ghostly fingers, urging her outside.

Daphne unlocked the back door and pushed through the screen on squeaky hinges. She glanced over her shoulder at Edwin.

It was undoubtedly the quintessential moment to say something kick-ass.

She only smiled, though, to assure him everything was okay. That she would be back.

Which she only half believed. The itch of her wound reminded her she was not invincible after all.

Edwin pulled both hands through his hair, grasping the ends in obvious frustration.

Daphne turned, letting the screen smack shut behind her. She hurried down the cracked stone steps. There was a dilapidated shed in the corner of the square yard and a short fence made of faded whitewashed wood between the Bergman property and the wild field that edged the forest.

The world wavered around Daphne. It became a surreal painting of lopsided objects and wheels of color.

Willoughby was giving her what she wanted.

She lurched forward, stumbling into the waist-high fence. It was easy to pull herself over—something, an unseen force, was helping her along.

Panic scratched inside her. She had forgotten something. A vital something that was more significant than what she had come to see. It was deadlier than a rusty axe. Yet as she tripped into the narrowing tunnel around her, she still couldn't remember.

Night slapped her in the face. It was cool and moist, like the spray of the ocean at Locust Beach in Bellingham.

"I'm in Minnesota," Daphne murmured to herself in an attempt to steady her mind.

Towering weeds tickled her wrists. She crouched down, waiting for her eyes to adjust to the black sky.

The nip in the air caused the fair hair on her arms to rise. She tasted the familiar, comforting flavor of autumn on her lips: smoke and the sweet tang of decaying leaves.

The brief moment of ease was fleeting, leaving Daphne alone on the surface of an alien world. She stood on tingling legs, surveying Willoughby by the light of the witch's moon. Her mom's childhood home had disappeared, as though the earth had opened its rotten, clammy mouth and eaten it up. All the other houses too.

Daphne squinted, spotting a flickering gaslight where she knew Main Street had been. A few structures hulked in the blackness.

She took in a deep breath, allowing the chill to invigorate her body.

Willoughby had chosen to bring her here, to show her an empty field in the night.

There had to be a reason.

Daphne glanced down at her sandals. She wiggled her toes, mesmerized by the magnitude of her vision. She was not there, not really, yet she tasted the air and heard the far-off whinny of a horse.

A rustling in the thick grass behind her made Daphne swivel around. Her heart pounded against her chest as she tried to silently remind herself that there was nothing that could harm her. This was a vivid movie, a sort of virtual reality.

But the adrenaline coursing through her said there was reason to be frightened.

The silhouette of a man appeared several yards away against the backdrop of the night. His long arms swung like pendulums as he ran across the open field. A derby hat fluttered off his bald head, swirling up on a gust of wind and settling in the brush.

Daphne watched as the man scurried across the landscape. He was breathing roughly, wheezing as he made a sharp left, heading toward a line of pines.

"Hey!" she yelled at his back. "Your hat!" It was a test. To see if she could affect the world in any way.

*To see if you can change it all. Take away the axe. Take away the minivan.*
She could not.

The man continued, practically tripping down a decline into the mouth of the forest.

Daphne hesitated, wondering if Willoughby was telling her to follow him. Or if she should investigate what he was running from.

Instinct told her to follow, to flee as he fled.

She stepped forward, her feet sinking into the soft dirt.

Another man shouted from where the first had run from. "Hart! You twit!"

Someone guffawed—a rumbling, enjoyable sound.

The fear in Daphne lessened. She was happy to see the glimmer of a swinging gas lamp in a man's hand.

It illuminated the field, creating a warm glow on the faces of the group forming in the knee-high weeds.

They looked like actors, dressed in costume and ready for a community theater production.

The man holding the lamp had a sizable belly straining the buttons of his old-fashioned waistcoat. He plucked at his moustache with his free hand, considering the night.

Daphne trembled, unable to comprehend that these men were from a time so long ago. Unlike the 1940s, where she could recognize a similarity to her own era, she was witnessing what she could only process as fiction.

The man beside the lamp bearer wore a wry smile, the apples of his cheeks pressed into his eyes.

*Frankly, my dear, I don't give a damn.*

The recognition shot through her. It was him! Not Clark Gable, but his sandy-haired doppelganger, Calvin Bergman.

Daphne studied the suspenders across Calvin's barrel chest and the severe cut of his chin, trying to make sense of the idea that she shared his blood. That he was her ancestor.

More than just their shared genetics, she recognized, as the light cast sharp shadows across Calvin's bristly eyebrows, that he was not good. That this group of men, carousing about in the blackness of a rural field, held no good intentions.

Finally, her eyes adjusted and focused on the man in the center. He stood before the others, his bony hands on his hips in a rather feminine stance. Daphne would recognize that weasel face anywhere: Fred Willoughby.

His top lip was stuck in a perpetual sneer as the others chuckled beside him.

"It can't hurt us!" Calvin bellowed toward the forest.

"Hush!" Fred pivoted and pinched Calvin's shoulder. "Let us not wake the town."

Calvin cleared his throat as he nodded his obeisance.

Daphne tiptoed closer to the men. There was no need to hide herself in the shadows, but they gave her a sense of protection, like wrapping herself in her trusty quilt back home.

They stank of skunky beer, cigars, and body odor. She gave a little thank you to the universe for allowing her to live in the twenty-first century where men smelled like Edwin: pleasant and washed.

"We're gonna find him in the morn halfway up a tree with piss in his trousers!" The man on the end, skinny with wiry white hair, doubled over in a coughing laugh.

Fred pushed the spectacles up his beaklike nose. "Don't be crass."

Self-conscious, the white-haired man straightened up.

"Where d'ya suppose it went off to?" The man holding the lamp scratched at his mole-speckled neck.

"Hart?" Calvin whispered.

"Nah, not that sissy! *It*, the . . . the, you know!"

Fred's shoulders stiffened. "That is no matter. It knows what to do, and it will stay within the confines of Willoughby. I made certain of that."

The men shared a conspiratorial look that turned Daphne's blood to ice.

"All right, should we go farther in?" Calvin gestured toward the tunnel of darkness where Hart had disappeared. "Into the woods yonder?"

Fred Willoughby gave an exasperated sigh. "That will not be necessary." He scanned the field, his rat eyes looking right through Daphne.

She shuddered at his gaze.

"Here, then?" White hair pointed to the ground.

"Not too deep." Fred walked away from the others, toward Daphne. She instinctually took a few steps backward, uncomfortable with his proximity.

Calvin and the plump man holding the lamp turned and bent down to pick up something behind them.

"We'll take good care." The man gave a hearty sneeze into the crux of his arm. "We assure you, Dr. Willoughby."

"Of course." Fred removed a handkerchief from the inner pocket of his pearl-gray coat. For the first time, Daphne could see that he held a leather-bound book close to his chest. The pages were edged in sparkly gold. "I must return home to Mrs. Willoughby. She detests when I'm not punctual." He wiped one side of his glasses with the handkerchief in a deliberate circular motion.

"What we did." Calvin began rolling a wheelbarrow into the shards of light. "It was good. It will be *good* for Willoughby."

The other men nodded in agreement.

It was an eerie movement, as though they were connected by an invisible string.

"We are in control, gentlemen. Our blood." Fred sniffed the air.

"I will leave you. Don't lollygag. I really do not like men out of doors past nine o'clock. It demonstrates a severe lack of decorum."

"Yes, sir." Calvin stopped the wheelbarrow. A beam of gaslight danced on the contents inside.

At the sight, Daphne grabbed her arms, wrapping herself in a violent hug. A hiccuping shriek climbed out of her throat.

A woman's legs were draped over the side of the wheelbarrow. They dangled there, jiggling from Calvin's movement. Daphne's eyes ran up the length of the woman's pale calves, and the rivulets of blood that descended onto the grass beneath.

The men's whispering conversation left Daphne's ears as she stepped forward to get a better look.

An inner admonishment came to her, that she was being a rubbernecker, one of those vile people who had come to watch when Oscar had died. They had stared and goggled and gossiped.

Daphne forced down her shame and took a good, lingering glance at the corpse. Willoughby, after all, had chosen her to see.

The young woman was freshly dead. A touch of pink remained in her sloping cheeks and at the end of her button nose. Her eyes were mercifully closed.

She could almost be asleep, if not for the offending gash in her abdomen. Her white nightgown, still buttoned primly at her chin, became a muddled mess at her center.

Blood oozed into the wheelbarrow, creating a grim-looking bath.

The men worked to shovel into the earth several feet away, yet Daphne could not take her eyes off the ragged hole in the woman.

She thought first of a violent C-section. The edges of the nightgown where the cavernous hole had been made were blackened. It was more like something had burst forth, like the woman had swallowed a bomb in a cartoon.

All Daphne's horror transformed into a clinical fascination. *How? Why?*

Calvin's deep voice interrupted her thoughts. "We'll toss it in as well, right on top a'her. It's better that way." He leaned on a shovel, pointing toward something in the darkened weeds.

Daphne pinched her nose as she caught the first whiffs of the dead woman's bloody stomach. She shuffled to the side, trying to see what Calvin was referring to.

The man with the wiry white hair wiped a dribble of sweat from his top lip. "Where did Hart get off to?"

"He ran off like a sissy boy, don't you recall, Florence?" The fat man adjusted the lamp closer to the hole in the dirt. "Scared of . . . something or other."

"Nah." The white-haired man shook his head. "I seem to be forgettin'."

Daphne trembled. Her hands fell to her sides as she finally saw what Calvin intended to include in the makeshift grave. It was *the* axe, blood tinged and not as rusty as it was in 2017.

It waited.

A patchwork of thoughts tried to sew themselves together in Daphne's mind.

These men had used that axe to help something along. Something that had come out of that woman, something that had clawed its way out.

And that thing, Daphne was certain, was skittering around the woods.

A smell—a pungent punch of death and rot—assaulted her, replacing the sharp, acidic scent of the woman's blood.

Daphne slumped down, tasting the familiar slick of saliva that came before she puked.

A memory, like a kernel stuck in her back tooth, ached to be free.

Needles. Needle teeth.

A growl tore through the night.

Then, suddenly, sunlight came, as bright as the gates of Heaven. Brilliant white light burned into her corneas.

Daphne curled into a fetal position.

Birds sang.

"Daphne!" A kind, worried voice enveloped her like a hug. She reached for Edwin. He held her, imbuing her with his infectious energy.

She raised her head and sat up in one fluid motion.

"Hey." Edwin cupped her chin. "That was longer, maybe ten minutes."

She nodded. "I better say it all, before I forget."

"Okay, yeah, did you see? The murderer?" He helped her to stand.

Daphne studied the squat, working-class house that was her unwanted birthright.

"I saw a very long time ago." They hoisted themselves over the fence, still arm in arm. "I . . . I think maybe 1890, or around there?"

"Holy shit," Edwin breathed.

"The men from the picture, they were all there." She pressed her sandals into the grass. It was just as real as her hallucination.

They turned to each other, holding hands.

"They made a thing; they created a . . . a mean, evil thing."

His eyebrows twitched. "What?"

"I don't know. The axe was there, the same one. I know it was the same, just newer. And they were all together—Fred and Calvin and all the rest—and they killed a woman."

"God."

"I don't know if she's important, whoever she is. But they used her, I think." Daphne rubbed her belly, not wanting to burden Edwin with the violent image.

"They used her?"

"Something came out of her, like a baby. But not." She bit her lip, shaking with happiness to be back in the warm spring sun.

She could see her disjointed story was confusing him.

Abruptly, he sucked in a deep breath and tightened his grip on her hands. "When you were lying there, I kept thinking . . . I'm such a chickenshit."

"What?"

"I should've said, just in case . . . I should've said, about earlier . . . about what Doris asked you . . ."

Now Daphne was confused.

"I know she put you on the spot, about me." His eyes locked onto hers. "Just know, I have those feelings for you too."

A delicious fire singed her cheeks. "Thank you." It was an awkward response, but sincere.

They shared a silent moment.

Suddenly, Daphne realized she was panting as a memory from her frightening vision struck through her.

"Something else." She looked over Edwin's shoulder, out onto the sea of wildflowers. "Fred said that whatever they did, or made, they had control over it. Their blood."

Edwin considered this, his brown eyes shifting back and forth will all the information.

"I know what that means." Daphne couldn't help the tears that spilled out swiftly down the sides of her nose. There was a goodness in Willoughby! And it had shown her what she needed so eagerly to know.

She could finally read understanding in Edwin's expression.

"You're the last," he said.

She let go of his warm grip. "And I'm the only one who can stop it."

# 51

DAPHNE AND EDWIN SPENT the day on the murder house's front lawn. She couldn't handle the inside; the air was dusty, and she could see her mom in every bauble and nick of wood.

She had taken a long nap, curled up with Edwin, unable to stop the exhaustion the vision had given her.

Once she had awakened, they sat watching the sun fall, and she remained constantly vigilant, aware that at any moment Willoughby could beckon her to see more.

Edwin kept one arm behind her, unconsciously she guessed, so that he might catch her if she fainted.

For hours they repeated all that they knew, which wasn't much.

"There's something we're forgetting." He pushed the heels of his sneakers against the cemented edge of the front path.

"It's what they made. I think . . ." She searched her memories. "I think it's supposed to be forgotten. It's a bad thing, I know, and it can't leave Willoughby. He said that."

"Fred Willoughby?"

"Uh-huh. I don't know if it can hurt me." She picked at the gauze at her ankle. "He said it couldn't hurt them, and he implied their family too."

"But it did that to you."

She swallowed.

"And it got people to die, somehow."

Daphne raised her head, taking in the beauty of the stars pushing through the twilight. She could sense the pull again, like the centrifugal force of a swing.

She patted his wrist. "I'm going to lie down."

"You're feeling it? You think you're going under again?"

*Under.*

She liked that way of describing it. It was like crawling under— underneath Willoughby.

"Yeah."

He kissed her forehead. She wished she could truly forget all of this. That they could run away.

And then she was alone.

She was still in the Bergman's front yard.

It was hot, summer hot, making the armpits of her eyelet lace blouse wet.

Daphne took in a deep breath, praying to keep her stomach contents where they belonged.

She jumped to her feet, listening for a clue as to when Willoughby had brought her mind, her senses, to see. Daphne cautiously made her way to the sidewalk.

A flash of sunlight rocked her back on her heels. It was intensely hot, causing the sweat gathered in her already clammy armpits to drip down her sides.

Daphne took in a breath, urging herself to be calm. It was hard not to feel like an object, like one of Doris's dead-eyed baby dolls, thrust about at the whim of a child. The summer day, not unlike the spring one she had been plucked from, revealed itself around her.

A muffled song grew louder. John Mellencamp's husky voice swirled about her, describing the pains of love.

She turned to see a Ford station wagon gliding down Oak. A man's fat elbow was propped in the open window. His head nodded to the beat of the song, jiggling his jowls.

As he passed, Daphne leaped forward and caught a glimpse of

the inside of the car, hoping for another clue to the date. On the passenger seat, next to a crumple of newspaper, was a sparkling empty bottle of Coke. It had the insignia of the Iowa Hawkeyes.

*1981 Big 10 Champions*

Before she could place the memory, her stomach tensed like a fist.

Was it 1981?

The murder house loomed beside her. The windows were blank eyes, and the small front porch was a gaping mouth.

She remembered a Coke bottle in the night, moved by invisible cords.

"No." Daphne wiped at the bangs sticking to her forehead.

It was not 1981.

It was the morning of July 13, 1982. She knew this as she knew her own name. It was a certainty. She knew this in a cavernous, shadowy place of her mind that was not wholly her own.

Her pulse pounded in her ears and the back of her throat itched. At least, she reassured herself, she would not have to worry about being axed. No one would see her. She could observe as one who watches a film or flips through a grizzly photo album.

The trip up the porch steps was interminable. She licked the stale roof of her mouth, struggling to keep herself from vomiting.

Mints would have been nice.

The front door opened easily.

Daphne stepped inside. A cuckoo clock ticked on the wall beside a hutch holding various glass and porcelain figures. It looked similar to how Doris had arranged the home, although there was more clutter, more clues of life. There were backpacks hung on hooks and a forgotten stitch work on the arm of a chair.

A woman appeared from the kitchen. She had young skin but haggard eyes. Just like the people in the other visions, she didn't see Daphne standing in her living room. They were only four, perhaps five feet apart.

It was Ida, her grandmother. Daphne knew this without ever seeing her picture. She would have been beautiful if not for the severe wilt of her mouth. Her light hair, much the same color as Daphne's, was rolled into a bun at the top of her head and covered with a mesh cap. She wiped her hands on the sides of her silken robe and turned her back to Daphne as she placed her bare foot on the bottom stair.

"Ida?" Daphne asked to test her surroundings.

Her grandmother didn't answer. Instead, she disappeared upstairs without a hint that she'd noticed the interloper, her watcher.

Daphne quaked. It had all been theories, names, dates, ideas. Now . . . it was real. Ida Bergman was flesh and bone. She was her grandmother.

"I don't want to see. I—can you take me back? Wake me up?" Daphne politely requested of the imperceptible force that had brought her there. She buried her face in her hands, regretful of more than just her foolish bravado. She was sorry to have ever come to Willoughby, to stumble into its gnashing maw.

Into its needle teeth.

Then came a squeak. It was a hesitant sound, drawing out much too long.

Daphne looked up. It came from the kitchen, from the screen door she had pushed through herself decades later.

Footsteps scraped upstairs as her grandparents readied themselves for a day they would not live through.

Someone tiptoed across the linoleum.

Daphne sniffed the air, pleased for some reason to not smell the putrid scent of death and soft, rooted earth.

The sharp wedge of the axe came into the living room first. Daphne skidded backward, holding a hand over her mouth.

A girl came next, holding the heavy tool with both hands. Her dark eyes were glassy marbles.

Daphne had never known such beautiful relief. She was soaked in the welcome acknowledgment of righteousness. Her mother was not the Minnesota Borden.

Tiffany was.

The waitress was a few pounds lighter and quite a few years younger, but it was definitely her. Her beady gaze crossed over Daphne as though she were made of air. She stepped cautiously toward the stairs, her large breasts heaving in and out.

A creak sounded at the top of the staircase.

Daphne bit her thumb, trying to figure out how to stop what she was about to witness.

A man's feet thudded down the stairs rather swiftly.

The girl dug her nails into the wooden handle.

"Tiffany? What in the—"

Time slowed, as though they were all trapped in a viscous jelly.

An image of green snot hitting linoleum flashed across Daphne's mind.

Then she watched as the man's blue eyes widened into two strained Os.

Tiffany waited a beat and then brought the axe back in a horizontal arc. Her dark hair swung as she charged up two stairs and buried the blade into Gunnar Bergman's stomach. Blood sprayed, a hitching fountain of red.

Daphne screamed.

Wordlessly, Gunnar fell forward, wrapping himself around the axe, but Tiffany pushed her weight into the handle and forced him back with a primal growl.

Daphne watched, disbelieving that a teenage girl could overpower such a large man.

Yet she had. Tiffany, the waitress, had killed Daphne's family.

He slipped on the gore and hit his head on a wooden stair, gurgling.

"Bitch!" Blood bubbled at the corners of his mouth. He reached out and grabbed for Tiffany. She curved away from his searching hands with a spry athleticism.

Tiffany gave a retching, humorless laugh as she used her superhuman strength to pull the axe from Gunnar's yawning belly.

"Stop!" Daphne begged. She waved her hands as though to enforce a time out. "Stop! Please!"

A river of blood poured down the stairs. It trickled toward Daphne, speckling her sandals.

So this was her punishment. The image of little Oscar swam before her eyes. She would walk in blood endlessly for what she had done.

She couldn't help him, but she had to help her grandparents.

Daphne couldn't live with herself if she didn't at least try.

She flung herself at the stairs, grabbing at Tiffany's bare ankle. Her hands went through her, like a ghost. A troublesome mosquito would've had more effect.

"Fuck you," Tiffany said flatly. She stood above him as she brought the axe down again. "Fuck you for saying you love me, and fuck you for being a shitty dad to Carrie."

. . . *for saying you love me.*

It was Tiffany! He hadn't been sleeping with Rosalee.

Daphne had a flash of sympathy for the teenager before her. She had been mistreated, and Daphne had a vile sense that she was being used now, not unlike that woman who'd had her insides hollowed out a century ago.

A blood bubble popped like gum from Gunnar's screaming mouth. The blade cut through the bridge of his nose, sinking deep into his cheeks.

Daphne fell backward, squeezing her eyes closed. Fat tears drizzled down her face.

The sound of water running through old pipes groaned above.

Ida was in the shower. She couldn't hear the carnage.

Daphne opened her eyes. She must take her medicine. She had asked for this. Awareness is what she had sought. Willoughby, or the force behind it, was granting it to her.

The man, her grandfather, gave a splatting cough as the axe entered his mouth. He kicked his long legs out in a death throe, and one managed to make contact with Tiffany's crotch.

The teenager's air was knocked out of her. She wobbled but kept a grip on the axe. She removed it from the dead man's split skull and brought it down, again and again, as she gasped for air.

Her tank top, her tanned arms, her ample cleavage—everything was a tacky red.

Daphne scooted away from the carnage. Bits of brain slid down the edge of the axe and plopped against the railing as Tiffany kept swinging.

Daphne stared at the pulverized head, wondering how anyone could be so vicious and cruel.

Tiffany ripped the axe out of the body. Gunnar Bergman might have been bad: a man who took advantage of a teen. But Daphne mourned for him, her grandfather, as his body slipped down the last few stairs.

Tiffany skipped backward, avoiding being tripped by the falling body.

What was left of Gunnar Bergman hit the floor. One arm reached out above him as though he were attempting to backstroke away.

Tiffany howled with laughter.

Any sympathy Daphne had for Tiffany evaporated.

Daphne sat, grabbing the sides of her head. She couldn't watch anymore. Her heart beat unevenly. Stomach acid burned her esophagus.

Blood lapped at her legs like the waves of the ocean.

"I know now. I know now. I don't have to see anymore, please. I know."

The other in her brain, the thing that lurked there, pulled a string at the base of her neck. Her head turned to the left.

Tiffany, cloaked in red, giggled as she regarded her work.

Daphne's neck was twisted further, gently, toward the kitchen.

There, in the doorway, sat another face, watching.

The watcher's mouth hung open.

Daphne stared at the teeth, white and not made of needles. "Shit!" the watching girl squeaked.

Tiffany took her bare hand and wiped a chunk of something off the axe. "Oh, fuck, I know!"

"Maybe we should stop," the watching girl suggested.

Tiffany huffed. "Oh, hell no! You want your mom. I'll do your mom!"

The girl's mouth pursed and then frowned. "Um . . ."

"Mom?" Daphne hiccuped. "Mu . . . mom?"

Her mom's eyes, so piercingly familiar, stared through Daphne.

"Can you see me? Mom?" It was a desperate attempt to connect.

Caroline tiptoed into the living room, trying to avoid the sea of gore.

Tiffany kicked Gunnar's dead leg.

"Mom?" Daphne tried to stand on her tingling legs but slipped back down, weak.

Caroline turned her head toward Tiffany, hiding her face with a curtain of brown hair. "You really did it."

"He deserved it! I got those voices too, Carrie, and they agree!" Tiffany was a red, grinning monster.

"Mom, please? Tell her to stop. She's going to kill your mom and Kyle too. She's . . . Mom, you have to get her to put it down."

They couldn't hear her, but she still had to try.

Caroline combed her hand through her hair. "Okay, but you can't hurt Kyle."

"Nah, I won't. I mean unless I have to." Tiffany sighed. "Oh, I think she's getting out. Listen."

The teenage girls stared at the ceiling, waiting.

"Mom!" Daphne watched as her young mom surveyed the room. Caroline had the same catatonic, glassy-eyed stare she had had later, when she would lie in her bed and wait for death.

"You *can't!*" Daphne managed to stand. The smell of blood gagged her. "You're guilty! If you let her do it . . . if you let her do it, then you're . . ."

"I'll forget," Caroline said as though in answer to her daughter. She stood beside her dead father, on top of a coil of his intestines. She spat. "I'll forget all of this." She wiped at what might have been tears. "Thank you, Tiff, for doing what needs to be done, and then I'll get to . . . I'll get to forget it all."

*It is the bad and the weak who cry the loudest.*

Her mother *was* the Minnesota Borden. Not in action, but in inaction.

Caroline Bergman was bad, yes, deep down Daphne already knew that, yet what bothered her more greatly was that her mother was *weak*.

"Quit talking to yourself, you crazy bitch, and get over here!" Tiffany dragged the axe along the wooden floor. "She's gonna see him first, and when she's knelt over him, wondering what in the blue blazes happened, we'll chase her into the kitchen!"

Caroline looked away from her daughter and nodded obediently.

Tiffany crawled into a corner, behind the chair with the stitch work.

"You don't want this to happen." The edges of Daphne's vision dulled. It wasn't Willoughby pulling her away, but her own shocked and pained consciousness.

"I won't remember wanting it." Caroline spoke to herself again, the young girl who would run away and become Jane. "If I don't mean it to happen, then it's like it never did."

A high-pitched scream of terror filled the small home. Ida's bare feet could be seen at the top of the stairs.

Daphne had seen enough.

She took one last look at her mother and ran through the front door and out onto the lawn of what would soon be referred to as the murder house.

A teenage boy jogged up the sidewalk, a basketball wedged under his arm. His brow furrowed at the sound of a shrill scream coming from inside his house.

"Oscar!" Daphne was on her hands and knees. "Don't go in there! Oscar!"

He didn't hear. He skidded up the steps, the ball rolling from his grip and bouncing into a bush.

His name wasn't Oscar, she realized as the world threatened to go black.

But he was just as dead.

# 52

"No! No!"

The raspy screams of her teenaged mother jarred Daphne from her spiraling grief. She stumbled toward the desperate sound, wondering why no one else on Oak Street emerged from their home, curious and able to assist.

Although she had resigned herself to her own ineffectiveness, she still felt a hollow ache at the notion that there was nothing she could do or say to change the inexorable march of fate.

Daphne rounded the corner of the Bergman home, the familiar bubble of nausea caught in her throat.

The sea of purple flowers swaying in the slight summer wind nearly hypnotized her as she made her way down the narrow strip of grass between the houses.

Kyle's head bobbed above the overgrown thicket as he carved a path to nowhere with his long youthful legs.

Tiffany followed behind him with the axe raised up by both her hands into the warm air, as though she were carrying something revered. As though she were carrying an American flag in a parade and not a weapon still clotted with blood and brains.

Daphne watched, as she ran her trembling hand along the fence, feeling the grooves in the whitewashed wood, as Kyle stopped and swiveled around to look at Tiffany close on his heels.

She pressed her eyes closed for a beat, knowing this was probably his crucial mistake. She understood the shock that was radiating through him and in fact recognized it on his ashen face as she pushed through the twist of weeds and grew closer.

No doubt Kyle couldn't accept the sudden and violent new reality that had swallowed him up like a great whale does krill. It was written in the rapid blink of his eyes and the slackened nature of his mouth.

In the seconds since he had surely seen his dead parents and his sister and Tiffany standing in the gore, the harmony of his predictable teenaged life had been ripped away. Daphne knew exactly how his brain was fighting to comprehend, to make excuses, to forget.

Daphne stood hip-deep in the weeds, several feet away from Kyle. The perfume of the flowers coated her nostrils, a peculiar detail that made her uncertain if she was having a vision or if she had somehow stumbled into reality.

"Hey! Kyle! Run!" she called out, still clinging to a hope that she could affect this strange, vivid place.

She was yelling into a vacuum, though. Kyle didn't even glance in her direction.

He balled up his fists and ground his heels into the soft dirt. "Stop!" he roared. Anger brought color back to his temples as he stared at a blood-soaked Tiffany.

She was a vision of madness: her pupils were dilated, and a clot of viscous blood rested in the hollow of her neck.

Daphne was surprised to see that Tiffany obeyed Kyle. She halted midstride, keeping the axe poised above her head. The blade glinted in the sunlight as it tilted forward, but she gripped it tighter, stopping it from falling.

"Tiffany, put it down." He panted, the muscles in his arms rippling as he spoke. "Put that fucking thing down." He choked on the last word, and Daphne knew he was probably thinking of his mother on the kitchen floor and his father on the stairs.

She was overcome with immense pride for her uncle.

Though he should have kept running.

Caroline appeared in the copse, breathless and the color of turned milk. "Tiff!" Her voice was strangled. "Stop, okay?" She reached out to pat Tiffany's shoulder but then pulled her hand back as though she might get burned by her friend's homicidal rage.

Daphne pivoted to stare at her mother. The affection she had had for Kyle turned cold at the sight of Caroline's pinched face and slumped shoulders.

"Please," her mother squeaked through her curtain of stringy hair.

A vision of Edwin came to the surface of her mind. *A vision within a vision, like Russian nesting dolls,* she mused.

He was an infant, mewling on a heap of trash in a Seoul alleyway.

Time seemed to slow as Daphne shook the picture away from her mind's eye.

She was not certain why she had thought of him then, but she guessed it had something to do with her own brain attempting to process the shock it had endured. Not the inevitable murders of her family, but the realization that her mother was as weak as she had feared.

Caroline was no more than a limp dishrag crumpled behind Tiffany.

"Just let it go." Kyle stepped toward Tiffany, his sneaker kicking up a bit of soil.

Tiffany rocked back on her heels and then forward on her toes, back and forth. Daphne ripped her eyes from Caroline and studied Tiffany's face. There was a battle erupting there, a series of grimaces and eye twitches that caused Daphne to hold her breath in anticipation of what was to come.

A feeble voice within begged her to run, to relish in the fluttery swish of the wildflowers on her knees as she escaped the sight of

Kyle's death. But Daphne resigned herself to staying, to witnessing what she must.

"Carrie?" Kyle had turned his attention on his sister. "Carrie, tell her to stop all this, okay?" he pleaded.

"I told her not to. Not to do you," she insisted. "Tiffany, please? It's Kyle; it's just Kyle."

Tiffany blew air forcefully from her nose, like a bull about to charge. Her eyes, which hadn't left Kyle, flickered and then rolled to the side.

For one heart-pounding moment, Daphne thought Tiffany could see her. Her blood became ice at the blood-drenched girl's sharp gaze.

"Hello?" she managed. As she uttered the last syllable, she realized Tiffany was looking through her.

In that same instant, the heady smell of the flowers was overpowered by something foul and oddly familiar.

Daphne swung around, dizzy with fear.

It was close, a lethal presence that she couldn't quite see or remember.

Several yards away, near the edge of the Bergman's fence, a cluster of creeping thistle shifted as though inhabited by another vision walker.

The pain on her ankle throbbed and Daphne rubbed at it mindlessly. She wrinkled up her nose at the putrid stink, unable to make out who it may be that was hiding in the brush. She then looked back over her shoulder at Tiffany, who was still staring past her at the movement.

Apparently emboldened by Tiffany's distracted gaze, Kyle rushed forward.

Caroline shrieked, flapping her hands as her brother bounded toward Tiffany. "Don't kill him!"

Tiffany, so slicked in blood she appeared newly-born, tripped backward at the sight of the tall, muscular boy coming at her. She hit the ground with her butt. The air was knocked out of Tiffany in a *whoosh.* As she instinctively reached to pat her sore bottom, the axe swayed and fell to her side.

Daphne couldn't subdue the flutter of hope that scratched her insides as she watched Kyle leap toward Tiffany.

His hands came down on the dirt as he attempted to grab the weapon, his chin grazing Tiffany's knee.

But the girl had been infused with a strength and resilience that Kyle's boyish aggression couldn't match.

Tiffany grabbed for the axe, and in the blinding sunlight, it appeared to Daphne as though the axe was meant for her hand. A willing participant in murder, it seemed to magnetize to her flesh.

Caroline remained fixed to her spot, moaning like an injured animal as she stood idly by. It was as though she were as helpless as Daphne, walking within a vision.

Daphne knew better.

"Don't do this!" Kyle cried, trying to find purchase on his knees in the rotted weeds.

Tiffany's thick eyebrows undulated as her face shuffled from confusion, to joy, to rage, and back again in a bizarre merry-go-round of expressions.

Daphne's heart ripped open at Kyle's sob. She ran to him, desperate to pull him away. He was so young, so good, and so unlike his twin sister.

In the span of two seconds, Tiffany brought the axe up over her right shoulder with both hands. Daphne felt the whip of air as she reached out for her uncle.

Kyle, kneeling before Tiffany, yanked at her left arm in a feeble attempt to stop her.

This only made the axe come down with more force onto his neck. The blade cut through his skin in an instant, causing a geyser of blood to spray onto Daphne just as she was crouching down to save him.

The hot liquid blinded her. Daphne stumbled backward, tasting the iron tang on her tongue. She wiped the blood from her eyelashes in time to see Tiffany up on her feet, hacking Kyle's head off with the blade.

She forced the vomit back down her throat. An invading blackness was diminishing her vision. The wildflowers danced in a hazy conga line.

"Mom?" She swallowed the bitter taste as she watched her teenaged mother cry into the crux of her elbow.

The brutal sound of Tiffany's work was too much to bear, so Daphne tried to listen for the thing in the thistle. She turned, not surprised to see it.

It was a monster, wholly *familiar*, and it was exultant.

It was the thing those awful men had made. The creature they'd created from the mangled body of that young woman.

It's beady animal eyes shone with accomplishment. Up on its hind legs, it sipped the sun-soaked air through its needle teeth like one would drink Diet Coke through a straw. *She* held up her snout and sniffed the blood, a snotty bubble popping in her mottled nostril.

Knife-like claws pushed out of the ends of her furless paws as she took in a deep, raspy inhale.

*She's enjoying it.*

*She's . . . eating it. She's eating the pain and the death.*

Daphne watched in awe as the stinking thing grew taller. Her legs, vaguely human, stretched slightly and her ugly head blotted out the sun. The muscles on her veiny, speckled chest rippled and formed into harder masses.

*Remember. Remember. Please, you've got to remember this.*

The wound on Daphne's ankle screamed in pain.

Caroline hiccuped behind her, causing a sudden terror for her mother to bubble to the surface of her consciousness.

What if the monster wanted more?

Though she had just witnessed Caroline's cowardice, the instinct to protect her mother gripped her soul.

She swiveled back around, keenly aware of the monster lurking behind her, to find her mother in the same spot, trembling.

Finished, Tiffany stood up straight. She kept hold of the axe as she turned to look at her best friend.

Daphne expected to see the same victory in Tiffany's eyes that she had recognized in the monster, but there was only fear.

"*Why?*" Caroline wrapped her hands around clumps of her own hair and pulled. "Why *Kyle?*"

"I don't . . ." Tiffany's voice was small, as though she were at the bottom of a well and not standing right there, two feet from Daphne.

Tiffany looked through her again, her eyes fixing on what Daphne knew was the ravenous monster.

A monster that snacked on people but became full on misery and death.

"Carrie?"

"Tiff! *Why?*"

"You're the last." Tiffany shrugged, the casualness of the gesture made gruesome by her thick coating of blood.

Daphne's eyes flitted down to Kyle's head. She allowed herself to look at his unkempt sandy bangs and nothing more.

"What?" Caroline screeched. "That doesn't make any sense! No! It's me! Tiff!"

Daphne's attention was brought back to the girls. Tiffany was inching closer to Caroline. "Carrie, I think . . . I think you should get out of here," Tiffany pleaded, her bottom lip jutting out dramatically.

Caroline shook her head. "We gotta clean all this up and clean you off, Tiffany."

"Go! Go to the lake. I'll do it!" Tiffany brought the axe to her chest, cradling it like a child. Tears slid down her face, streaking through the gore. "I feel like I might kill you. I really might. And I don't wanna."

Daphne heard a pained snarl behind her. The monster had moved closer.

The sky grew darker. She had to squint to see her mother.

Caroline was backing away from Tiffany, her hands up and her eyes bulbous. She was in fear for her life. She believed her best friend would kill her.

Daphne fought to stay, to see it through. Yet Willoughby was pulling her back. She was a struggling fish on a hook, hauled out before she was ready.

The edges of Daphne's vision became shadows, and soon she was falling into a blackened, cold abyss.

*I can't forget. I can't forget any of this.*

# 53

DAPHNE CAME TO, CHOKING on the taste of vomit in her mouth.

"Okay?" Edwin sat on the floor, his face pale.

She pulled herself up.

They were in the house. The wood planks were mercilessly free of blood and guts.

"Edwin?" She could sense a wrongness.

"Sorry, bad timing. The ground's starting up."

"Shaking?"

"Uh-huh," he stuttered.

She noticed the change in the light filtering across the wood floor. It was night.

The door of the kitchen swung open. A woman came out, dressed in khaki pants, which were tight on her thick legs, and a white work-style shirt straining to remain closed over her chest and belly.

Tiffany grinned, carrying a washcloth in one hand. "You're stirring."

Daphne gasped. Every alarm in her body clanged and thrummed.

Tiffany's dark eyes, unchanged by time, became slits at the sound. "What's wrong with him?"

Daphne didn't take her eyes off the woman who had killed her family. "He needs a glass of water. Can you get him one?"

"Well, aren't I Nurse fucking Nancy?" She laughed. It was the same hollow vibration of teenage Tiffany's mirth.

Daphne tried to compose herself. "Please?"

Tiffany tossed the washcloth. Daphne caught it.

"Gimme a minute." Tiffany disappeared back into the kitchen.

"Okay, Daphne?" Edwin yelled as though she were on the other side of a vast canyon. "Tiffany saw us, helped me carry you in!"

Daphne shook her head. She pointed to the kitchen door.

Edwin raised an eyebrow.

Daphne pretended she held an axe. She swung it with one hand while pointing with the other.

They both leaped up. Edwin lurched forward. He struggled to stay upright. Daphne pulled his arm as they thundered toward the front door.

As Daphne reached for the handle, the kitchen door crashed open behind them. The walls of the house shook.

She watched Tiffany run across the room in three easy steps, grasping *the* axe above her swinging ponytail. Her face was a mask of rage, even more vengeful than when she had murdered Gunnar.

The sight short-circuited Daphne's mind as she tried to understand where the axe had come from. Had Tiffany climbed the stairs to find it? Or had it been waiting for her patiently in the kitchen sink like a well-trained dog?

Edwin turned. His mouth formed a shocked O as he watched the City Café waitress bring the axe down and bury it into his right thigh. Blood sprayed.

He gave a hoarse shriek and stumbled backward into Daphne.

Daphne hit the door with her back. She watched, dumbstruck, as Tiffany pulled at the axe embedded in Edwin's leg.

Edwin punched at his attacker as he fell. "Run! Go, Daphne!"

*She's not as strong as before. She's weaker.*

Time had altered more than just memories. It had caused Tiffany to grow fat and slow.

*You got this.*

Daphne jumped over a thrashing Edwin and lunged at Tiffany.

The axe came out of Edwin's leg with a sickening squelch as Daphne threw herself against Tiffany. They tripped backward, into a side table, knocking down a pile of murder pamphlets.

Frantic, Daphne brought her knee up and hit Tiffany in the stomach. As the older woman listed to the side, the momentum of the axe sent her back on her heels. Daphne shoved into Tiffany with both hands. They hit the floor in a tangle of limbs. The back of Tiffany's head hit the floor. She lost her grip on the weapon for a moment and then clawed for it. The tips of her fingers wrapped around the handle.

Daphne hoisted one leg over Tiffany, straddling her, and then drove her knee into Tiffany's armpit, causing her to drop the axe again. Daphne ground her butt down onto Tiffany's chest, pressing down with her full weight. The woman pounded her fists into Daphne's sides.

Daphne stretched forward. When she realized she couldn't reach the axe, she used every ounce of her weight to keep Tiffany pinned to the floor.

Edwin, panting, scrambled behind her. She could hear his hands scraping, trying to find purchase on the floor.

"Oh, you stupid bitch." Tiffany wiggled. "If I don't kill you, it will. It will!"

"Shut up!" Daphne slapped her ugly, snarling face. Then she called over her shoulder, "Are you calling? Edwin? You getting 911?"

"I got it out," he answered. "I got it . . ."

Tiffany bucked beneath her. Daphne found a hidden strength and kept the big woman down. She felt like a splayed starfish, holding one knee into Tiffany's armpit and the other between her legs. Her hands were clasped around her pudgy wrists. She ground the toes of her sandals into the floor.

"Edwin?"

Tiffany cackled.

"*Edwin?*"

The pit of her stomach dropped out. Daphne braved a moment of vulnerability to look over her shoulder.

Edwin was slumped in the doorway unconscious—*or dead*—in a puddle of dark crimson blood. His iPhone glowed on his lap.

"Shit! Wake up!" Daphne hollered.

Tiffany's left hand came up and grabbed hold of her hair. Fiery pain encapsulated Daphne's scalp. She watched in mute horror as the large woman got the better of her. In slow motion, the room flipped as Tiffany sent her into a somersault. Daphne's back hit the floor, and the violent usurping ended in the world becoming topsy-turvy.

Daphne screamed as a chunk of blonde hair, pulled out at the roots, floated down onto her face like fresh snow. The back of her head rattled against the hardwood, causing her to chomp down on her tongue.

Tiffany slammed a fist into Daphne's diaphragm. Daphne spit out a string of blood, hoping it would fly up and hit Tiffany in the eye. It only dribbled down her own chin, instead.

Tiffany got control of Daphne's arms, stretching them out over Daphne's head. While holding Daphne's wrists with one hand, she pinched Daphne's nose with the other. "Did your momma tell you she watched? Hmm? She liked watching."

Yes, Daphne's mother might have been weak.

But, she wasn't.

*You got this.*

Daphne was imbued with both a dizzying fury and an innate power of will.

She wriggled her right arm free from Tiffany's grasp and clocked the fifty-year-old woman in the side of the head, hearing her knuckles snap as she made contact with Tiffany's jaw.

She ignored the pain in her fingers.

"Christ!" Tiffany roared.

Daphne pulled her legs up between them, right at Tiffany's soft middle, and kicked with every fiber of her being.

Tiffany was flung backward, inches from Edwin.

There was a moment—less than a second—when Daphne had to decide to pick up the axe or run.

Time slowed. The choice was presenting itself. She had to decide. She didn't want to kill.

Edwin's blood dotted the sides of her sandals. This was her punishment, to swim in an infinite sea of blood.

She ran.

Daphne sprinted into the kitchen. She flung herself at the door leading to the backyard.

Her mind couldn't comprehend the series of locks and bolts waiting for her.

She grabbed randomly, trying not to think of Tiffany finding purchase on the slick floor. Of her coming for her with that gleeful smile she had held while killing her family. She thought of Kyle's detached head, of Gunnar's bloody mouth, of Oscar dead beneath her wheels.

The kitchen door swung open.

She didn't look over her shoulder, not this time.

Daphne yanked at the screen door. A hook and eye kept it from opening.

She held her trembling body up by clutching the doorframe with her left hand as her right unhooked the latch.

The gentle swish of an axe tickled her ear.

*I'm dead.*

It landed in the doorframe beside her head, splintering the wood.

Daphne pulled her hand away as she pushed out into the night. She ran and toppled over the whitewashed fence.

She ran through the weeds blindly, vaguely aware of them thwacking against her aching legs.

A searing pain, not unlike the sting in her ankle, surged up her arm.

Hot liquid squirted against her left palm.

Still moving, Daphne looked down in the starlight and realized the top of her middle finger was gone. The axe had gotten her after all.

Regret, throbbing and more painful, ballooned in her chest.

She should have grabbed the axe. Or reached over Tiffany and got the iPhone from Edwin's lap.

*Oh, Edwin. Oh, God, Edwin.*

Tears threatened to descend.

The sound of her own running made it difficult to discern if Tiffany was close behind.

Daphne dropped down low, holding her breath. The complete darkness reminded her of the men, hiding their deeds in that same field. She wondered if the bones of that nameless woman were buried just beneath her. She could see nothing but unhelpful streaks of moonlight, sparkling on the dewy flowers.

*You shouldn't be alone! Not now!*

That was the intruder speaking. The other in her mind.

"Shut up," she hissed in the tall grass. Her tongue was swelling against the inside of her cheek.

Satisfied that Tiffany was not close behind, Daphne began to swerve right and then back toward the glimmer of the house.

It seemed like an opportune time to have a plan.

Her mind sputtered, searching for viable options.

*You're alone at night. I warned you.*

*Fuck off!* she said without opening her mouth.

Edwin. She'd left him alone in there, helpless. What if Tiffany was burying the axe inside him again? Over and over? Pulverizing his face?

The flare of rage returned.

How convenient for Tiffany to find them. And where had that murderous bitch even come from?

Daphne crept along the back chain-link fence of the murder house's neighbors. She stuck her face out of the twisting weeds and looked from side to side. No one. Despite all the screaming, every window of this house was black.

This fence was a bit higher and demanded that she hoist herself up a few feet. She favored her bleeding left hand as she climbed and then tumbled into the lawn, a jagged link of the fence catching, for a second, on her wrapped ankle.

Her ears perked—not at a sound but at the enveloping silence. There were no running sprinklers, no barking dogs, no passing cars.

Daphne ran between the two houses, hoping to see a citizen on the sidewalk out front.

No one.

*You're alone.*

She shivered.

Her plan was forming. She would make certain Tiffany was not in the front room of the house and then inch open the door. Edwin would be easy enough to drag down the front steps.

If the universe was fair, his phone would still be with him.

She clutched the siding of her mother's childhood home, running through the pitfalls and advantages of her strategy.

*You SHOULD NOT be alone, Daphne. Not here.*

The interloper within was so loud, so intrusive, that Daphne whipped her head around, half expecting to see Tiffany with the blood-soaked axe right behind her.

Light from the nearby porch shone on her hand, revealing the extent of her injury. Her middle finger had been severed beneath the nail, and the tops of the surrounding fingers were sliced to ribbons. The blood pumped like a tiny spigot.

It hurt like a bitch.

She was leaving a trail. Red sparkled on the freshly mowed lawn like strange starlight, a festive decoration celebrating tonight's attempted massacre.

Yes, she thought as she held her mangled fingers to her chest, she would never be released from all this blood-soaked cruelty. It was in her DNA.

On tiptoe, she skirted along the front of the house. Her blood plopped on the woodchips of the small garden beds. She might as well have drawn a map for Tiffany. Or made a blinking neon sign for the *other*—the one she had forgotten yet inherently knew was stalking her.

Daphne gave a hurried look at both sides of Oak Street and then took a moment to remove her lacy blouse with her good hand. Her lip trembled from the pain as she wrapped the blouse around her weeping fingers and tucked the fabric in at her wrist.

Dressed only in a floral-patterned bra and skinny jeans, she crouched down at the corner of the large window overlooking the lawn. She carefully crawled beneath it, in case Tiffany was surveying the street from inside the house.

Her body was a symphony of sensations: aching, fiery, and moist with blood.

Halfway to the porch steps, she braved a peek into the front window above. Through a sliver of glass between the drapes and the frame, she could make out Edwin's canvas Vans. He was still there.

Somewhere, the leaves of a tree rustled.

Daphne's stomach pulsed. She begged herself not to puke. The uncontrollable retching would give her away. Tiffany would slice her head off in one cool stroke as Daphne knelt like a French woman at the guillotine.

She could *not* let herself puke.

The sight of blood haphazardly staining her white blouse-bandage threatened her resolve. She pinched her eyes closed and thought about Edwin. She had to save Edwin.

Edwin.

A memory.

His hand on her lower back, slipping down to her butt.

Daphne dug into her jeans pocket and found the most beautiful gift. It was cold and smooth.

Unbelieving, she brought the pearl-handled folding knife up to her face and stared.

Edwin—smart and clever man.

Things were turning around in their favor.

Daphne struggled to open the old-fashioned blade with just one hand. She held the handle in her teeth and popped out the blade with her fingernail.

She continued to crawl, knife jutting up in her fist, toward the porch. Her left hand screamed with every movement.

A few more agonizing moments on her palms and she would have to get herself up the porch steps and to Edwin in a lightning-quick motion.

The aroma of a slimy, leaf-choked marsh tickled her nose. A slight breeze picked up, sending the gagging sweet scent of death to mingle in the strands of her hair.

Daphne's mind opened into a vast black hole. A vision rippled on the surface of memory. The blade hung limp in her grasp as she stood.

A concentrated spray of moonlight illuminated its face, like a thespian on a stage.

It was both foreign and familiar, a monster and an acquaintance. *You.*

She remembered: its stink, its wolfish snout, and its prickly yellow eyes.

Daphne stepped toward the monster on Oak Street. She—*yes, it is a she*—stood on her hind legs, thick tail swinging like a jungle vine. She was a tall and sinewy behemoth, nearing seven feet.

Daphne took in their surroundings. Every window of every house was black. The neighborhood lay silent as a dead thing. The street empty, a forgotten road to nowhere.

They knew, all of them. The Willoughbians locked themselves inside, away from the punishment.

She was out at night, alone, when she shouldn't be. *The rules, enforced with cruelty.*

Daphne got closer, mesmerized. Doris's words stamped across her soul like the bar of a typewriter.

Syrupy green spittle seeped down from the monster's mouth and onto the pavement.

"I'm . . ." Daphne waggled her swollen tongue. "I'm not alone."

The creature pulled back its greasy lips and revealed an infinite spiral of teeth. Shining, razor-sharp needles.

Daphne stopped at the curb, remembering the little old lady dragging the shotgun behind her on the school's tiled floor. The monster had been right beside her, sharing in her murder. Feeding off it. Wanting it.

"You didn't make her do it. You can't change a good heart, right? You can lead them there, the bad ones, to do what you want. But they have to do it."

Muscles undulated beneath the surface of its ashen, veiny skin.

"I'm sure you try, though." Daphne tightened her grip around her measly weapon. If the monster wanted to eat her, the knife would do nothing more than provide a toothpick. "You talk to them, through the axe, through whatever you can."

It waited, watching her with the patient, mocking grin of a lioness.

Realizations bloomed, infusing her with a giddy wisdom.

"Hello?" she called into the vacuum of night. "Someone?"

There was not one light, not one footstep.

She was certain.

"They made you. To take care of them."

It snorted hot, noxious air out of its snout.

"Like a . . . like . . . a . . ." The word was on the edge of her throbbing tongue.

*Mother.*

*No. You're a golem. A golem made to protect and help weak people. You did not create Willoughby. The people here—the scared, bad people—they created you.*

A clattering wheeze, the surreal sound of a train whistle, came from its throat.

She had annoyed it.

This, Daphne supposed, would be her last victory. For soon she would be eaten and swallowed, and she would swish and tumble with the others in its stomach acid.

The irony of this was not lost on her.

She looked down at the blood-soaked blouse wrapped around her hand, her naked belly, and the swell of her breasts in a bra she had hoped to remove, in time, for Edwin.

She was happy she had driven his Toyota and enjoyed the purr of the engine beneath her.

She was happy she had kissed him and raked that lush, beautiful hair with her fingers.

She was happy that Oscar, if even for only a short time, had lived a good life of love and choo-choo trains.

In the end, she had found the truth. That her mother had been weaker than her. In a way, she hated her for it, but she loved her too. Because in the end, her mother was her mother.

Daphne allowed herself to laugh. The joyous sound echoed off every angle and nook of Willoughby, from the bridge over Pelican River to the fluttering flowers laid at the foot of Moira's library.

The monster bent forward, allowing its sharp front claws to grasp the road. It growled, from somewhere deep, deep inside. From a place, she imagined, that would soon be her bloody future, to match her bloody past.

She watched as the hungry monster came toward her.

The sound of footsteps interrupted. A voice—Tiffany's—hollered from nearby.

"Oh! I told you! If I didn't do it, then it sure as would!"

Daphne concentrated on the monster's opening and collapsing mouth.

"Ha-ha! Oh, yes!"

Doris's words came to Daphne, comforting her.

*It is the bad and the weak who cry the loudest.*

"Wait." Daphne held up her right hand. She didn't realize until she saw her splayed fingers that she had dropped the knife.

"You have to listen to me."

The monster's tail swatted back and forth, a cat ready to pounce. It was so close, Daphne could see down into the void of its stinking maw.

"You have to listen to me! Because I'm a Bergman. I'm the last. You were trying to get rid of us, huh? But I'm here. And you have to listen. I'm a Bergman, and I'm bad, just like them."

From the corner of her eye, she could see Tiffany shaking with laughter. She held the axe on her shoulder as she guffawed.

"I know you know. You've been inside." Daphne pointed to her temple. "My mom's a murderer. And . . . and . . . and I'm a murderer. You saw it."

It exhaled rotten breath into her face. A chunky glob of its toxic saliva pooled at her feet.

It could bite her. But it could not kill Daphne. It had its own set of rules, devised by those men, and although it had used bad people to circumvent this, she could play against its weakness.

"I want you to kill her!" Daphne's eyes rolled to the right, where Tiffany watched with an increasingly pale face. "I hate her! I want to watch you tear her apart!"

Daphne summoned every ounce of fury she held in her heart. She thought of her mom, of that damned van, of Edwin, maybe dead, on the floor.

She stomped her foot. "I command you!"

It huffed. Its jaundiced eyes flickered.

*Murder her,* Daphne said through the impossible umbilical cord connecting them.

*Murder her because you have to. Because I'm a Bergman and I am telling you. Because I'm a murderer and you HAVE to.*

When it lowered its haunches like a guilty dog, she knew.

She had cried the loudest.

Its neck creaked like a door on ancient hinges as it zeroed in on its new meal.

Under the creature's foreboding stare, Tiffany shook her head in disbelief, her disheveled ponytail swaying. Her eyes bulged from their sockets as the thing sprung toward her like a panther. It covered the space between them—twenty paces—in a blink.

Tiffany swiveled to run. It cut her down before the axe clanged to the pavement.

The waitress's mouth was distorted in anguish as it clawed at her arm.

Showers of blood streamed into the monster's vast and waiting mouth.

The Minnesota Borden emitted a high-pitched, squawking scream. She fell onto her back, reminding Daphne of Gunnar violently thumping against the stairs.

"I'm sorry! I'm sorry!" Tiffany begged. "I'm sorry I'm alone!"

On tingling legs, Daphne scurried up behind the carnage.

The monster snacked on Tiffany's head. It slurped, as though devouring a plate of spaghetti.

The nearly lifeless woman lay surprisingly docile, her shredded arm twitching.

Daphne looked down at the blood on her sandal. The gummy crimson squelched underneath her weight.

*Just a little bit more.*

She bent down and picked up the axe that had been used to kill her family.

*And Edwin. It hurt him too. Maybe killed him.*

Daphne blocked out the sounds of the crunching monster and the moaning woman. She ran her hands over the smooth wood, intoxicated by it.

This is what she had been afraid of, of course. To hold the axe in her hand and understand that she was capable of being a cold-blooded murderer. That her mom was not the only one.

Her stomach was remarkably calm.

*Just a little bit more blood.*

Daphne pulled the blouse off her hand with her teeth. It drifted to the ground on the soft breeze.

She wrapped both her good hand and her injured one around the handle and brought it up over her head.

*This is for listening to the dark hearts instead of the pure.*

The creature flinched at her telepathic message.

Daphne brought the axe down into its back.

336

Its nightmarish scream filled both her ears and her brain. Her bones rattled from its shrill frequency.

That did not stop her.

She was bathed in fresh squirting blood as she yanked the axe up and let it fall again on its slender neck.

Oily black liquid seeped from the gaping crevice.

It struggled. In one last desperate move, it swiped its claws across her bare belly.

Instant electric pain seized her.

She did not stop.

She pulled the axe free and chopped again and again and again. It's bald wolflike head rolled between her sandals.

Daphne staggered back, observing what she had done.

She was happy she had done it.

# 54

## Doris

DORIS KNEW, FROM THE SECOND her addled and fuzzy brain
registered she was awake, that she wasn't alone.

Over time, she had grown to not be frightened of this and
accept it for the gift it was meant to be. She clicked on the crystal-
beaded lamp beside her bed and was shocked by the magnitude of
her guests. There were many of them, lined up in a neat row as
though waiting for communion. They all gazed down at her.

"Hello. Does this mean it's my time?" Doris looked from face to
face. There was Moira, her brassy-orange hair still vibrant as ever.
There was Kyle Bergman, forever a teenager, just like the girl in black
beside him. Kasey held up both hands and waved.

Doris sighed. "It's all right. I'm ready."

"No." Franklin, her beloved husband, was farther back by the
door. He stood between a young woman in a fancy promenade dress
and Doris's mother-in-law, Devorah. "We need your help, my
dearest."

Moira's smile crumbled into a concerned frown. "Could you call
an ambulance, Doris?"

Confused, Doris pushed the quilt off her legs. "Oh my, yes, right
away."

Kasey stepped closer to Doris. "Better make it two."

338

# 55

THE NEEDLE MADE HER ARM itch beneath the medical tape. Daphne scratched around the site of her IV, at the crux of her elbow. This made her itchy on her belly, where she had been nearly gutted. She scratched there, gingerly, and then unplugged the IV drip from the wall.

Her left hand didn't itch. Instead, it whimpered in a nagging, ceaseless pain across the uneven peaks of her severed fingers.

Daphne wheeled her IV pole down the corridor, sniffing at the other patient's recently delivered meals. An elderly man in 408B shoveled glistening hospital green beans into his mouth as he watched the *Nightly News*.

Her stomach groaned.

"Hey, Ms. Forrest. Nice to see you up and about." Nurse Krista looked up from a computer screen at the nurse's headquarters, where they flitted to and from as the patients chimed their buttons all day and night.

"Going for a walk," Daphne responded. Cool breeze slapped her bare legs. She wore her hospital gown, thin robe, and a pair of crinkly slippers.

"Good." Krista pushed up the bridge of her glasses. "I saw your dad leave earlier. I hope he went for a nap."

"I forced him. Hey, can you ask Dr. Leasure if I can have toast in the morning? Or anything? Oatmeal? I'm healing up."

The nurse gave a wise, knowing smile. "Sick of your liquid diet?"

Daphne stuck out her bottom lip. "Even the food in this place smells like heaven."

"Oh, my. I'll ask." Nurse Krista returned her eyes to her work.

"Thank you." Daphne trailed away toward the elevator. She punched the button and waited, wondering if she should have bothered to go through the agonizing process of putting on a pair of sweatpants.

Just thinking about it made her skin prickle with sweat. The wound in her abdomen blazed, and her left hand was a useless club of gauze.

Daphne boarded the elevator. A teenaged volunteer in a maroon vest helped drag her IV pole over the threshold.

She rode up three floors thinking of dry toast.

Once on the seventh floor, Daphne thanked the same volunteer for helping guide her rolling contraption back out.

She made her way past an identical looking nurses' station and maneuvered herself and her IV around a cart full of fragrant dinners under circular plastic shells.

Doris Woodhouse stood in the open doorway of 713A, stooped over from the weight of her enormous crocheted purse.

She turned at the sound of Daphne's papery slippers on the tile. "Hello. I was just coming down to check in on you."

"Aw, you're sweet." Daphne hugged Doris with her untethered arm. The warmth of the old woman's embrace gave her an instant rush of good vibes. For just a moment, her pain and itchy flesh were forgotten.

Daphne sighed. "You smell like peppermint tea."

Doris smiled. "I brought you some." She unsnapped her purse and began to dig through the jumbles of receipts and wrappers.

"Yes!" Daphne pulled the pole farther into the room and peeked over Doris's shoulder.

"You're walking." Edwin had been propped up against a mountain of pillows in order to eat his dinner.

"No wheelchair for me!" Daphne rushed past Doris, nearly forgetting her metal companion. She remembered just in time, grabbing it before the IV cord could be ripped from her vein.

Edwin reached out his arms and she fell into him. Her abdomen stung and her legs were shaky noodles as she climbed up over the bedrail.

"Can you push that food away, just for a minute?" Her request was muffled against his matching hospital gown.

Edwin obliged, pushing the rolling table away from his lap as he wiped his hands with a napkin.

"If I ever get pukey again and reject food, just remind me of this moment. I'm starving." She tucked herself against his left side, careful of his wrapped leg.

"If it helps, the meatloaf is truly shitty." He ran his fingers through her hair as she laid her head on his chest.

"It doesn't help."

Doris gave a victorious shriek. "Here! The tea!" She crossed the room and placed the box beside Edwin's meal.

"You're so nice, Doris. You should go home; it's a long drive and it's going to be dark soon." Daphne pointed toward the venetian blinds, where the evening's shadows were growing long over Minneapolis.

Doris snickered. "Oh, that's not a bother for me."

"Doris was just filling me in on some updates." Edwin's voice was a pleasant rumble against Daphne's face.

"Oh?"

"She says after we told the police about Tiffany . . . confessing, the sheriff did a more thorough investigation of the house."

Doris waved her tissue-stuffed hand. "They have so many newfangled devices."

"They searched the shed, you know in the back?"

Daphne nodded. She knew her memories of the murder house would never fade.

"I guess they used some sort of device that reads irregularities in the wall. Anyways, they found a hiding spot."

"There were bloody clothes." Doris frowned. "Wrapped around an old Coca-Cola bottle."

"They think maybe, even after all this time, they can get some DNA off the bottle. And the clothes." Edwin squeezed Daphne's shoulder.

Daphne closed her eyes. She tried to remember what Tiffany had worn that day, but she could only see her mother navigating over the rivers of blood.

"It's good you killed her, dear."

"Hmm?" Daphne glanced up at the old woman.

"It's very good. The police agree. You killed the Minnesota Borden."

That was partly true. She'd told Edwin, and only him, that her mom had been a part of it too.

Daphne remembered the axe in her own hands: up and down, up and down.

She couldn't remember Tiffany beneath the blade. Only her own rage and determination.

And the fear. The fear that the smooth wood in her hands felt somehow right.

She couldn't even remember how and when Tiffany cut her belly.

"Well." Doris rubbed her nose with the tissue. "I'm off. Willoughby needs me." She gave a cheeky wink.

"It sure does," Edwin agreed.

"Bye, Doris." Daphne waved. "Thanks for my tea. I'm going to have lots for my supper."

"Good." Doris patted them both on the head. "Willoughby needs you two even more, you know."

Daphne and Edwin laughed together.

"Uh, no, I'm good." Daphne burrowed herself deeper underneath Edwin's arm.

Doris tapped her soft shoe on the floor. "We need good people. More good than bad. Don't you think so, dear?"

Daphne thought of her mother. She thought of the angry teenage girl watching as her father died. She thought of the woman, both the one who struggled with her own culpability and the one who made Daphne popcorn and wiped the fever from her brow. "Bad people are complicated. They have the ability to change. So do weak people, I think."

"Precisely." Doris revealed a craggy set of yellowing teeth. "Goodnight, my dearies."

She hobbled out.

Edwin and Daphne sat in silence, listening to the reassuring beeps of the hospital machines.

Finally, Edwin spoke. "I'm glad you rescued me." He rested his chin on her head.

"I didn't!" Daphne fought back a barrage of tears. Something Doris had said had snagged in her mind.

"You did."

Daphne swatted his chest with her bandaged hand. "Do you think it's good I killed her?"

"Yes."

"Me too. For once."

Her mind flashed to all the times she had stood in blood: her own, Edwin's, Oscar's, Tiffany's. Something black churned in her memory. An *other's* blood.

Again, she saw the image of her mom tiptoeing over the red.

"I was brave," Daphne whispered.

"Yes."

"We'll get out of here soon, I think. Once I can eat and you're not so anemic." She snuggled even closer.

He ran a hand through her hair.

"They wanna give me another bag or two of blood before I go."

*Blood can fix things, sometimes. Make them better. Make them good.*

It was not her inner mother speaking. It was her own voice and her own words.

"Well, wherever we do go, Edwin, if we stay here or go to Bellingham, or God, even if we go back to Willoughby." She raised her head and looked up into his affectionate eyes.

"Yeah?" He smiled so brightly, her heart sputtered and burst.

"Wherever we go . . ." She weaved her fingers into his, reveling in the sight. "I want to drive."

To Be
Continued
in
# Daughters of
# Darkness

Award-nominated horror and suspense author Meg Hafdahl was raised in both British Columbia and Minnesota. She is a member of the esteemed Horror Writers Association, and her female-driven horror stories have been produced for audio by *The Wicked Library* and have appeared in anthologies such as Spider Road Press's *Eve's Requiem: Tales of Women, Mystery, and Horror*. Her first short story collection, *Twisted Reveries: Thirteen Tales of the Macabre* was released by Inklings Publishing in 2015. *Twisted Reveries Volume II: Tales from Willoughby* arrived in 2016. *Her Dark Inheritance* is Meg's debut novel. She is also the co-host of the podcast *Horror Rewind* and a regular contributor for *Spider Mirror Journal*. Meg lives in Minnesota with her husband, her two young sons, and a menagerie of pets.

Follow her at:

www.meghafdahl.com

twitter.com/MegHafdahl

www.facebook.com/meghafdahlhorrorauthor

Excerpt
from
Daughters of
Darkness

"Daffy."

Daphne leaned forward, unbelieving. "What did you call me?"

Officer Blackwood stared forward. The ragged nails of his right hand dug into the leather steering wheel. "Daffy, it's me."

Hysteria, real and fervent, vibrated through the core of her being. "No! *No!*"

"I know I'm not your favorite person." He spoke in a raspy, whispering voice.

Daphne gagged, tasting vomit at the back of her throat. *Oh my god, oh my god, oh my god, oh my god.*

She writhed, instinctually tearing at both the handcuffs and the seat belt. "Lady! Wake up! Please, help me!"

Officer Pope blinked mildly, ignoring Daphne.

Blackwood, the brawny policeman who had carried himself with the confidence of a soldier, now turned to Daphne with the look of a beaten remorseful child. The grief in his gray eyes pierced Daphne through the metal grate between them. Daphne could never forget the expression of someone defeated by death.

Of someone who'd given up.

"Daffy," he continued in the soft voice that didn't match his sinewy body. "You have to listen."

"I don't have to. I don't have to! Go away!" Sweat, both hot and cold, dribbled from her armpits. She knew her cheeks had turned the color of freshly spilled blood. Her abbreviated middle finger throbbed with memory. "You lied to me!"

The body of Officer Blackwood trembled.

Other books
by
Inklings Publishing
and
Inklings Children
Division

The Twisted Reveries Series by Meg Hafdahl debuted in October 2015 with *Thirteen Tales of the Macabre*. In October 2016, *Tales from Willoughby* followed. Get your copy of these spine-tingling volumes today and enjoy short stories by this great female voice in horror!

This epic fantasy novel, *Tarbin's True Heir*, is the first of Kelly Lynn Colby's The Recharging series. Follow a pair of royal twins as they go head-to-head to prove to all peoples which of them, older sister or younger brother, is the True Heir.

THE RECHARGING
BOOK ONE

TARBIN'S
TRUE
HEIR

KELLY LYNN COLBY

Kira has been given up by her parents as an infirm, to live out her days as a ward of the government. But how many days does she have? And is there a secret haven where her limited time might be extended? Get *Infirm*, and join Kira as she fights to live in this first installment of the Kira Chronicles.

The *Smiley Face Blatoon*, now available in a bilingual Spanish/English edition, launched Inklings Children Division in Summer 2015. First-place winner of the Texas Authors Association's Best Picture Book for All Ages, this, and all Inklings Children Division books, contains extensive activities, discussion questions, and cross-curricular work, as well as other tools for parents and educators.

The anthologies in the Perceptions Series are collections of short stories, poems, and nonfiction articles based on themes written for children grades three through six by a variety of authors. As with all Inklings Children Division books, each volume contains questions and activities for parents and educators to extend learning.

SPECIAL NEEDS

Perceptions Series
Volume One

Edited by: Fern Brady

# Follow Inklings Publishing by:

 Signing up for our newsletter at www.inklingspublishing.com

 Liking our Facebook page /InklingsPublishing

 And following our tweets

Made in the USA
Middletown, DE
08 December 2020

26969005R00227